USA TODAY BESTSELLING AUTHOR

JENNIFER PEEL

To Justin, my favorite son and big guy.

Prologue

1935 MULBERRY LANE, LOVELAND, COLORADO. It just sounds nice. Living on Mulberry Lane in a town named for the most prized emotion on earth was even better. And for me, it really was perfect. At least until . . . well, we'll get to that part. I won't go into all the boring details like the first day we moved in; I was nine, by the way, and it was the day after Thanksgiving. Let's start with something better, like that prized emotion I mentioned earlier.

It was the summer of my fourteenth year, you know the one when you were about to start high school and you were barely coming out of that awkward stage. The braces had just come off, and I was learning how to apply make-up correctly, and not like a painted lady of the night. And, of course, my chest was finally coming along nicely. I moved up one whole cup size that summer. So life was good, but in July of that year my life was about to get a whole lot better.

The "For Sale" sign had finally come down next door, and with that came the Carter family, a family of four with two of the most beautiful men that had ever graced the earth. The only problem was that Kaye and Guy Carter started having their children way too early. Evan, their youngest, was nineteen, and Ryan, the godliest creature to ever walk on the face of the earth, was twenty-two. When you're fourteen, twenty-two is like forty, and obviously pedophilic, so I knew it was never happening. But that didn't stop me from discussing him at length with my other neighbor and best friend, Krissy, who had gone up *two* cup sizes that summer. I hated her, but loved her like a sister.

Neither of them really paid attention to us, although like idiots, Krissy and I did our best to make spectacles of ourselves that summer.

We laid out on my trampoline in our bathing suits whenever they were in their backyard—like they were really interested in looking at the not-fully-formed bodies of juveniles. I honestly try not to think about our stupidity anymore, especially since, at the time, we thought we were beyond cool. And had they been interested, there would have been something really wrong with them. My only saving grace was that I'm pretty sure they had no idea we existed.

The only time either of them talked to me that summer was once, when I was out front shooting hoops. You see, my parents were only blessed with one child, me. They wanted a slew of children, and my dad especially wanted a son to groom as his legacy. But my mom almost died in childbirth, and to save her life, some of her lady parts had to go, so no more kids. My dad got over his disappointment that he would never have a son, but he decided his daughter could be all he'd ever wanted a son to be. That meant I got stuck with a boy name, Charlee. At least my mom insisted it have a somewhat feminine spelling, not that it really mattered, because most people called me CJ (short for Charlee Jensen). I was taught to dribble a ball from the time I was two. My dad and I spent countless hours running drills and playing one–on-one. Believe me, I'm not complaining, my dad was the best. Let me stress *was*, but we'll get there. I was the epitome of a daddy's girl, and I had the man wrapped around my little finger.

Back to the first time Ryan Carter ever noticed me. Doesn't "Ryan Carter" sound perfect? Never mind. I had just made a perfect three-point shot, swish, nothing but net. It was beautiful, and so was he. He was tall, which was good, since I was five feet eight already. I would only grow one more inch, but add heels with that, I could stand close to six feet. Back to Ryan. He had to be at least six feet two, with light brown hair that glistened in the sun, and he was perfectly tan with bright white teeth (dental hygiene is a must). But it was his eyes that did it for me. They were green, but not any green, they were bright like the first buds of spring.

"Nice shot," he called out as he was getting into his little sporty-looking red car.

The red sports car only added to his beautifulness. Why, oh why did his parents have to have kids so early? It's not like they were old. In fact, Kaye and Guy looked too young and beautiful to have kids that old. The family was genetically blessed, but mystery shrouded them. Guy seemed to travel a lot, and as the years passed, government people would come to our house and interview us about him. They asked my parents things like, "Have you noticed any strange activity?" "Does he make a lot of large purchases?" "How much contact do you have with them?"

My guess was that Mr. Carter was a CIA agent. I thought it was a pretty educated guess, too. Once, my parents had them over for dinner and my dad offhandedly mentioned a news report about waterboarding. I noticed that Mr. Carter turned a tad red, pulled on his collar and cleared his throat. He also changed the subject really quick. All he would ever say about his job was that he worked for the Department of Defense. Yeah, right . . . I'd seen every Jack Ryan movie with my dad.

No matter, I wasn't interested in the spy next door. I was only upset with him for not waiting a bit longer to start a family, because I knew in my teenage heart that Ryan and I were meant to be together. It became even more apparent when we found out that he had recently graduated from the University of Southern California with his Accounting degree and he was getting ready to take his state board exams to become a CPA. It was like fate. You see, my dad owned a large accounting firm, and guess where Ryan was going to be working? You're right, Jensen Accounting. This made me love Jeffrey Jensen even more.

I suddenly became very interested in going in to work with my dad whenever possible. Of course my dad thought this was terrific; he had not only wanted me to be a star basketball player like him, but he was hoping that, someday, I would love numbers as much as him, too. He used to point to the sign outside his office and say, "Someday, baby girl, that will say Jensen and Jensen Accounting." I always promised him I would never change my last name and he would always be the number one man in my life. It was a stupid promise to make.

Fast forward a few years. At seventeen I was past that awkward stage, and my chest had grown to the perfect C cup. Not too big, but still ample and perky. I looked more like a woman than a kid; my dad would always say I looked too old for his liking. I was the starting forward and all-star for my high school team. Life was just about perfect, or at least it was for like two minutes. My unrequited crush for Ryan was as strong as ever, though I knew he only saw me as a kid, and I knew I *was* a kid. I knew I would never realize my dream of becoming Mrs. Jensen-Carter (for Ryan I would at least hyphenate), so I had a boyfriend, Chance Wallace. He was gorgeous and tall. He played basketball, too, but he was nothing compared to Ryan. Even though I knew it was hopeless, I would daydream that when I turned eighteen and legal, Ryan would magically see me as a woman and discover that I was perfect for him.

My dreams ended up being crushed that summer before my senior year. First, Chance broke up with me; I guess I accidentally called him Ryan one too many times. He kept asking who Ryan was, but I could never say. I tried to play it off like he reminded me of Ryan Reynolds, which was sort of true, but he didn't buy it. The only person who knew about my Ryan obsession was Krissy, and I didn't even really talk to her about it anymore because she, too, realized how farfetched it was. Besides, she thought I was crazy for not being in love with Chance. By the way, Chance and Krissy, let's just say there is another story there, but first we have to discuss why my whole world came crashing down in a matter of mere months.

So, the summer before your senior year is supposed to be what Neutrogena commercials are made of, but mine was turning out more like a horrible infomercial about digestive issues; it was truly nauseating. You already know about the no boyfriend thing, which wasn't a big deal, but admittedly I kind of missed him, or at least the making out part. Hey, I was seventeen, don't judge. But while I was breaking up, Ryan was hooking up. Ryan still worked for my dad and was quickly working his way up in my dad's firm. My dad loved him. There was a time or two he mentioned that he kind of thought of him like a son. It didn't hurt my feelings. I honestly thought it was perfect. Son-in-law was just like a son.

Anyway, I digress. I had been spending my summer working at my dad's office, just like I had the summer before, soaking in ledgers, credits, debits, balance sheets, payroll, taxes, you name it. I had a knack for it even though I found it tedious and dull, but the scenery more than made up for it; and by scenery, I mean Ryan. Of course, I loved spending time with my dad and making him proud. My dad really had his heart set on me being an accountant, so I faked it.

There I was one day, in my own little cubicle, and in walks Victoria. Ryan only dated women that had proper names like Elizabeth, Josephine, Francesca, or Isabelle. Definitely not Charlee or CJ. Coincidentally, Victoria looked like a Victoria's Secret model: long, flowing red hair (Ryan had a thing for redheads, that's all I ever saw him with, remind me to tell you someday about my hair dying experiment); tall; flawless skin; bright blue eyes—you get the picture. She was perfect. I couldn't help but compare myself to her. I felt plain next to her with my ash-colored hair and hazel eyes. She was even a little taller than me.

I watched her walk into Ryan's office. She greeted him with a small kiss on his cheek. Even from where I was, I could see his beautiful green eyes light up. I had never seen him behave in such a way with any of the other women that had come to visit him. He certainly didn't lack for female companionship, but Victoria had been more of a permanent fixture. I had seen her at his parents' house, too. With all of that, I shouldn't have been surprised that they announced that they were engaged and were planning a wedding for the end of August, right before school started in the fall.

I won't lie, I cried a little in the privacy of my bedroom when I found out. In public I was all smiles.

"Congratulations, Ryan," I said as he dropped off a stack of papers at my desk the day after the big reveal. He smiled like he was the happiest man in all the world.

I'm not going to lie, that hurt. I mean, why couldn't he wait one more year, you know, to see how I turned out and all?

"So, Charlee, we need someone to serve punch at our reception. Would you be interested?"

I tried my hardest not to let my shoulders slump or my head drop. Of course I wasn't interested. I didn't even want to go to his dumb wedding. In my heart, I knew Victoria wasn't the woman for him. She was so serious, and she always looked like someone had peed in her Cheerios. I mean, seriously, if Ryan had asked me to be his wife, I would be turning cartwheels and have a permanent smile on my face.

But it didn't matter what I thought. What did I know? I was only a kid. "Yeah, sure," I responded.

"Great, I'll give you more details the closer we get."

I smiled, and he walked away.

Ryan's nuptials were only the tip of the iceberg of bad news that summer. Soon my life would come crashing down around me. Everything I ever thought I knew and believed in would be brought into question. August Twentieth of that year would go down in the History of Charlee as the day the sky came tumbling down.

It was Ryan's wedding day, a day I prayed wouldn't happen. The more I saw of Victoria that summer, the more I knew in my heart and gut she wasn't the right person for him. She didn't seem that into him. She didn't act how I would have expected a bride-to-be to act. She was kind of bossy, and anytime I saw Ryan try to give his opinion, she acted like it didn't matter and was completely dismissive. A couple of times, I wanted to jump in and say, "Hey lady, look how nice he's being to you, can't you see how much he loves you? The least you could do is try and deserve him." But I never did. My dad even offhandedly mentioned once, on our way home in the car, how he thought perhaps Ryan should think twice.

Ryan never gave it a second thought, so I found myself sitting behind Jeffrey and Monica, the best parents ever, or at least I thought so at the time, in my dad's new Audi, on the way to the Fountains of Loveland to some stuffy wedding. It was so stuffy, Victoria ordered me to wear a horrible eggplant-colored satin full-length gown just to serve punch. It cost two hundred dollars, and I would never be caught dead in it again. In fact, I was planning on burning it in tribute of their unholy union.

So, there we sat in the hoity-toity ceremony room that was sprayed with different shades and hues of purple. It looked like Barney had thrown up in there. I'm sure I remember it being more horrible than it really was, due to my frame of mind, but even my mom arched her eyebrow in scrutiny.

The ceremony began. There was my lovely Ryan standing up front with his brother by his side. They were both handsomely decked out in black tuxedos, again stuffy. I was having a much more fun and relaxed wedding when my time came. Ryan looked like he was the luckiest man in the world, and Evan was looking around for his next conquest. Oddly enough, he looked my way and winked. He had been paying a lot more attention to me that summer since he had been home on break from Georgia Tech. He was still as gorgeous as ever, but he knew it, while his brother never seemed to let it go to his head.

Did I mention Victoria had nine bridesmaids, and they were all gorgeous like her? They also had that air about them, too. Apparently they'd all eaten peed-on Cheerios. I couldn't believe this was the life my sweet Ryan was destined to live. He was too nice and fun to be around such stuck-up boringtons. The wedding march started, and all eyes turned to the bride. There she was, in all her redheaded glory, in a dress fit for a queen. It was mermaid style and fussy with more beads than a bedazzle factory, but she looked stunning. She also looked bored and stiff. Really? If I had Ryan waiting for me at the end of the aisle, and smiling at me like he was smiling at her, I would have been running and jumping into his arms and kissing off his face. Not her, though. She moved at a snail's pace and looked more at her bridesmaids than she did at the man who looked at her like she was his everything. I felt so sorry for Ryan, but as he took her hand from her father, he only had eyes for her.

The actual ceremony was long, flowery, and quite honestly, fake and insincere. They both read poems from somebody I'd never heard of. They had nothing to do with love, joy, or even romance; it was more like how a business contract read. As they and the priest droned on, I looked at my parents, who were sitting close together. My dad held my mom's hand in his like he never wanted to let go. His other arm was around me and he would squeeze me from time to time. That was what love was. At that moment, I felt sorry for Ryan. I knew he wasn't getting what my parents had. Sure my parents had their issues like everyone, but I knew they loved each other. I vowed then that I would make sure to never settle for less. My mom had told me for years, the most important decision you'll ever make is who you decide to spend your life with.

Well, rings were exchanged and the "kiss the bride" moment happened; sadly, Victoria pulled away before Ryan was done, but he took it in stride. They walked back down the aisle together as Mr. and Mrs. Carter. He looked like he was on top of the world, and she looked haughty, with her head held high and stiff. She didn't even crack a smile.

I sighed.

My dad looked over to me and smiled. "Don't go getting any ideas. You're still way too young to think about marriage." I guess he mistook my sigh. I wasn't envious of what I just saw. In fact, I was a little sad.

After the long procession of bridesmaids and groomsmen, we all followed them into the ballroom. There I took up my duties serving punch. I don't know why I agreed to it, but my mom said it was the neighborly thing to do. Easy for her to say. She didn't have to stand all night in ridiculously high heels. I looked like a grape fruit roll up.

My only source of entertainment came from Krissy. She and I scanned the crowd and dance floor for attractive guys that were relatively our age. Unfortunately, there weren't many. I guess I really had been born too late. Admittedly, I also watched Ryan and Victoria. A lot. I was fascinated, not in the good way, with her behavior. She spent more time chatting with her friends than she did with Ryan. Sure, Ryan stood near, but she seemed to ignore him. I also watched Guy and Kaye. I got the feeling they weren't all that impressed with their new daughter-in-law's behavior. Then I watched my parents on the dance floor and the way my dad held my mom close. I sighed again, but this time it was a happy sigh.

My parents seemed to fit. My dad was tall, dark, and handsome, and my mom was light and feminine, with a willowy figure. You could see that they were in love.

As I was oohing and aahing over my parents, I had a surprise. Evan, Ryan's playboy brother, requested punch, although it looked like he'd had plenty to drink from the other side at the bar. "Charlee, you are looking fine tonight. How old are you now?"

Part of me was flattered because I was seventeen and stupid at the time. I think I even blushed. "I turned seventeen in March."

He smirked. "Let's dance."

"Oh, well . . . I'm kind of busy serving punch."

"No problem." He left and asked some woman I didn't know if she wouldn't mind serving punch while we danced. She quickly agreed, and I was relieved of my duties for a moment.

Evan held out his hand to me. I took it with unease. I had little beepers going off in my head telling me that maybe this wasn't the best idea, but again, I was seventeen, naïve, and flattered that a very attractive older man was paying attention to me. Evan was tall, like Ryan, and they looked similar, but Evan was darker and had brown eyes.

Evan led me to the outside of the dance floor where it was a darker and less populated. He pulled me close and rested his hand awfully close to my gluteus maximus region. I could smell the beer on his breath—it was real classy. I placed my hand on his shoulder anyway. He smirked again and applied more pressure with his hand near my nether regions.

I smiled nervously, and that seemed to give him satisfaction. He grinned wickedly. Those beepers went off again.

"You filled out nicely," he whispered in my ear. "I always knew you would."

I didn't know how to respond to that. That should have been my clue to walk away. My mom had warned me that a decent man would never make a woman feel uncomfortable, and I was very uncomfortable at the moment.

"So what are you doing after this shindig?" His breath reeked.

"Oh . . . uh . . . you know. Going home with my parents." That sounded so lame.

He laughed low. "Sounds dreadful. How about a change of plans?"

"Like what?" I knew that was the wrong thing to say as soon as I said it, but I was nervous.

He pulled me tighter to him and his hand inched lower. He crossed the zone.

I reached back and moved his hand back up. Maybe I was a lot younger than him, but I wouldn't stand for that nonsense.

He laughed devilishly. "I like a girl with a little spirit. Why don't you meet me by the gazebo after I make the best man toast."

The loud buzzer sounded in my brain to not go anywhere alone with him, especially in his obviously inebriated state. "I promised your brother I would stay and serve punch until the reception was over."

His hand slid down again. "That can be easily remedied."

I once again moved his hand up and pulled away.

Just as he was pulling me closer again, I heard a deep angel voice say, "Evan." The voice didn't sound happy.

I looked over to see Ryan walking our way. Evan let go of me, but immediately grabbed my hand, like he was telling me I should stay put.

Ryan didn't look happy at all. "Evan, it's time for the toasts to begin."

"Give me a minute, I'm a little busy here."

Ryan looked over to me, and I let go of Evan's hand. "I'm going back to the punch table now."

Evan reached out and took my hand again. "The dance isn't over yet." He looked over to his brother. "Do you think you could get someone to take over for Charlee?"

I shook my head no. "That's okay."

"Let's go, Evan." Ryan wasn't taking no for an answer.

I let go of Evan's hand, and this time he didn't take it back, but instead smirked at me. "I'll come find you later, sweet thing."

His words and look made me feel dirty.

"Evan, leave her alone. She's a kid."

I did appreciate him protecting me, but that kind of stung, although it was true.

"Look at her. She's not a kid anymore, and the age of consent in Colorado is seventeen."

Age of consent? Holy crap. That was his intention?

Ryan looked disgusted with his brother. I concurred, but I took that as my cue to leave. I didn't even look back. I rushed back to my punch-serving duties.

Ryan followed me and caught up easily. "Hey, Charlee."

I stopped and looked at him. We were almost eye level, with me in heels. "Congratulations." I tried to keep the nerves and disappointment out of my voice.

He smiled, and I reminded myself he was married and not to have any thoughts about him. "Thanks, Charlee. I'm sorry about my brother."

"Oh . . . it's okay."

"No, Charlee, it's not okay." He was completely right. "Did he do anything to you?"

I shook my head no.

He looked relieved. "Do me a favor and stay away from my brother."

I nodded my head yes. I had become a functional mute.

He smiled and showed off his perfectly white teeth. "You look very pretty tonight." He said it like I was his kid sister. Of course, that's how he should have said it. He was married and you could tell he loved Victoria, just like he should.

"Thanks." I nervously tucked a strand of hair behind my ear.

"You know, I have a really nice cousin here that's your age. I'll send him your way."

"That's okay. Thanks."

"All right. Just let me know if you change your mind."

I quickly walked back to the punch bowl, thanking my lucky stars I hadn't done anything stupid and reminding myself to quit obsessing over my crush. He was married. End of story. Off limits. Period.

The rest of the evening was a total bust. The toasts were drunk-laced and filled with crude humor from both Evan and the maid of honor, Trixie. Was that even a real name? They were both completely inappropriate, and people only seemed to laugh because they felt obligated to. I won't even insult your intelligence by repeating what was said.

I was so happy when the clock struck ten and it was time to throw the bouquet; then we could all go home. To add insult to injury, guess who caught the bouquet? Yep, me. I was only standing there because Krissy made me. I wasn't even trying, but it was like the flowers zeroed in on me and I couldn't get away. I pretended to be excited about it, but once the commotion died down, I gave the flowers to Krissy.

On the way home that night, my parents discussed at length how off the whole night seemed. They, too, had noticed the unseemly behavior of the bride. They both hoped out loud that it was an off moment for her and that she and Ryan would be blissfully happy for eternity. I could only listen, not because I didn't hope that. I honestly did. My whole life my parents had tried to instill in me the importance of commitment and what it means to be married. I wanted that for Ryan, and Ryan had made his choice. I knew I was never even in the running, but in my head we would have been perfect together.

I went to bed that night a little depressed. As I lay in bed trying to think of all the boys my own age who I could throw my attention at, I heard a very unfamiliar sound in my house. I heard my parents' raised voices, in particular my mom's. I had rarely heard my parents argue. That was something they did behind closed doors, and even then it was mild, but this was anything but mild. I couldn't make out the words, but there was some volume. My parents' room was upstairs and on the other side of the house. I had been in the basement since last year when my parents remodeled and made the basement like the coolest place ever for a teenage girl. It was perfect for slumber parties and hanging out with friends. My house had become the go-to place for team parties. I think that's why my parents did it. They wanted our house to be the gathering place—this way they knew we would all behave.

Without warning, I heard doors slamming and then crying. The puzzling part was, it was my dad who I heard crying. He must have been in the family room which was above me. I felt completely unsettled. I wasn't sure what I should do. This was so out of the norm. I lay there and worried for several minutes. My parents seemed happy all night. My dad had even sent my mom flowers earlier in the day, and she kissed him fervently when he got home from the golf course. It kind of grossed me out.

I decided to just stay there. I was sure whatever it was would blow over and in the morning it would all be okay. I woke up Sunday morning to an eerily quiet house. Sunday was our big breakfast day, and I would normally hear and smell the sounds of something wonderful being made in the kitchen. For some reason, I had this sinking feeling in the pit of my stomach. It made me not want to go upstairs, but on the other hand, I felt like I needed to.

I slowly got out of bed and ran my fingers through my overly hair sprayed and styled hair from the night before and made my way upstairs. The basement door was right off the family room. The first thing I saw was a blanket and a pillow on the couch, but no one there. The family room was sunken and off the kitchen and eating area. I made my way up to find my dad in the kitchen, looking at the Sunday paper and drinking coffee.

"Good morning, Daddy." I looked around for my mom.

My dad looked up at me from the breakfast bar. His eyes were red and swollen. He looked terrible.

"Daddy, what's wrong?"

He stood up and immediately took me in his arms, hugging the air out of me.

I knew something wasn't right. "Daddy, where's Mom?"

My dad began to cry, and I felt like I couldn't breathe. I felt ill, and I wasn't even sure why. "Daddy?" I was starting to freak out.

"She's out for a walk, clearing her head."

Well that wasn't so bad, but why was my dad bathing my head in his tears?

"Daddy, please tell me what's going on."

He hugged me tighter. "I need to tell you something."

Why did I feel like I didn't want to hear what he had to say?

He took my hand and led me to a stool at the breakfast bar. He took the one next to me. He kept on crying, making me cry, too. I had rarely seen my dad cry, and I'd never seen him cry like this. Whatever it was, it was terrible. I thought someone had died, but it was worse.

My dad took both of my hands. "Baby girl, I've done something that I'm not proud of at all. I deeply regret it. You don't know how sorry I am."

I hated this. I wanted him to say it all, while not wanting him to say it at all. I knew whatever it was, it was life changing. I just had no idea how much at the time.

"CJ, last month I had a dinner meeting with the owner of one of our largest accounts."

That didn't sound bad.

"And . . .," he could hardly speak. He was practically full-on sobbing.

"Daddy, please tell me what's going on. You're scaring me."

He looked up into my worried and watery eyes. I think he wanted me to get it without him having to admit it to me. But admit it to me he did.

"I drank too much and I wasn't thinking straight. One thing led to another and I left with *her*."

Oh. I got it. It was a *her*. I jumped up. I didn't need to hear the rest. I was smart enough and old enough to get it. I ran outside in my pajama shorts and t-shirt, I didn't even bother with shoes. I did what I always did when I was upset, I started shooting hoops. I wasn't making any shots. I was crying too hard. How could this have happened? My dad and mom loved each other. They said it every day, and more importantly they acted like it. I felt hate, hurt and confusion. What did all this mean for my family? *My poor mom. She must be devastated.* I knew how much she loved my dad. She had always told me to find someone like him when I got older.

My dad joined me after a few minutes. He looked weak.

I threw the ball at him as hard as I could. "I hate you!" I ran past him back to the house, but not before I saw the utter defeat in his hazel eyes, eyes that were just like mine.

In a matter of a week, my whole life and world came crashing down. I found myself being whisked away by my inconsolable mom. My parents gave me the choice to stay, it was my senior year after all. And I was going to be the team captain that year, but I meant what I'd said. I hated my dad. I felt I would betray my mom if I stayed. She was relieved when I chose her. My dad was just as devastated, but he agreed I should go with my mom. He begged us both to stay, but my mom couldn't bear the thought. She was broken.

The whole week before we left for my grandparent's home in Overland Park, Kansas, my dad stayed home from work. He begged and pleaded with my mom to try and work it out. It was horrible. I kept to myself. I couldn't even talk to Krissy about it. I was embarrassed and ashamed of what my dad had done. My mom was even sleeping in my room with me. I remember laying there and wiping her tears as she kept me close, like I was all that she had. My dad tried to talk to me, but I was too angry. He threw my whole world off kilter and he hurt my mom. Yes, I was a daddy's girl, but what he had done killed me and seeing what it had done to my mother worsened it all for me. My mom had always seemed prone to mild depression and insecurities, but this threw her over the edge.

I remember packing up my mom's minivan and thinking this was only a nightmare and I would eventually wake up, but the pain was too real. Then to add insult to injury, the newlyweds showed up at Ryan's parents' house next door. Ryan held Victoria's hand and waved at me with the other. I didn't return it. I vowed then and there I would never think about him again. He was married, and married men should stay married and true to their wives. And sneaky awful women shouldn't take married men to dinner and drink with them and then sleep with them. I would never, ever be a home wrecker.

So that was that. My last memory of 1935 Mulberry Lane was of my dad and Krissy standing on our perfectly manicured lawn, in our perfect neighborhood, crying and waving. I could barely see through my tears, which was bad since I was driving. My mom was like a zombie and barely functioning. Life would never be the same again.

One

"... HEALTH, GOOD HUMOR, AND CHEERFULNESS began to reappear at Longbourn." Oh wait, we weren't in a Jane Austen book. But it was true, eventually those things did reappear. It just took a long time, not the fortnight like in *Pride and Prejudice*. It was more like months, I would say even years. My senior year of high school was a blur to me. I only functioned. I did well in school and got good grades, but that was about all. I didn't make any real friends. I didn't even attend the graduation ceremony. I was mourning what I was missing out on in Colorado: my friends, the parties and celebrations. I especially missed Krissy. We talked and texted every day, but it wasn't the same. I didn't even try to make it onto the basketball team. I wanted nothing to do with the sport that had meant so much to me and my dad.

My mom was doing better by the time I graduated, and by that I meant she was getting out of bed almost every day. She and I even moved out of my grandparents' home and into our own townhouse. The divorce was finalized the summer before I started school at KU. My first school of choice had always been CU, but my mom couldn't bear to be without me, and I didn't want to be near my dad. He had come to visit me several times, but those visits were anything but pleasant. I resented him with a fiery passion. He eventually gave up and wrote me some very lovely letters and called me on a regular basis, though I rarely answered.

For those first few years, I was lost and confused. I wanted my perfect life back on Mulberry Lane. I missed Loveland and my mountains. I didn't particularly care for the plains. I missed Krissy, and mostly I missed my dad and even my mom, my mom from before our lives were obliterated.

By my junior year in college, my mom had found her new self. She shed her motherly image, lost twenty pounds, and decided to hit the single scene. At first I was happy for her, but she took to the single life in what I considered an unhealthy way. It was about this time I decided I needed to live on my own. There's nothing like coming home to find your mom making out on the couch, or worse. Besides, I had been the parent long enough.

My dad set me up with my own place. In a way I felt guilty about it. I hardly talked to him, but he always seemed to want to do whatever he could to help me out. I didn't even have to work while I went to school, which ended up hurting me more than helping, but we'll get to that momentarily.

So, there I was in my junior year, not sure what I wanted to be when I grew up, like really grew up. That's not entirely true. What I really wanted to be was a psychologist or counselor. I loved every psychology class I had taken so far. It made sense. I had felt so screwed up, and being able to analyze my situation from a research point of view helped. And I liked the thought of being able to help other people with their problems. The only problem was, everyone around me, and especially my mom, kept telling me not to waste my time on a degree that I couldn't support myself with, at least not for a long time to come. My mom was worried—she had never graduated from college and was always a stay-at-home wife and mom. She never expected to be out on her own, so I was constantly reminded that I needed to stand on my own and never depend on a man.

Don't get me wrong, my mom wasn't a man hater (in fact, she had come to love men a little too much); she just saw life through a different lens now.

I hated doing it, but I ended up majoring in accounting. It was kind of in my blood. My dad was obviously one, but oddly my mom's dad was, too, and his dad before him was. Seriously, someone needed to stop the cycle, but I guess it wasn't going to be me. I was a natural at it anyway, and it didn't require a lot of thinking on my part; which was good because I was in no state of mind for thinking.

Fast forward two years later. I'd earned a degree in a field I'd barely tolerated and I had no real work experience. So what did I do? I decided to get an MBA. There's nothing like pushing off real life for as long as possible. My dad was once again willing to help fund my juvenile delinquency. By this time, my mom was remarried to, you guessed it, an accountant. It was weird, like an epidemic. At least she was happy and behaving more like a woman her age should.

Mark was a decent enough guy. He was a little older than my mom, and he had four grown kids that were all married and had kids of their own. My mom was in grandma heaven. It was like she was meant to be a grandma, which was weird for me. I always assumed she would only dote on my children. That is, whenever I got around to getting married and having them. Nothing in my life was turning out the way I had imagined.

Two more years passed and cheerfulness really had returned for me. I had met a really nice guy named Jay Danbury, and he reminded me that, once upon a time, I was fun and spontaneous. He was an All-American boy, or I guess I should say "man" since he was twenty-six and I was twenty-five. He had beautiful blonde hair and deep blue eyes, and, of course, he was tall. He was in my MBA program and just what the doctor ordered. The only problem was, I wasn't in love with him. He was ready to make plans for the future, and he wanted to include me in them. I cared for him deeply, but no matter how hard I tried, I just couldn't love him.

I had come to a crossroad in my life. I was about ready to graduate with a master's degree, but I had no job prospects because, guess what? I had no job experience. See how that came back to bite me in the butt? No one cared that I TA'd for two years. And I had a really good guy that wanted to make me a permanent fixture in his life, but I knew it wasn't right. Marriage seemed hard enough, even when you're totally in love with someone.

It was at this time my mom and Mark had a little intervention with me. I was annoyed Mark was invited. Yes, he was a decent guy, and I was glad he made my mother happy, or at least kept her stable, but he wasn't my dad. I didn't even look at him like a stepfather. He had entered the picture way too late. They both sat me down and basically told me to grow up, get a job and get over the past. And most importantly, forgive. Apparently my parents, the real ones, Monica and Jeffrey, had discussed me at length, and they both thought it was a good idea that I move back to Colorado, at least for the summer, and work for my dad.

I stared blankly at my mother. "Huh?"

She took my hands in her newly manicured ones. "Charlee, honey, it's time to forgive your dad and grow up."

I wanted to object, not to the growing up part per se, but objecting seemed childish, which would have only proven my mom's, and apparently Mark's, point. He had sat there and nodded his head at everything my mom said. I won't even mention how hypocritical she was being. It seemed rich coming from the woman who went through a second teenage phase and only got her act together a couple of years ago. Who was the responsible one then? Oh yeah, that would be me.

I stood up. "Fine."

As I walked away, my mom called out, "Someday you're going to thank me for this. I love you."

Yeah, yeah.

I guess it was good timing, and it helped with the whole break-up with Jay. I felt terrible about breaking up with him, especially when he pulled me close and whispered, "I love you," in my ear.

I wanted to be in love with him. I really did, but it wasn't there. I don't know why.

On a more positive note, Krissy was getting married and I was going to be her maid of honor. Being in the same state would be much more convenient. And by the way, remember when I mentioned her and Chance, my old boyfriend? You guessed it. They ran into each other last summer, in Target of all places, and the sparks flew. Krissy's parents still lived next door to my dad, but Krissy lived in Fort Collins, which was only twenty-five to thirty minutes from my dad's house. That was at least exciting for me. I had missed being close to Krissy.

With my degree and loaded down Jetta, I hugged my mom goodbye in the middle of May. She held on extra tight. I was glad it was only her. I had said goodbye to my grandparents, Mark, and his family the night before. They had a little graduation celebration for me. It was still so weird that my mom was part of that. It had only been the three of us for so long, and now my mom was in the middle of a semi-large family. I had to admit, I missed being an only child and I still mourned the life I thought I should have had.

"I love you, CJ. Thank you for being my rock." My mom held me to her. It was the first time she had ever acknowledged what I had done for her. She almost seemed hesitant doing it then.

I tried not to think about that time in my life. "I love you, too, Mom."

She pulled back, held my chin, and looked me in the eye, which meant she had to look up. I was a few inches taller than her. "Go home. Be happy. Forgive your dad, he's a . . . good guy."

I wanted to disagree with her, but her look silenced me.

"He made a terrible mistake, but he's not a terrible person. And I'm sorry if I made you believe that." I caught the reluctance in her voice.

"I'll try my best, Mom."

She tapped my nose like I was two. "I have a feeling that good things are in store for you. Just don't mess it up." She had to throw in a snarky comment.

I shrugged my shoulders and smiled closed-lipped. I hoped she was right, but I didn't see how moving back in with my cheating dad and working for him was a good thing. Unfortunately, it felt like the right thing to do. I knew I had to forgive my dad. I needed to find peace with the life I had, not the one I thought I should've had or wished for. I needed to be happy in the moment. Jay had helped me realize that, and now I needed to remember it. *Why couldn't I be in love with Jay?*

I got into my car, and my mom stood and watched me until I couldn't see her anymore. I had a ten-hour drive ahead of me. My dad had offered to fly in and drive back with me, but I felt like I needed the alone time to contemplate, not to mention I hadn't spent ten hours straight with my dad since I'd moved to Kansas almost eight years ago. I felt kind of guilty for that, especially when I thought about all the things my dad had done for me, including buying me the car I was currently driving. It was a graduation gift when I earned my undergrad. He drove it all the way out to me, and I probably wasn't as kind as I should have been to him. But no matter how indifferently I had treated him over the years, he still tried to make an effort with me. He tried to keep connected.

I think I cried half of the way there, partially out of fear, but mostly because I had missed home; I knew it wasn't going to be the home I remembered. I knew a lot had changed in my absence. I'd already mentioned my dad's neighbors to the left, Krissy's parents, but what about my dad's other neighbors, the Carters? Well, the Carters moved to D.C. I'm just saying, CIA. But some Carter decided to stick around and buy his parent's house. My favorite Carter, Ryan. And to top it off, Ryan and Victoria had divorced the previous year. I only knew this because of my mom. I had been very good about not thinking about Ryan, other than to cringe when I thought about how stupid I was to ever have had a crush on such an older guy. Ryan sent my mom their family Christmas cards over the years, so that's how I knew Ryan was a dad. I thought his son's name was Josh, and he was the most adorable kid I'd ever seen. He had red hair like his mom, but he inherited his dad's green eyes, like spring buds. I was pretty sure he was three years old. And Ryan still worked for my dad. He was a partner now at my dad's accounting firm. I knew this because my dad still emailed me the company newsletter.

I swear the drive between Kansas and Colorado is the longest, most boring drive in all the United States. I could have probably set the car on cruise control and napped all the way there. Thankfully the speed limit was seventy-five, which meant I could do like eighty-five and most likely not get busted for speeding. Honestly, though, I didn't feel any desire to speed toward my destination. I kind of wanted to prolong the journey. I knew once I got there I was going to have to deal with things my heart had purposely not dealt with for many years, mainly my dad. I was going to have to find a way to get over the hurt and betrayal I had felt for almost a third of my life. I wasn't sure how I was going to take it.

After miles and miles of plains, desert, and monstrous windmills that, in my opinion, should be banned because they're terrible for the landscape, I could finally see my mountains. I was almost to Denver, and there they were, in all their majesty. I could still see some snow on the caps. I shed a few tears. I was home. Sure, I had been back to Colorado for a few weekend visits with friends, but I'd never been back home.

I carefully waded my way through Denver's rush hour traffic. I probably should have left earlier, especially since this was Friday. As I sat in bumper to bumper traffic on I-25, a little apprehension crept in. I wasn't sure how to behave around my dad anymore. I knew he was anxious for me to get there. He had already called me six times to check on me, twice in the last hour. He sounded excited. I tried to be a little emotive. I'm not sure how well I did.

Eleven long hours later I was about ready to pull onto Mulberry Lane. I took a deep breath and tried to dry my eyes. Everything looked so different, but the same, if you know what I mean. The trees were larger, there was a new subdivision behind our neighborhood, and a newer shopping complex close by, but it still felt like how I remembered.

My dad was waiting for me in the driveway when I pulled up. He was at my car door before I even turned off the ignition. My emotions overwhelmed me as I looked at him. I don't think I had really looked at him in forever. I had done my best to ignore him, but there he was. He looked so distinguished and handsome. His hair was almost completely gray now, but he still had plenty of it. He looked ecstatic as he pulled me out of my car as soon as my seatbelt was off. He didn't even hesitate to pull me to him, and I didn't hesitate in reciprocating.

"Daddy." I hadn't used that term in almost eight years. He had been dad or father. In my mind, he hadn't been deserving of daddy. Maybe it was silly for a twenty-five-year-old woman to use the term, but it seemed right in the moment.

He pulled me tighter. "Baby girl, I've missed you."

I couldn't help it. I cried like a baby. I had missed him, too. More than I had wanted to admit to myself. I soaked him in. He still smelled like Irish Spring and Old Spice.

I'm not sure how long we stood there embracing each other, but I got the feeling it wasn't nearly long enough for him. I suddenly felt like a little girl again.

"Do you want to unpack first or go get something to eat?" He reluctantly let me go.

"I don't think I can even think about getting back into a car right now."

He laughed. "So unpacking and takeout?"

"Sounds like a plan."

We both seemed unsure around each other as we unloaded the car. These next few months were going to be interesting, to say the least. I had eight years of hate to get over. Part of me felt like I didn't even know this man, yet he was just like I remembered him from before *it* happened. I was so torn. My heart, and even my head, were telling me I needed to let go and forgive, but there was that part that said, *How can you forget everything you had to give up? And what about watching your mother lie in bed for days because she felt completely worthless and betrayed*? I would sit there and stroke her hair and beg her to get up. I would tell her over and over again how wonderful and beautiful I thought she was and that my dad was wrong and horrible. She would list all the things that she thought were wrong with her. She felt unworthy. It was heart wrenching, but that wasn't even the worst of it. My mom changed. She was no longer the mother she had been most of my growing up. I felt robbed in a sense, but I guess if my mom could forgive him, I should at least try to. Hating him for so long hadn't done me much good.

It didn't take us long to unload the car. I was still down in the basement. It looked the same right down to the charcoal gray sectional and pool table. Even my room was the same—my dad had left the Denver Nuggets posters up. Sadly, or almost comfortingly, the rest of the house looked the same, too. It even smelled the same. I noticed all our family pictures were still on the walls, even the ones of only my mom and dad. It made my heart ache.

He smiled at me as I looked around. "Feel free to decorate any way you want. And if you want to spruce things up, we can go shopping, or I can give you my card."

"No, that's okay. I brought stuff from my apartment." Besides, I already had a card from him. I had tried to be responsible with it.

"Well, I'll let you get settled in. Is it okay if I pick up burgers from Harry's Pub?"

"Perfect." I smiled.

My dad pulled me to him once more. "CJ, I'm so happy you're home. I love you, kiddo."

I nodded my head against him. I hadn't told him I loved him in a very long time.

He kissed the top of my head and left me to look around and unpack. I started with my bedding. My old full-size bed was devoid of any coverings. As I started to make my bed, I noticed a gift bag on my nightstand. I sat on the edge of my bed and peered into the contents. I smelled it before I saw it. That sounded weird, but the smell of a new basketball was unmistakable. The tears came again. I reached in and pulled out an official NBA Spalding ball. Those balls weren't cheap.

I held it in my hands, almost reverently. I hadn't held a ball in forever, and it was like my hands came to life. I spun it on one finger and smiled to myself. I still had the touch. I even dribbled it a couple of times on the hardwood floor. I loved the sound of the ball against the court, and I could almost hear the screech of shoe soles against the wood. I ached to run out and shoot a few. I had noticed first thing that the basketball hoop was still up; it even looked like it had a new net. However, I refrained and placed the ball back in the bag. There I discovered a note:

Here's to new beginnings and taking a shot on or at your old man, I'll let you choose. Love, Dad

I held the note to my chest. I would decide later whether to give him a shot or shoot him, but I was leaning toward the first option.

Two

I WOKE UP, AND FOR a small moment I felt seventeen again. I could hear Supertramp on the surround sound upstairs—that was Saturday morning chore music. I hadn't heard it in forever, and it was my favorite song of theirs, "The Logical Song." I slowly sat up and looked around. I was home. I stretched and ran my fingers through my medium-length hair. I made a quick stop in my bathroom and threw on a bra. I had to remember I lived with my dad now. I had a feeling he wouldn't appreciate being reminded how womanly I was.

I ran up the stairs to find my dad in the kitchen, already dressed for the day, and from the smell of it, already cleaning. It smelled like Pine Sol and cinnamon swirl pancakes, my favorite.

He turned around from the griddle when he heard me approach. "Good morning, CJ."

"Good morning, something smells good."

"Sit down, breakfast will be ready in a few minutes."

"Do you want me to make juice or anything?" I sat down on one of the stools at the breakfast bar.

"I got it. Just relax."

"Okay. Dad?"

"Yes?" He turned back around.

"You know you don't have to wait on me and take care of me, right?"

He grinned. "Don't worry, I have a whole list of chores I've been saving until you got here."

I rolled my eyes. "Thanks."

"And, I know you're an adult."

25

"I just want to feel like I'm doing my part, you know?"

"Do me a favor and let your old man spoil you for a while, okay?"

"Okay, Dad." I smiled.

He turned back to the griddle and flipped the pancakes. "So what do you want to do today?"

I shrugged my shoulders. I hadn't really thought about it. "I don't know. I did promise Krissy we would meet up for dinner tonight, but other than that, I don't have any plans."

"Do you want to take the boat out on Boyd Lake or maybe hit the trails there with the bikes?"

I had missed the lake and our boat, and the Colorado scenery in general. To me, Colorado was like heaven. The sky even seemed bluer here. "Sounds perfect."

My dad didn't turn around, but I could see his shoulders relax, like he thought I might say no.

"All right." Excitement ran through every word. "We'll head up after we've eaten and you're ready."

We scarfed down our food. It tasted like home.

I hurried to get ready. Since we would be out on the boat, all I had to do was shower and throw my hair up in a messy bun. My dad said it would be warm and in the eighties, so I put on my red one-piece and some white shorts. I looked at myself in the mirror. I could use some color on my skin. I threw a t-shirt and towel, along with suntan lotion, in a bag and headed upstairs. My dad was ready with a cooler and some fishing poles. I shook my head. He never wasted an opportunity to fish.

"I called the marina at the lake, so we should be set." He beamed.

"Great."

We walked out together to the three-car garage. My car occupied the single slot. In the double area was my dad's old Silverado and his Audi. I was surprised he still had the same car as when my mom and I left. He usually bought a new car every few years, but I didn't bother asking why he hadn't. He threw our gear in the back of his pickup, and we pulled out. We had just pulled out onto the street in front of our house when I noticed my dad's neighbor was mowing his lawn. My dad noticed, too, and stopped.

"Ryan," he called out his open window.

Ryan let go of his lawn mower, and the engine stopped. He smiled and began walking our way.

Oh wow. He looked good. No, better than good. I think "godliest creature" still worked for him. I took a deep breath and told the butterflies in my stomach to behave. The butterflies said, *"Why? Remember, he's not married anymore."* I told them to shut up. I didn't need the reminder.

Ryan walked right up to my dad's side. "Hey, Jeff." He did a double take in my direction. He shook his head. "Charlee?"

"Hi, Ryan." I tried not to stare.

Oddly, he seemed embarrassed.

"We're heading out to the lake." My dad filled the momentary silence.

Ryan's eyes traveled from me back to my dad. "Looks like a perfect day for it." He turned back to me. "Charlee?"

"Yep, I'm still Charlee."

He ran his hand through his hair. "Sorry, it's just. Uh . . . you look . . . grown up."

"Thank you . . ." That sounded stupid. Why did I thank him for telling me I looked grown up?

He must have thought so, too. He turned his attention back to my dad and patted the truck. "Well, have a great time. I better get back to mowing my lawn."

"Don't work too hard," my dad called out to his retreating figure.

His backside looked as good as the front. Dang, he did his khaki shorts justice.

"You know Ryan's a partner now, right?" My dad headed out of our subdivision.

"I remember reading that in one of your newsletters." I may have glanced back trying to catch another glimpse of Ryan.

"He's been a great asset. Best hire I ever made. That is until you." My dad winked.

"I think that's called nepotism." I faced forward.

"Guilty." My dad laughed.

"Did you know Ryan and Victoria divorced?"

"Yeah, mom told me. That's too bad."

My dad shrugged his shoulders. "Maybe. I think it might be for the best. Victoria wasn't the easiest person to be married to. I don't think their marriage was filled with a lot of love. At least not on her part."

That didn't surprise me. I still remembered his wedding day. She sure didn't act like a woman in love.

"He has a son, right?"

"Oh yeah, cutest little guy ever. His name is Josh."

"Does he live with his mom?"

"They share custody."

"So does she live nearby?"

"Yes."

I sat back and thought about Ryan Carter. I hadn't thought about him in years, just like I shouldn't have, but I figured since he was divorced now, my mind could have free reign. His hair was a tad darker, but his eyes still shined. It looked like he hadn't shaved yet this morning, and it totally worked for him. He had an angular and perfectly proportioned face. I wasn't expecting this reaction to him. I thought he was a stupid crush, and I guess he still was, but geez looking at him again made me realize that I had every right to have crushed on and fantasized about him. Now that I was mature, I was admiring him.

My dad's deep voice brought me out of my thoughts about my new coworker. Hey, maybe working for my dad wouldn't be so bad after all.

"CJ?"

"Yeah, Dad? Sorry. What did you say?"

He looked over my way and smiled, like he knew something. "I was just asking how your mom is."

"Oh . . ." What should I say? "She's . . . happy."

"I'm glad." He didn't sound all that glad. "Do you like Mark?" He didn't seem like he really wanted to know.

"Yeah."

"You're not convincing me."

"Mark's great for Mom. It's just . . ." How did I put it into words? Especially to my dad. I wanted to say, "I don't like having another man in our lives. A man who has a big family that takes time away from me, and in some ways I think Mom likes them better because they have babies and their acts together and they don't remind her of the past. And mostly I hate it because it's not you, Dad," but I didn't say any of those things.

My dad glanced my way. "I'm sorry, CJ."

I wiped at my eyes.

He reached over and held my hand, and I let him. I missed his big strong hands. "You want to change the subject?"

"Please."

He squeezed my hand tight and let go. "Well, I have all the necessary information for you to apply for your CPA license. You'll just need to sit for the exam. I can help you study if you want."

"Yeah, sure." I still wasn't sure why I was becoming a CPA, but since I had nothing else going for me, I went with it.

I was grateful we didn't talk about anything else accounting related for the rest of the day. I was already dreading Monday. Well, maybe not so much now that I knew I had something fine to look at from time to time, but not even Ryan Carter could make me happy about being an accountant.

The sun and water were just what the doctor ordered. I forgot how much I loved being out on the lake, especially with my dad. It was a little awkward. We had lots of lags in the conversation, but I think you're supposed to be quiet when you fish and soak in the sun. I wasn't really one for fishing, but my dad convinced me to give it a try again. I think he was hoping age would have changed my mind on the sport; he was going to be disappointed.

In the spirit of trying to build a relationship with him again, I decided to at least pretend, but I refused to bait the hook. No matter how old I was, I wasn't gouging a worm.

My dad laughed at me and sacrificed the slimy earthworm. I reluctantly sat up and grabbed the pole.

I was happy to sunbathe all day on our old Sea Ray. There were so many good memories associated with the old boat. I could picture my mom reading and my dad fishing while Krissy and I laid out and talked incessantly about boys and maybe a couple of men with the last name of Carter. We had code words for them; I would have died if my parents knew I was checking out my much older neighbors. Ryan was Zeus, for obvious reasons, and Evan was Hercules. I think we were studying Greek Mythology at the time. I know it was dumb, but I plead teenage girl.

I couldn't help but think about my dad sweetly kissing my mom in front of us and her pretending to be embarrassed by it all those years ago. You could tell she loved it, though. It had been apparent they loved each other. How did it all go so wrong? I think my mom was happy now, but I'd never seen her look at Mark the way she looked at my dad. Why did my dad have to ruin everything?

I tried not to let my emotions and hate get the better of me. I had to remind myself I needed to move on and forgive, but it was difficult.

"Are you okay?" My dad brought me out of my thoughts.

I shook my head. "No . . . I mean yes."

He looked concerned.

I turned my attention back to the pole in my hand that now had a squirming worm on the end. It almost seemed cruel. Okay, it was cruel.

"Do you need a refresher course on how to cast your line?"

"You're not the only guy that has taken me fishing."

He arched his eyebrow. "Someone I should know about?"

I wish. *Why couldn't I be in love with Jay?* I shook my head. "No, just a friend that liked to fish and thought I should, too."

"Sounds like a good friend."

"He's the best."

We both pulled back and sent our lines sailing across the water as if we were in sync. We also reeled in the same amount at the same time. We looked at each other and smiled. My heart ached for how much I had missed him. I noticed the extra creases and lines as he smiled, but he'd really aged well. Very distinguished.

"So, no other men I need to know about?" My dad reeled in his line and threw it back out there.

"Nope."

He looked at me like he couldn't believe it.

"Seriously, Dad. I'm not seeing anyone."

"Then there are a lot of fools out there."

I lazily reeled in my line. "I was seeing someone, but I broke it off."

"What was wrong with him?"

"Nothing, he was about as perfect as they come."

"Then what was the problem?"

I shrugged my shoulders. "He wanted to marry me and . . ."

My dad dropped his pole.

I laughed.

He quickly picked it up. "I wasn't expecting that."

"Obviously."

"So was there someone else?"

"No. I would never do that to anyone." I realized too late that was probably not the nicest thing to say to my dad.

My dad's head dropped. "You don't know how sorry I am."

I shook my head. "I didn't mean to—"

"I know, CJ."

I casually tossed my line out again. "I couldn't say yes to Jay because I didn't love him. At least not how a wife or even a girlfriend should love someone she wants to spend the rest of her life with. I care deeply about him, but there was something missing. Does that make sense?"

My dad nodded his head.

"I wonder if there's something wrong with me. I mean, Jay is the whole package, and I know he loves me and he would do whatever he could to secure my happiness, but it's just not there."

My dad reeled in his line and set his pole down. His eyes were warm and thoughtful. "Baby girl, there's nothing wrong with you. You did the right thing. When the right person comes along, you'll know."

"I hope so. It's not like I'm looking to get married right now, but I'm worried I let my one chance walk out the door."

"Unfortunately for your dad, I don't think you'll have to worry about that. I've already noticed several men staring at my daughter today. I may have to get out to the shooting range some more and do some target practice."

I rolled my eyes at him. "I think you're obligated to say that."

"Obligated or not, you have grown into a beautiful woman."

"Thanks, Dad."

My dad turned back to the water and his pole. "This is what

happens when you take women fishing. Too much talking and not enough fishing." He turned to me and winked.

My dad caught several nice-sized rainbow trout throughout the rest of the afternoon. I caught some nice branches and an old can of Budweiser, which was fine with me. Most importantly, I caught some rays—my skin had a nice healthy glow going for it at the end of the afternoon.

On our drive back home, I could tell my dad was a happy guy. He was singing along to the classic rock station and intermittently smiling at me. I had to admit it felt good to be with him; it was helping me to remember that he wasn't the monster that I'd made him out to be in my head. I knew our fishing trip wasn't the cure to our relationship, but I think it was a start.

Three

"HEY, DO YOU MIND IF I invite our neighbors over tomorrow night for a fish fry?" Dad grabbed his tackle box from the back of the truck.

"The Lawtons?" The Lawtons were Krissy's parents.

Dad grinned. "No, our other neighbors."

I shrugged my shoulders, but my insides were dancing. "I don't mind." I tried to act casual about it.

"Great. I'll see if Ryan and Josh can make it."

I smiled and ran into the house to get ready to meet Krissy. I hadn't seen her in two months, and I couldn't wait to see her. We talked and texted every day, but I needed some massive real-time Krissy. I showered and dolled up a little. Krissy was the hot best friend. Tiny, big boobs, small waist, perfect flowing golden blonde hair. If we weren't best friends, I would probably hate her.

I went with a navy-striped white dress, paired with a yellow belt and a cute jean jacket that hit me at my waist. I wore sandals with no heel, so I didn't feel like an Amazon woman next to Krissy. She was a cute five-feet-three. I grabbed my yellow bag to match and was ready to hit the town, or at least Chili's. It was our favorite hangout. We were addicted to their chips and salsa and strawberry lemonade.

I hurried up the stairs and found my dad with the Rockies game on, chips and soda in hand. Not much had changed.

"See you later, Dad."

He looked up from the game. "Wowza! Are you too old for me to tell you not to leave the house looking like that?"

"Looking like what?"

"Gorgeous."

I rolled my eyes, but I was flattered. I missed my dad's bias. "Thanks, Dad. I'll see you later."

My dad's smile faltered. "Are you too old to kiss your old man goodbye?"

I smiled, walked over to him, and bent down and kissed his cheek. "Bye, Dad."

He reached up and touched my cheek. "I love you, kiddo."

"I know." Why couldn't I say it back? I knew he wanted me to, and part of me wanted to say it, but I couldn't make myself.

He looked dejected, but understanding. "Do you need some money?"

"No, I'm good. I think I've taken enough of your money."

He reached into his pocket, grabbed his wallet, and handed me two twenties. "Take this."

I hesitated.

He pushed it forward some more. "Please, it will make me feel better."

I snatched the money. "Thanks, Dad."

He winked at me and went back to watching the game.

I took that as my cue and headed up to the main level and out to the garage.

"Hey, you still have your pepper spray?" my dad yelled out as I was walking out the door.

I shook my head to myself. "Yes, Daddy." Okay, so I missed this. It was nice to have someone worry about me for a change and not the other way around. I could understand why my mom behaved like she had, but understanding and approval are two entirely different things.

As I opened the garage door and walked out to my car, our *neighbors* were passing by in front of our house. Ryan stopped when he saw me walk out. He held the hand of the most adorable kid I had ever seen. I waved to them both.

I was surprised when Ryan approached me. "Charlee?"

I wasn't sure why he kept saying my name like it was a question. "Last time I checked, yes." I smiled.

He smiled back, albeit some embarrassment was mixed in.

34

I noticed he still had the perfect smile and gleaming white teeth. His dentist must love him.

"Dad . . . dee!" his son squealed.

Ryan picked him right up. "Hold on buddy, we'll go to the park in a minute,"

Ryan was becoming more and more attractive by the second.

"Charlee, this is my son, Josh."

I reached out and touched Josh's soft, chubby little hand. "It's nice to meet you, Josh. How old are you?"

He tried to hold up three fingers. It was cute to watch him. Ryan helped him keep his pinky finger down.

"I's three." His little voice was completely adorable.

"Well, you are the cutest three-year-old ever."

He smiled at me like he knew.

"Josh, this is Charlee." Ryan smiled at his son. "Can you say Charlee?"

"Cherry," Josh said, proud of himself.

"No, Charlee," Ryan corrected.

"I think I like Cherry." It had a ring to it.

"Cherry," Josh repeated while trying to wiggle out of his dad's arms.

"I think someone wants to get to the park."

Ryan concurred. "Well, it was nice to see you again, Charlee."

"Don't you mean Cherry?" I teased.

Ryan flashed those pearly whites at me and my stomach went *whoa, baby*. I reached down, held it, and subconsciously told it to settle down.

"See you later."

"Yeah, I guess we'll see you for dinner tomorrow night."

Ryan looked confused.

"Oh, I guess my dad hasn't talked to you yet. Well darn, I guess I ruined the surprise."

His eyes questioned me again.

"He just wanted to invite you over for dinner."

Ryan shook his head at me like he wasn't sure what to make of me. "Oh . . . that sounds good."

"Okay, but when he asks you, make sure you act surprised."

He stared at me again like he was trying to figure me out, but after a few seconds he smiled. "I'll do my best."

"Thank you. I would hate to disappoint my dad."

He shook his head at me again. "See you tomorrow."

Tomorrow can't get here soon enough, I thought. "Bye, Josh." I waved at him.

Josh was now down and trying to drag his daddy to the park, but his daddy kept looking at me. "Bye-bye, Cherry. Come on, Daddy."

"Have fun at the park." I kept waving.

"Bye, Charlee." Ryan still said my name like a question.

"Bye, Ryan."

I couldn't help but watch him walk away. The butterflies in my stomach applauded, like a standing ovation. He was beautiful.

I got into my car and blasted the air, I needed to cool off.

On the drive up to Fort Collins, my mind kept being drawn to my "neighbor." I wasn't sure how he ended up in his parent's old home, but gosh was I glad. I needed to remind myself to act like the mature twenty-five-year-old I was, at least I was most of the time. I mean, sure I knew it was never happening between us, but I was going to be enjoying the scenery.

I made it to Chili's in no time and there waited the best friend ever in her cute little white convertible that fit her personality to a tee.

Krissy hopped out of her car as soon as she saw me. Yep, she was perfection. She was wearing a cute pink sundress, and her cascading golden locks would fit into a Pantene commercial.

We ran to each other, jumped and hugged, like we were five, but a very mature five. The only awkward part now was that Krissy's head hit my boob line, but what the heck, we were best friends.

"Oh. My. Gosh. You look gorgeous!" Krissy gushed.

That was what made Krissy the best friend ever— she thought I was the most gorgeous creature. She really needed to look in a mirror.

"Right back at ya, babe."

"Let me get something out of my car before we go in." She headed back toward her car and I accompanied her.

She sneakily reached in and grabbed a black garment bag.

"What's this?"

"Your maid of honor dress."

"It's in already?"

"Yes . . .?" There was on odd tone to her voice.

"What was that?"

"I don't know what you mean."

I narrowed my eyes. "Liar."

She smiled and giggled.

"Seriously, what's up?"

"It's a surprise. I'll show you once we get in."

"Just show me now. You don't want to take my dress into the restaurant."

"Of course I do. I want you to try it on."

"Where?"

"In the bathroom. Where else?"

"Krissy, I'm not changing in a public restroom."

She grabbed my hand and pulled me into the restaurant. "Oh come on, it will be fun."

"Public nudity in a filthy bathroom? Fun is not the word I would use."

She laughed at me. "Come on, CJ. It's your duty as my maid of honor to do whatever I say."

I rolled my eyes at her. "Okay, bridezilla, but you owe me like five strawberry lemonades."

"Deal."

She hauled me and the dress into Chili's and talked the enamored seating host into a booth right by the bathroom. I guess the guy didn't notice the huge sparkler on her ring finger, or he didn't care. I had a feeling everything we ordered tonight would be on the house. Krissy had this way with guys.

With seating reserved, she dragged me into the bathroom. I didn't even like to pee in public restrooms, I couldn't believe I agreed to strip down in one. As soon as we walked in, I instantly wished for the musty smelling locker room at our old high school. I thought changing in there was bad, but this took the cake.

I'm sorry to say, I used the handicap stall. Yes, I felt guilty about it, but it was the cleanest and by the far the roomiest. Besides, Krissy insisted on coming in with me because it was okay if I touched the dirty, germy floor, and walls, but heaven forbid the dress did.

I started by unrolling practically a whole roll of toilet paper on the floor while Krissy laughed at me. Yes, I would heavily tip to pay for the wasted toilet paper. There was no way my bare feet were touching that floor. Then I stripped down to my skivvies. Thankfully I wore the cute lacey undies. "Okay, now hand over the dress before someone comes in here and exposes me."

She grinned evilly. "I don't know why you care, if I had your body, I would probably walk around like that."

"Seriously, Krissy, look in a mirror. You have a rockin' bod. Now hand over the dress."

She slowly unzipped the garment bag to my irritation. I barely saw the beautiful deep red satin before she turned to me. "Now before you see the dress, just know this was for the best."

"What are you talking about? I've already seen the dress."

Krissy had chosen a dress from a chain bridal store, that way, even in Kansas, I could go in and get fitted for it. For a bridesmaid's dress, I thought it was tasteful—definitely not dreadful, and the color totally worked for me. The style was flirty, A-line, and almost to the knee with a sweetheart neckline. Probably nothing I would wear again, but for a day, completely doable.

"Well . . . I got to thinking that I wanted something a little more sleek and sophisticated. And since we already had your measurements, I chose a different dress."

I tried not to be annoyed. I mean, it was her big day, but a heads up would have been nice and even polite. "Fine, show me what you've got, and hurry." I was covered in goose bumps. There was a vent directly above me, blasting cold air, and let's just say my ladies were awfully perky.

She turned around and pulled out the dress. I thought *what a weirdo, it's just a dress*. She turned back around and held out a dress made for . . . well . . . those that frequented Colfax. Colfax Avenue in Denver had the reputation for those that liked to get paid for their night-time services. I don't know if that was true, but everyone said it growing up. For all I knew, Colfax was a lovely street, but anyway.

"I thought you said sophisticated, not hooker."

Her face faltered. "So you don't like it?"

I reached out and touched the red satin. "There's not a lot there to like, if you get my drift."

"All the other girls like it, and it covers them plenty."

"Krissy, all your other bridesmaids are tiny like you. I'm like five to six inches taller than the rest of them." Krissy was a cheerleader in high school and then for CSU. Three of her bridesmaids were on her old squad, then there was her sister, and they all looked like her.

"CJ, just try it on. Please."

I huffed and I puffed and I tried on the Barbie doll dress. I wriggled into the tiny dress and held my breath in while Krissy zipped it up. When I looked down, I saw a lot of skin. The dress had the tiniest spaghetti straps, it cut straight across the chest, and it felt like it barely covered my bum. Breathing was also apparently optional. I turned around to a beaming Krissy.

"You look amazing." She was nothing but sincere.

It was then I knew I couldn't object. This was her wedding, and for her I would look like a painted lady of the night. She's the only person I would do it for.

"You have to see yourself, let's go look in the mirror."

"I'm good. I'm not walking out there."

"I almost forgot." She reached back into the bag. There she pulled out the red strappy high hooker heels to match.

I shook my head at her. "Are you trying to kill me on your wedding day?"

She gave me her pouty look.

I took the dang shoes out of her hand. As I bent down to put them on, I felt a lot of air in the back. First order of business was buying Spanx. Second order of business was looking for the worst bridesmaid dress ever and putting it on hold for when I got married. Payback was going to be painful for her.

I walked out of the stall and prayed no one would walk in. I had already heard one lady snickering at us in another stall. My ankles already hurt. I was going to have to take the next six weeks to practice walking in the hooker heels. It was a good thing Chance's best man was his brother and tall, just like him, or else I would really look like a freak. I was already going to look like an Amazon woman compared to all the other ladies in the line.

I took a deep breath and looked in the mirror. It was as bad as I thought. Lots of skin and nothing left to the imagination. I think I would almost be more comfortable in my bathing suit.

Krissy knew I wasn't impressed. "I don't know why you don't like it. Look at yourself. If I had your legs and curves, I would show them off all the time."

I rolled my eyes. I was of the "let's leave it to their imagination" mindset. I mean, I wasn't a prude and I sometimes showed some skin, but never like this, unless you counted at the pool or beach. "I love you, Kris." It was all I could say as I stared at my reflection and tried to yank the dress down a little more. Yes, it showed off my curves and my long legs, but this was so not me.

"Well, you should thank me for letting you look so hot next to me on my wedding day."

I looked at her through the mirror. "Thanks wasn't the word I was thinking of."

"Believe me, you're going to be thanking me someday that I finally got you to wear a dress that shows off your assets."

"I think you should have left off the last three letters of that word. That's more fitting."

We both started laughing, but it was true. I would be doing squats like no one's business the next six weeks. If everyone was going to see my butt, it was going to be at its finest.

I carefully redressed and kind of wished the dress would accidentally-on-purpose fall into the toilet, but Krissy made sure to prevent me from causing any harm to the tiny garment. I wasn't even allowed to take it home with me. She knew me all too well. I did insist on taking the shoes home. I was serious about practicing walking in them.

I was more than happy to be fully clothed and sitting in our booth.

Of course, the service was excellent, because our server was male. And like I said, Krissy had this way with people. I don't think she'd ever met a stranger, especially of the male variety. Honestly, though, I wasn't jealous of her. Krissy was the sweetest girl I knew and I loved her—there was no room for the green-headed monster to pop up. It didn't even bother me that she was marrying my ex-boyfriend. We had discussed at length about how weird it was that she was marrying someone I had made out with on several occasions, but if she was okay with it, I certainly was. And I promised I wouldn't make mention of it during my toast. Besides, Chance never really did it for me anyway, obviously, since I kept calling him Ryan. Now that was something I wished he would forget. The last time I saw him and Krissy, he'd brought it up. Krissy had given me a knowing look, and like the best friend she was, she didn't rat me out.

"So how is it being back home with your dad?" Krissy snagged a chip as soon as our server brought them out.

I eyed the chips, wondering now if I should eat them. I could barely breathe in the loin cloth I was going to have to wear for her wedding, but I threw caution to the wind and grabbed a chip and double dipped. "So far, better than I thought. He isn't as bad as I made him out to be."

Her smile lent to some sadness. "He told my parents how excited he was for you to come home."

I tucked my hair behind my ear on one side. "I know, and I'm trying."

She reached across the table and touched my hand. "I'm glad you're home."

I smiled wide. "Being close to you is the biggest perk of all."

She arched her eyebrow. "Really? What about your dad's other neighbor? That has to have you pretty perky." She laughed at how funny she thought she was.

"You mean Ryan? As in my dad's partner and divorcee Ryan?"

"No, I mean the hottest man on the planet Ryan that you were totally in love with that's now single."

I rolled my hazel eyes at her. "Okay, first, I was young and immature and I wasn't in love with him, I just had a crush on him."

41

It was her turn for eye rolls. "So now that you're mature, what do you think?"

"He's still very handsome." I tried to remain nonchalant, but the butterflies in my stomach were saying *liar, liar, pants on fire*.

She smirked at me. "Is that all?"

"Of course. I mean, the guy's a dad now, and when he saw me this morning, all he could say was, 'You look grown up.'"

"I'm sure he meant it as a compliment."

"Ha ha. It's fine. I know there will never be anything between us other than being neighbors and co-workers for the next few months." And I'm sure he would show up from time to time in some of my sultry dreams of the night, but that didn't need to be said out loud. In fact, if he didn't, my subconscious and I were going to have a serious discussion.

Her demeanor dropped. "Are you really only staying for a few months?"

I sighed heavily. "I don't know. I really don't want to be an accountant."

"I still don't understand why you ended up with a degree you hate, and then to top it off, you got an MBA."

"I know, but at the time I just needed something I didn't have to think about, something I knew I would be good at." That, and I had applied to grad schools for Psychology and was rejected. I never told anyone. It wasn't because of a lack of excellent grades, it was because I didn't have enough psychology classes under my belt, but still, to be rejected wasn't something I wanted to admit to anyone. Not even Krissy.

"Maybe you'll like working for your dad and *Ryan*."

I shrugged my shoulders. "Maybe."

She grinned evilly. "Come on, CJ."

"So maybe the scenery will be nice at work."

"Are you kidding me? If I wasn't engaged and I was working with Ryan, I would make sure I wasn't only looking."

"Well, I'm sure if it was you, and not me, Ryan would be amenable."

"You really don't get how gorgeous you are, do you?"

"This is why we're best friends."

"I think you may need to clean off your mirrors because your vision is cloudy. CJ, you need to get over the way your mom's issues messed with your head. You're gorgeous inside and out. I bet even Ryan Carter has noticed."

We both giggled way too loud for twenty-five-year-olds, but she was right. I needed to get over my issues. Not that I needed to think I was gorgeous, but I needed to remember who I was. I looked at Krissy and was so grateful for our sixteen years of friendship. If it hadn't been for her, I don't know where I would be. She was the one that convinced me to move out of my mom's place, or more like she threatened she would tell my dad the whole truth if I didn't agree to it. It was hard for me to ask my dad for the help, especially because it seemed selfish and like I was some spoiled brat wanting my own place. But I had to get out, and I couldn't tell my dad the real reason why. I probably should have gotten a job and taken out student loans and done it on my own, but I just couldn't think about it. Emotionally, I had been totally spent at the time.

Four

I WOKE UP EARLY SUNDAY morning. I needed to run off chips and salsa and strawberry lemonades. My incentive was that stupid dress. I still couldn't believe Krissy changed dresses like that, and this close to the wedding. She was already behind. I was meeting her at her parents' house later for brunch and an invitation addressing party. I loved how she called it a party, like it would make it more fun. The invitations were supposed to go out two weeks ago, but Krissy abhorred how the pictures turned out, so she talked the photographer into redoing them, all free of charge. The girl had a gift. Hence I would be wearing a hoochie dress for her wedding.

My dad was already up when I made it upstairs. He was one of those old-timers that still had the Sunday paper delivered. Seeing him sitting there drinking coffee and reading the paper reminded me of the day my life changed forever. I tried to shake off the crushing feeling. *Breathe, Charlee*, I told myself.

"CJ . . . CJ . . . Charlee."

I shook my head when I realized my name was being called. "What?" That came out harsher than I intended.

My dad cocked his head. "Are you okay, baby girl?"

"I'm fine."

"You know, when a woman says she's fine, that's always a good indicator she's not."

I plastered a fake smile on my face and decided to ignore his comment. "Did the Rockies win last night?"

He took off his reading glasses and peered into my eyes. "Honey, tell me, what's wrong?"

I stood at the counter and looked back at him. For a moment I wanted to tell him everything, but I couldn't. "Nothing's wrong. I'm going to go for a run."

His look said he knew I was lying. I could tell he considered calling me on it and then thought the better of it. He smiled closed-lipped. "Okay, kiddo. Make sure to take some water and your cell phone."

"I will."

"Do you want to shoot some hoops when you get back?" His eyes flooded with hope.

"I can't. I promised Krissy and her mom I would help with addressing her wedding invitations."

My dad's head dropped. "I remember now. But you'll be home for the fish fry, right? Ryan and Josh are coming."

That thought made me smile. "I plan on it. Do you want me to make dessert or anything for it?"

I think he was going to say no, but he changed his mind. "That would be great."

"See you in a bit." I turned to walk out the back door.

"By the way, Ryan wanted me to tell you he was surprised by the invite." My dad caught me before I walked out the door.

I shook my head and smiled. "See you later."

"Love you, kiddo." He didn't even wait for my response before he turned back to his paper.

I stood there for a second and grappled with whether I should reciprocate. In the end I didn't have the courage. I turned and walked out the door and across our perfectly lush green lawn to the back of the yard where we had a gate that led back to the greenway. As soon as I opened the gate, I felt this wash of happiness come over me. I looked at the leafy trees and grass and even the well-worn concrete path. I loved it all. So much so, my eyes welled up with tears as I stretched the muscles in my legs.

I thought back to the many hours I had spent running on the greenway conditioning for basketball. My dad used to run with me on occasion. We had a schedule of long distance running and sprinting and would alternate. My dad made sure I could endure a full game of running up and down the court. At first I balked at him, but it had paid off. My coaches always remarked how impressed they were with my ability to play hard for all four quarters. I was rarely taken out of a game. Really, the only time I was taken out was when we were so far ahead that the coach felt comfortable sending in the second string.

I wasn't in that kind of shape anymore, but I still enjoyed running. I planned on doing plenty of it the next several weeks in preparation for the wedding. I normally put on my running playlist on my phone and threw in some earbuds, but this morning I found I just wanted to take in nature. The sounds of the birds singing and the bubbling of the little brook that ran along the path. I started off slowly, but quickly sped up. It was like my body became more and more alive the farther down the path I got. I felt free, as well as a sense of belonging. I hadn't felt like I belonged in so long.

Kansas never became my home. I always felt out of place and nothing ever fit there, but here everything was in sync with me. Well, except my dad, but maybe we would get there. I used to be more in tune with him than anyone.

After a good thirty minutes of serious running, I was feeling the runner's high (or Rocky Mountain high, take your pick). I was reveling in it, lost in my thoughts, and not paying attention to my surroundings, which probably wasn't the best thing for a woman out running by herself. Thankfully, my perpetrator was innocent, or at least I think he was. He did save me once from his handsy brother.

"Charlee."

I jumped out of my skin and held onto my heart as I felt company to my right and heard my name.

He chuckled. "Sorry, I didn't mean to startle you."

"That's okay." I took in a big breath and steadied myself.

"It's just, I noticed you running and I thought I would say hi."

I looked over to him, and this time I really looked. He was glistening in sweat. My dreams were about to get sultrier. "Hi." I smiled.

He smiled back, and it sure had me feeling the heat.

It was then I realized I probably didn't look my finest. I sweated a lot when I worked out, and I could already feel it dripping off me.

"So you run." He kept pace with me nicely. His breathing patterns were perfect— he was obviously a skilled runner.

"Is that what this is?" I teased him. I thought it was better than outright making fun of him for his lame comment.

I think he realized how that all came off. "Why do I get the feeling you like to keep people on their toes?"

"Well, you did ruin my dad's surprise."

He laughed. "Case in point."

I liked his laugh. There was something melodic to it, but it was completely manly. I also noticed how lucky his clothes were. His running shorts and t-shirt clung quite nicely to him.

"Okay. How's this then? Yes, I run. Better?"

He narrowed those gorgeous green eyes at me. "You're different than what I remember."

"Yeah, you know those formative years between seventeen and twenty-five. There's a lot of growth."

"Maybe we should just run. I feel like I need to sharpen my skills before I talk to you anymore."

"Okay, but you started it."

He shook his head at me.

We ran together in silence for a minute. All I could hear was his controlled breathing. He was definitely a runner. I bet he ran races.

"So where's your son?" We ran through the small tunnel under the bridge on the path.

He looked at me for a moment. I could see the wheels turning in those amazing eyes. "I figure since he's three now, I can leave him at home." He cracked and smiled.

I shook my head at him. "If you're going to be a smart aleck, you can't smile like that. It gives it all away."

He threw his hands up in surrender. "I give up. He's with his mom. Do you remember Victoria, my wife? I mean ex-wife," he corrected.

How could I forget the woman who crushed my teenage dreams into oblivion? "Yes. I'm sorry about your, uh . . . divorce." That came out awkward. Is that something you say sorry for?

"Thanks. I would normally have Josh today, but he's going to his cousin's birthday party on his mom's side. I'll get him back this evening." His tone was melancholy.

"It must be hard to share."

"It's definitely been an adjustment."

I knew about adjusting, or at least about not adjusting to sucky situations like divorce.

We both began to slow down as we made it around the loop and back to our houses. It was weird in a way that we seemed in sync. I was breathing a lot harder than him, which was a little embarrassing, but he didn't mention it. If he did, I was going to blame it on the elevation, which could have been a contributing factor, but it sounded like an excuse.

We both stopped at my gate, which meant we went past his.

"Thanks for the company." He stretched out his hamstrings. "You've certainly grown up." He sounded like he was my uncle or some other family relation. I almost thought he might pat my head or something. It was certainly not what I was hoping for. Sure, I wasn't holding out any hope for the two of us, but I guess I at least hoped he looked at me like a woman now and not some long-lost niece.

I half smiled in return. I had plenty of smart aleck comebacks, but since he didn't see me like the witty adult I was, I figured why waste my time. "Well, I guess we'll see you later." I opened my gate.

He dropped his leg he was stretching out and cocked his head sideways. "Yeah. See you later."

I did my stretching in my backyard before I went in. Normally I felt pumped after a run, but for some reason, I was feeling a little deflated. I guess I didn't like to be thought of as a child, especially at that particular time of my life. Not that I didn't like myself then, I liked myself a lot. I thought I was a fun girl, but I was so naïve about life. Part of me still ached to have that girl back. But just as I felt that ache, I remembered something Jay said to me. "Charlee, embrace the beautiful, wonderful woman you are now. The bumps in your road have only made you that much better."

Why, oh why wasn't I in love with him? Yes, I loved him, but like a brother. Maybe not like a brother because we kissed frequently, and it was nice. But when he kissed me, I never had the desire and passion that kept me wanting more. It was like I almost felt obligated to kiss him because we were dating and because he wanted to kiss me.

I walked in to find my dad at the sink washing dishes.

"Hey, kiddo, how was your run? I see you had company."

I raised my eyebrow at him. "Were you spying on me?"

He turned back to his task at hand. "No, just doing dishes."

I couldn't help but smile. "It was a good run."

"Good. So did you and Ryan talk about anything interesting?"

I thought about it for a second as I downed my water bottle. "Not really."

"Oh." Was he disappointed?

"Well, I'm going to hit the shower and then head over to the Lawtons."

"Okay, honey. I may head out to the golf course." He still sounded disappointed, which kind of made me feel bad, like I should stay home, but Krissy really did need my help and I was the maid of honor.

"Well, maybe we can shoot some hoops after dinner tonight," I offered, though my prideful stubborn side was kicking my sweet side for doing so.

My dad looked over to me with eyes alight. "It's a date."

I gave him a smallish smile and tried to keep my sighing down. I retreated to the basement where my stubborn prideful side chewed out my sweet side for caving in so quickly. I told that side to shut up, it had been like eight years. My stubborn side said, "Whatever."

After some massive squats, I practically crawled into the shower. I could feel the burn, but I reminded myself it was better than everyone seeing my cellulite at the wedding. They were already going to be seeing way too much of me. Which reminded me. I needed to start searching the internet for horrid bridesmaid's dresses. Not that I would ever make Krissy wear a monstrous dress to my wedding, but she was going to think she was for at least a while. I mean, it was going to be my wedding and I would never truly have hideous dresses, but it was going to be fun to mess with her. I had plenty of time to search, especially since I had no prospects. That wasn't true, I had *one*. I just didn't want him.

Going over to the Lawtons' was like coming home for me. Growing up, I had spent as much time at their house as I did my own. If I didn't like what we were having for dinner at my house, I went to their house and vice versa for Krissy. Their home reminded me of sleepovers, double dates, prom, and all-night talks. It was a piece of me.

I stopped for a moment and looked at their home before I went in. All the houses on the block were custom built. The Lawtons' home had several large windows all around the house. In a way, it was odd, but beautiful. It was modern looking, whereas our house was a traditional-looking house made with stone and wood—it had a rustic feel to it. I had always loved it. I had also loved that my mom always kept it clean so I was never embarrassed to have friends over. My mom had prided herself on her home. I could tell she missed it when we left. My dad offered to let her have it, but she wouldn't take it. The house she and Mark lived in now was nice, but it was plain in comparison.

I walked right in. I hoped that was still okay. Krissy and I never knocked on each other's doors, and we always called each other's parents mom and dad.

Ann Lawton came right out and squeezed me tight. "Charlee, you're home!"

I hugged her back tighter. "Hi, Mom."

She stepped back and touched my cheek. "You're as pretty as a picture."

I knew she was going to say that. She always did. "Thanks."

She shook her head. "I can't believe how grown up you and Krissy are. It seems like only yesterday I was fixing up scraped knees and telling you two to wash up for dinner."

I bent down and kissed her cheek. She was short, like Krissy. "You're the best."

She smiled, grabbed my hand, and led me back to their kitchen table that was piled high with invitations. Looked like it was going to be a long day.

"Krissy and everyone else went out to grab the food. They should be back soon."

I assumed by "everyone" she meant her husband and twin son and daughter who were now twenty-one, which was weird for me. In my mind, Mason and Maviny were twelve. They used to bug us all the time, so it was odd to think of them as adults.

We both sat at the high glass table. Their furniture was modern to match the house.

"So, how are you sweetie?" She patted my hand.

"I'm good."

"Really?"

I gave her a knowing smile. "Yes. I'm happy to be back in Colorado."

"You know your dad is thrilled to have you back home."

"I know."

"He's talked nonstop about you for the last eight years, he's so proud of you."

"I don't know what for."

She scrunched her face. "Are you kidding? Dean's List, grad school, scholarship recipient, the list could go on and on."

"Yeah, well, now I'm living in my dad's basement, and he's paying me to do so."

She laughed at me. "Oh, sweetie, you're doing the right thing, and if anyone says different, you tell them to talk to me."

This is why I loved this woman. She was a mom, and I kind of needed one at the moment.

We were soon joined by the rest of the Lawtons, and they were bearing breakfast sandwiches, fruit, juice and muffins. It all smelled wonderful, but I had to remind myself that I was expected to be half naked at a wedding soon, so I didn't indulge the way I wanted to. I was the best friend ever.

I hadn't seen Mason and Maviny in forever, they were both gorgeous like the rest of the Lawton family. I was surrounded by gorgeousness in this neighborhood. I hoped I caught it. Mason and Maviny had taken after their dad and had some height to them—well at least they were taller than Krissy and her mom—but they were all blonde with blue eyes. Mason and Maviny were both at CU, and by the sounds of it, they were loving life. I always liked coming over to the Lawtons'. I had wanted siblings, even though I thought Mason and Maviny were annoying at times. Now looking at them all, and how well they got along, I really felt like I had missed out on something. I knew I technically had step-siblings, but honestly, I would never see Mark's kids that way.

After we ate, the men, Ken and Mason, escaped—more like Ann shooed them away. Their handwriting was deemed unworthy for the invitations. That left four of us and four hundred invitations. My hand hurt thinking about it, but I couldn't think of better company. The conversations were fun and lighthearted, as always, when we were together. I think Ann Lawton was the nicest woman on the planet, and she always had the funniest stories to tell. She was like Krissy and never met a stranger, and for some odd reason, people always seemed to spill their guts to her. We also got to hear all about Maviny's man drama. It must be rough to have so many men in love with you. She couldn't decide who should be her date for her sister's wedding.

"Speaking of dates," Ann said. "Who are you bringing?"

I looked up from what felt like the nine hundredth envelope. "Who me?"

They all laughed because, seriously, who else was she talking to?

"No one. I'll be too busy with my maid of honor duties."

Everyone was still staring at me.

"What?" I wasn't sure what the fuss was about.

Ann's smile was subtle. "It's just, I saw you running this morning with your attractive single neighbor."

Was everyone spying on me this morning? This was neighborhood watch in overload. "I wasn't running with Ryan, we just happened to be out running at the same time."

They all shook their heads in a mocking sort of fashion.

"Seriously. Besides, he still thinks I'm twelve, and he's divorced with a kid and a lot older than me. Oh, and I don't think my dad would appreciate me dating his business partner."

Ann laughed. "If he thinks you looked twelve in the little running shorts and tank top you were wearing this morning, then he needs glasses . . . Va va voom!"

Everyone laughed, including me.

"Believe me, Ryan isn't interested in me, and I'm barely out of a relationship."

"Yes, but you aren't broken up after ending things with Jay," Krissy pointed out.

"True, but I still don't see where Ryan fits in."

"It's just a date to the wedding," Ann said. "Do you want me to talk to him?"

"No!"

"Okay . . . but if you change your mind, let me know." Ann's eyes twinkled.

I couldn't even believe we were having this conversation. The last time I sat around this table it would have been a taboo discussion because of the age difference. I guess twenty–five and thirty-three was acceptable, but judging by Ryan's words and reaction to me, he still saw me as seventeen and off limits. Even if he did see me as datable in age, I'm sure he wouldn't be interested. I wasn't his type. I wasn't a raving red-headed beauty, and experience told me I never would be. Believe me, I'd tried, and red hair color and I don't mix.

After hours of meticulously filling out envelopes, we were done. Chance showed up and he and Krissy needed a room, so I took that as my cue to go home. I needed to make dessert, anyway. I got home to find my dad not there, so I headed to the store and purchased the necessary items for individual no-bake raspberry lemon cheesecakes. Does it sound weird that I even missed the grocery stores in Colorado?

By the time I got home, my dad was back and looking pleased. He must have had a good day on the golf course. "Hi, baby girl. Do you need help bringing in bags?"

"No, I only had the one, but thanks."

"Did you have fun at the Lawtons'?"

"Yep. The invitations will be in the mail tomorrow. By the way, yours is on the counter there." I pointed at it.

He opened it while admiring it. "Is it weird that Krissy's marrying Chance?"

I laughed. "You don't know how many people have asked me that. The answer is, not at all. I wasn't really that into him, and it was a long time ago. I'm happy for them. They fit."

He came over and kissed my head. "You're a good girl."

"Thanks, Dad. How was the golf course?"

His grin was wide. "I shot eighty today."

"Impressive."

"You'll have to come out with me sometime."

"Plan on it."

"Next weekend?"

"Sure, Dad."

He kissed my head again and headed off to take a shower.

He really was trying. I knew I needed to as well, but it was hard for me.

While my dad got ready, I cranked up the surround sound and went to work on dessert. It was both pretty and somewhat light. I made my portion smaller than everyone else's. Krissy owed me. First, no muffins and now smaller dessert, but all I could think of was my butt hanging out of that dress.

My dad came down looking handsome in his polo shirt and shorts. I wondered why he never remarried. I guess part of me was glad he hadn't, and part of me hoped he didn't even date. I already had to go through that with my mom, and it was a miserable process. We worked on dinner together, and before I knew it, our guests had arrived.

Josh immediately tore through the house, but he stopped when he saw me in the kitchen. His dad and my dad trailed behind him. "Cherry." He sounded so proud of himself.

I was becoming fond of that name, and it sounded adorable coming out of his three-year-old little mouth. "Hi, Josh."

"Do you want to see my stickers?" He pointed to his chest.

I knelt down. "Yes, of course."

He approached me and showed me ten stickers of Spiderman on his little blue t-shirt.

"Those are very nice."

"I know," he agreed

He made me laugh.

"Hi, Charlee." Josh's dad made my insides do a dance.

I looked up and saw him hovering over us. "Hi."

He dazzled me with his smile. The butterflies in my stomach said, *Holy crap!*

"Josh was showing me his sticker collection." I stood up.

Josh pulled on his dad's shorts. "Let's jump."

Now it made sense why he was excited. I looked out our patio door and there sat my old trampoline. I had noticed it earlier and was surprised my dad had kept it. I doubt he ever used it, but it looked like Josh had before.

"Okay, buddy."

Why are men with kids so attractive? Like I needed more reasons to have sensual dreams about Ryan.

All the males went out the door, while I finished making the salad I'd been working on. I watched my dad at the grill on our deck, Josh on the trampoline, and Ryan standing on the grass nearby watching him and telling him to stay in the middle. I rolled my eyes. He needed to be on the trampoline. I decided he needed to be shown how it was done.

I walked out with salad, plates, and silverware in hand. It was quite the juggling act, but I managed. My dad looked happy at the grill as he looked out at Ryan and Josh. I wondered if he still wished he had a son, or maybe he was ready for grandchildren. I know my mom seemed to enjoy being surrounded by babies. Admittedly, I did too. It was the only thing that endeared me to Mark's family. I loved babies and little kids.

"So, does Josh play over here a lot?" I set the table.

My dad smiled over at me. "Once in a while."

"I can't believe you kept the trampoline. I'm surprised it hasn't fallen apart yet."

"I replaced the springs and mat."

"Well, I guess I better put them to good use. I'll be back."

My dad grinned as I walked down the steps of our deck.

As I approached Ryan, he smiled at me again, and seriously, my stomach was having a party. He needed to quit doing that.

Josh called out, "Cherry!" as he bounced and bounced, albeit not very high. He seemed cautious, which surprised me.

When I reached the trampoline, I slipped off my flip-flops and jumped right on.

Ryan raised his eyebrow at me.

"You obviously need a lesson on how to have fun on a trampoline."

"I'm too old to jump."

I rolled my eyes at him. "If you say so." I turned my attention to Josh.

He smiled big at me. He was seriously adorable, and I had a feeling someday he would be a lady killer. He was a good mixture of his gorgeous parents.

I took his little hands in mine. "Do you want to sing a song?"

He nodded his head.

"Okay, ready?" I began jumping in a circle with him. "Ring around the rosy, a pocket full of posies, ashes, ashes, we all fall down!" I bounced on my bum and Josh followed me.

He giggled loudly. "Again!"

I happily complied with his request. We did it a few more times, until he got the hang of the song. By the fourth time he was shouting, "We all fall down."

I looked over to Ryan. His gaze was fixed on me. "Do you want to join in? I promise we'll go easy on you, old man."

He thought about it for a moment, then Josh said, "Please, Daddy."

You would have to be heartless to say no to that sweet little voice, and did I mention his chubby cheeks and dimples? If he were my kid, he would get away with everything.

Ryan slipped off his boat shoes and hopped on. "Go gentle on me, this is my first time."

My eyebrow raised. "You may make a good smart-aleck yet."

Josh immediately took his dad's hand. It was then I realized, *Hey, I get to hold Ryan's hand.* The butterflies were so happy, they swore. I won't repeat what they said, but let's just say it was salty. It was kind of awkward when Ryan hesitated. It didn't do much for my ego, or my self-esteem, but I tried to play it off. "You can wash your hands after we're done."

He grabbed my hand and half smirked at me. "I don't have to sing, do I?"

"Of course you have to. It's not fun if you don't sing."

He looked wary of the idea.

"What? Do you need help with the words?" I wasn't going to let him off the hook.

"I think I've got it."

"Great, you can start us off then."

He narrowed his gorgeous eyes at me before turning to his son, who was not so patiently waiting for us to start. "Okay, buddy, ready?"

Josh was beyond ready, and he started jumping and singing, "Rings da rounds da rosies . . ."

So cute!

His dad was obviously out of his element, and sang quietly as we jumped. He barely fell down, but I noticed he dropped my hand as quick as he could.

I shook my head at him. "Now we have to do it again."

"Why?"

"Because that was lame."

"Are you calling me lame?"

"I'm sorry to say this, but yes."

"Daddy lame," Josh repeated, though I'm pretty sure he had no idea what that meant.

"Now my kid thinks I'm lame, thanks."

I shrugged my shoulders. "I'm sure he would've figured it out sooner or later."

"You're really not how I remembered."

"You keep saying that."

Ryan stood back up. "Well, I guess I better prove to my kid you're wrong about me." He held out his hand to me and helped me up.

I'm not going to lie, I liked the feel of my hand in his. It kind of did something to me, or maybe for me. I knew it meant nothing, but I was thinking about how many times I could get him to keep doing this without looking like an idiot. We only ended up doing it a few more times, but by the time we were done, Ryan was jumping the highest and singing the loudest. I guess he wanted to prove he wasn't lame. He did an excellent job, and it was quite comical. I did my best not to laugh. I figured I looked just as silly jumping, falling, and singing ridiculous songs about the plague.

"Dinner's ready," my dad called out.

Ryan made his way off the trampoline and carefully lifted his son off. I loved how he hugged him tight when he picked him up.

"What are you smiling about?" Ryan brought me out of my thoughts about him.

I jumped off the trampoline in my embarrassment. "Do I need a reason to smile?"

"I suppose not." He smiled back.

Gosh, he really needed to quit doing that.

Dinner was fun and delicious. I forgot what an excellent cook my dad was. He made up his own recipes. He was a genius. He came up with this homemade batter that he used to cook the fish in, and it was to die for. It probably wasn't helping my butt cause, but it was tasty. Even Josh liked it. I was surprised, I didn't think a three-year-old would eat fish, but Ryan told me Josh ate about anything. He was lucky. I had taken enough child development classes to know that wasn't always the case, and I had seen plenty of Mark's grandkids throw a fit about eating vegetables and even noodles.

The conversation topics varied. It ran the gamut from sports to, of course, the office. I was hoping we wouldn't talk about the office, but I suppose it was inevitable. Sadly, I understood everything they were talking about. The pros and cons of being a C Corp versus an S Corp, the maximum limit on social security taxes, and the new Medicare tax. It all made me feel a little nauseated. I would have rather talked about mental illness, personality disorders, the neocortex and phobias, anything but accounting. But I tried to stay engaged. I even threw out some of my acquired knowledge. It made my dad proud, and Ryan looked mildly impressed with my tax code lingo.

One thing everyone, including Josh, was impressed with was my dessert, even though I think more got on Josh's face than in his mouth. I guess he was still fine tuning his skills with the spoon.

"Well, I guess I better go and get Josh cleaned up before Victoria comes to get him." Ryan gave up trying to clean Josh's face with a napkin. He turned to my dad. "Dinner was excellent as always. Thanks, Jeff." He said it like this was a common occurrence. I also noticed how the two of them acted like the best of friends. It was a little odd. I mean, my dad was practically old enough to be Ryan's dad, but the age gap didn't seem to hinder their relationship at all. I guess a lot had happened since I had been gone. Then Ryan turned his attention to me before he picked up his son. "Dessert was delicious."

"Thank you."

"I guess we'll see you tomorrow."

"That's the plan," I said without a single sigh of resignation regarding my fate.

"I look forward to working with you."

"Me, too." At least that was true, but only because it meant I could ogle him on occasion.

Ryan smiled at me and carefully picked up his very messy son.

I stood up and grabbed Josh's messy hand. "Bye, Josh."

"Bye, Cherry." He waved with his other dirty hand.

"Cherry?" My dad questioned.

"At least it's more feminine than Charlee," I teased my dad.

"Hey, Charlee is a perfectly feminine name."

I rolled my eyes. "Sure, dad. Tell that to all the guys named Charlie."

Ryan and my dad chuckled.

On that note, we saw our guests out.

Five

As soon as they were out the door, my dad turned to me with excitement in his eyes. "We still on for some b-ball?"

I took a deep breath. "Yes."

My dad's whole countenance shone. It was like I'd handed him the grand prize. Did it mean that much to him? He was so eager, he suggested we clean up after we played. I agreed to the suggestion. I ran down to the basement and threw on my running shoes. I hadn't owned basketball shoes in forever. I grabbed the new basketball my dad had given me. That smell made my senses come to life. Oh, how I had missed the game, and oh, how I had missed the man who taught me how to love the game.

I almost felt ten again when I ran up the stairs with my ball. How many times had my dad gotten me out of chores so that I could practice basketball? I knew it annoyed my mom, but my dad had this way of talking her into it. My dad was the best coach and fan. He never missed one of my games, even if it meant traveling around the state and missing work. How did everything get so turned around? How could one careless act ruin so much? I pushed those thoughts to the back of my mind and met my dad outside. *I can do this*, I thought. *I can move past the past and the hurt and confusion.*

My dad was anxiously waiting for me by the basketball hoop, the one that was installed before we even moved in. I'm pretty sure the house was designed around the driveway and basketball hoop.

I did a bounce pass to my dad, and suddenly the game was on. I felt like myself as I got in my defensive stance. It was like yesterday. I could still hear my dad say, "Butt low to the ground, CJ, put the weight on the balls of your feet. Make sure you slide, but never lose contact with the ground."

And, the smack talk was on. "Come on, old man," I chided my dad when he tried to get past me for a layup. He did a fast break, but not fast enough. I easily took the ball from him and dribbled back, and without almost any effort, I made the prettiest shot—nothing but net, two points.

I had forgotten how much I missed my sport. I think we both missed it. We were out playing until the sun started to set. We could have stayed out longer because we had lights installed, but two hours of playing was my limit. My legs were still burning from squats earlier in the day. I had burned off any extra calories I had taken in throughout the day, and the bonus was I beat my dad, if only by two points. I think he let me win by calling the game over as my last shot went in.

My dad put his arm around me as I downed my second water bottle of the game. "You still got it, kiddo."

"You're not so bad yourself, for an old guy."

"Old guy? I could have had you."

"Sure, Dad."

He kissed the top of my head. "Let's stop by the shoe store tomorrow and get you some real shoes."

"I'm not a kid anymore."

"Woman or kid, you're going to sprain an ankle or worse wearing those shoes when we play."

"Fine, but take it out of my first paycheck."

His wink meant he wouldn't.

When we were ready to walk in, I noticed Ryan walk out with Victoria. He had a sleeping Josh in his arms. Victoria, from what I could tell, still looked like a Victoria's Secret model. Her hair was maybe a tad shorter, but she was still gorgeous, and Ryan still looked at her like he had feelings for her. She, on the other hand, acted aloof. After Ryan placed his sleeping buddy in the car, I could tell he tried to engage her in conversation, but she wasn't having it.

I probably shouldn't have stared, but I was still puzzled by their relationship. Ryan watched them drive off, and to my embarrassment, we locked eyes when he turned around. I waved before I turned around and followed my dad in. I really needed to watch myself around him, but it was so easy to get lost in him. I didn't know what it was about him, but he'd always had that effect on me. I had thought it was only a silly teenage crush, but now that we were both older, I wasn't so sure. He made me feel different than any other man I had ever been around. I thought back to all our interactions throughout the day, especially on the trampoline and at dinner, and there was something about his mannerisms. He was a thoughtful person, and I admired what a good father he seemed to be. He was attentive and loving to Josh.

I went to bed that night and prayed for two things: first that my dreams would be fabulously steamy and the main star would be Ryan. Second, that when I woke up in the morning, I would be a psychologist, not an accountant. Apparently, I hadn't been very good because I dreamt I was naked at Krissy's wedding, and it wasn't pretty. Do you know how mortifying it is to walk down the aisle nude, carrying one single rose? I mean, my brain couldn't even think to give me a large bouquet to cover up part of myself. And the other bad news? I was going to be an accountant.

With that, I dragged myself out of bed at five-thirty, stretched, and got ready to run. If I was going to be naked at a wedding, I was determined to look my best.

My dad wasn't even up when I walked upstairs. It was too dang early to be up. I guess that made me a real adult now. I left my dad a note, just in case he worried where I was.

I crept out of the house and out the back fence. The sun was barely up. I yawned and thought of that stupid dress, and trudged forward, although I was sore from the day before. Between running, squats, and basketball, I was wiped by the time I made it to bed, but it had been a good day. I needed that game with my dad. I think he needed it more than me.

To my surprise, when I opened the gate, Ryan was coming out of his gate. I needed to quit meeting him with no make-up on.

"Good morning." He walked my way.

I looked at him in all his glory, the sun illuminating him from behind. Yes, it was a very good morning. "Hi."

We stood there awkwardly for a moment, neither of us saying anything. Of course, we decided to speak at the same time.

"Well, have a good run," I started to say as he said something I didn't quite catch.

We both smiled.

"I'm sorry, what did you say?" I asked.

"Do you want to run together?"

Uh, this was good. "Sure, that would . . . "

"It's really not safe for you to run by yourself."

Oh, so this was *not* good. He was doing it because he saw me as a kid that needed protection. That was disappointing. I didn't say anything. Instead I headed out on the trail. He followed and kept pace by my side. His presence annoyed me, well maybe not totally, he looked too good to be a complete nuisance.

I got the feeling I was holding him back. I was a good runner, at least I used to be, but I wasn't at my peak now. "You don't need to babysit me, I've been running for years by myself."

He looked over at me with brows furrowed. "Consider this a neighborly gesture."

I shook my head at him and faced forward.

"No quips this morning?" he taunted me.

"I'm saving my wit for worthier opponents."

He faux stabbed himself in the heart with his hand. "That hurts. And to think, I've been practicing comebacks all night in preparation for seeing you today." He looked over at me and dazzled me with his smile.

I was suddenly not annoyed with him anymore. "So, let's hear some of your brilliance."

"That's not how it works. First you have to say something worthy of the gems I came up with."

"Who uses words like gems?" I laughed.

"What's wrong with gems?"

"Well, nothing if you're in an AARP commercial."

He looked down at me with wide eyes.

"That was your opportunity to throw out one of your gems."

He thought for a moment and then another moment. Before he could come up with something, I spoke again.

"I think you may have to practice some more. I bet you can google 'comebacks.'"

He laughed. "Okay, you win."

"That wasn't much of a competition."

"You're really bruising my ego this morning."

I wanted to say the same thing to him, but I kept it to myself. "I'm sorry. I'm sure you came up with some really great gems."

"How about this, I'll race you to the bench about a quarter of a mile up."

"Are you serious?"

"I have to earn my man card back somehow."

"Fine. On your mark, get set, go." I picked up my pace around 'mark' and took him off guard.

"Hey, cheater," he called out to me.

I was barely ahead of him. My lead only lasted for a moment. He breezed by me, smirking. That I couldn't have. I dug in deep and caught up to him. He put his arm out to hold me back. I ducked under it and ran past him. With seemingly no effort, he caught up to me and pulled me back. By now I was laughing and couldn't sustain my pace. He was laughing, too, but he was a much better runner than me. He beat me, hands down.

I bowed down to him once I reached him. He took great delight in it.

"At least now I won't go into work feeling emasculated."

"Yeah, you can tell everyone you beat a girl."

"There's no shame in it."

From there we had a pleasant run, except for the stupid stitch in my side, which I tried to ignore. I wasn't going to give him the satisfaction by drawing attention to it.

"You should run the Bolder Boulder this year," he threw out there when our houses came into view.

"Isn't that next week?"

"Yeah, on Memorial Day."

The Bolder Boulder is a huge 10K race that takes place every year in Boulder.

"I don't know if I'm in good enough shape to do a race right now."

He slowed and looked me over. "You look in good shape to me."

I raised my eyebrow at him, but my insides were saying, *Yes!*

He ran his fingers through his sweat-dampened hair, which made it stick up some. Dang he looked good. "I only meant you wouldn't have any problem finishing it."

Now I was back to being annoyed, and my insides swore again. They did that a lot lately. "Maybe next year."

"If you change your mind, let me know."

I nodded my head. We were back to our houses by then. This time he stopped at his house. I kept going the several yards to my house and waved goodbye on my way.

"See you later." He waved back.

Yeah, yeah, I thought. I walked into our backyard and tried to nurse my wounded ego by reminding myself that there was a man or two out there that found me to be womanly and even beautiful. Where was Jay when I needed an ego boost? I left him, I reminded myself. I knew it was the right thing to do, but part of me missed him. Unfortunately, it wasn't how I *should* miss him.

I decided to dress extra womanly for my first day. I didn't want to be treated like a kid, or worse, the boss' kid. I wore a black pencil skirt that hugged the curves nicely, and I paired it with a form-fitting coral blouse. It made my girls stand out. Unfortunately, I needed to wear heels. I figured I'd better work on walking gracefully in heels. I normally stayed away from them due to my height, but I needed the practice for the wedding. I slipped on some respectable black peep-toe pumps, and my feet protested. Sorry, I told them. They would thank me later when they were prepared for the red hooker heels I would be sporting at the wedding.

My dad's eyes bugged out when he saw me come up the stairs to the kitchen from the family room. "Wowza."

"Good morning, Dad."

He shook his head. "Whoa! You look grown up."

Well, at least someone noticed.

I smiled.

"I think I may have to add a new office policy. No looking at my daughter."

I rolled my eyes. "I don't think that's going to be an issue." Considering half of his employees were women, and from what I remembered, most everyone was married. Of course, we know that could have changed, just ask Ryan. One thing I knew for sure, the guy I wanted to look at me saw me as a child.

"So, are you and Ryan running partners now?" Dad perused his paper.

"Uh, no. Apparently, Ryan feels it's his neighborly duty to watch over the young girls that run by themselves in this dangerous town. And when did you become such a Peeping Tom?"

He set his paper down and laughed. "I forgot how cheeky you are."

I raised my eyebrow at him from the fridge. "Cheeky? I prefer witty."

He smiled at me and went back to his paper.

"Do you want me to make your lunch?"

He looked up, surprised. "I was planning on taking you out for lunch, to celebrate your first day."

I closed the refrigerator. "Oh. Okay . . . but somewhere healthy."

Dad narrowed his eyes in concern. "You're not on a diet are you?"

"No. I don't believe in them. Let's just say Krissy owes me."

My dad shook his head. "That sounds like something feminine I need to stay out of."

"Good call."

Dad and I drove in together. I almost said no, only because I didn't want to feel more like a child, but my dad was fond of the idea and I didn't want to disappoint him again. The drive was barely fifteen minutes. Not much had changed, except when we pulled into the parking lot, the sign now read, Jensen and Carter Accounting.

I looked over to my dad. I hadn't been expecting that.

"Don't worry, there's still room for one more Jensen on that sign."

Yeah, that's not what I worried about. I nodded my head in silence and tried not to grimace. There were already quite a few cars in the parking lot. I took a deep breath and braced myself for what waited for me through the double doors of Jensen and Carter Accounting.

The first thing I noticed when I walked in was that the décor had been updated. It looked nice. The furniture was now darker instead of the old oak furniture. The paint was a neutral, but there were pops of green in the chairs and artwork that made everything look clean and classy.

"I love what you've done with the office."

"I figured it was time to get out of the nineties."

I agreed.

My dad walked me around the office and introduced me to some of the newer employees, and there were some I already knew, including Felicity, my dad's secretary who happened to love me. I think she may have crushed a rib in greeting me.

"Look at how beautiful you've grown up to be." She touched my cheek. "It seems like yesterday you were ten."

"Thanks, Ms. McLaughlin." For some reason she had never been married. I could never figure out why. I always thought she was an attractive lady, and she had a great personality.

"You should call me Felicity now."

"Okay." I nodded.

Ryan was already there, too. It looked like he and my dad had offices next to each other now. He came out and greeted us. "Good morning, Jeff." He turned his attention my way, and his eyes kind of popped out a little as he cleared his throat. "Charlee?"

Why does he keep saying my name like it's a question? "Ryan."

I wasn't sure if he had allergies or a cold, but he cleared his throat again. "You're looking well . . . I mean, you look different than you did this morning." He rubbed the back of his neck and turned a few different colors.

"I did try to talk my dad into changing the dress policy to a more athletic bent, but it was a no-go."

Both my dad and Felicity laughed. Ryan, on the other hand, smiled nervously. "Well . . . uh . . . welcome."

"Thanks, Ryan."

My dad got me settled in my own office. It was Ryan's old office, which was kind of weird for me. I was glad I didn't have to work in a cubicle, but I'm sure somebody there was hoping for the empty office, and they were probably seething that the owner's daughter got it. I didn't plan to be there that long, so whoever was up for it wouldn't have to wait too much longer.

I was going to be working with some of the smaller companies that hired the firm to handle all their payroll services. My dad said if I proved myself, he would throw a mid-size company my way. I tried to act eager, as if I wanted the challenge, but it was hard to muster up the enthusiasm. I promised myself I would give this job and my dad one hundred percent, though. Besides, we were constantly warned in school about the trouble and penalties we could cause for ourselves and our future clients if we weren't careful. The government doesn't mess around where money is concerned.

As soon as I was settled and waiting for someone named Debra to come in and train me on the software that the office used, my phone went off. It was a text from Jay.

Good luck this morning. I'm thinking about you. Miss you.

I held my phone to my heart. He was such a good guy.

Thanks, I texted back. Then, I hesitated. *I miss you, too.* It was true. I wasn't sure if I should say it back because I didn't want to give him the wrong idea, but he said all along he could tell I wasn't as into him as he was into me. That made me feel terrible, but it was true.

He didn't text back. I'm sure he was busy. He had landed a great job in Overland Park as an Operations Research Analyst. On top of everything else, he was smart, too.

Krissy was next. Her text was much more comical. *I hope you're enjoying the scenery. By the way, my mom says she saw you running this morning. You should ask him to be your plus-one at the wedding.*

I rolled my eyes. I was beginning to think I was living in a fish bowl. *Ha! Don't you have some pyramid you need to be on top of?*

Krissy ran cheer camps. Her dream was to be a Denver Bronco's cheerleader, but for some reason, that was the one thing that had eluded her. I wasn't sure why; she had the skills and the looks. Oh well, she seemed happy doing what she was doing, and besides, I think Chance was hoping his bride-to-be would forget about that dream. I don't think he was too keen on Krissy showing off her assets for the whole world to see on national television.

I spent the rest of the morning learning the software. It was straightforward and intuitive. I had lunch with my dad, and then that afternoon I was on the phone with my dad introducing me to the companies I would be taking care of. Eventually, I would be meeting with them face to face, but my dad thought it was good to at least have an initial phone introduction. My dad talked to everyone like they were old friends. I supposed that was why he was so successful. People knew they were getting someone that genuinely cared about them and their needs. It made me more determined to do a good job for him.

Six

JUNE BEGAN AND WE WERE T minus thirty-four days until the big day. Krissy was getting married on the Fourth of July—it fell on a Saturday that year. She was even planning on shooting off fireworks at the end of the reception as she and Chance rode off into the sunset, as it were. My days were filled with work and my evenings were spent trying to calm Krissy down and helping with wedding preparations. I swore if I ever got married, I was having a simple wedding. None of this everyone-needs-their-own-personalized-wedding-favor. I mean really, who needed or even wanted a hand-stamped gift bag that included things like lip balm with the couple's names on it and personalized candy? I loved Krissy, but I didn't need her name and wedding date plastered on my ChapStick. But there I sat, stamping bags. Even worse, we were personalizing the wine glasses that everyone got to take home. I'm just going to say, I hate vinyl.

I was still running my butt off, literally. The running also had another positive side effect—Ryan joined me every morning. I enjoyed our little tete-a-tetes. He was still trying to outwit me, and I was still trying to beat him to the dang bench. I also got to learn a little about him, like how he ended up buying his parent's house. They had given him an incredible deal and he wanted Josh to have a house to grow up in, no matter which parent he was with. Apparently, Victoria got their home in the divorce. I also learned that Victoria was a part-time private tutor and a fulltime mom. From the sounds of it, she was a good mom and Josh was her life. It sounded like financially, Ryan was still quite supportive of Victoria. I respected that.

Ryan also liked to talk a lot about work and our clients. I did my best to be engaged, and admittedly, I tried to show off how smart I was. I had to say, I think he was impressed. I'm sure he, like everyone else, was thinking I was just the boss' daughter and didn't have any real skills. He even offered to help me study for my CPA exams. I didn't really need it, but I accepted the help because time spent with Ryan was time well spent. I was hoping that perhaps he was beginning to see me as a woman. I was even contemplating making a fool of myself and asking Ryan if he wanted to be my plus-one at Krissy's wedding, even though he had his own invite. I was going to ask him as friends . . . and if my lips accidentally fell on his at the end of the night, so be it. I would blame it on the champagne I wouldn't be drinking. Alcohol and I didn't mix, and in light of my dad's tryst, I wasn't a big fan of losing control of my faculties.

My courage was being bolstered by Krissy and her mom. You know the kind of encouragement I'm talking about: "You two would look so well together" and "Of course he sees you as a woman, look at you." "Any man would consider himself lucky to be your date." And then there were the dreams. Finally my brain was getting it right, so much so I couldn't wait to go to bed sometimes. Dream Ryan was muy caliente, and to top it off, Ryan had asked me a couple of times during our runs who I was going with. From the sounds of it, he didn't have a date either.

So, halfway through June, when he came into my office to find me, not quite focused on my work, I was thrown for a loop. First, I wasn't really messing around. I had kept my promise. I was a model employee, and so far the clients I had were pleased. I had already helped one save some money by getting them into a cafeteria plan that they had no idea they were eligible for. I was also getting a jump on quarterly reports for each of them. But anyway, back to why I was a little preoccupied. So my favorite band ever, One Republic, was coming to Red Rocks Amphitheater, which was made even cooler because they're from Colorado. Their first show had sold out, and they were adding a second one for the middle of July. I was stoked, so at ten, when the tickets went on sale online, I knew I had to get in on that action. I had already received my first couple of paychecks, and what better way to waste them than on concert tickets?

It was at that time Ryan walked in. I was so torn . . . look at beautiful Ryan or my computer screen where I was in a virtual waiting room, that's how fast the tickets were selling. Ryan was yammering on about something accountant-related, I think he was asking if I wouldn't mind taking on a new account, which I nodded in response to. I knew as soon as I was out of the waiting room I would have to act quickly or I could kiss my tickets goodbye. Then, there it was, I was out of the waiting room. I went to typing, and this was when I heard something like, "Hey, I have these two tickets and . . ."

Suddenly Ryan was getting my full attention. Ryan asking me out was better than One Republic. I'm sorry Ryan Tedder (the lead singer), but it was true. I guess I had a thing for Ryan's.

Ryan rubbed the back of his neck as he stood in front of my desk like he was nervous. I liked this. ". . . I know this is short notice."

Who cares, I thought. I would go with him at the last second if he asked.

"It's just, Jacquelyn has really wanted to see this French film, and it's only playing at the Mayan this weekend, and I have Josh tonight, and my normal babysitter isn't available, and Josh really likes you, so I was wondering if . . ."

OH. MY. GOSH. He was asking me to babysit. What was I, thirteen? And to think I was going to ask him to be my date for the wedding. I shook my head like I couldn't believe what I was hearing, and it was then I caught a glimpse of my screen. I quickly turned to it and typed in that I was looking for, two seats in the best available category. I didn't know who would go with me, well I knew who it wasn't going to be . . . Ryan Carter. My first search came up empty. I panicked, quickly typed in one seat at the highest price. I just wanted to go. It was then I heard Ryan say, "So are you available tonight?"

I shook my head no, but at the screen not him. There were no tickets available. I lost my chance all on my silly unrealistic hope that my teenage crush was finally coming around. I looked up at him and glared.

"What?" He was obviously confused.

"You made me lose tickets to One Republic, my favorite band ever."

"Oh, so you're available to babysit then?"

I gave him a blank stare. He was so dense.

"Again, sorry about the short notice, but I'm in a bind."

"Fine." I waved my hand at him.

He looked relieved. He must really like this Jacquelyn. It reminded me he only dated women with proper, snobbish-sounding names. I should have remembered that and got my head out of the clouds.

"Okay, so can you come to my house tonight at six?"

"Yeah, whatever."

He smiled. "Thanks, I owe you one. Oh, and by the way, I won't mention your using company time to purchase concert tickets."

"Well, thanks to you that didn't happen. And I'm going to plead boss' daughter on this one."

He laughed at me as he walked out. If only I had something to chuck at his head. I eyed my stapler, but that could have gotten ugly.

On the way home with my dad, I stewed. I knew I was delusional, but really. Babysitting?

My dad must have noticed. "How was your day? You seem out of sorts."

I turned from wistfully looking out the window, to him. "It was fine."

He grinned. "There's that word again, fine. By the way, I've been hearing very good reports about you. You're doing a great job, kiddo."

"Thanks, Dad."

"So what do you want to do tonight?"

"Oh, well I told Ryan I would babysit for him."

My dad looked at me in confusion.

That's how I felt, too. "Maybe I should start up my babysitting business again," I teased. Krissy and I had had a babysitting service when we were teens. We'd made some pretty good money. I think I would have liked being a babysitter better than an accountant.

My dad chuckled.

We got home, and I changed into some shorts and a t-shirt and scarfed down some leftovers from the previous night's lasagna. What had my life become? I was supposed to be in my prime, but here I was babysitting on a Friday night. I kissed my dad on the head and headed out the door. I walked to Ryan's house, but not before I admired Mulberry Lane. It really was the best place ever. I looked around and saw kids riding their bikes and moms and dads out walking with their kids and babies. It was a beautiful neighborhood, too—large, leafy trees and pine trees filled everyone's yards, and there were flowers blooming like crazy everywhere. It also smelled wonderful, like barbecue.

I practically skipped to my dumb neighbor's house. At least I got to spend the evening with the cutest kid ever. He and I were becoming good friends. His dad had been bringing him over to our house frequently to jump on our trampoline. I was also teaching him how to dribble a basketball. Last weekend I held him up, and to my surprise, he made a basket. He was strong for a little guy. I don't think most kids his size could push a full-size ball up and into a hoop. He was so excited. "Cherry, I did it!" He'd giggled when he hugged me.

I knocked on Ryan's door, and he answered it almost immediately. He must have been anxious to get on his date. He had to look good, too, and he smelled divine. I think I was going to sneak into his room or bathroom to see what cologne he was using. It was yummy, and I was going to insist any boyfriends I may have in the future use it.

"Charlee," he greeted me.

"Hey."

He opened the door wider and motioned for me to come in. I was interested to see that the Carter's old place looked quite a bit different. It was much more open than it had been. Some definite remodeling had been done. There was now a large great room with a beautiful stone fireplace that was the centerpiece, and it was framed by large windows. I bet in the winter, when it was lit, it was a beautiful sight.

Josh came running out. "Cherry!"

I picked him up as soon as he got to me.

He put his sweet little arms around my neck.

"Hi, Josh." I snuggled him close.

"Daddy says if I'm good I can have ice cream."

I smiled. I had no doubt he was having ice cream.

"So, I'll probably be back late," Ryan said. "Josh's bed time is eight, and his room is the first one on the left down the hall." He pointed in the direction of his room.

"Okay." I kept my focus on Josh.

"Make sure not to give him anything to drink right before bed."

"Yeah, I got it. This isn't my first rodeo."

He smiled that gorgeous smile of his at me. "Thank you. You really don't know how much I appreciate this. Jacquelyn and I have been trying to get together for a while now, and it has never worked out between her schedule and mine."

What a pity, I thought. "It's no problem."

"Well I better get going. Feel free to help yourself to anything."

The only thing I wanted to help myself to was leaving, but I didn't mention that. I only nodded and smiled.

Ryan kissed Josh on the cheek while he was still in my arms. We briefly locked eyes. Ryan seemed to gaze into my eyes, confusion clouded his. "Charlee?"

"Yes?"

" . . . I'll see you later."

"I'll be here."

He smiled and touched his son's hair gently. "Be good for Charlee."

"I will, Daddy."

"Love you, buddy." Ryan walked out the door.

I almost sighed. Dads that love their kids are a total turn on, especially when they look and act like Ryan.

"All right, it's just you and me kid. What do you want to do?"

"B-ball," he shouted.

A kid after my own heart. We walked back over to my house, and my dad was happy to have the company, and play basketball. I think he loved the idea of training the next generation, and he seemed to really like spending his time with me. I was remembering how much I liked to spend my time with him. My dad and I had a great time trying to teach Josh how to dribble with his fingertips and not his palms. We also tried to get him to take his focus away from the ball when he dribbled, but he was three so that wasn't happening.

My dad hoisted Josh up several times and tried to help him make a shot. When he finally got one to go in, I don't know who was more excited, my dad or Josh. I really think my dad was looking forward to the time when I had kids. From the looks of it, he would be a terrific grandpa. Once we were done with hoops, we hit the trampoline. Josh was so worn out by the night's activities, we didn't even have ice cream. I got him in his jammies and helped him brush his teeth, and by the time I was done reading him a book about fire trucks, he was sound asleep. I kissed his little forehead, pulled a light blanket over him, and swiped his beautiful hair.

I walked out into the great room and wasn't sure what to do with myself. It seemed weird to be there. I remember when I was younger, Mrs. Carter sometimes invited me over. She said she needed girl time or she just missed her own kids. I remember helping her make cookies and banana bread. I liked her. The house now looked like a man lived there. It was nice, but more masculine. Very straight lines, minimal artwork, leather and metal, and, a TV that was way too big, but it was clean and even inviting with the warm lighting.

I settled on Ryan's black leather couch and turned on the TV for company. I was delighted to find *The Sisterhood of the Traveling Pants* was on. Krissy and I loved that movie when we were growing up. I curled up on the couch and enjoyed a piece of my wonderful childhood. I really was so lucky; I guess it was just too good to last. It made me wonder if good things did last.

When the movie ended, I heard Josh call out for his daddy. He sounded scared. I jumped up, ran to his room, and found him sitting up and crying. I went to him and held him to me. All he kept saying was, "mean doggie." It was clear he'd had a bad dream. I tried to get him to calm down and go back to sleep, but he didn't want me to leave him. I decided to pick him up and take him back to the couch with me. His toddler bed was too small for the both of us.

I wiped his wet cheeks and held his little body close to me and sang to him a song my dad used to sing to me when I was little. It was an old song by James Taylor called, "You Can Close Your Eyes." I loved that old song. I sang it repeatedly until he fell back asleep in my arms. There was something wonderful about having a little one sleep in your arms. They looked so angelic. Well, at least I had someone to cuddle up next to on a Friday night.

I watched one more movie, and close to midnight I heard the garage door open. Ryan walked in a minute later. He looked happy. I took it his date went well. He looked my way and walked toward Josh and me. His dress shoes tapped on the wood floor as he approached.

"Is everything okay?" He looked down at his sleeping son.

"I think he had a nightmare, and he had a hard time falling back asleep."

Ryan knelt next to us on the couch and stroked his son's hair. "He's been having those lately."

"I think it's pretty normal for kids his age to have nightmares."

Ryan looked up at me and smiled. "And you know this how?"

I was offended. "Uh, child development classes, thank you very much."

He smirked at my annoyance. "Other than that, was he okay?"

"Better than okay. We had great time."

"Thanks, Charlee. He doesn't usually take to people so well."

"You're welcome. So . . . how was your date?"

Ryan stood up and sat on the couch next to us. "It was nice. It's weird to watch a movie where you have to read the subtitles though."

"Sounds dreadful."

He looked at me, surprised. "Don't women typically love foreign romantic films?"

"Not this woman. I typically don't like movies at all for dates."

"Really?"

"Yep. If a guy asks me on a first date and that's his plan, I say no."

"Why would you do that?"

"Because how can you get to know someone if you're watching a movie? And seriously, if that's all you can think of to do, then I'd just as soon pass."

"Well, I guess I'm glad Jacquelyn doesn't feel the same way."

"You mean this was your first date with her?"

"Yes. We met at the park a couple of months ago and our kids played together, but like I said earlier, it has never worked out until tonight."

"Oh."

"So . . ." he said. "What do you consider first date worthy?"

"Lots of things."

"Care to elaborate?"

"Why, do you need some tips?"

He arched his eyebrow at me, and I laughed.

"Well, here, the possibilities for non-lame first time dates are endless. There's boating, hiking, biking, picnicking, and, of course, you have Estes Park nearby which is the most romantic place ever. Even just walking down the river walk there would be perfect."

"So, you're saying I'm lame once again."

I shrugged my shoulders. "I didn't say anything."

"Well, for your information, I must not be too lame; she agreed to go out with me again."

That was lame, but I didn't say anything. "Well, I should get home."

"Here, let me pay you."

I shook my head in disgust. "I'm not twelve. I don't take babysitting jobs."

He put his wallet back into his pocket and looked at me. "No, you're definitely not twelve. Thank you. I owe you one."

"You don't owe me anything. I love being with Josh."

He smiled and took Josh out of my arms. He came too close for my own good. Our faces were mere inches apart as he bent over to get Josh. For a brief second, I had a thought of pure insanity—my unbridled side said, *Reach up and kiss him. You know you want to.* And did I ever, but my rational side, thankfully, overruled the dumb thought.

Ryan paused for a moment. I could see the flecks of blue in his green eyes. Oddly, he stared into my own eyes and bent his head. "You have very unusual eyes." His breath was warm, and it smelled of honey when he spoke.

"I'm not sure how I should take that."

He stood up with his son, but he smiled down at me. "I've never seen so many colors in one iris."

"Well, I've always been an overachiever."

He laughed quietly as to not wake up Josh. "I never know what you're going to say."

I stood up, too. "Goodnight, Ryan."

"Goodnight. Thanks, again."

I walked toward his front door and proceeded to exit, but he called out my name. I turned back toward him.

"Are you planning on running tomorrow?"

"Yes, but don't worry, I don't need you to be neighborly and watch over me."

"I just wanted to see if you could go later, like eight. I don't want to get Josh up too early. I'll have to bring him in his jogger."

"Oh . . . sure. See you tomorrow."

"I look forward to it."

I looked forward to our morning runs, too. He made getting in shape for the wedding fun, even if he didn't see me how I wanted him to.

The next morning our run was like the many others before, except better because Josh was part of the package. It's amazing what little kids notice and how excited they get about the smallest things that we as adults take for granted, like birds and even colorful rocks. To see the world through Josh's eyes made me appreciate my surroundings even more.

My appreciation for Ryan grew, too, as I watched him take care of his son and respond with enthusiasm to all his questions. Besides "again", "why" was Josh's favorite word of choice. Ryan took the time to answer each of his questions and encouraged more. No wonder Josh was so smart for his age.

It was all well and good, actually more than good. Then I had a rude awakening as we neared our houses. I was laughing at Ryan after he had informed me that he had an 'N Sync album on his iTunes playlist. Not that I didn't like that band. I mean who didn't love Justin Timberlake, but I was embarrassed for Ryan.

He nudged me with his shoulder and at the same time I felt this horrible stinging pain in my other arm. "Ahhh," I cried out. I stopped dead in my tracks, not sure what had happened.

"Charlee, I didn't mean to hurt you. Are you okay?"

"It wasn't you, it's my other arm."

Ryan gently turned me toward him and we both looked down at my arm. It was red and swollen, but I was confused as to why.

Ryan delicately touched the affected area.

"Ow."

He smiled at me and suddenly I felt better. "I think I found the culprit. You've been stung."

"By what? I didn't see any bees."

"My guess is a yellow jacket, they'll sting without being provoked."

"It packs a punch."

"Let me take you back to my place. I'll get the stinger out for you and make a paste."

"Make a paste?" I smiled.

"With meat tenderizer, it will help with the pain."

"Did you say meat tenderizer?"

"Trust me."

"Okay, Davy Crockett."

He shook his head at me.

We jogged the short distance to his house and I tried not to be a baby, but seriously, my arm hurt. I had never been stung before and let me say, I was okay missing out on that before now.

"Have a seat at the table." Ryan waved to his table when we walked into his kitchen from the backyard.

Josh tore through the house and said something about getting his owie kit.

I looked to Ryan for clarification.

"He has a doctor kit."

I smiled. That made sense.

"So, are you like a Boy Scout or something?"

Ryan looked up from the concoction he was mixing and grinned. "I earned my Eagle Scout when I was sixteen."

"Really?"

"Are you surprised?"

"Honestly, no." He seemed like the do-gooder type. I bet he helped senior citizens cross the street and everything.

It didn't take too long for him to join me. First, he used a credit card and removed the stinger, then he carefully cleansed the area. Every touch from him made me hold my breath. I'm pretty sure I was biting my lip, too, as he worked his magic. He kept looking up and flashing those pearly whites at me. He sent me over the edge when he blew on my arm. I'm pretty sure I shivered like an idiot.

My saving grace came in the form of Josh, who had his pretend thermometer out and insisted I put it in my mouth. He didn't have to convince me. Did I mention chubby cheeks and dimples?

Ryan administered his meat tenderizer paste and I instantly felt relief from the pain of the sting.

"Thank you," I mumbled with the plastic toy in mouth.

"My pleasure."

Josh took out the thermometer. "You all better now."

I looked between him and his father and I felt plenty good.

Ryan peered into my eyes. "Charlee?"

"Yes?"

He acted like he wanted to say something, but he stopped and shook his head. "Just make sure to keep an eye on the site to check for infection or an allergic reaction."

"Thank you, Dr. Carter."

He smiled at me, but he stood up and acted as if he wasn't sure what he should do. It was odd, but I didn't call attention to it. I just said my goodbyes, went home, reminded myself he liked redheads with snobbish names, and tried to get him out of my head. It didn't work.

Seven

I HAD THE PLEASURE, OR DISPLEASURE, as it were, to meet Jacquelyn the following week. She came and met Ryan for lunch at the office. Yep, she was his type, a redheaded raving beauty. Her curly red hair framed her perfect head, and she was tall and thin. She fit his type to a tee. She even seemed aloof.

I was standing in my dad's office doorway when she and Ryan walked by.

"Hey, Charlee, I would like you to meet Jacquelyn."

I gave them both a charming smile and held out my hand. "Nice to meet you," I lied.

She eyed my hand before she reluctantly held out her own. She squeezed mine awfully tight.

"Jacquelyn, this is Charlee."

She kind of gave me sneering sort of look. "Yes, you've mentioned her."

Okay, Miss Snotty Pants. I didn't know what her problem was. I turned from her and looked at my dad. He, too, looked a little confused. Ryan introduced her to my dad as well, and then they headed off to lunch.

When they left, Felicity commented, "Well, wasn't she a little ray of sunshine."

My dad and I both laughed.

I went back to my office and pondered why Ryan always picked women that seemed awful. I knew I wasn't being fair, because I was completely jealous of her. I was even more jealous when Krissy told me he returned his response card and named Jacquelyn as his plus-one.

I really needed some ice cream, but I couldn't have any because I was going to be half-naked in ten days. I had to give myself props, my butt and legs were looking pretty good. I was even getting good at walking in hooker heels. My dad kept making fun of me for walking around the house in them, and once Ryan came to the door and I made the mistake of answering it while still wearing them. I looked real classy in cut-offs, a tank top, and sky-high heels. Ryan smirked at me, looked me over from head to toe, and then chuckled.

I really needed to quit thinking about him, but it was hard not to. I mean, we worked together, ran together practically every day, and frequently he and Josh came over to hang out or eat with us. He was everywhere. Heck, I even babysat for the guy. I decided, after all this wedding nonsense, I was going to start going out more. I needed to find people my age that were single to hang out with.

I also started looking at psychology programs. I was toying with the idea of going back to school. I got so giddy every time I would see that there was a new edition of *Psychology Today* or *In Mind* available. I knew that's where my heart truly lay, but I was torn. I had spent a whole lot of time and my dad's money on the education I already had. Sure, I had scholarships, but they nowhere near covered everything, and my dad was beyond happy that I was following in his footsteps. I only fed the monster by doing my job well.

I decided to push off any decisions about school until after the wedding. The closer it got, the more hectic my life was becoming. Besides the wedding, there was the bridal shower, bachelorette party, and rehearsal dinner. I was in charge of the first two, at least mostly. Ann and Maviny were helping quite a bit with the shower, and they were hosting it at their home. I was more than grateful for their help, because I wasn't the best party planner or decorator in the world. And, to be honest, I really kind of disliked showers with the silly games and endless lingerie, but this wasn't about me. I hoped when I got married, I married someone who didn't mind me wearing t-shirts to bed; lingerie looked awfully uncomfortable, and from the looks of it, you might as well be naked.

Krissy's wedding colors were red and aqua, so we decked the

Lawtons' house out in her two signature colors the Saturday before her wedding. We even made the food to match. At least I could bake. I made strawberry cheesecake, chocolate covered strawberries, and a beautiful berry trifle. Did you notice a theme there? Ann even made a red punch. When it all came together, it looked perfect, and it was what Krissy wanted. I had even worked with Chance on one of the games. I taped him answering a bunch of questions. At the shower we were going to ask Krissy how she thought Chance would respond to each question and then we would play his answer and see if she was right. They were silly questions like, "How many kids do you want to have?" and "Should the toilet paper hang over or under?" By the way, they disagreed on both. Chance wanted two kids and Krissy said four. She was also an under-the-toilet-paper-roll kind of girl and he was over. I guess they would have a lifetime of working out their kinks.

The following week we were in serious wedding mode. I had a nice boss, and he let me take Thursday and Friday off. It was a good thing, too. Krissy called me early on Thursday crying and in crisis mode. First, her period had started early and she was bloated. That was going to make for a fun honeymoon, but secondly, and most importantly to her, she decided she hated the shoes she bought originally. And apparently if she didn't have the perfect shoes, the wedding was going to be a disaster. I didn't even try and reason with her. I got ready and headed to her apartment with dark chocolate and a willingness to go to every shoe store on the eastern slope of Colorado, if necessary.

Krissy opened her apartment door with red swollen eyes. "You're the best." She clung to me for dear life.

I patted her back. "I know."

She laughed. "I'm so glad you're home."

"Me, too. Now go clean up. We have some serious shopping to do."

She sniffled a little and then went off to finish getting ready. I looked around her packed apartment, and for a moment I was sad. I knew we would always be the best of friends, but I knew things were going to change this weekend. She would be married, and I would be single. She and Chance would find married couples to hang out with, and I would be that weird loner friend.

Krissy and I went from store to store to store. I swore she tried on hundreds of pairs of shoes, but each one had some minor defect, from too much heel, to too little heel, or one had too many embellishments, another not enough. She was driving me crazy, but I was in supportive mode. After the ninth store, I suggested that perhaps some Midol may do us both some good. Thankfully, she laughed instead of hitting me or freaking out on me. It honestly could have gone either way.

We stopped for lunch, and I loaded her up on protein and foods high in potassium to try and see if we could beat the bloat. I thought she looked great, but she wasn't thinking rationally, so I was doing my best to try and talk her off the ledge. With some nutrition in her and yes, some Midol, we finally found the perfect pair of shoes at the eleventh store. Chiffon ruched shoes with a tiny crystal embellishment was apparently the ticket. They were beautiful, but they looked like thirteen other pairs she had tried on. And not to be nitpicky, but her ball gown wedding dress was so long, no one was going to see her shoes anyway. Believe me, though, I didn't mention it.

With the crisis averted, I went home to get ready for the bachelorette party. This wedding was taking over my life. Bachelorette party tonight, rehearsal dinner tomorrow night, and then all of Saturday would be nothing but wedding. In a way, it was good, it kept my mind off myself. I was still bugged about Ryan. I knew I should forget about him, but my steamy dreams were making it hard. Plus, we spent a lot of time around each other, and besides being physically attracted to him, I liked him. I liked how he treated people at the office with respect and kindness, and I loved how he was with Josh. He was an all-around great guy.

I was also irked at my mom at the moment. She was supposed to come for the wedding. Krissy had been like a daughter to her, and Ann was a good friend of hers. But no, she and Mark decided to go to Branson, Missouri. Really? The Osmond Brothers were more important than Krissy? My mom was not the woman I had grown up with, and I missed that woman terribly.

Krissy and Chance promised each other no sleazy bachelor or bachelorette parties, and I'm grateful I had the foresight to book us a spa night. It couldn't have come at a better time for the bride, or the maid of honor. The Midol was only going so far. I was going to move onto tranquilizers soon, if need be.

When I opened my garage to leave for the party I had a sweet treat waiting for me. Josh came running up the driveway yelling, "Cherry!" He ran right into my arms.

I picked him up and squeezed him tight. "What are you doing?"

"Can I jump?"

I looked between him and his dad who now stood close. "Sure, but your daddy will have to jump with you today. I'm leaving."

"Where are you headed to?" Ryan asked.

"Bachelorette party."

He nodded. "I remember you mentioning that now. I take it you won't be in any shape to run in the morning."

I rolled my eyes at him. "It's not that kind of party."

"So, I'll see you in the morning?" There was some anticipation in his voice.

"If you're lucky."

Ryan took Josh out of my arms, but not before I kissed his cute cheeks. "I'll see you in the morning."

"Okay." He wasn't making it easy for me not to think about him.

"Bye, Josh."

"Bye, Cherry."

"Bye, Ryan."

He looked at me for a moment. "Bye, Charlee. Be safe tonight."

I cocked my head slightly at his concern. He didn't sound brotherly, and I liked it. "I don't think I can get into too much trouble at the spa, but I'll tell the masseuse to be gentle."

He shook his head from side to side and laughed.

I watched him and Josh walk toward the park. I guess Ryan wasn't in a jumping mood.

See how hard it was not to think of him? My insides were like goo. I reminded myself he was dating Jacquelyn, and took off to indulge in some much needed relaxation.

I struck a deal with the spa, so it would only be the bridal party. I admit, my dad's credit card helped there. He told me to think of it as part of Krissy's wedding gift. The place was great enough to let us have dinner delivered there. I was the first one there to make sure everything was set up and ready to go. I wanted to make sure Krissy had a stress-free, fun night. It was only going to be her four other bridesmaids, Dana, Amy, Tasha, and, her sister, Maviny, and then the two of us.

Everything was in order, right down to the salads and lemon water I'd ordered. As soon as the party arrived, we ate, and then we were whisked away for some serious pampering. We started with mani-pedis. We sat in a long row of chairs and talked and giggled like women do when they get together. Most of the conversation revolved around men, and mainly our celebrity crushes.

Maviny was the most vocal. "I'm telling you, Adam Levine is like the hottest man on the freaking planet."

"Yeah, he's sexy, but I could never be with a man who has thinner thighs than me," I countered.

Everyone laughed, but it was true. I thought about Ryan's perfectly muscular legs and how lucky I was to see them almost every day as we ran.

"So who do you like?" Maviny asked me.

I gave her a wry grin. "We're not in junior high."

She smiled evilly. "That's okay, we all know."

"You all know what?"

"My mom told us about the time you spend with Ryan Carter."

"Your mom needs to get some shades for the windows in your house."

Maviny and Krissy laughed.

"So, who's Ryan?" Dana asked.

"He's no one."

"Don't listen to her," Krissy said. "She's only been in love with him since we were fourteen."

I threw my head over to Krissy and gave her the vilest look on the planet. That was a secret. Like lock-in-the-vault secret between best friends. She at least had the decency to look a little ashamed.

"Wow!" Maviny exclaimed. "I didn't know that. Isn't he like way older than you?"

"Ooh, an older man," Tasha threw in.

I was suddenly not enjoying myself. The worst part was that I couldn't even let Krissy have it because she was the guest of honor and PMSing. I picked up the magazine next to me and started perusing it in hopes of ignoring them all. That was a nice thought, but . . .

"So are you bringing Ryan to the wedding?" Amy asked.

"No." I spoke into the magazine.

"He's coming, though," Krissy informed her friends. "He's bringing someone else."

"Ouch," they all echoed each other.

I was beyond annoyed now. I lowered the magazine. "For your information, Ryan and I are just friends. He thinks of me like a sister. The time we spend together is purely platonic and," I glared over at Krissy, "I'm not in love with him." I just really, really liked him and he made me feel like I'm on fire when I'm around him, but no one needed to know that.

"So we need a plan for how to take care of this other woman at the wedding," Dana said.

I shook my head. "No, no, no." But no one was listening to me. They were coming up with idiotic things like accidentally spilling wine on her. The more I objected to their lunacy, the more it fueled them. When this wedding was over, Krissy was getting smacked. I felt like we were in high school again and I was afraid that the guy I liked would find out I liked him before I knew if he liked me. The worst part was I knew the guy didn't like me like that, and it would be way more uncomfortable if Ryan ever found out that I had feelings for him that went beyond friendly.

"I'll point him out to you guys at the wedding," Maviny offered.

I got up with my newly painted toe nails and carefully headed over to the drying table. They all called after me, but I ignored them.

I thought we were supposed to be talking about the bride and groom, not teasing the maid of honor, who by the way paid for all of them tonight. So my dad helped, but that still counted, right? This was some way to be paid back. I probably should have been a better sport about it, but I knew it was never happening between Ryan and me and I was disappointed by it.

When we were done and walking out together, Krissy held me

back and hugged me as tight as she could. "Thanks for being the best friend ever. I'm sorry for spilling the beans about Ryan."

"It's fine. I love being humiliated."

"Don't worry, what happens at bachelorette parties, stays at bachelorette parties."

I scrunched my face at her.

"Seriously, CJ. Don't worry about it. And besides, if Ryan doesn't see how amazing you are, then he's an idiot."

I hugged her one more time. "Okay, bridezilla, you better get home and get some rest. Tomorrow's another big day. Make sure you bring your happy pills to the dinner."

She smacked me on the arm. "I love you."

"I know, and I suppose I still love you."

I got in my car and sighed. I was tempted to head straight for ice cream, but then I thought of that Barbie dress I was expected to wear and breathe in. All I knew was Sunday I was eating ice cream with every meal in between sleeping. I was exhausted.

Not exhausted enough to miss my run with Ryan, though. He kind of got my blood flowing. I met Ryan back behind the fence, per our usual. And per his usual, he looked perfect. I wondered if he knew how attractive he was. He didn't act like one of those men that knew he was God's gift to women. In a lot of ways he acted unassuming. Even at the office, where he was number two, you would have thought he was just another accountant. He was approachable and more than happy to help when a problem arose. Like the other day, when our intern, Garrett, practically had a meltdown because he filled out a 940 instead of a 941 and transmitted it to the IRS. Ryan stepped in and first, calmed him down and then explained to him how to go about correcting it. Ryan could have easily scolded him for filing an annual form versus a bi-weekly form, but he didn't. In fact, he helped him find some humor in it, and then he took the guy out to lunch. I thought maybe I should make some errors so Ryan would take me out to lunch. Unfortunately, I was a perfectionist when it came to my job that I didn't love, not to mention the boss' kid, so the fewer mistakes, the better for everyone.

I did think, though, about all the lunch hours he had spent helping me study for that ridiculous CPA exam I didn't want to take. He had even worked up a study guide and flash cards for me. I'm sure he spent hours on both. I had asked him why last week and he actually said something witty like, "It was the neighborly thing to do." But then those green eyes of his bore right into me and he touched my hand. "Charlee, I—"

"You what?" I smiled.

He had squeezed my hand. "I just want you to do well. In fact, I know you will. I think you may know this stuff better than me."

Suddenly, I was brought out of the memory.

"Did the masseuse go easy on you last night?" Ryan jogged beside me.

I shook my head and refocused in on the present. "Yes, it was heavenly."

"You know, it's so weird for me to think that Krissy is getting married. She's just a kid in my mind."

I threw him a dirty look. "Krissy and I are the same age, and it's not like you're that much older than us."

He looked over at me, surprised. "I didn't mean to offend you."

"I'm not offended." I was ticked that he thought of me like a kid.

He cracked a smile. "You know, I'm almost a whole decade older than you."

"Well, you really rounded up there, didn't you?"

"I never knew you were so touchy about your age."

"I'm not touchy."

He stopped running and tugged on my arm. "Is something bothering you? You seem . . . unhappy."

I stopped and stared into his eyes as we both jogged in place, and I inadvertently touched my arm where his hand had touched me; it left an invisible mark. For a second I wanted to lay it all out there and let him reject me to my face, on the very off chance he could ever see me as something more than a kid, but I didn't. "I'm sorry. I'm really stressed out, with wedding stuff, you know."

He smiled like he got it. "Just wait until it's your turn, then you'll really know what stress is."

"I've decided I'm not having a wedding, at least not like any I've ever been a part of."

"Let me guess, weddings are too boring for you."

"Very good, and don't forget pretentious and ridiculously costly."

He laughed at me, and I took that as my cue to begin running again. As much as I wanted to stay there with him all day and listen to him laugh, I had a full day on tap.

"So, what kind of wedding do you want?" He stuck close by my side.

I shrugged my shoulders. "I haven't put that much thought into it."

"Sure you haven't."

I nudged him with my shoulder. "Not every woman is obsessed with getting married, thank you very much."

He looked at me and narrowed his eyes. "You're an unusual girl, so maybe I'll believe you."

"Did you just call me an unusual *girl*?"

"I didn't mean it in a bad way."

"You know, I think we should just run." I faced forward and put a little more effort into my running and pulled ahead of him slightly.

He lagged behind for several seconds before he decided to catch up. He didn't say anything until we were almost back to our houses. "Hey, Charlee. I didn't mean anything by unusual. Really, I think you're a great girl."

I turned and gave him an ice-cold stare. "I'm not a girl."

His eyes widened.

I walked off without another word and disappeared behind my gate.

As soon as I was safely away from him, I stopped, bent over, and tried to get a hold of my emotions. I felt so stupid. I don't know why I snapped like that. He looked at me like I had lost my mind, and I had. I took some deep breaths, but it wasn't helping. I gave up and walked into the house.

There sat my dad. "Hey, baby girl. How was your run?"

"Don't ask."

He tilted his head. "What's wrong?"

I walked to the refrigerator without answering and pulled open the door with a vengeance.

"Hey, what did that refrigerator ever do to you?"

"Sorry, Dad."

"Honey, what's wrong?"

I spun around to face my dad. "Say you just met me, would you say I look like a girl?"

My dad opened his mouth, not sure what to say. "Is this a trick question?"

"No, Dad!"

My dad stood up and walked over to me with extreme caution. He stopped just short of me. "Honey, you look all girl to me, I don't know how anyone could mistake you for anything else."

I started laughing. He wasn't getting it.

My dad shook his head confused.

"Never mind, Daddy." I kissed his cheek and left to get ready for the day.

"What time do we need to be at the rehearsal dinner tonight?" he called after me.

"Six."

"Okay. I'll be home early."

"Sounds good. Have a good day."

"You too, baby girl. And if anyone mistakes you for a boy again, tell them to come see me."

I shook my head and headed down the stairs. Men were so dense sometimes.

Eight

I WAS HAPPY TO HAVE my dad by my side for the rehearsal dinner. I was beginning to feel very out of place. It seemed like everyone had someone; even Mason and Maviny had dates, and, all the other bridesmaids had boyfriends. Krissy offered to set me up with someone, but I didn't think this was the proper venue for blind dates. It was pointless, anyway, since I couldn't get Ryan out of my head. Ryan. The man who saw me as a child, Ryan. I was so dumb!

I walked up the stairs in my little black dress and the red strappy heels. I wanted to practice walking in them down the aisle tonight.

My dad was waiting for me on his recliner, but stood as soon as I entered the family room. "Wow, honey! You're gonna give your old man a heart attack looking like that."

"Thanks, Dad." I ran my fingers through my beach-waved hair. If this dress gave him a heart attack, tomorrow's dress was going to be aneurysm worthy.

He held out his arm to me. "Shall we go?"

I nodded my head yes and put my arm through his. He reached across and patted my hand. "You remind me of your mom when she was your age, but don't tell her, I think you're even more beautiful."

"Thanks, Daddy."

"So . . ." My dad reached for my hand on our drive over to the country club, where the wedding would be the next day, and where the rehearsal dinner was being hosted. "I had an interesting conversation with Ryan today at lunch."

I looked down at my hooker heels. "Oh, really?"

"Yes, and your inquiry in the kitchen now makes more sense."

I sighed aloud, mostly out of embarrassment.

My dad chuckled. "Do you like Ryan?"

I whipped my head toward my dad. "Does Ryan think that?" I was in full panic mode.

My dad smiled at me. "No . . . but he's awfully confused about why you're upset with him. Which is surprising, because I thought he was smarter than that."

"What does that mean?"

"I may be old, kiddo, but I can still tell when someone is attracted to another person."

I cringed. "Have I been that obvious?"

"Neither of you have done a very good job of hiding it."

I shook my head. I was sure I'd heard my dad wrong.

My dad noticed and laughed again. "Yes, both of you."

"Ryan isn't attracted to me, Dad. He thinks of me like a little girl."

"Believe me, CJ, he recognizes that you're a woman. I don't think he wants to admit it to himself, but there's no doubt he notices you. Why do you think he spends so much time at our house now? I can assure you, it's not me."

"Okay, let's say hypothetically you're right, which you're not, but let's pretend you are. How would you feel about it?"

My dad took a deep breath and let it out slowly. "Well, it could definitely make things interesting since he's my business partner and we all work together, and then there's the age difference, but I think you might be good for each other." He squeezed my perfectly manicured hand.

"It doesn't matter anyway. He's dating Jacquelyn, and honestly, he doesn't see me like that."

"I wouldn't be too sure of that, but promise me you'll be careful. I love Ryan like a son, but I think he's still reeling from the effects of his marriage and divorce."

"Again, Dad, there's nothing to worry about, other than your daughter being a complete idiot. You won't say anything to Ryan, will you?"

"My lips are sealed."

"Thanks."

I didn't know why, but I felt better. I was a little embarrassed, but mostly it was nice to have a parent to talk to, one that focused on me and not just himself. It was nice not to feel like I was in a competition. I loved how my dad made me feel beautiful. I did wonder, though, if he was delusional. There was no way Ryan was attracted to me.

The rehearsal went off without a hitch, thank goodness. I wasn't sure if Krissy's state of mind would have settled for anything less than perfection. I even made it down the aisle in my ridiculously high heels somewhat gracefully. I knew tomorrow would be a different story as I would be half-naked; I was trying not to think about it. I had been praying the dress would magically grow in my absence.

Dinner was amazing, and I wasn't only talking about the lobster tails—the company was even better. It made me so happy to be home. These were my people. This was where I belonged. I decided then that even if I didn't stay working for my dad, I was staying in Colorado.

I felt mostly content as I got ready for bed that night. Sure, I'd apparently made an idiot out of myself with my very attractive neighbor, and apparently the whole neighborhood could see it, but I felt a sense of belonging, and I had so desperately missed that.

While brushing my teeth, I heard the doorbell. I looked at my phone and it was eleven, a little late for visitors. Then my dad called my name.

I threw my bra back on and walked upstairs. I was greeted by a crying Krissy. My dad stared at her blankly, not sure what to make of the scene.

I went to Krissy, wrapped my arms around her, and mouthed to my dad, "Go to bed, I've got it."

He looked beyond relieved.

"Krissy, what are you doing here? I thought you and Chance were going back to your place to finish packing?" They were moving into a townhome closer to the pharmacy where Chance was doing his residency to become a pharmacist.

She cried harder, and I'm pretty sure some snot was left behind on my t-shirt. I pulled her to the kitchen and sat her down at the breakfast bar. She looked like heck. I did the only thing I could do, I pulled out the best cure: ice cream. I didn't even bother with bowls, I just grabbed two spoons. I sat next to her and took the lid off the dark chocolate ice cream carton. "Okay, spill your guts."

She sniffled and took a bite of the ice cream.

I took a large bite, too, and it was ecstasy. I may have even sighed.

"I can't get married tomorrow."

"What! Why?"

"I got a call today from the Denver Bronco Cheerleaders. They had someone drop out, and they asked if I would be interested in auditioning again."

"That's terrific."

"I thought so, too," she cried. "I was excited to tell Chance tonight when we were alone. I thought he should be the first to know." She looked at me like she was sorry.

She didn't need to be sorry. He was going to be her husband, he should be the first to know. I was already prepared to be second in line. I gave her a warm smile.

She gave me a weak one in return. "Well, anyway, he said he didn't think it was appropriate for a married woman to be part of that squad and if that's what I wanted to do, then maybe we shouldn't get married."

"So what did you say?"

"I told him where he could go, and I drove straight over here." She shoved another spoonful of heaven in her mouth and cried some more.

"Oh, Kris, I'm sure he didn't mean it. You're both just stressed."

"No, it's over," she cried.

I stood up and hugged her. "I think we should call him. I'm sure he's worried about you."

"My dream has been to be on that squad for as long as I can remember. How can he tell me to forget about it? It's like he doesn't trust me, and if he doesn't trust me, how can we get married?"

I wasn't sure what to say. I could see her point, but I could understand why, perhaps, Chance had reservations, though I didn't agree with his almost ultimatum. They really needed to talk this out. "Honey, I'm sure you can work this out. You're tired and you're in the middle of a huge life change, not to mention Mother Nature's having her way with you. I think you need to take a deep breath and call Chance."

We didn't have to call him—within a minute there was a knock on my door.

I opened the door, and without even a hello, Chance rushed in, picked Krissy up, and held her to him. "Krissy, baby, I'm so sorry. If you want to be a professional cheerleader, I'll support you one hundred percent."

"Really?" She spoke against his chest.

He didn't answer, at least not verbally. That's where I took my leave. I waited for them in our living room. I didn't wait too long; within a few minutes they were walking out my door hand-in-hand, but not before Krissy bear-hugged me. "I love you, CJ."

"I know. I love you, too."

Chance waved goodbye to me, and I watched them walk out my door. For a moment, I longed to have a love like that. I walked back to the kitchen and eyed the ice cream on the counter. I was tempted to eat the whole carton by myself, but I resisted. I placed the lid back on it and whispered that we would get reacquainted on Sunday.

It was well after midnight before I made it to bed. Even though I was exhausted, I couldn't sleep. If it weren't so late, I would be tempted to shoot hoops. I needed to clear my head. I think tonight was the first time I'd ever felt a little envious of Krissy. Not because of Chance; I wasn't attracted to him at all. No, I wanted someone that loved me like he loved Krissy, someone I could love back with the same passion and desire. I couldn't help but think of Ryan, but it was a fruitless thought. He didn't see me that way.

Saturday morning came way too early. I didn't get enough sleep for the day I had ahead of me. I longed for Sunday and sleeping in and eating whatever I wanted to. I got up and showered, but I didn't do my hair or makeup—that would all be done at the country club with the whole bridal party. The only thing I did at home was meticulously shave my legs and underarms, and moisturize until I shined like no one's business. I felt like I was getting ready for the swimsuit portion of a beauty pageant.

I ate a light breakfast with my dad before I was off for the day. The wedding was at five that evening, but as the maid of honor, I had my duties to attend to, mainly keeping Krissy from freaking out. I hoped she and Chance hadn't had any more blow-ups in the eight hours since I'd last seen them.

"Everything okay with Krissy and Chance?" My dad took a sip of his coffee.

"As far as I know, but the day is still young."

He chuckled. "Pre-wedding jitters are normal with emotions running so high."

"Yeah, I've noticed. I think I've decided to skip the wedding nonsense when and if my turn comes."

He looked up from his paper. "You're going to deny your old man a trip down the aisle with his baby girl?"

I grinned. "Think of it this way, I'm saving you a whole lot of money."

His eyes brimmed over with love. "I would pay any amount of money to have the honor of giving you away."

"You know that could be taken in a bad way."

"You know what I mean."

"I do, but I don't think we'll have to worry about it for a long time."

"You never know about these things; sometimes love pops up when we least expect it to."

I knew what he was talking about, or at least I thought I did. He and my mother had met each other while they were each on a date with other people. They both said it was love at first sight. I washed my mind of it. I couldn't think about my parents and the demise of what seemed like an almost perfect relationship this morning. I especially couldn't think of the aftermath and how it had altered my life.

"Just as a warning, my bridesmaid's dress . . . you're probably not going to like it."

He focused back on me with a question in his eyes. "And why's that?"

"Oh, I think I'm going to leave it as a surprise." I walked over and kissed his head. "I'll see you later."

"Love you, kiddo." He looked up at me with hope.

"I know." I took a deep breath and tried to let go of my pride. "I mean . . . love you, Dad."

He stood up and pulled me right to him, and for some reason that released a tidal wave of emotion. I began to cry. I stood there and bathed his shoulder with my tears. He rubbed my back. I think he was crying, too.

I reluctantly pulled away. "I need to get going, and I don't think the whole puffy-eye look works for me."

He gently touched my cheek. "You'll be the most beautiful woman there today."

I shook my head at him and his bias.

"I'm not just saying that. It may be Krissy's day, but I have a feeling you'll have your fair share of attention."

"I love you, Dad."

He kissed the top of my head. "I love you more than you know."

With that, I ran downstairs to brush my teeth. I grabbed my bag full of necessities for the day, and headed over to the country club. On my drive over, I thought about my dad and forgiveness. I thought about how freeing and wonderful it felt to tell him that I loved him. It was weird, but I felt I could breathe a little easier. I didn't even realize what I had been holding onto was having a physical effect on me.

I met Ann and Maviny when I got there. Krissy was already inside, apparently fussing over the tablecloths. Ann and Maviny begged me to go in and calm her down. I didn't delay and went in to see what I could do. I found my best friend personally measuring the aqua-colored tablecloths to make sure they were perfectly even on every single side of the round tables.

"Drop the measuring tape and step away," I called out to her.

She looked up at me. She looked like a wreck, as if she hadn't slept at all last night. I hoped she and Chance didn't get into another argument.

I walked cautiously toward her. She had a caged-animal look, and I didn't want to spook her. "Krissy, no one cares, honey, if the table-cloths are perfectly even, and if they do, they have serious issues."

Yep, she lost it. Huge crocodile tears streamed down her pretty face.

I pulled her to me, took the measuring tape out of her hand and hugged her tight. Her mom and sister ran in and retrieved the measuring tape from my hands and hid it. I let Krissy get it out of her and then walked her to the bridal room where I got her a cool damp towel and some cucumbers for her eyes.

"I just want everything to be perfect." She cried as she laid on the couch with the cucumbers on her eyes.

I held her hand. "Krissy, why are you getting married?"

She took the cucumbers off her eyes and looked at me like I was insane or something. "Why do you think? Because I love Chance."

"That's an excellent reason. And would you still love Chance and marry him even if nothing went as you planned today?"

She cracked a small smile.

"That's what I thought. So why are you driving yourself and everyone else crazy worrying about things that don't really matter at all? I guarantee that the only thing Chance cares about is that he loves you and he gets to spend the rest of his life with you and . . . the honeymoon."

She laughed a little. "Yeah, well, Mother Nature's gone and ruined that."

I rolled my eyes. "I'm pretty sure Chance won't care."

"He said he didn't."

"See. You need to relax and enjoy this day. Hopefully, it will be the only wedding day you will ever have." I winked at her.

She took a deep cleansing breath. "You're right."

"Of course I am."

She sat up. "When you get married, I promise to be as good a maid of honor as you've been."

"Oh believe me, I know you will. And you're also going to wear the lime green dress I picked out specifically for you."

"You know I wouldn't be caught dead in lime green; it looks terrible on me."

"Why do you think I picked it out?" I grinned evilly.

"Again, you should be thanking me. You're going to look like a runway model at my wedding."

"Hmm . . . I'm still thinking hooker on Colfax."

She laughed at me.

With the reset in mood and priorities, we did a tour of the ceremony hall and reception area where there would be dinner and dancing. Anytime Krissy started to get nitpicky or maniacal, I reigned her in and reminded her the real reason she was having this wedding. And honestly, she had nothing to complain about—everything looked fantastic right down to the red rose centerpieces on each table.

By then the other three bridesmaids had arrived, and we went to work on each other. We each helped each other with hair and makeup, and we pampered our bride, who thankfully, was chilling out some. Midol and chocolate are godsends.

Krissy and I stood in the floor length mirror and stared at each other. This was really happening. We did our best not to cry. It was as if time stood still for a small moment as we held hands there. A million happy memories flooded my mind. I knew we would have more, but they would never be the same. I felt as if we were really saying goodbye to childhood. Thank goodness for waterproof mascara.

Krissy looked absolutely stunning in her off-the-shoulder winter-white princess ball gown. Her hair was swept up romantically, and she had to have her tiara. It so perfectly suited her. I kept looking at myself, too. I still couldn't believe I was wearing a dress that left hardly anything to the imagination. I was so unbelievably grateful for Spanx and that I didn't finish off the ice cream carton the night before.

Krissy and I hugged once more and each took a deep breath, which was a little difficult; even with all the working out that I had done, my breathing still needed to be shallow.

Once we were decked out, it was time for pictures of only the bride and her bridesmaids. Krissy and Chance opted not to see each other until the ceremony. I thought that was weird, but hey, it wasn't my party.

The photographer wasn't quite sure what to do with me. As I predicted, I looked like an Amazon woman in comparison to Krissy and her other bridesmaids. She suggested I take off my heels, but Krissy wouldn't hear of it. There were several pictures with us sitting down on the benches throughout the gardens.

"I hope you have some tall groomsmen," the snarky photographer commented.

I bit my tongue and refrained from shoving her camera down her throat. It was bad enough I was half-naked, but now I was being singled out because of my height. Did she even realize how uncomfortable I was?

"Don't let her get to you," Maviny whispered. "She's jealous because you're gorgeous."

"Thanks." I smiled. "You're the best little sister I never had."

As we walked back in from the gardens to freshen up before the ceremony, I ran into someone I didn't expect to see yet. Someone I had been trying hard not to think about all day.

Nine

"CHARLEE." RYAN PERUSED ME FROM head to toe and then back up again. His arm accessory did the same, and her look said peed-on Cheerios. Ryan's was more of shock. I had never seen his eyes so wide. It looked like he had been to the optometrist and had his eyes medically dilated.

I never felt so self-conscious in all my life. "Ryan."

"We came early to walk through the gardens." That came out nervous. "Oh, and you remember Jacquelyn, right?"

Jacquelyn tightened her grip on his arm.

"Yes, of course. It's nice to see you again," I lied.

She sneered at me and nodded her head. What did I ever do to her?

"Come on, CJ," Dana called after me.

I bit my lip. "I guess I better go."

Ryan smiled, and my insides melted. It didn't help that he looked all sorts of handsome in his light gray suit and his viridian-colored tie.

"I'm sure we'll see you later." He kept staring at me.

I nodded my head and tried to walk off with grace and composure. I wasn't sure how I did on the outside because my insides were having a dance party, and I think some of the butterflies were drunk.

"Who was that fine man?" Dana asked once I caught up to the group.

"That's Ryan." Maviny laughed.

"Dang, girl, he is fine!" Tasha shouted a little too loud.

"Shhhh," I begged. All I needed was for Ryan to hear.

"Who was the priss he was with?" Amy asked.

"Jacquelyn," I tried to say without derision.

Krissy, who had been leading us, turned around. "Well, we need to come up with a plan tonight on how to get little Miss Priss away from Ryan and you into his arms."

"Stop it right there. Ryan doesn't see me like that, I'm completely not his type."

"Please, girl," Tasha cut in. "Did you see the way that man was looking at you? He's definitely into you."

Everyone was smiling at me, including Ann and Ken, Krissy's parents.

I could feel myself turning red.

Ann took my hand. "Honey, any man would be a fool not to be attracted to you. You're a beautiful girl, inside and out."

Everyone nodded his or her head in agreement.

"Thank you, but don't we have a wedding here to get to?" I was trying to turn the attention back to where it belonged.

Krissy grinned wickedly at me. "Wedding or not, I have a plan," and with that, she turned around.

"Krissy," I called after her as she hightailed it down the hall back to the bridal room. I easily caught up to her; my legs are much longer than hers. "Please don't do anything to embarrass me. I already feel like an idiot around him."

She turned and looked up to me. "I would never embarrass you, but this is so happening tonight."

"What is so happening?"

"You'll see," she winked.

"Just remember, I still have to give your toast, and it might change from the sweet sentimental version I was planning to use." I smirked at her.

"It'll be well worth it."

"Ugh!" I didn't even try and argue with her. This wedding was becoming more than I bargained for. I felt completely vulnerable, physically and emotionally.

I felt ill as we touched up our makeup and hair. At least my hair and makeup looked good. Everyone thought we should leave my hair down in soft curls. I was sporting a nice tan, so the makeup was minimal, too. At least I didn't look like a painted lady of the night. I preferred a more natural look, and I was happy that I didn't go glam like the other women in the party. They all looked gorgeous, it just wasn't for me.

The wedding coordinator came in at fifteen minutes 'til five and let us know it was show time. I hugged Krissy one more time before I exited. She wanted a private moment with her parents. It was the only time of the night I would be envious of her. I knew I would never have that moment with my parents when it came time for me to take the plunge. I was at least happy to see that maybe, just maybe, true love lasted and weathered the storms of life.

The guests were all seated, and we took our places outside the double doors to the wedding hall. The other four bridesmaids were all walking down the aisle with a groomsman; I would be the only one going solo. Brandt, Chance's brother and best man, was already waiting by his brother's side. I felt a little awkward about it, but Krissy said I deserved my few moments in the spotlight. I disagreed, but she was the boss.

I watched each couple go, and before I made my appearance, I looked back at my beautiful best friend and smiled; she already had tears in her eyes. I turned around and took the deepest breath I could in my glorified Barbie dress and prayed I wouldn't trip or stumble or anything else that would cause me irreparable emotional damage. The doors opened just for me. I took my first steps into the beautifully decorated hall. I held my flowers close, just as they told me to do, and smiled.

All heads turned my way, and a couple flashes of light went off. I thought they announced no flash photography. Oh well, nothing like being blinded when you're walking in hooker heels. Thankfully, there was no harm done. I tried not to look at anyone directly, but halfway down, I locked eyes with Ryan; it was like my body homed in on him. I couldn't read him. He was staring at me all right, but it was as if he looked confused. I had to look away from him, he was causing major fluttering and swearing on my insides. The only other person I really made eye contact with after that was my dad. He was in the family section, and boy, did he have wide eyes when he looked at my dress. I did my best not to laugh at his raised eyebrows and stunned expression. I wanted to say, "Yes, Daddy, I'm not a little girl anymore."

I made it! I took my rightful place right next to where the bride would be momentarily. I smiled out into the audience, and again I locked eyes with Ryan. I could see his dazzling smile from where I was. I also noticed his date's look of pure disdain. It only made me smile wider, though I'm not sure why.

As the wedding march began, everyone stood and turned toward the doors. First came the cutest little ring bearer and flower girl. They were the children of one of Krissy's cousins. The little flower girl basically dumped all the petals in the first few steps—she was just grabbing fistfuls. There was a low murmur of laughter at her antics.

Then there was Krissy with her dad. She was picture perfect. I looked over to Chance and could see he thought so, too. I saw him wipe at his eyes. For that, I would always think highly of him. That is, unless he ever hurt my best friend, but I was giving him the benefit of the doubt today. Krissy's mom was wiping furiously at her eyes; she looked like the perfect mother of the bride in her aqua-colored skirted suit. She was a beautiful woman. No one was crying harder than Krissy's dad, though, poor guy. I think he was really taking this hard. It made me wonder how my dad would take it if I ever got married. I looked over to him, and he was already looking at me. It answered my question. I smiled at him, and he winked back.

As Krissy and her dad drew near, Chance eagerly met her earlier than he was supposed to, but it was perfect. It was the way it should be. Krissy's dad could barely choke out, "Her mother and I do," when the pastor asked who gives this woman. Ken was reluctant to let his daughter go, but Krissy only had eyes for Chance; she radiated as he took a hold of her.

The ceremony was all it should have been: intimate, lovely, and full of joy and laughter. It made me think maybe weddings weren't all that bad.

I was happy to walk back up the aisle on Brandt's arm, and I was even more grateful he was taller than me, heels and all.

"I'm glad I got the hottest chick in the line." Spoken like a twenty-one-year-old frat boy.

I refrained from rolling my eyes. Besides, I caught another glimpse of Ryan, and he kind of waved at me as I neared him. In response, I winked at him, and he smiled back. I turned from him and tried to refocus, but being near him made my senses go completely out of whack.

The wedding party was ushered out for more pictures while the other wedding guests were served hors d'oeuvres. I was a little envious; I was starving and not fond of the photographer.

On the way out the doors to the gardens, I heard my dad calling my name. I let go of Brandt, turned, and waited until he caught up to us. He wrapped me up in his big strong arms. "You weren't kidding about the dress," he laughed in my ear.

I laughed with him.

"I can't say I love the dress; it's giving me heart palpitations, but you're beautiful, honey."

"Thanks, Daddy."

He eyed Brandt. "I don't like the way all the men have been ogling you, but I guess I can hardly blame them with such a beautiful woman in front of them."

"You're so biased, Dad."

"No, baby girl."

"We have to get out to the gardens."

He kissed the top of my head. "Save your old man the first dance."

"You got it."

I turned back to Brandt, and he held out his arm to me. "You know your dad's right, you're freaking hot. You're at the top of all the guys' lists of who we want to hook up with tonight."

"Please tell me you didn't just say that." I was disgusted.

He looked confused, like I should be flattered. "What do you expect, looking like you do? I'm sure you're used to it."

"You know, I think we shouldn't talk anymore." I most certainly wasn't used to being treated that way. I wasn't some object, and I certainly wouldn't be hooking up with anyone. I never remembered Chance being piggish like his younger brother, thankfully. For a teenage boy, he was quite gentlemanly, and he never pushed the limits.

Brandt shrugged his shoulders and escorted me outside.

It seemed like the pictures would never end. It had begun to cool off, so standing outside was much more pleasant. That, and the fact the gardens were breathtakingly beautiful, not to mention that the backdrop was the Rocky Mountains. I'm telling you, Colorado is synonymous with heaven. I was tempted to take off my shoes and walk through the cool grass and maybe just stay out there, but I knew that would be a no-go with Krissy.

The best part of the pictures for me was when the Lawtons insisted I be in the ones of only their family. They don't know how special that made me feel. I couldn't wait to get my own copies of those.

After what seemed like forever, we made our grand entrance into the reception hall. Everyone stood, clapped, and cheered for the blissfully happy couple. The room was centered on the dance floor with all the round tables outlining it strategically. At the head was a long rectangular table for the wedding party. You know, this way we could lord over all the other guests. Or I guess so they could admire the bride and groom. Either way, I wanted to be off my feet for a while. I had warned my feet we needed all the conditioning we could get.

The Lawtons were thoughtful once again and placed my dad at their table right next to the bridal party's table. I hoped he didn't feel awkward sitting there with Chance's and Krissy's parents, but he seemed happy. At least I assumed he was, because he smiled at me a lot through dinner.

As hungry as I was, I couldn't eat as much as I wanted to— the dang dress was my nemesis. I had a feeling that the ice cream in the freezer at home was going to be my best friend tonight, that and ice for my feet. My stomach was also having issues with massive fluttering. You see, I had a clean shot of Ryan from where I sat, and my eyes frequently drifted toward him. I wasn't sure he was having a good time, he and his date didn't seem to interact much, and when they did, it looked stiff. She had this air about her that was awfully reminiscent of Victoria. The only real emotion she seemed to show was toward me. I'm not sure what she had against me, but she kept shooting me dirty looks. I loved smiling back at her, it only seemed to irritate her. I found it amusing. I knew she was older than me, and for her to behave in such a way was comical.

As soon as dinner was cleared, the fun began. I was so happy Krissy and Chance decided against a formal procession line; they opted for a night of dancing, instead. Chance led Krissy out onto the dance floor as everyone oohed and aahed, me included. Their first dance was to "God Gave Me You," by Blake Shelton. Krissy and I had gone over and over the dance list to make sure it was perfect, and this was their song. They looked so in love as they barely swayed to the music amidst the flashing lights of phones and cameras.

After their moment in the spotlight, the party was on—that was, of course, after I danced with my dad first.

"Do you think I could talk you into going home right now?" he teased as we danced.

"Why?"

"Because you're going to give your old man a heart attack."

I rolled my eyes. "Daddy."

"I'm serious, baby girl. Watch yourself tonight. I've already had to tell a few men that's my daughter they were talking about. I would hate to end up in jail."

"I love you, Dad."

He smiled and kissed my cheek. "I love you, honey. Always remember that."

With that, he left me on the dance floor, and to my surprise I had a line of men waiting to take his place. Not the one man I really wanted to dance with, though. With each dance and each man, I couldn't help but notice Ryan and Jacquelyn. They didn't dance often, but mostly stuck to their table, and from what I could tell from my limited vision of them, they still weren't having a good time. I so badly wanted to go over and talk to him, but I figured it was bad form since he was on a date. Besides, I didn't have a moment to spare. As soon as one song ended, I always had someone there asking me to dance the next. I did make time, though, to dance with my girl. We showed them all how to do the Electric Slide and the Wop. It was the most fun I'd had in forever. Krissy and I took our bows and hugged each other amid the applause. By that time, I was exhausted and my feet were begging me for a reprieve.

Chance was eager to wrap this party up and start the honeymoon, so it was announced that everyone fill their glass for the toasts. As I looked around, I was thinking there were some that didn't need any more alcohol for the evening, including most of the groomsmen and bridesmaids. I specifically requested sparkling cider or water for the event.

It was my honor to start off the toasts. I had been practicing it for days. I only hoped I could get through it without completely bawling my head off. I hadn't succeeded in practice, so I knew it was a long shot. I was right. Just looking at Krissy and Chance had me choking up, but I stood up, mic in hand, and looked to my dad for moral support. He smiled, and I began.

"Krissy and I have been friends since we were nine years old. It is my longest and most treasured friendship. I would not be the same person without her. Everyone knows when Krissy arrives because she lights up the room. She is the first one to act whenever you're in need and she is the last one to leave."

Krissy reached over and held my hand. It didn't help with the tears, but it was perfect.

"I've known Chance since junior high, and I've always had a lot of respect for him. He was a star on and off the court. I always admired his sportsmanship and dedication. And though Krissy and Chance knew each other as we grew up, it wasn't until last year and a chance meeting in Target that they would find in each other their soul mate. Target has always been our favorite store," I threw in as an aside. It drew quite a bit of laughter.

I looked to the both of them and raised my glass. "So tonight, as you begin your journey as husband and wife, I wish you a lifetime of joy, friendship, love, and happiness. Know that I will be your biggest fan and friend. I love you both. Cheers."

The clanging and raising of glasses could be heard and seen throughout the hall. Krissy stood and hugged me tight. I sat back down and wiped the tears away and watched as Brandt barely stood upright. What an idiot. I could tell Krissy and Chance didn't look too impressed, either.

Brandt looked my way and winked. "That was a beautiful speech, CJ. And I have to say how smokin' hot you looked saying it." There were a few spatterings of laughter, but you could tell the room was getting uncomfortable. Believe it or not, that wasn't even the worst part. "For those of you that don't know, my brother here," he slapped Chance on the back, "used to date CJ."

I cringed.

"And let me just say she's only gotten hotter."

I dropped my head in embarrassment.

"Then he scored the best friend. Cha ching. He's the luckiest ba . . ."

There was a lot of coughing and clearing of throats to mute the idiot.

"All I have to say, brother, is enjoy the honeymoon."

You could tell Krissy and Chance and Chance's parents were mortified. I felt a little that way, too. From the looks of it, I think Chance wanted to punch his brother. The parents each got their turn and it was all lovely and classy. I would not be serving alcohol at my wedding.

After the toasts and cake, it was time for the throwing of the bouquet and removing the garter. The whole garter thing I didn't get either, especially after we googled the origin of it. I'm just going to say, it's a little twisted, but hey, if you want your husband to reach up your dress for the world to see, I say go for it.

Before the tossing of the bouquet, I noticed Krissy and all the other bridesmaids having a little pow-wow as I stood on the dance floor holding the bouquet she was going to toss. I decided I needed to be part of it. I was a little put off that I wasn't already, but as I approached their huddle, they all smiled at me and dispersed.

"What was all that about?" I handed Krissy her the throw-away bouquet.

"Nothing." She was lying.

I narrowed my eyes at her and she laughed. "Good luck," she said.

"I'm not going to try and catch your bouquet."

"Yes, you are. Now get out there."

I found myself being pulled back out to the dance floor by Maviny. "Stand right here," she demanded. I was in the middle of the group of desperate girls and women all clamoring for the bouquet. I wanted to tell them all it meant nothing to catch one. Believe me, I knew. The only time I'd ever caught one, my whole world came crumbling down in a matter of hours.

Not only did I find myself smack dab in the middle, I was also flanked by Maviny, Dana, Tasha, and Amy, and they kept looking at each other conspiratorially. Okay, something was definitely up.

"Maviny, what's going on?"

"Nothing." She grinned. "Just get ready."

"Ready for what?" I asked, but it was too late.

The bouquet was tossed and sailing right toward me. The ladies around me pushed out from me, leaving a clear path for the flowers to sail right to me. I had no choice but to catch the dumb thing, and the worst part was, I found myself having to pretend like I was happy about it. I smiled toothily and held it up like it was a prize, but what I couldn't understand was why it was so important to Krissy that I catch it. That is, I didn't understand until I watched a well-coordinated plan unfold with the tossing of the garter.

To my horror and embarrassment, I watched as the other bridesmaids went and grabbed my neighbor, who obviously didn't want to be tossed the garter, and pulled him out to the dance floor. I also noticed that his date looked none too happy about it, either. I watched as Chance seductively reached up Krissy's dress and removed the red satin garter. He obviously enjoyed himself, as did she. He stood to the hoots and hollers of all the pigs in the crowd, and by pigs I meant Chance's brother and his idiot friends. Krissy winked at me, and mouthed, "You're welcome."

I gave her a questioning look, but then I realized what she meant as the garter sailed directly to Ryan and he clumsily caught it. I don't think he knew what to do with it, poor guy. He kind of held it up as several men around him patted him on the back. Once the commotion settled down, the DJ announced it was time for the final dance, and he invited the recipients of the bouquet and garter to take their rightful place together on the dance floor and start the dance off.

My heart pounded erratically as Ryan looked up at me and smiled. The butterflies were beyond excited and swearing like sailors. I bit my lip nervously and watched Ryan walk my way. I felt like I couldn't breathe. I knew it didn't mean anything to him, but not to sound cheesy, it was like a dream come true for me. All I needed was some fog behind him as he sauntered over to me.

He held out his hand as soon as he approached me. "Will you give me the pleasure of dancing with me?" I think that was the sexiest thing I'd ever heard in my life.

I couldn't talk very well, which was saying something. I always had something to say. I nodded my head and held out my hand, that I prayed wasn't sweaty. Before he led me away, I tossed the bouquet to Amy, who wore a sly grin.

As we made it to the middle of the floor, I heard the DJ say, "Now don't they make a lovely couple? Maybe there will be another love connection tonight." I think I turned about ten shades of red. Ryan didn't seem fazed by it as he pulled me to him and held me firmly, but gently. His hand rested on my mid-back. With his other hand he took my hand, and instead of holding it out, he brought it in, more intimately, against our bodies. Ed Sheeran's "Thinking Out Loud" began to play. Ryan was obviously an experienced dancer as his steps kept in time with the rhythm of my new favorite song.

Ryan's eyes seared into mine. "I was hoping I would get to dance with you tonight."

"You were?"

"Yes, but you've been quite popular." He pulled back a tad and looked down at my dress. "You look very . . ."

"Please don't say grown up."

He smiled and shook his head. "I wasn't going to say that, I was going to say . . ." he tried to think of something.

"You were going to say it, weren't you?"

He sighed. "Charlee, you really know how to make a guy feel inadequate, don't you?"

"I'm sorry."

"Don't be. I find I like it."

"You do?"

He nodded his head. "I also find you to be very . . ." he hesitated.

"Very what?"

"Beautiful and annoyingly charming."

"How can somebody be annoying and charming at the same time?"

"See what I mean?" He held me close.

In my heels, we were practically eye level, and our faces were only inches apart. I could smell the sweet scent of honey on his breath. I wanted more than anything to taste it, and the way he was looking at me at that moment, I thought maybe he felt the same way. His eyes turned to confusion, though, before he pulled me closer. I rested my head against his and swayed against him. It was even better than I imagined. I wanted the dance to last forever.

"By the way," I whispered in his ear. "I find you beautiful, too."

He laughed low while his hand slid down to the small of my back. It was perfect. That is, it was perfect, until I noticed Jacquelyn. She was shooting darts at me with her eyes from across the room.

"I don't think your date likes me very much," I informed Ryan while the other dancers weaved around us.

He turned us so that he was now facing her. "No, I don't imagine she likes you very much at all."

I was surprised by his agreement. "Why is that? I don't even know her."

"I have a feeling not many women in this room like you tonight," he whispered in my ear. It sent shivers coursing through my whole body. I had never felt such a way.

"What a thing to say."

"They may not like you, but believe me, they all want to be you."

"Have you been drinking? I think you're a little off."

He pulled back and looked into my eyes. "I haven't had a drop, but I am feeling intoxicated."

We both stood still. I was about to tell him I felt the same way, but I guess his date had hit her limit.

"I'm ready to leave." Jacquelyn appeared by my side and glowered at me.

Ryan cleared his throat and reluctantly released me. "Thanks for the dance, Charlee."

I didn't want to let go of him, but I knew how tacky and probably desperate it would have looked if I didn't right away. For a split second I thought it may be worth it.

In the end, I stepped back. "Thanks for having good hands."

He arched his eyebrow and Miss Snotty Pants clucked her tongue at me. It was then I realized how that could have been taken, but I really was referring to his ability to catch the garter. I decided not to clarify. He did have amazing hands, and I loved how I felt in them. "Goodnight, Ryan." I waved as they walked away. I didn't even bother saying anything to Jacquelyn. I had a feeling she may have ripped my throat out if I did.

I walked back to where all the conspiring bridesmaids stood watching me, and they were obviously quite pleased with themselves. Krissy stepped away from Chance for a moment and joined us, too. She grabbed me and hugged me tight. "You guys looked so amazing together."

"Really?"

"Oh my gosh, yes. I could feel the heat coming off you."

I hadn't even noticed she and Chance danced close to us. It was as if for a moment I was in my own little Ryan world. I think I'd like to take up residence there.

Ten

THE CARTON OF DARK CHOCOLATE ice cream came to bed with me that night, as did ice packs for my feet. I sat propped up, indulging in delicious fat-filled calories, enjoying the feel of being in shorts and a tee and no shoes. The wedding was wonderful and everything it should have been, from the cake to the fireworks, but I was exhausted and happy for it all to be over with, except for the dance that could have gone on forever.

I couldn't get Ryan out of my head. I could still feel his arms, as if they were still around me. His words kept ringing in my head. He thought I was beautiful and annoyingly charming, all adjectives I was okay with. I sat there and wondered if perhaps it would lead to more or if I was just delusional. Everyone at the wedding was saying how "into" each other we looked as we danced, but sometimes looks are deceiving. I didn't want to put my hopes into a pipe dream, if that's what this was, but couldn't help myself. I hoped Ryan was finally coming to see me as a woman and not the kid next door.

I'm not sure when I finally drifted off to sleep, but I didn't wake up until noon. I don't remember the last time I had slept in that late, but my body needed the rest. I looked over at the empty ice cream carton and rolled my eyes at myself. Then I looked over at the wilting bouquets on my dresser. I wasn't sure what to do to preserve them, and besides, I liked having the "one" where I could see it any time I wanted. It invoked a very pleasurable memory. I could still feel Ryan's warm breath against my skin and the way he gently placed the errant strap from my dress back on my shoulder. It had been sliding off all night.

His hand glided against my skin as he commented how soft my skin was.

I threw off my covers and got out of bed. My feet said, *You've got to be kidding me!* I promised them a short walk to the bathroom where I would take a bath and soak them. I spent an hour in the tub. When I got out, I threw on some cut-offs and an old college tee. I figured I wasn't going anywhere, and no one was coming over, so it was okay to look like I didn't really care about my appearance. I didn't even bother with makeup; my hair was lucky to get combed and a little bit of styling spray.

I found my dad in his usual position on his leather recliner, watching a game.

"She lives," he commented when I opened the basement door.

"Hey, Dad."

"You hungry, kiddo?"

"Yes." That came out more enthusiastic than I intended, but I had been hungry for six weeks.

He chuckled. "I'll make you something." He started to get up.

"Relax, Dad. I've got it."

He sat back down and smiled.

I walked up to the kitchen to find something to eat that would require hardly any effort.

"What do you have on tap for today, my little troublemaker?"

I looked down at him from the kitchen. "Troublemaker?"

"You caused quite the stir last night."

I shook my head in confusion. "What are you talking about?"

"Your dance with Ryan set off a firestorm."

"I'm still confused. All we did was dance."

My dad grinned up at me. "It didn't look like you were just dancing."

"And what did it look like we were doing? We were completely appropriate."

"Calm down, baby girl, I wasn't implying you were anything but appropriate."

"Then what *are* you implying?" I ripped the peel off my orange.

"Honey, it's just you and Ryan didn't look like friends. There was a low buzz that perhaps the superstition was true and you both would be the next to marry, and to each other. His date didn't take it well."

"Oh . . . well, that's completely ridiculous. It was only a . . . dance."

My dad smirked. "If you say so, but his date really let him have it as they walked out. I felt kind of bad for the guy."

That made me feel horrible. "Really? I didn't mean for that to happen. Ryan said she didn't like me, though I'm not sure what I ever did to her."

My dad laughed.

"Why are you laughing at me?"

My dad stood up and met me in the kitchen, where he sat on the stool closest to me. "Honey, Ryan and every other guy there last night, except for the groom, had eyes only for you. And again, I already had my suspicions that Ryan was attracted to you. Last night only confirmed it. He did a terrible job hiding that from his date."

My spirit soared at the thought. "I don't know, Dad."

"Again, I may be old, but I have eyes."

"I feel terrible that I ruined his date."

My dad shrugged. "I wouldn't worry about it too much. It was probably good for him. He has lousy taste in women."

I raised my eyebrow at him.

"That is until now." He winked. "Again, just be careful."

"I'm not sure there's anything to be careful about."

He tapped my nose. "You didn't see the way he was looking at you last night. It was the first time I've ever had any negative feelings toward him."

"I'm not going to lie, I really like Ryan, but I don't want to do anything to rock your relationship with him. You know, that is if he likes me, too."

"Believe me, he likes you, and don't worry about the end game. Okay?"

I nodded.

"Great, how about we watch some baseball?"

"Sounds perfect, just let me make a sandwich. Do you want one?"

"You're going to spoil your old man."

I found I wanted to.

We spent a great afternoon yelling at the umps, even though they couldn't hear us through the TV. It didn't do any good—the Rockies still lost. After the game my dad put on some old western starring Ronald Reagan. It was enough to make me doze off. In my dream, or what I thought was my dream, I heard the doorbell ring, but I was too out of it to move. I wasn't quite sure if I was awake or asleep.

"Cherry!" I heard before I felt the cutest kid ever pounce on me.

I opened my eyes to find a grinning Josh inches from my face. "What are you doing here, big guy?"

"I want you to play with me."

I sat up and realized his dad was with him, which I should have known, but again, I was kind of out of it. I nervously ran my hand through my hair, prayed I hadn't slobbered in my sleep, and smiled at Ryan who was standing near my dad. Ryan smiled, but he seemed nervous, too. I decided to turn my attention back to Josh. "So what do you want to do?"

"We're sorry we woke you up," Ryan said before Josh could answer. "Josh really wanted to see you."

I looked back up to him and smiled. "I'm glad you *both* came over." Even though I probably looked like a train wreck.

"I want to jump," Josh exclaimed loudly.

"Josh, I think Charlee's tired."

Oh I was, but for Josh I would muster up some energy. "It's okay. I need some fresh air anyway."

"How about I throw some burgers and dogs on the grill?" my dad offered.

I looked at Ryan to answer. I more than liked the idea, but I wanted to see how he would respond.

Ryan looked at my dad. "Thanks for the invite."

I guess that meant they were staying for dinner.

Josh was impatient and pulling on my arms, trying to get me up. I complied and took his hand. We walked toward the stairs and up to the kitchen. My dad and Ryan let us pass before they followed. I noticed Ryan seemed unsure whether he should look at me or not. I wasn't sure how to feel about it because I wanted to look at him. I wanted him to reciprocate even though I looked like a mess. I wished

I had at least put on some mascara and maybe pulled my hair up, but, oh well, I guess he'd seen me with sweat dripping out of every pore. He, on the other hand, looked perfect in cargo shorts and a tight t-shirt.

Josh dashed out the patio door, and I walked after him. I wasn't running anywhere today; my feet were already threatening to strike. They even balked at the thought of flip-flops, so I stayed barefoot. Josh waited for me at the trampoline. I lifted him up and placed him on it before joining him. It really was a beautiful day, or rather, evening. I looked at my mountains and sighed; I loved this place.

"Ring around da rosies," Josh said, getting me out of my own thoughts.

"Sure, but I'm going to sit down okay?"

"Aww."

"Josh." Ryan approached.

I turned to him, I hadn't realized that he had followed us.

"Let's give Charlee a break tonight." Ryan joined us on the trampoline. He sat crossed-legged across from me.

Josh was in between us bouncing.

"Hi." I tucked some hair behind my ear.

"Hi." Out came the smile I loved.

"Cherry, you're not singing," Josh cut in.

"I'm sorry. Are you ready?"

He vigorously nodded his beyond adorable head.

"Okay . . . Ring around the rosy pocket full of posies . . ." This went on a few more times. I even got his daddy to sing.

Ryan finally grabbed his son and placed him on his lap. "Let's take a break for a minute."

Josh didn't think that was the best idea, but he was obedient.

"How are you?" Ryan asked me.

"Besides tired, I'm well. How about you? Did you have a good day? Did you enjoy the wedding?"

"Josh and I spent a fun day at the zoo."

"I saw zebras, and lelephants." Josh could hardly contain his excitement.

"That sounds like fun."

"More fun than the wedding," Ryan interjected.

I bent my head slightly. "I take it you didn't have a good time last night?"

"Not really."

"Oh. Sorry."

Dawning illuminated his handsome face. "I did enjoy part of the evening very much."

"The cake was good." I smiled.

His eyes danced with delight. "Some of the best I've ever had."

"I brought some home with me if you want another slice."

"Maybe later."

Josh wiggled out of Ryan's arms; he was tired of grown up talk and being ignored.

I took Josh's hands, and he jumped as high as he could while I kept him upright and steady.

"Charlee?" Ryan said.

"Yes?" I peeked around his son and looked at his smiling face.

"Thanks for the dance last night."

The butterflies in my stomach felt like throwing up. "My pleasure."

We spent the rest of the evening talking, laughing, and eating with my dad. At times it was a little awkward, it seemed as if we all weren't sure how to act, but for the most part, we acted normally, even though I wanted to reach under the table and grab Ryan's hand. I usually wasn't so forward, but there was something about him that had me feeling like I never had before. I was drawn to him, plain and simple.

When it was time for them to go, I walked them to the door. My dad lingered back and started the dishes. I loved that man. I picked up Josh and squeezed him tight. "Thanks for coming over to play with me."

"You're welcome." He hugged me back.

I kissed his cheek. "Bye, Josh."

"Bye, Cherry."

I set him down and looked up to find his dad carefully considering me. I smiled at him. "Bye, Ryan."

"Are you going to run tomorrow?"

I thought about it for a moment. My feet were begging me to say no, but when I looked into his eyes, I lost my senses. "I might not be the best partner tomorrow."

"I'll go easy on you."

"Then I guess I'll see you in the morning."

He grinned and left with Josh.

I was suddenly looking forward to getting up at five am.

Eleven

WHEN MY ALARM SOUNDED AT the ungodly hour of five in the morning, I almost threw my phone, but then I remembered who would be waiting for me behind my fence, and suddenly I was very perky. I jumped up, changed into my running attire, brushed my teeth, and threw my hair up into a cute bun and called it good. My poor feet cried when I put on my running shoes, but it was the price that had to be paid. I promised them no heels for at least a week in return for their cooperation.

I opened our gate to find Ryan waiting for me. His hair looked wet, like he had already showered and gotten ready for the day. I smiled. "Good morning."

He looked me over. "You ready?"

"Remember you promised to be gentle today."

"I'll do my best."

"You know I just set you up to throw out one of your gems." I grinned wickedly.

"There you go making me feel inadequate again." He started to jog.

I kept pace with him. "I thought you liked it."

"Did I say that?"

"Yes, you said you found it charming."

"I think I said annoying." He looked over at me and winked.

I nudged him with my shoulder. "I'm sorry you didn't enjoy the wedding, and I'm sorry if I did anything to ruin your date."

He chuckled. "Are you really?"

"Yes. And if I remember correctly, *you* asked *me* to dance."

"I was obligated to."

I stopped running and gave him an incredulous look. This wasn't going in the direction I wanted it to.

He stopped and grinned at me. "If I'm going to toss gems out there, you can't take them seriously."

I rolled my eyes at him.

"Charlee, dancing with you was the highlight of the night, and you didn't do anything to ruin my date, that was all me."

"My dad mentioned she kind of let you have it and my name was mentioned."

"That it was, but again, that was my fault, not yours. I probably should have been more of a gentleman and averted my eyes when it came to you, but in my defense, you made that difficult."

"How's that?"

"You looked very grown up and you dance well."

"That's what happens when your best friend is cheer captain and on the dance team. And by the way, I prefer beautiful to grown up."

He reached up and touched my cheek. "I'm sure you do, it's just I'm having a hard time reconciling how I feel about you right now."

"I'm not a balance sheet."

"No, you're not, but you're my partner's daughter and quite a bit younger than me. And most importantly, I'm a dad. Anything I do affects Josh. I need to be careful."

I thought for a moment of all the things I could say to help put him at ease, reasons why we would be good together, but then I realized that no matter how much I wanted to be with him, I wanted it to be in the right way. I didn't want to be with anyone that was unsure about me. I remembered Jay trying to convince me of all the reasons we were perfect for each other, and it all sounded wonderful and right, but in the end I couldn't, because it didn't *feel* right. "I understand." I turned to finish our lazy jog.

He didn't follow right away, but he easily made up the hundred yards that separated us. "So that's all you have to say?"

"What do you want me to say? If you're not sure, I'm not going to throw myself at you."

"I would never accuse you of that, but tell me what you think. Don't you have any reservations?"

"Other than your hesitation, no."

"Really?"

"Really. And if you're looking for me to convince you, I won't." I sounded more mature than I felt. I really wanted to convince him, but I knew that was wrong. I found it in myself to run rather than jog, the adrenaline helped.

Ryan kept pace, but he didn't say anything, and neither did I. My hopes had been dashed, but I was proud of myself for not acting like a silly schoolgirl.

As we neared Ryan's fence, he slowed down and reached for my arm. "Hey, no matter what, I still want to be friends."

I nodded my head. "See you later." Saying you wanted to be friends was like a death sentence to any relationship.

"Yeah, see you in a bit."

Oh yeah, work was going to be pleasant. I mean awkward.

I spent longer than normal stretching out in the backyard. That *so* did not go how I wanted it to. I had been hoping he would be asking me out, and I felt kind of moronic now that there was no doubt in his mind how I felt about him. No pain, no gain, right? Too bad this was all pain and no gain.

I was more than grateful my dad wasn't in the kitchen when I came in; it allowed me to retreat to the basement, nurse my wounds, and regain my composure. Maybe Ryan was right, we shouldn't even consider dating while we worked together. If things went south, it could be all sorts of uncomfortable. Even still, I knew in my heart we could be great together. I decided to really start looking at psychology programs and for an apartment.

"You're quiet this morning." My dad noticed on our drive in together.

"Long weekend."

"Is that all?"

"No."

"Ryan?"

"Yep."

"Do you want to talk about it?"

"Nope."

I could see him grin before I turned and looked out the window at our fellow motorists.

"You want to do lunch today?" My dad was doing his best to make me feel better.

"If it includes French fries, yes."

"Lots of them."

"It's a date, then." The only date I would be getting.

My dad reached over and touched my knee. "Don't worry, he'll come around."

I looked over to him with a questioning glance.

"I'm pretty smart for an old guy."

I laughed quietly, it helped lighten my mood.

I was feeling better as I settled in and started my day with finishing off second quarter reports. It was mind numbing, but at least it kept my mind off Ryan. Right before lunch, my mom called. She rarely called me first anymore, so I was pleasantly surprised. Too bad, it was anything but pleasant.

"Mark and I just saw some of the wedding pictures that you posted on Facebook and Instagram. We were shocked."

"Why?"

"You looked like a hussy."

"Wow. Thanks, Mom."

"I'm just saying, I thought you knew better than to dress like that. What did your dad say?"

"He said I looked beautiful."

"Well, nobody's saying you aren't."

Except for her. Ever since she and my dad divorced, it was like suddenly I was competition and complimenting me meant lessening her. I had put up with it for years, but I was done.

"You know what, Mom? I would like it if, for once, you called me to see how I'm doing instead of pointing out what you think my perceived faults are. Heck, I'd like it if you just called me at all."

"Well," she said. "I didn't realize what a terrible mother I was."

Here we go again. The guilt trip. This time I wasn't falling for it. "I've got to get back to work. Talk to you later."

She hung up. That was mature.

The day was getting better and better.

By the time my dad and I made it to lunch, I was ready to order a double order of fries, ice cream, and for good measure, a stick of butter. Just kidding about the butter, unless it came with popcorn.

"You still upset about Ryan?" My dad perused his menu.

I was still huffy and puffy about the phone call with my mom. I had to stop myself from crying several times.

"No."

"CJ, you're not a good liar."

I set my menu down and looked at my dad's concern-filled eyes. "Did you find what I wore to the wedding distasteful or slutty?"

His eyes widened to the max and he coughed a little. "Why are you even asking that?"

I couldn't tell him the truth. As much as my mother had hurt me over the years, I still felt like I needed to be loyal to her. I still blamed my dad for what he did to her. "You didn't answer the question."

"No, honey. You could never be either. Sure, as your dad, I would like to see you in body armor every day, but you were lovely beyond words, not only in dress, but in your mannerisms."

A tear escaped. I quickly wiped it away. "I love you."

"I love you, kiddo."

A dad, fries, and milkshakes are the cure for almost anything.

I went back to work feeling much better, but the afternoon dragged on as I feared it might. I spent a lot of it on the phone talking to a poor woman named Shelley whose husband died recently. Apparently, he was the one who had handled all the payroll items for their company; she had no idea what to do. I walked her, step-by-step, through the process of compiling and then transmitting their data to us. It literally took about ten times before she got it. I had a feeling I would be walking her through it again the next pay period. I didn't mind. I felt terrible for her.

Besides, we had an interesting conversation about the man who frequented my thoughts. Ryan managed this account long ago, and he made quite the impression on Shelley and her husband Barry. From the sounds of it, Barry had been sick for some time. When he first became sick, Ryan personally went to their place of business and streamlined their accounting and payroll processes to make life easier for Barry. He also visited Barry in the hospital and even attended his funeral. I had no idea. I think Shelley was as big of fan of Ryan as I was. She was in tears talking about the kindness he had extended to her family. I wasn't surprised by the news. Ryan was a good man. He was kind and thoughtful, but in a quiet unassuming sort of way.

Sure I was attracted to him physically, but the attraction was more than skin deep. I was attracted to the kind of person he was, even if he was frustrating me at the moment.

Right before it was time to leave for the day, I had a surprise visitor. I hadn't seen him all day, which I would have normally considered a tragedy, but not today. I was still feeling a little awkward with where we had left things that morning.

"Hey." He stood at my door, running his fingers through his hair.

I wouldn't mind giving that a go. *Focus*, I told myself. "Hey, how was your day?"

He stepped into my office, if only just barely. "Productive. How about you?"

"Same."

"Great." He sounded unsure.

"Did you want my list of transmitted reports? Because I already emailed them to you."

"No." He smiled. "I saw them. I'm sorry I didn't respond, I've been wrapped up with some clients that extended their annual tax returns, and they aren't being very forthcoming with the remaining items I need."

"Sounds like fun."

"Not really."

"There's always tomorrow."

"Speaking of tomorrow." He walked closer to my desk. "I hope that you'll still run with me. I don't want to lose the relationship we already have while I'm trying to figure things out."

I thought about it for a moment. It was hard for me to be around him. I didn't like limbo land, but I did value our friendship and him. "I'll see you tomorrow morning. I'll be the one in the pink shorts."

He smiled in relief. "Those are my favorite pair." He walked off without another word.

I smiled to myself, and the stupid butterflies did a small happy dance. I told them there wasn't anything to be happy about yet and not to get their hopes up.

We met every morning to run, but Friday. We both tried hard to keep our conversations light and platonic. For me, it was easier said than done. I felt like what I'd wanted for so long was so close I could taste it, but on the other hand it seemed further away than ever.

I drove myself into work since my dad had a business dinner with a potential new client. I admit that thought gave me heartburn. I didn't even know who it was with and he wasn't married, so what he did was his business, but it brought back a lot of very painful memories. It didn't help that I had received a scathing email from my mother the night before outlining how hard it was to be a mother in her situation. I would never understand, and she just prayed that I would never have to endure the heartache and humiliation she had to, but that I was asking for just that if I kept dressing like a floozy. I didn't even respond. I deleted it and counted the days until Krissy was back from her ten-day honeymoon in the Bahamas. I needed a friend.

On the drive in, my phone rang and I picked it up on the Bluetooth.

"Hello."

"Charlee?"

I didn't recognize the voice. "This is she."

"Hey, this is Aidan, Chance's old roommate. We danced at the wedding."

"Oh, hi." I remembered who he was, but I wondered why he would call me or how he got my number.

"Maviny gave me your number." That cleared it up. "I know this may seem last minute, but I was hoping you would like to go out tonight."

Huh. Did I? It's not like I was dating anyone, even though I really wanted to be. But, the thought of being home on another Friday night by myself depressed me. "What did you have in mind?" *Please don't say a movie.*

"My parents own a ranch near Estes Park. How does horseback riding and a picnic sound?"

Uh, perfect. This guy was good. "Sounds lovely."

"Great. Can I pick you up at five?"

"Yes. I'll text you my address."

"I look forward to it."

I kind of did, too. I didn't know how long it was going to take Ryan to work through his issues, if he ever would, but I wasn't going to sit around and pine for him in the meantime.

I walked into the office with a little spring in my step. Aidan, from what I remembered, was handsome and tall, which was a must for me. I also remember he had cowboy written all over him, which totally worked for me, too.

I stopped by my dad's office first. "Hi, Felicity, is my dad with anyone?" His door was closed.

"Well, don't you look pretty today."

I loved Felicity. She looked very pretty, too, in yellow.

"He's meeting with Ryan," she informed me just as my dad's door opened and Ryan walked out.

Gosh, did he look good. He smiled when he saw me. "Hi, Charlee."

I tucked my hair behind my ear. I felt my heart rate increase exponentially. He had that effect on me. "Good morning." I noticed Felicity smiling between us, like she knew something. I took that as my cue to walk past Ryan and into my dad's office.

Ryan didn't move, he just let me pass by. Oh, he smelled good. I really needed to get the name of that cologne.

"Hey, kiddo." My dad was happy to see me. "What can I do for you?"

Ryan still wasn't going anywhere, so I wasn't sure what to say. I looked between both men. Why wasn't Ryan leaving?

"I wanted to let you know that I probably won't be home when you get back from your dinner appointment tonight. I didn't want you to worry." I was going to leave it at that and tell him later where I would be and who I would be with. That was a nice thought.

"Big date tonight?" There was a gleam in his eye.

I turned so only my dad could see my face and gave him my what-do-you-think-you're-doing look. He smiled like he knew exactly what he was doing.

"Something like that." I tried to play it cool.

"I hope you have a good time, honey."

"Thanks, Dad," I said through gritted teeth. I turned to find Ryan looking at me with some intense confused eyes. "See you later." I wasn't sure what else to say to him.

He didn't respond other than to nod his head.

I walked to my office feeling warm. I wasn't sure if it was out of embarrassment or being around Ryan. Probably a good dose of both. My dad and I were going to have a little chat later.

I had a hard time concentrating on my work, which seemed dumb. Ryan and I were only friends, and it was perfectly fine for me to have a date. Ryan hadn't given any indication he had decided that he wanted to date me. We were basically running partners and friends.

I skipped my lunch break since I was leaving early. Leaving early meant I unfortunately ran into Ryan in the parking lot. He always left early on Fridays so he could get Josh. I waved at him. "Have a good weekend."

He turned from his Ford Explorer and began walking my way. Why couldn't he just leave? My waving goodbye wasn't an invitation.

He met me at my car. "Josh was hoping to see you tonight. Are you going to be busy the *whole* night?"

"That's the plan. Can Josh come and play tomorrow?" I felt like I was making a playdate for myself.

"That's a long date, I guess I can safely bet it's not the movies." He ignored my request for a playdate with Josh.

"We wouldn't be having this conversation if it were."

"Yes, of course. That would be too boring for you. So what does this guy have planned that is first-date worthy for you?"

I wasn't sure what to make of this conversation and why I was even having it. Didn't he get that it was him I wanted to date and for him I would have even gone to the movies, yet there he stood asking me what my plans were for the night with another man? Why did he even care?

I decided to play along, though I was annoyed with him. "Horseback riding and a picnic."

That wiped the smirk off his face. "Hmm . . . It seems a little overkill for a first date."

"It's terrible that there's a man who feels I'm worthy enough to ask out and then heaven forbid he tries to impress me on our first date."

He stepped closer and took off his aviators. "Charlee, I'm sorry. I didn't mean for you to take it that way."

"I'm going to be late. I need to go."

He reached up and touched my arm. "I'm sorry I kept you."

"Tell Josh he can come over tomorrow or Sunday if you're not busy. I would love to see him."

"He'd like that . . . I'd like it too."

"See you later." I turned, opened my car door, and got in. I sat there for a second. I wasn't even sure now that I wanted to go on my date with Aidan. I was drawn to Ryan. I was about to turn on my car when my phone's text alert went off. I picked up my phone.

Your date is one lucky guy.

There was no luck involved. He asked and I said yes. I texted back. Then I threw caution to the wind and put my heart on the line. *You should try it sometime.* I hesitated to hit send, but at this point I figured I didn't have anything to lose. My thumb made direct contact with the send button. I tossed my phone in the passenger seat. Why couldn't he be the lucky guy?

I rushed home and changed into jeans, a t-shirt, and boots. I tried hard not to think about my neighbor who I got along famously with. Our morning runs were basically long, drawn out talks.

As I looked into my floor-length mirror and did one more hair and makeup check, I thought maybe I should give up on the whole Ryan thing. Who cared that he made me laugh and that we both loved spicy food? Or that we both saw the genius in John Hughes movies? Not to mention that I was completely in love with his kid and I loved how he loved his son. Who cared that when he touched me I felt connected in a way that I never had before? I cared, that's who. These were not good thoughts to be having when a different man was on his way to pick me up.

When the doorbell rang, I reminded myself it was better than being home by myself, but then I remembered, I wouldn't have been home by myself, Josh and Ryan would have been with me. *Ugh.*

I opened the door to a very handsome cowboy holding a bouquet of daisies. It was picture perfect, well almost. When he smiled, I noticed he had one dimple, and his copper colored eyes lit up.

"Hello, Charlee, these are for you." He pushed the sweet bouquet forward.

I gladly took them and breathed in their scent. "Thank you, Aidan. Come in and I'll put these in a vase real quick."

He took off his cowboy hat and walked in. It was then I noticed his muscular physique, particularly his biceps. So maybe this was going to be good.

We walked out to his large Dodge Ram truck, the side of the door advertised his parent's ranch, Bailey Ranch. He was a gentleman and opened my door and helped me in the truck, which sat high off the ground. His hand was strong and smooth, but his touch did nothing for me. Darn that Ryan Carter, he was ruining me for other men.

We headed west up US-34; it was one of my most favorite drives. I loved Estes Park and had been missing it. I hadn't had the chance to get up into the mountains since I'd been home due to work and wedding nonsense. I loved the scenery, the rushing river to our left and the cute little towns we passed on our way up. The weather was fantastic too. Tonight had all the makings of the perfect evening. I tried to focus on Aidan and not the other guy. It helped that Aidan kind of fascinated me. To look at him you might think hick, but he was anything but. He was currently studying to get his PhD in chemistry. He was doing an internship at a pharmaceutical company this summer, and on the weekends he worked at his parents' ranch.

"Have you heard from Krissy?" he asked as we wound our way through the quaint town of Estes Park.

I pulled myself away from looking at all the little shops I used to visit with my parents when I was growing up. In particular the Christmas shops that were open all year round. I laughed a little. "No, not at all, but I didn't expect to. Besides, I'm not sure I want any reports on the honeymoon."

He chuckled. "I don't blame you."

"But I'm definitely looking forward to them coming home."

"So did you and Chance really date?"

"Why is everyone so fascinated with that?"

He glanced at me and grinned. "I wouldn't say fascinated, but you have to admit, it's unusual for a guy to date two best friends and for the girls to still remain best friends."

"I suppose, but it was high school, and honestly, I wasn't that into him."

"Ouch. Just what every guy wants to hear."

"Well, it's not like I told him that, and he did break up with me."

"Really?"

"Yep."

He glanced my way again. "And here I thought he was a smart guy."

I think I may have blushed. There was some definite lip biting going on. "Well, thanks, but really, he got the better of the two."

"Beautiful and modest."

This guy was good.

"Again, thank you."

His parent's ranch was situated right outside Roosevelt National Forest, and it was breathtaking. The main house was a giant log cabin with a wraparound porch. There was a small pond in the front with tall grass and wildflowers. I rolled down the window and breathed in the cool mountain air and the smell of the pine trees. It also smelled like someone was barbecuing, and the aroma was tantalizing. Aidan informed me this was a guest and working ranch. Each night they provided dinner for the guests staying there.

He pulled his truck around to the stables and corral. There were already a few horses meandering in the corral. They were beautiful specimens.

Before he even turned off his truck, he turned to me. "Don't move, I'll get your door."

He was good—really, really good.

He helped me out and released my hand as soon as I was safely on the ground. I liked that, it meant he wasn't forward.

A haggard-looking man came out and greeted us. Aidan called him Earl and introduced him as the boss. The boss of what, I wasn't sure, but he informed Aidan that he had saddled up the horses and they were ready to go. "Your shotgun is loaded and packed, as well," he added.

I gulped and looked between the two men. I had never had a date that involved firearms, and I wasn't too sure how to feel about that.

Aidan gave me a reassuring smile. "There have been some reports of mountain lions in the area."

Yeah, I still wasn't feeling better about the situation.

"Don't worry ma'am, Aidan's a crack shot and mountain lions usually like to be left alone. You're in good hands."

"We can stay at the ranch," Aidan offered.

I shook my head. "A little adventure is good for the soul."

Earl smiled and slapped Aidan on the arm. "This is a good one here."

Aidan nodded his head.

I hadn't been on a horse in years, but I found it was like riding a bicycle. I even mounted Butterscotch correctly. Aidan's horse was named Thunder, and you could tell he was livelier than the sweet paint I was on. Thunder was a purebred and had an air to him, but Aidan commanded him well. I was grateful they thought to give me a gentle spirit.

Aidan's horse carried the food and yes, gun. I hoped this guy really was a good guy and if that's true, I hope that if we see a mountain lion, he's quick on the draw.

"You don't need to worry about mountain lions, they're usually more afraid of us." I guess he noticed my frequent glances.

"Are you just saying that?"

"I wouldn't bring you out here if I didn't think it was safe."

Good guy? Yes.

We didn't talk a lot, which was fine by me. There was too much nature to enjoy, and talking would have ruined it. Once in a while Aidan would point out a different type of bird, and we even saw some elk, but other than that, he too seemed to just enjoy being out on the trail. The trail led us to a beautiful lake in the middle of a meadow. It was so stunning I took out my phone and snapped a few pictures. It was the picture-perfect place for a picnic. It looked like a postcard with the evening sun reflecting on the still water and a light breeze that barely nudged the tall grass. It was a piece of heaven. Too bad my first thought was, *I would love to bring Ryan here. Focus*, I told myself.

Aidan and I enjoyed chicken salad sandwiches, fruit, and I daresay the company. Aidan was a thoughtful speaker and well read. I almost felt like I needed a thesaurus handy to speak to him, but he never made me feel stupid or inadequate, as Ryan would say. I couldn't believe this cowboy was a chemist. He didn't fit the image in my mind. Maybe I should have taken more chemistry classes in college.

We didn't only talk about him, although I was intrigued with the world of drugs, that is the legal kind (he knew all sorts of long names for penicillin, ibuprofen and so on). He was a courteous date and asked a lot about me. I tried to steer the conversation away from accounting, in fact I liked talking to him about drugs that treated different types of psychosis.

"Are you sure you're in the right profession?" he asked after a lengthy discussion on the side effects of depression medication and his opinions on the best options available.

"No," I sighed. It was weird telling a practical stranger that. The only other person who knew was Krissy. I never even told Jay.

"So, why are you an accountant?"

I looked out over the lake and watched a fish jump out of the water. It reminded me of my dad. "It's a long story, but I guess the short answer is family."

His smile said he knew exactly what I meant. "I understand that. My dad wasn't too thrilled when I decided I didn't want to be a rancher."

"Did he come around?"

"Eventually. I think he likes telling everyone his son's going to be a doctor, even though it's not that type of doctor."

"I'm sure you've made them proud."

"You know, it's not too late for you to change your mind."

I sighed again. "Honestly, I've been looking at different programs at CU and CSU, but again, it's complicated."

"Choose CU." That was his Alma Mater.

"If only that was the complicated part." I smiled.

He skimmed my hand, and yep, nothing. "I'm sure you'll figure it out."

I'm sure I would, too, but I wasn't sure how long that was going to take or how I would accomplish my dream. I couldn't ask my dad for money, and I couldn't live with him forever. It's not like he was in any hurry to kick me out, but out of self-respect, I needed my own place. With what my dad paid me, I could more than afford a place of my own, but if I went back to school, I could only work part time. I think I could still manage if I cut my hours, but then there were the student loans, and I would have to pay out-of-state tuition if I went back in January. I was looking into different scholarships, but there were no guarantees. Then there was the whole, I don't want to disappoint my dad thing. He was already nudging me about taking my CPA license exam. I had studied quite a bit with Ryan. I had no doubt I could sit the four-part exam and pass it, I just didn't want to.

We had to get back to the ranch before the sun set. It had been a pleasant way to spend the evening. I liked Aidan, he seemed like a great guy. In fact, he reminded me of Jay, which was great on the friend spectrum, not so much on the romantic end.

Why couldn't I fall for nice guys, not that Ryan wasn't nice, he was beyond nice, but not so available.

I had the pleasure of meeting Aidan's parents briefly before he took me home. Evelyn and William were a lovely older couple. They were definitely proud of their son. They made sure to throw in how smart he was, and for good measure, that he would one day own the ranch. I tried not to laugh at their overt attempts to sell their son to me. I think it embarrassed Aidan, but he took it in stride.

"You're welcome back anytime," they said.

I would love to come back and explore, but I wanted to bring Josh and Ryan. I wondered how they would feel about that. Not that I wouldn't go out with Aidan again. He was a super date, but I needed to get over Ryan, which was dumb since we weren't anything but friends.

The dreaded part of the evening came for me when we hit

Loveland's city limits. You know, the part where you decide if there was any sort of connection and if you would like to see each other again.

"I had a great time." He smiled my way.

"Me, too. Your parents' place is incredible. Thank you for inviting me."

"Can I ask you a question?"

Here it comes.

"Maviny mentioned that perhaps you were already involved with someone, but it wasn't exclusive, is that true?"

Okay, so that was not what I expected. And boy was Maviny getting an earful from me. "I'm not technically involved with anyone." I stared out the window. This was a little awkward for me.

"What does 'technically' mean?"

I turned toward him. He kept glancing at me when he could as he drove. "I know it feels like I keep saying this, but it's complicated."

"Is it that guy who caught the garter?"

I tilted my head. "How did you know?"

"It was obvious from the way you two danced together."

I let out a deep breath and twisted my hands together. "I hope you don't feel like I've led you on or anything."

"Hey, it's just a date. Not that I wouldn't want another if you're up for it. And I don't mind a little competition."

I laughed. "You're a good guy."

"But?"

"There's no but. I need to figure out my feelings."

"I can respect that, and you have my number. I hope you'll use it."

Twelve

I WALKED IN, AFTER I had been walked to my door and sweetly kissed goodnight on the cheek, to find my dad pretending to watch Jimmy Fallon, but I knew he was up waiting for me.

"Hi, Daddy." I walked down the few steps it took to reach the sunken family room.

He sat up from his lying down position on the couch. "Hey, baby girl. How was your night?"

I sat down next to him. He put his arm around me. I reveled in the safety and comfort I felt there with my head on his shoulder. "It was really nice."

He rubbed my arm. "Nice, huh?"

"Yep, nice. How was your evening?"

"I scored a big account tonight."

"Exciting."

"It's not as exciting as it used to be."

"Yeah, I guess success gets boring after a while."

He chuckled. "I missed your cheekiness."

"I thought we agreed I was witty, not cheeky."

He laughed again. "You going to go out with this guy again?"

"He wants to."

"Ahh. I take it you don't."

"I know, I have problems."

"Why would you say that?"

"Because, Aidan is a great guy. He seems like the whole package exactly like Jay, but I'm not interested. But give me a guy that's not interested in me and he's all I can think about."

My dad squeezed me tighter. "Honey, Ryan's interested, he's just gun shy."

"I don't know, Dad."

"I do know. I saw the look in Ryan's eyes when you announced you had a date this morning. He wasn't happy to hear that particular piece of news."

"Then why doesn't he ask me out himself?"

"Honey, dating you puts a lot at stake, and I think he's having a hard time coming to terms with the fact that you were his teenage neighbor once upon a time. And he's still dealing with getting over his divorce."

"He's dated other women."

"True, but with you it's different."

"Why?"

"Because you're different."

"I'm not sure how I should take that."

He kissed my head. "It's a good thing. I think you're just what the doctor ordered for him, but sometimes medicine can be hard to swallow."

"So now I'm different and horrible tasting medicine?"

"No. You're perfect and wonderful."

"No need to exaggerate."

"I'm not."

"Thanks, Daddy."

"I have a feeling Ryan will be coming around real soon."

I woke up and enjoyed the feeling of not having anything to do. My only plans were Saturday chores, some grocery shopping, and laying out on the deck. I got up, showered, and dressed for my super casual day. I only bothered with mascara and lip gloss. I made it upstairs just in time for the Saturday morning music playlist. First up, Boston's "More Than a Feeling."

My dad and I made omelets together and then commenced cleaning the house, which didn't take long at all. The two of us were both generally tidy people. After I threw a load of laundry in the washer, I sat down and started to make the grocery list for the week. I had insisted on buying the groceries and doing at least half the cooking. In my mind, it was the least I could do. My dad was uncomfortable with it, but relented. Halfway through making my list, the doorbell rang. My dad was mowing the backyard lawn, so I got up and answered it. I opened the door to find two of my favorite people.

"Cherry," Josh yelled as soon as I opened the door.

I immediately bent down, and he ran into my arms. I picked him up and squeezed him tight while I looked at his daddy, whose smile was melting my insides. "Hi, big guy. I've missed you." I kissed his chubby cheek.

He gave me a sloppy one in return.

"I hope we're not interrupting anything?" Ryan asked.

"Not at all. Do you want to come in?"

"Actually, we were hoping you would want to come to the park with us."

"Pwease, Cherry."

Believe me, I didn't need to be asked twice. "I'd love to. Just let me tell my dad."

I kept a hold of Josh as I made my way to the backyard.

My dad was bagging some lawn clippings when I walked out. He looked up and grinned when he saw who was in my arms.

"I'm headed to the park with Josh and Ryan. I'll see you later."

"See. What did I tell you?" My dad winked.

"Bye, Dad," I kind of sang. I met Ryan back at the front door where he waited.

"Are you ready to go?" he asked.

I nodded and smiled. I set Josh down and took his little hand in mine. Gosh, I loved that kid.

On our way out, Ryan picked up a full backpack he had left waiting on our porch.

"What's that?" I inquired.

"Rumor has it that you like picnics."

I'm not sure if I've ever smiled so big. "So that's the word on the street, huh?"

"I'm afraid so," he teased.

"Very good. Did you practice that gem?"

"All night."

I was loving the playful banter. "I can't wait to see what else you've come up with."

Ryan smiled and took Josh's other hand. The three of us headed toward the neighborhood park. I hadn't been there for years, but back in the day, Krissy and I had spent our fair share of time there, even as we got into high school.

The weather matched my mood: bright, sunny, and warm. Colorado summers were the best.

Ryan and I kept glancing at each other and smiling; sometimes we would look down at Josh. It was perfect.

"Cherry, will you swide with me?" Josh's little voice drifted up.

"Yes, of course."

"See, daddy."

I looked at Ryan for clarification.

"I told him you were too old to slide."

"Oh . . . You think so?"

"Don't you?"

"You're never too old to slide, that is, as long as your butt still fits."

Ryan laughed at me and then surprised me by carefully looking me over. "I don't think you'll have any issues."

I looked him over in return. "So I guess that means you're sliding, too?"

"No, I really am too old."

I rolled my eyes. "Yes, ancient. Come on. You've never gone down the slide with Josh?"

He shook his head.

"We need to change that as soon as possible."

"Not happening."

"I'm sorry to say, but that sounds like a challenge."

"I knew asking you to come to the park with us would liven things up."

"Are you regretting that now?"

He gave me a meaningful look. "Not in the least."

"By the way, thanks for asking me."

"Thanks for coming."

The park came into view, and Josh let go of both of our hands. He made a beeline for the slide. "Come on, Cherry!"

"Are you coming?" I asked Ryan before I chased after his son.

"I'm just going to watch for now."

"Enjoy the show."

"Believe me, I will."

I raised my eyebrow at his somewhat seductive comment. I liked this Ryan very much. So did the butterflies in my stomach, they were adding new swear words to their vocabulary. I took off and easily caught up to my favorite three-year-old and picked him up and tickled his tummy. He had the most addictive laugh ever.

"Cherry, stop, it's time to swide," he said through his giggles.

"Okay, let's slide."

I stood behind Josh as he climbed up the stairs to the slide. I felt very protective of him. I made sure he didn't fall climbing or getting situated on the top before he went down. I watched him go down and then caught him at the end.

"Again," he shouted.

As Josh climbed the second time, I snuck a quick glance at Ryan who was setting out a plaid blanket. I was hopeful this meant that he was getting on board the Charlee and Ryan train.

It was nice that the park wasn't too crowded, so Josh had free reign of the slide.

Ryan joined us after a few minutes and stood at my side. "I thought you were going to show me how it was done," he whispered in my ear.

My body said, *dang*. "I was just waiting for you, so Josh had someone to catch him on the way down."

He gave me that alluring smile of his. "Thanks for being so great with my son."

"It's my pleasure. Now watch and learn."

He grabbed Josh, and I made my ascent up the ladder. It didn't take much as my legs were so long. I admit, I felt a little ridiculous as I climbed, and some of the other adults were staring at me, but I got over it when I looked down at the only adult that mattered to me at the moment, and at his son, who was looking at me like I was the coolest person ever. I got my butt situated at the top of the long slide that wasn't really that long for me. To prove my point, I pushed off, raised both hands up high and shouted, "Woo hoo!"

Ryan grinned and met me at the end with Josh. He held out his hand to me, and I didn't hesitate a bit in taking it. He helped me up and shook his head at me. He held onto my hand for just a moment longer than necessary and squeezed it before letting go.

"Thank you. Now it's your turn."

His smile faltered. "I don't think so."

"You don't want Josh to think you're L-A-M-E do you?" I figured I better spell it out, so Josh didn't repeat it again.

"Actually, I figure he eventually will, so I'm okay with it."

"I suppose that's probably true, but your reputation with me is on the line, and I could go either way right now."

He fixed his gaze on me and studied me. "You don't play fair do you?"

"Did you expect anything less of me?"

"I'm learning not to underestimate you."

I smiled in delight before picking up Josh, and swinging him around. There was that giggle again. When I turned back around, Ryan was still looking like he wasn't sure what he should do.

"You know if you slide down with Josh on your lap, you would look like the world's best dad."

He didn't hesitate. He walked toward the slide, and then up the steps. I handed Josh up to him as soon as he was settled at the top. The look on Josh's face was priceless. He was so excited his daddy was sliding with him. They were down within a couple of seconds. I took Josh out of Ryan's hands and held him close while Ryan stood up.

"How was that?" Ryan grinned.

"Just about perfect."

The rest of the day could be summed up with that exact phrase. We played hard at the park and then ate a delicious meal of homemade quesadillas made with marinated steak and bleu cheese.

"Did you make these?" My taste buds gave their overwhelming approval.

"A guy's got to eat."

"You do it very well."

He flashed those pearly whites at me and that was it, I was completely smitten.

The only damper, and it wasn't really a damper, more like a blip, was that Jacquelyn showed up with her two kids as we were getting ready to leave. I didn't realize that she lived nearby and this was the park they had met at. I already knew she didn't like me, so her poisonous look wasn't a surprise, but she wouldn't even look at Ryan. That was fine with me, I didn't want her looking at him. Ryan was definitely uncomfortable. He picked up Josh and hurried his pace.

"Sorry about that." Ryan apologized once we were a good distance away.

"You don't have anything to apologize for."

He stopped for a moment and gazed my way. "Being around you is easy."

That was one I had never heard, and for once I wasn't sure how to respond other than to smile.

Playing hard left Josh wiped out. As we walked home, the poor little guy was dragging. Ryan picked him right up, and we walked slowly home. Josh fell asleep against Ryan right before we made it to Mulberry Lane. Ryan holding a sleeping Josh was the most attractive thing I had ever seen.

My weekend was filled with attractive sights, whether it was running the next morning with the two of them, or a rousing game of basketball where Josh and I kicked the butts of our dads. Not really, but who's going to beat a preschooler on purpose?

The only thing off for me was I could tell Ryan wasn't sure about what he should do about me. I could tell he enjoyed being with me, but he was comfortable with the friendship aspect of our relationship. Once in a while, he would say something that was more than friendly, but he never followed through. My dad even gave him the prime opportunity to spend some alone time with me on Sunday as we watched the Rockies game.

"You know, if you two want to go catch a movie or something, I'll watch Josh," my dad offered.

For a moment, my insides felt like Mardi Gras, but the party was squashed almost instantly. I looked with hope in my eyes at Ryan who was sitting close to me on the couch, but not too close. He, on the other hand didn't look at me, only my dad. "I have to drop Josh off at his mom's soon, but thanks for the offer."

In my head, I kept thinking, *We could go after you drop him off.* But I wasn't going to throw myself at him. I looked at my dad, who shrugged his shoulders. I decided it was time to jump on the trampoline with Josh, by myself. Josh thought it was a great idea. At least one Carter man liked spending one-on-one time with me.

Thirteen

MONDAY DAWNED, AND I WAS puzzled by the weekend's events, so much so I almost decided against running with Ryan. That, though, would have been a terrible misstep.

We didn't say much at the beginning of our run. I was a little annoyed with him, and for some odd reason, he was acting nervous.

Then out of the blue he said, "I have two tickets."

I had heard this before. "And you need a babysitter?" I couldn't keep the ice out of my voice.

He laughed at me, reached down, and grabbed my hand. "Hold up for a second."

I stopped and faced him. He kept my hand in his; his touch wasn't lost on me or the butterflies.

"I'm not asking you to babysit Josh." He smiled. "I'm trying to ask you out."

I bit my lip. "Like on a date?"

He stepped closer as a fellow runner passed us and grinned.

Just keep on going, buddy, there's nothing to see here, I thought. I didn't want any distractions for the moment I had been waiting for since before I was even old enough to date.

"I think that's what they call it when a man and a woman go to see One Republic."

That was it, Ryan had officially ruined me for life. I squealed and threw my arms around him, not thinking that we were both sweaty. Actually, that was a bit of a turn on, I'm not going to lie. "How did you manage to get tickets?"

147

He reciprocated the hug. "I know a guy. So does this mean you'll go with me?" he whispered in my ear, which drove me crazy.

I let go of him, but not before kissing his cheek.

He reached up and touched his cheek where my lips just departed. "I'll take that as a yes."

"Heck, yes! Oh my gosh, I'm so excited."

"I couldn't have our first date be to the movies, and I had to top Friday night's date."

I rolled my eyes at him. "Believe me, this wins best first date ever. Not like it's a competition though."

"Best ever, huh?" He grinned.

"Don't let it go to your head." I jogged away.

He followed me. "Better than horseback riding?"

"Are we still on that?" I smiled over at him. "Thank you, by the way."

"It was my fault that you missed out on the tickets in the first place."

"Well, at least you got to see your foreign film."

"Are we still on that?" he threw back at me.

I nudged him and he chuckled.

I think I floated into the house. I didn't even bother with stretching. I think I was going to wear a permanent smile on my face for, like, ever. In two days, I was going to be with both of my Ryans. I had to text Krissy. She was coming home the next day, but I knew she would want to know this. She could spare a few minutes for her best friend, right?

Krissy was going to have to be second in line though. My dad was up and eating a bagel when I glided into the kitchen. I walked right over to him and kissed his cheek. "Good morning, Daddy."

My dad lowered his bagel and grinned. "You're in a good mood, baby girl."

"Am I?" I smiled toothily from the sink.

"I take it your run with Ryan went well."

"You could say that."

"Are you excited about the concert?"

I swallowed the water I was drinking. "How did you know?"

"Ryan told me about it last night after you left with Josh. I told him he was being foolish and if he didn't watch himself, he was going to waste his chance with you."

I set my water bottle down and my euphoria went out the window. "So he only asked me out because my dad told him to?"

My dad shook his head. "Not at all. He was already planning on asking you, he just wanted to get my take on it, or more like my permission. He also mentioned something about you finding movies to be inappropriate first dates, so that's why he didn't take me up on my offer last night."

Dang it. I could have already been out with Ryan. Oh well. "So he asked for your permission?" I laughed.

My dad wasn't laughing. In fact he looked serious. "Honey, I don't want you to worry about dating Ryan, but I need to caution you. Dating a divorced man with a child, and someone you work with, isn't going to be easy." He sounded like he knew what he was talking about.

I paused for a moment and took a few more sips of water. "Do you think this is a bad idea?"

"I didn't say that. The best life has to offer is always hard. I just want you to be aware."

"Thanks, Dad," I said—though I wasn't feeling very thankful. His warning kind of took the excitement out of my triumph this morning. It's not that I didn't think it was wise or good counsel, but it's not what I wanted to hear this morning.

My dad reached out and took my hand as I walked by sullenly. "Honey, I think you and Ryan are a terrific match."

I gave him a tight-lipped smile.

"I mean it."

I kissed him on the cheek and headed for the shower.

I took longer than normal in the shower. I was contemplating the morning's events. On the one hand, I was excited out of my mind. In two days I was finally going to have my first date with Ryan, but my dad's words kept playing over and over in my head. I hadn't really stopped to think about all the nuances of dating Ryan. I had never dated a divorced man or somebody that was a dad, at least not that I knew of. I guess I was a little ahead of the game, because I already knew Josh and we had mutual affection for one another. I also knew that

Ryan's time wasn't just his, and I was okay with that. One of the things I really dug about him was that he was really into his kid.

That was all the positives, then I started to think about the what-if's. Like what if things went south? How could we work together? Would my dad hate Ryan, his partner? What about Josh? I loved Josh and I would hate to not be part of his life. Or what if things went really well and we decided we wanted to be a couple in the "till death do you part" kind of way? How would I deal with him having an ex-wife? And what about the kids we would have? Would he love them less because I was the mom? And what about Victoria? I could tell he still had some type of feelings for her.

Then I thought, You're being stupid. You haven't even gone on a date yet and you're worrying about things that'll probably never happen. Just enjoy this, I told myself, and take it a day at a time.

With some of my giddiness back, I texted Krissy, *Don't feel the need to respond to this, I know you're preoccupied with things we don't ever need to discuss, and I mean like ever, but I thought you would want to know that Ryan asked me out. And guess where he's taking me? The One Republic concert. That's right! Can't wait to see you! Lots of love.*

I swore Monday and Tuesday were the longest days ever. I felt like I was a seven-year-old waiting for Christmas to get here, but in my mind this was better than Christmas because I already knew what the gift was, and he was amazing. I was trying not to act like some idiot around him when we ran or when I saw him at work, but it was hard. I was having these urges to pull him to me and kiss him senseless, or me senseless, but I resisted. I also hoped I didn't look like some fan girl every time I saw him in the office. I wondered if anyone could tell that I was totally into him. I think Felicity might have had her suspicions, but she never said anything directly, she just seemed to give me lots of knowing glances.

I worried, too, if it looked completely obvious, since Ryan and I were leaving work together Wednesday. The concert started at eight and Ryan had gotten us reservations at the Ship Rock Grille at Red Rocks for six-thirty. He must have a really good friend to get us in there and get us tickets. We needed to leave right at five to make it there on time.

I was a mixed bag of emotions that day. I was extremely excited, but I was also nervous. I brought five different outfits to change into because I couldn't decide that morning what would look best on me. I texted Krissy pictures of each, since she had returned from her honeymoon. She may have been more excited than me. She wanted a full report. I couldn't wait to hear about the honeymoon, well, at least the PG parts. We had plans to meet for lunch on Friday. After a lot of thought, and fifty texts from Krissy, I went with the white lace shirt dress. It was flirty, showed off my figure and tan, and I felt feminine in it. I paired it with some comfortable wedges, pulled my hair into a sexy messy bun, touched up my lip gloss and called it good.

Ryan decided we should meet at his car at the designated time. I guess he, too, was worried about how it would look. I teased him that perhaps he was embarrassed to be seen with me. His response was, "I don't know of any man who would be." That scored total points with me.

I threw my leftover stuff in my dad's Audi before I walked over to Ryan's deep blue Ford Explorer. He stood at the back of his SUV, handsomely waiting for me in jeans and a nice fitting black tee. I think he would look good in anything. He waited for me to reach him, and from there he walked me to the passenger side door. I took a deep breath and held my stomach for good measure.

"Hi there," I greeted him.

"Hi there back. You look good, Charlee."

I tried to act coy. "Thanks. You look good, too."

He opened my door for me and smiled as he perused me. "Real good."

For a second, I felt like I couldn't breathe. I had never felt this way. It was a little overwhelming.

He joined me seconds later, on the driver's side. "Here we go." He sounded as nervous as I felt.

Yes, here we go.

He headed up 287, since there was a report of an accident on I-

25, which wasn't a huge shocker. I-25 seemed to get worse and worse as the years went on, no matter how many extra lanes they added.

"How was your day?" He glanced at my bare legs.

"Today was the day for last minute changes. I had three companies send me new data files today after I had already finished their payroll. Thankfully, I hadn't transmitted anything yet."

"You were smart to wait."

"I guess."

He must have picked up on my frustration. "How about we don't talk about work."

Perfect. "How's Josh?" I changed the subject.

"He's great, but I'm missing him this week. Victoria's parents are in town, and I won't get to see him until Sunday."

"Can't you go over there and visit with them all?"

"It's not really a good idea. Her parents and I don't really get along."

"I'm sorry. Did you ever get along?"

"Not really. Our families never meshed well. Victoria didn't get along with my parents, either."

That didn't surprise me, but I can't imagine why Victoria's parents didn't like Ryan. I would think he was the model son-in-law. "Speaking of your parents, how are they?"

"Interesting you should ask. My mom was asking how you were when I talked to her last night on the phone."

"Really? And what did you say?"

"I told her you were all grown up." He looked my way and winked.

I scrunched my face at his feeble attempt at wit and he laughed at me.

"Honestly, I told her that you were smart and beautiful and she said, 'Tell me something I don't know.'"

"I always did like your mom. So, what new piece of information did you throw her way?"

"Only that I decided to rob the cradle and take you out."

"You know, you're not that much older than me."

"Are you kidding me? When I graduated from high school, you were still in elementary school."

"Okay, that sounds a little bad, but when you're seventy-eight, I'll be seventy."

"I'm not sure that makes me feel better."

"Does our age difference really bother you? I thought guys liked to date younger women. Did your mom say something against it?"

"Not at all. In fact, she thought it was great."

I love that woman.

"I just don't want to be one of those guys."

"You need to elaborate."

"You know, divorced and desperate."

"Did you say desperate?"

"Wrong word."

"Yes, let's pick a different word, please."

"Charlee, being here with you has nothing to do with desperation. I just don't want people to think I've preyed on you."

That made me laugh out loud, maybe even snort. "If it makes you feel better, you can tell them I preyed on you."

He gave me a wry smile. "Have I ever mentioned how annoyingly charming you are?"

"I think so, but feel free to remind me."

He surprised me and reached over and held my hand. Our fingers interlaced perfectly. "You're so annoying . . . and charming."

He kept my hand in his practically the whole drive. It drove my senses crazy. I think there is something lovely about holding someone's hand. In a way, it's even more intimate than kissing for me. He only let go when we hit I-70 and the traffic became congested and tricky to maneuver. It seemed like everyone was headed to the concert. I wasn't surprised, One Republic was amazing, and this was their hometown.

I didn't mind the extra time with him in the car. We were having a riveting conversation on the sordid affairs of his brother, Evan. I still thank my lucky stars I never snuck off with him at Ryan's wedding. He hadn't grown up like his brother. He was successful, but he sounded like a real louse. Never married, but with three kids, all from different mothers. He had been really busy, apparently.

"What do your parents think?"

"I think they try not to think about it. They do their best to try and have some contact with their grandkids. Two of the moms are amenable, but this last one won't let anyone, including him, have anything to do with their daughter."

"That's terrible."

"Yeah, well, my brother only has himself to blame. He's great on making promises, but not on following through."

"So you're the favorite son."

He chuckled. "Probably, but my parents are too good to ever say it."

"Well, I always knew you were the better of the two."

"I'm glad, because my brother always had an eye for you."

"Really?"

He laughed to himself. "I always warned him to stay away from you because you were too young. Now look at me."

I didn't respond. He was going to have to get over the age thing on his own. I for one didn't have an issue with it.

We parked in the top lot near the visitor's center where the restaurant was located. It was beginning to fill up quickly. Ryan was every bit a gentleman. He came around and opened my door for me. He held his hand out to me, and I gladly took it and didn't let go. He looked down at our entwined hands and smiled.

"Don't worry, I don't think anyone will guess how much older you are than me."

"Come on annoying woman, let's eat."

"You know you like it." I leaned into him and breathed him in. I could get drunk on that smell.

"That I do."

Everything on their menu looked yummy. It made it hard to decide what to choose, but I finally went with the Blue River Salmon Salad and Ryan chose the Chipotle Turkey BLT sandwich. We talked easily while we waited for our food. I was still impressed he swung reservations and tickets. I needed a friend like his. The restaurant was filled to capacity, but the service was excellent and timely, as was the food. I was still enjoying the freedom of eating whatever I wanted, within reason. The red dress and I parted friends, but I was happy not to ever wear it again.

We split a piece of to-die-for apple pie, topped with ice cream and caramel. For a moment, it was like I really had gone to heaven—perfect man paired with the ultimate dessert.

Ryan paid our check, and I made a quick trip to the ladies' room. While washing my hands, I looked in the mirror. I don't think I ever looked so happy. I hurried out to my waiting and smiling date. He held his hand out to me and pulled me close to him. "You really are looking quite grown up," he teased and whispered in my ear as we walked out into the warm night air.

"You know, it's a good thing I like you."

"I like you, too."

I had to say Red Rocks is the most amazing place to see a concert. For one, it's called Red Rocks for a reason. The red rock formations are incredible, I can't even begin to adequately describe them, so I won't. The amphitheater was set against the foothills of the Rockies, another amazing feature, and then there was the structure of it all. The amphitheater was sixty-eight rows of perfect acoustic sound and unobstructed views of the stage, so no matter where you sat, the show would be amazing. That's why I was completely blown out of the water when we kept walking closer and closer to the stage. Ryan kept grinning at me as we made our descent. We landed at row five, center stage.

"Ryan, you didn't mention how good of a friend you have. I have to insist on paying for my ticket." I knew how expensive those seats were.

"Not a chance, Charlee. I wanted our first date to be memorable."

I kissed his cheek before we sat down on the stadium cushions Ryan brought with us. "I'll never forget it. Thank you."

He flashed his breathtaking smile at me. "Don't thank me yet, the night has only begun."

"Oh, don't worry, I plan on thanking you again."

He raised his eyebrow at me, and that breathtaking smile turned seductive; I went a little weak in the knees. Seriously, best night of my life so far.

While we waited for the opening act to come out, the skies began to darken as the sun set behind the glorious mountains and some nonthreatening clouds rolled in. The mood of the amphitheater shifted the darker it became. Inhibitions were lowered as blood alcohol levels rose all around us. Ryan and I observed and commented on all the hooking up going on.

"There's going to be some serious regret in the morning. I guarantee it."

"Are you speaking from experience?" he asked.

"Uh, no. I never drink or leave with random men I meet at concerts, or anywhere else for that matter."

"Why don't you drink?"

"For one, alcohol and I don't get along well, and most importantly, I don't ever want to lose control of myself or my surroundings."

He nodded. "I'm impressed. Do you mind if your dates drink?"

"As long as it's responsibly and they act appropriately with me, I don't mind at all."

He reached up and touched a tendril of my hair that framed my face. "I promise, whenever we're together, I'll always do both."

"Are you saying you want to see me again?"

He leaned in closer and the butterflies in my stomach said, well we won't mention it. Let's just say I didn't need alcohol, his breath and everything about him was intoxicating.

"I think you can say that's a safe bet."

I almost leaned in and kissed him. Our faces were inches apart, and I had the feeling he wouldn't mind as he gazed into my eyes, but in a split second, he broke the connection and sat up straight and looked forward. At least he took my hand.

"Just so you know, I'm amenable to that."

He glanced my way and grinned.

It was about that time. Music began to play, and the crowd's focus and attention shifted to the stage, at least momentarily. I felt sorry for opening acts; even if they were good, most people hardly paid attention to them, and some people didn't even show up until the main attraction was ready to come on. Admittedly, I was anxious for the main attraction as well, but having Ryan by my side helped pass the time in the best sort of fashion, though it was getting harder to hear each other. That was okay too, it meant we had to be closer to each other.

Finally it was dark, everyone around us was thoroughly trashed, and the set on the stage was primed for my favorite band. The excitement was building up. There was an energy in the air when the music started. The crowd all jumped up, including myself. There was a roar when my other favorite Ryan and all his bandmates took the stage. They sounded even better on stage than the radio, and that's saying something. Ryan Tedder had the most amazing voice. When he hit the high notes, I wanted to swoon. Not like Ryan Carter swoon, but pretty close.

I think Ryan watched me more than the show as I sang along and danced to every song. Once in a while, I got him to let loose a little. His cell phone even came out, and he waved his hands with me during one song. I could tell he felt ridiculous doing it, but he was a good sport about it. I had to laugh at him when, after the last song of the night and the band exited the stage, Ryan made his way to leave.

I tugged his hand and pulled him back. "When's the last time you've been to a concert?"

"It's been a while. Why?"

"Because you can't leave yet. The band always comes back out and does one or two more numbers."

"But if we leave now, we'll miss all the traffic, and I'm pretty sure any minute now it's going to start to rain."

I looked up at the cloud-covered sky and then back to Ryan. "A little rain never hurt anyone. Come on, live a little."

He shook that gorgeous head at me. "Why do I always find myself doing the exact opposite of what I normally do when I'm with you?"

I took his other hand and pulled him closer to me. "I don't know. You tell me."

Ryan stared down at my lips and for a moment, I could sense I was finally going to get to taste the sweetness of his breath. I held my breath in anticipation, but I almost turned blue in the face. The kiss never came. In its place were confused, almost worried, eyes. I wasn't sure what to make of it, and I don't think he knew either.

He let go of both of my hands and backed away. "I'm up for staying."

I faced forward and found it hard to get back into the anticipation and calls for the band to come back out. I was wondering if I kept doing something to turn Ryan off. Fortunately, the band came back out and I had something else to throw my attention at. Their last two numbers were incredible, as I knew they would be, and they ended as I felt the first raindrop on my cheek.

Ryan reached for my hand as we maneuvered with the crowd of people toward the exits. "I told you it was going to rain," he yelled back at me so I could hear him.

I shrugged my shoulders. The rain didn't bother me in the least bit. I enjoyed being out in a good rainstorm. When the drops became many, Ryan tried to protect my head with the stadium seats. I laughed and told him it wasn't necessary. He gave me that look again that made me think he thought I was off my rocker some. It wouldn't have mattered anyway; the rain went from a sprinkle to pouring in seconds. You gotta love the Colorado weather. We were drenched as we ran across the parking lot.

In a way, I found it very romantic. I wanted to stay out in the rain and dance closely to Ryan, but he was practically dragging me to the car, trying to get out of the elements. Once we reached his car, he dropped my hand and the stadium cushions as he fumbled to get his car keys out. I couldn't help but laugh at him in his hastiness.

He paused for a moment and looked over to me. I'm sure I looked like a drowned rat at this point, but I had to say he looked sexy when wet. The look he gave was sexy too. He purposely shoved his keys back in his pocket and, to my shock and utter delight, he took me up in his arms and this time he didn't hesitate. His lips collided with mine, but I barely caught a taste of how sweet his lips were. Just as my lips were about to part, he released me.

"I'm sorry." He backed away.

I took a deep breath in. Though the kiss was short, his touch had left me feeling a little breathless. "Why are you sorry?" I wiped the water from my face. I had never had a guy say that to me after we kissed, especially the first time.

"I'm not usually this forward, but there's something about you."

I stepped closer to him, pulled on his wet shirt, and drew him to me. "Please don't apologize for kissing me."

He smiled before he leaned down and hovered over my lips, teasing me with his indecisiveness. My heart was racing and I wanted nothing more than to meet his lips, but there's something about anticipation and that moment before you kiss that's magical. I didn't have to wait long, he kissed me once more. Again, it was brief, but sweet. He hugged me quickly and looked me over. It was then that I realized I was wearing white and soaked. Thank goodness for slips, but it was still a little uncomfortable. Ryan helped me in, grabbed a jacket from his backseat, and handed it to me like a gentleman. He got in the car, and as soon as he started it, he turned the heater on to blow on me. One thing about rain in Colorado at night, it can cause a chill. I hadn't noticed, until we got in the car, that I was cold. Ryan had done a great job of warming me up outside.

I pulled his warm fleece-lined jacket over me as we waited in what looked like a never-ending line of cars. "Sorry, I didn't mean to turn this into a wet t-shirt contest."

He chuckled and looked my way. "As always, where you're concerned, I get more than I bargained for."

"Is that a bad thing?"

He reached over and ever so gently, touched my cold, wet cheek. "Not at all."

Fourteen

"THERE'S ONE FOR THE BOOKS" perfectly summed up my first date with Ryan. We didn't get home until right before 1:00 a.m. I would say the only thing that was a little off was Ryan's unsure way of handling me. At times he was all in, but then suddenly it was like he thought about it and decided caution was more appropriate. Even when he walked me to my door, he was thoughtful, gentle, and held my hand, so I assumed he would be kissing me goodnight. Then we got to the door and the confusion returned to his eyes. He kissed me on the cheek and left me there. I had to call out "Thank you," to him, though thank you seemed inadequate for the kind of evening he had shown me. I tried not to think about how much he'd spent on our date. I wasn't used to someone spending that kind of money on me, and I'd been surprised by it.

Sleep didn't come easy. The butterflies were on an all-night bender with all the excitement of being kissed and held by our favorite Ryan. Second favorite Ryan had also done his job admirably. I loved a man who could sing. First favorite Ryan did not sing well, but I wasn't holding it against him. He did plenty of other things well, and they more than compensated. I was drawn to him like I never had been drawn to anyone else. I wasn't sure exactly what that meant, but I wanted to keep exploring it with him. From the sounds of it, so did he, though we didn't set another time to see each other again, well, at least not as in a date. We would see each other regardless, except we decided against running in the morning, or I should say later that morning.

I rode in with my dad; I was too tired to drive, and I knew my dad liked the company.

"So, are you going to tell your old man how your date went last night?"

I was leaning my sleepy head on the window. I sat up and smiled. "It was fabulous."

"So I take it there will be another?"

"I hope so, but I'll leave that up to Ryan."

"Just no making out at the office, okay?"

"Daddy! Why would you say something like that?"

He laughed at me. "I know how you kids are today," he teased.

I rolled my eyes. "You don't need to worry about that. Besides, Ryan is totally old school, he thinks he's ancient, and I'm sure he's above such antics." I probably was too, but I could see if the moment was right, and it was discreet, I probably wouldn't turn him down.

"You think so, huh?"

"Yeah. Ryan has some hang ups about our age difference."

"And what do you think?"

"It doesn't bother me at all."

"So, you think it's okay if men and women that fall within different decades date?"

I lowered my shades and looked at him. The way he asked felt different, like he was asking something else.

My dad cleared his throat.

Hmmm. . . "I don't see any issue with it. Honestly, I think as a society we're too caught up in age. I say if it's within legal bounds, you shouldn't let age be a factor."

"Interesting."

I eyed him carefully. "What's the interest?"

He shook his head as if he was trying to clear out a thought. "Nothing, I'm just making small talk with my girl."

I had the feeling there was more there, but I didn't push. I was a little worried about how to be around Ryan today. I knew it was only one date, but I wanted to explore the idea of seeing him more, and even exclusively. I hoped that didn't sound desperate. I figured since we had spent copious amounts of time together for the last couple of months that could at least be an option. I wouldn't push for it if he wasn't interested, but I was up for it. Being with him had made me realize that with all my other relationships, there was something missing. I wasn't sure what that missing piece was, per se, but Ryan had it. I didn't want to blow it, so I was going to let him take things at his pace, since he was the one with reservations. And I admit, they were valid reservations, but we also had some pretty valid reasons for at least giving it a go.

I didn't see Ryan until late morning when he dropped by my office. He peeked his head in. "Hey, have you recovered from last night?"

I held up my can of Diet Coke. "I've had some help. How about you?"

"I'm ready to run the Bolder Boulder again."

"Really? So, do you want to do a 10k after work?"

He gave me a crooked little grin and invited himself into my office. Before he spoke, he looked around. I did, too. I was wondering what he was looking for, but the mystery was soon solved. "How about instead of a 10K, we do something boring like dinner and a movie tomorrow night?" He tried to act covert.

"Boring sounds good," I grinned mischievously.

"Great. I'll pick you up at six?"

I nodded my head in agreement.

"We're still on for running tomorrow, right?" He was heading for the door.

"Of course." Could I smile any bigger? This was what I had been hoping for. The butterflies perked up and I found I no longer needed caffeine. Ryan was my new stimulant of choice.

I was giddy, like schoolgirl giddy. It made concentrating on work hard, but now, more than ever, I needed to do a good job. I didn't want my dad, or Ryan, getting the wrong idea. I wanted them both to see me as responsible and competent. I even took the first part of the CPA exam and passed it with flying colors. I was planning on surprising them both when it was a done deal. Part of me wasn't sure why I was bothering, because my long-term plan was psychology, but I figured it was a good plan B, and everyone always needed a good accountant. Besides, if I ever had my own practice, accounting skills would come in handy. I could offer tax tips as a bonus to my patients.

I crashed early on Thursday night, but woke up with a purpose and vengeance on Friday. First, run with my gorgeous neighbor.

Second, lunch with my best friend and former gorgeous neighbor. Last, but not least, make dinner and a movie the most non-boring date ever with current gorgeous neighbor and object of my desire. Don't worry, I wasn't objectifying Ryan. I was admiring him. Thoroughly.

My run with Ryan was our usual: good conversation, great view, and a great work out. Nothing special to report other than Ryan suggested we sign up for the local 10k in September. I agreed we should, not because I was a fan of races, but because it meant he saw us together in two months.

Work was work. I was counting down the minutes until Krissy and I would be reunited, and until my date. A noteworthy mention of the morning came in the form of Felicity asking if I would like to have lunch with her. She seemed nervous, and my dad scattered when she approached us. I asked her for a rain check since I already had plans with Krissy. We made a date for the following week. She seemed relieved, and hugged me. Weird.

Krissy and I met at our favorite soup and salad place. I figured I better go easy at lunch since I wasn't sure where Ryan was taking me. He said he was still looking at options and would let me know when he picked me up. I trusted his judgment, so I didn't mind the element of surprise.

Krissy and I met in the parking lot, and man, did the Bahamas look good on her, or maybe it was married life. Either way, she was tan and glowing like the northern lights. I had never seen her look so good.

"Krissy, you look amazing." I embraced her.

"I was thinking the same thing about you."

We got our favorite table on the patio and munched on fruit and shrimp salad while we caught up. She pulled out her iPad and showed me picture after picture of white sand beaches, crystal blue water, and palm trees. She and Chance made several appearances. Most of it had been documented on Facebook and Instagram, but it was fun to hear her personal account of what sounded like the time of her life.

She brought me some souvenirs. She handed me a canvas bag filled with lots of goodies, my favorite was the conch shell necklace. I wasted no time putting it on.

"It's beautiful. Thanks, Kris."

"You're welcome. But enough about me and my perfect life. Tell me about Ryan. I still can't believe you're dating him."

"I don't know if we're really *dating*, but yeah, it's pretty surreal."

"I used to think you were so crazy for having a crush on him, but look at you now."

I stuck my fork into a nice big, juicy, red strawberry. "I'm still crazy, but there's just something about him. You know?"

"Yeah, I know," she sighed dreamily. I knew who she was thinking about as she eyed the rock on her finger. "He's obviously into you, though. The way he looked at you when you danced at my wedding left no doubt. If I didn't know better, I would have thought you were already a couple."

I thought back to that moment. It was one of those moments I would relive over and over in my mind until the end of time. "It really was perfect," I sighed.

She grinned. "I'm happy for you. You deserve to be happy."

"Thanks, I'm just trying to remind myself that others can't make us happy or miserable, it's really our choice, but I admit being with Ryan has a very positive effect on me."

She reached across the table and held my hand. "You know, it's okay to get lost in someone, even if you don't know what the outcome will be. Let go and see where it takes you."

"When did you get so smart?"

"I just want to see you happy like this for a long time to come. You've had so much to deal with in your life the last several years, I want you to finally be able to leave that all behind and move on . . . and even find love."

I wiped an errant tear. She had been my sanity and sounding board for many years. I didn't think I would ever be able to fully express what she'd meant to me. She was a sister to me, in every sense that mattered.

As we hugged in parting, she brought up a novel idea. "We should double date sometime."

"Huh. Yeah, that would be fun. I'll talk to Ryan about it."

"How about tomorrow night?"

I thought about it. That seemed awfully soon.

"Oh, come on, CJ. We all know each other and we'll do something low key like dinner or bowling."

"Bowling?"

"Chance loves it."

I laughed. "Well, that's something I didn't know about him."

"Promise me you'll ask."

"Okay," I said in exasperation. She always got her way.

CHARLEE AND RYAN DATE, TAKE two. This go around I decided to forgo white, in case of rain. Instead I opted for a more romantic look, with a cream lace shirt and some flare jeans that hugged my curves. I also loved that he was tall enough that I could wear a shoe with heels.

He knocked on our door at precisely 6:00 p.m. My dad teased that he would get it and grill him about his intentions with his daughter. I didn't buy it for a second.

"Goodnight, Dad. Don't wait up." I called out as I went to answer the door.

"Have a good time, baby girl."

I opened the door to find Ryan standing there looking very handsome and holding one white rose. Now that was romantic.

"Hi." I smiled.

He held out the rose and seductively smiled. "Hi."

Yes, I wanted to swoon right then and there, but instead I took the perfectly shaped, almost fully bloomed rose and drank in the scent. It was nothing compared to the way Ryan smelled, but it was a close second. "Thank you."

"You're welcome. Are you ready to go?"

I nodded and followed him back to his house where his car sat ready in his driveway. He opened my door, but before I got in he said, "You look beautiful tonight." He paused. "I mean you are beautiful."

I almost teased and thanked him for not saying I looked grownup, but I didn't want to ruin the mood. I liked the feel of this moment when our gaze was fixed upon each other. Where I could see in his eyes he spoke the truth. For a moment, I felt beautiful.

"Thank you, Ryan," I spoke softly.

His hand ran down my cheek making me shiver.

Once we were both settled in his car, I turned to him. "So where are we going?"

"I thought we would head up to Boulder."

"Why? We have a great movie theater here."

"Boulder has a great theater, too," he stumbled on his words.

"Yeah . . . but its forty-five minutes from here."

He cleared his throat. "There's a . . . great Mediterranean restaurant there I want to take you to."

I narrowed my eyes at him.

He was acting suspicious, not looking my way. "Seriously, you'll thank me."

"If you say so."

He reached over and held my hand. "Does it really matter where we go?"

I looked down at our hands, and I felt that wonderful sick feeling in the pit of my stomach that only he seemed to invoke. I shook my head no.

Upon arriving at our destination, I forgot why I even thought about objecting. The restaurant was near the Pearl Street Mall and there was a great vibe going on. Bands were playing and lots of people were out and about, enjoying the summer evening. Not to mention, Boulder is just one more beautiful city in my home state. Can you tell I'm biased? It sure beats cornfields, I'll tell you that.

Ryan looked happy as we walked hand-in-hand.

"How set are you on seeing a movie?" I asked him as we strolled to the restaurant.

"What do you have in mind?"

I looked around at the activity that surrounded us. I was totally digging the live music and street performers. "It seems a shame to be indoors when we could enjoy all of this." I waved my hand around.

"Life is never boring with you, is it?"

"Gosh, I hope not."

He smiled and kissed the top of my head. "There wasn't anything good playing anyway."

"You know, I think I may like you."

He wrapped his arm around my waist and pulled me to him as we finished our short walk to the restaurant. It was packed on a Friday night, but Ryan had made reservations, and we were seated right away. He was obviously well connected. I guess I needed better friends, or maybe more of them.

Ryan was right, I was thanking him profusely. The food was to-die-for amazing. We stuffed ourselves on paella and smoked chicken. Don't even get me started on the bread and the lemon pound cake with raspberry mousse for dessert. I was going to have to run ten miles the next day to burn it all off, but I would never regret it. And the company was wonderful.

We talked mostly about Josh. I loved how he talked about how it felt to hold him for the first time or the first time Josh said "Dada" or took his first step. My heart also broke for him because he felt like he was missing half of Josh's life. He was especially missing him this week. Their only communication was by phone.

"Josh has asked about his Cherry."

"He's staked his claim, has he?"

"I'm raising him right," he teased.

"You can tell him I'm all his."

"All his?" Ryan arched his eyebrow.

"You know, until perhaps someone older that doesn't drive a tricycle comes along."

He laughed at me, and I loved every second of it. It ranked right up there with Josh's giggle.

After dinner, we started at the east end of Pearl Street Mall. We enjoyed the artwork on display by some of the local artists. Well, at least most of it. Some people really took interpretation a little overboard, and then there were those that liked to bare it all, if you get my drift. I was happy to see my date avert his eyes and gaze upon me when we happened upon the exhibitionists. We found safer fare when we headed west. What would a street fair, of sorts, be without face painting? There was a lovely older couple set up offering just that. I had to do it. It amused Ryan when I took my seat in the folding chair.

"So what will it be young lady?" The gentleman of the pair, named Henry, was the artist.

"Hmm," I thought. "You choose."

Henry grinned and showed off his dentures. "I like you. You have a lot of spirit."

"That she does," Ryan agreed.

Henry looked between the two of us and smiled.

Ryan's phone went off in the midst of my face painting project. "Charlee, do you mind if I get this?"

"Not at all." I watched him walk away and pick up the phone. I bet it was Josh by the way his eyes lit up. The thought made me smile.

Henry went to work and talked while he painted. I had a hard time holding still, the brush tickled. I also followed Ryan's movements.

"So who is that fella?" Henry asked.

"A friend."

Henry gave me a scrutinizing glance.

"A very good friend," I amended.

"Ahhh. There's something wonderful about a new 'friendship' isn't there?"

"Yes, very much so."

"Do you know how to tell if a man is in love, dear?"

I shook my head no.

"It's all in his eyes. He will look at you like you hold the stars and the moon in them."

He turned from me and gazed at his wife. It was a perfect demonstration.

I sighed wistfully, and with that, he handed me a mirror. He had painted a moon near the corner of my right eye with tiny stars trailing down my cheek.

"It's beautiful. Thank you."

Ryan rejoined us as I was about to pay. He stepped in and paid for me instead. Henry smiled at the both of us, but he gently grabbed my arm. "Remember, sometimes people can't see the forest for the trees."

I shook my head, confused. What was that supposed to mean? I wanted to ask him, but he turned from me to greet his next customer.

"What was that all about?" Ryan asked when we walked away.

168

"I'm not sure. Anyway, how is Josh?"

"Victoria says he's having a great time with his grandparents."

"Oh . . . that was Victoria? Not Josh?"

"Josh was already asleep."

"I guess it was late." I knew it shouldn't bother me that he talked to her, and I guess it didn't. What bothered me was his reaction to her. It had excited him that she called, or so it had seemed.

"So where to next?" Ryan looked around.

My sights and ears fixed on the bluegrass band playing down toward the west end of the mall. I reached for Ryan's hand and led him to the small crowd that had gathered around them. I didn't listen to a lot of bluegrass, but I was intrigued with the four-part harmony from the all-women band performing. Their voices blended, but in dissonance, if that made sense; it was hauntingly beautiful. The song was lamenting the loss of love. I was mesmerized by it. Maybe I would have to listen to more bluegrass.

Their next song surprised me because I recognized it. It was a cover of "When You Say Nothing at All" by Alison Krauss. I adored that song. I turned to Ryan. "Dance with me."

His eyes widened. "Here?"

"Yes."

"No one else is dancing."

"So?"

He froze. Meanwhile, I took matters into my own hands. I wrapped my hands around his neck and pulled him to me in the middle of the small crowd.

I could feel him sigh when he wrapped his arms around my waist and drew me closer. "Why do I let you talk me into these things?"

"Because you know you want to."

He reached up and lightly ran his finger across my moon and stars. "I don't think that's it."

"Then why?"

He didn't answer, at least not verbally. He barely skimmed his lips across my own before he rested his cheek against mine. I was so wrapped up in him that I barely noticed the stares and the oohing and aahhing around us. My senses were completely fixed on the man who held me in his arms and perfectly kept in time to the rhythm of the song. He surprised me by twirling me out. He dazzled me with his smile when he drew me back to him. That smile turned heated as his hand held mine; he drew our hands in and held them close to my heart. I felt like I was on fire. If we weren't in a crowd, I would have kissed him until I needed to breathe, though I was finding breathing at all difficult at the moment. My insides felt like a roller coaster that I never wanted to get off.

Then the music stopped and just like that, the magic of the moment ended. Ryan was quick to let me go, and my body was slow to regain its equilibrium. Ryan didn't seem as affected by me as I was by him. It gave me some pause.

"Do you mind if we look at some of the handmade toy booths?" Ryan's question brought me out of my thoughts of him.

"No, of course not."

We walked in silence toward the booth.

"Thanks for dancing with me." I should have said that earlier.

He smiled over at me, but didn't say anything.

I wasn't quite sure what to make of him.

When we drove home that night, he seemed to be in a thoughtful state. It was almost as if he didn't want to be disturbed in his thoughts. He wasn't rude, but he was awfully quiet. It made me nervous to ask him if he wanted to hang out the next day with Krissy and Chance. I almost didn't, but Krissy had texted me earlier saying how much she and Chance were looking forward to going out with us.

Ryan walked me to my door from his house. He held my hand during the short walk over.

"I had a really great time. Thank you."

"Me, too," he said absentmindedly.

"Really?"

He stopped on my driveway and met my eyes. "Yes."

"Okay."

We finished the walk up to my porch. I wasn't sure what to expect from him in parting. I knew what I wanted, but I wasn't sure that was on the table for him. He seemed to be stingy with his kisses. As he peered into my eyes, he looked unsure of how to proceed as well, but he leaned in. At the last second, he turned his head and kissed my cheek. My waiting lips rubbed themselves together and managed a weak smile.

"Well, goodnight." He turned to walk home.

"Oh. I wanted to ask you something." That sounded lame.

He paused and faced me.

I nervously ran my fingers through my hair, which was very unlike me. I wasn't usually this nervous around men. "Krissy and Chance want us to hang out with them tomorrow night. They were thinking dinner or bowling."

Ryan's brows furrowed.

"Yeah, I know bowling seems a little weird, but who knew, Chance loves it." I tried to play it off lightheartedly.

Concern overtook his features. He let out a huge intake of air. "Charlee, I like you. I really like you."

"I really like you, too," I returned.

He didn't even crack a smile. "I don't know if I'm ready to announce to the world that I'm dating you, and I really need to talk to Victoria about it."

Suddenly it all made sense, or at least the whole going to Boulder thing did. I wasn't sure why he needed to talk to his ex-wife about me. "Oh, my gosh. I get it now. I guess when you said you couldn't think of anyone that would be embarrassed to be seen with me, you should have added, except yourself."

His face turned red. "No, it's not like that. I meant what I said. It's just, you were a kid and my neighbor and . . . Victoria . . . and . . ." he kept stuttering like an idiot.

I reached inside my bag for my keys and shook my head. I didn't need this or him. "You know what? You don't need to worry about it, because I don't think we should continue dating."

He reached for my arm. "Come on, Charlee, don't be like that."

I shook my head in disgust. "Don't be like that? What? Self-respecting? Goodbye, Ryan." I left him standing there, stunned, on my porch. I wanted to slam the door, but I didn't want to wake up my dad. At least I hoped he was asleep. I was too upset to talk to anyone. I felt so foolish.

Fifteen

WELL, THAT WAS A SUPER short-lived dream. I knew I was stupid to even think we would ever be anything more than neighbors, but in my defense, he kind of gave me some hope. But I wasn't desperate and I had dignity. I refused to be with someone that was embarrassed to be seen with me. I mean, really? Not once had I ever had a man behave like that toward me. Jay always was proud to have me by his side, and even Aidan seemed to think it was an enviable position.

I stomped down to my room. The first thing I saw was the dried-out bouquets from the wedding two weeks ago. I grabbed the stupid one I caught and threw it in the trash along with the ticket stubs Ryan let me keep from the concert. Ryan Tedder was back to number one Ryan, and I . . . I . . . was . . . unbelievably sad. I sat on my bed after my little tirade and willed myself not to cry. I reminded myself that I wouldn't let a man make me cry unless it involved the happy kind of tears. I had watched my mother lose herself over not only my dad, but a string of losers after him. That would never be me.

After several minutes, I got up and readied myself for bed. I looked in the mirror at the beautifully painted moon and stars. I knew there was no hope that Ryan would ever look at me that way. For a second, the tears threatened to appear, but I held them at bay. Then I remembered Henry's odd advice after he had painted the moon and stars on my cheek. I knew what couldn't see the forest for the trees meant, but why would he say that to me? Oh well. I got a makeup remover wipe out and scrubbed my face with a fury.

It took forever to fall asleep; the sting of Ryan's embarrassment of me wouldn't let me be. Self-doubt and insecurity were running rampant, and I was cursing Krissy for being married. If she was still single, I could have called or driven to her apartment. She would be consoling me or at least stuffing my face with ice cream—anything to dull the pain of rejection and humiliation. Instead, I was left to nurse my own wounds. I took to tossing and turning and punching my pillow. When that didn't work, I found my basketball, bounced it against the wood floor, and ran old drills in my head.

I took the ball to bed with me and kept throwing it toward the ceiling, only barely missing the ceiling fan. Finally exhaustion set in. I clung to the ball like a doll and fell asleep with it in my arms. It wasn't the first time that had happened, but it had been years. I woke up, with basketball marks on my arms, and to the sound of chore music. Today's selection was Kansas' "Dust in the Wind." It seemed fitting. My short-lived relationship with Ryan was dust.

Within minutes I joined my dad upstairs. He was busy making French toast, bless him. I loved that stuff.

"Hi, Daddy."

He turned from the griddle. "Hey, kiddo. How was your night out?"

I sank into the stool nearest me and leaned my head against my hand. "Which part?" I sighed.

His eyes narrowed in concern before he turned back to the griddle and flipped a couple of pieces of French toast onto a plate. He turned back around and served them to me. "What happened? Trouble in Loveland?"

"Oh, ha ha." I don't know how many times people in Kansas thought I was joking when I said I grew up in Loveland. I thought about whether or not I should tell my dad what happened. Would he be upset that Ryan was embarrassed to be seen with me? How would that affect their friendship and partnership? "Don't worry about it, Dad. Just know that Ryan and I won't be seeing each other anymore. Oh, and thanks for the French toast." I reached for the syrup bottle near me.

My dad stood there, apparently at a loss for words.

I, on the other hand, dug in. "Mmmm . . . This is good." My mouth was somewhat full.

"CJ, you can talk to me."

"Really, there's no need."

He didn't believe me. "Do you want to go for a bike ride or hang out on the boat? I had plans, but I'll change them if you need me."

"Daddy, I'm fine, really. Don't change your plans on account of me."

He reached over the counter and tipped up my chin. "Charlee, you are the priority in my life."

A dumb tear escaped. I supposed a dad was worth crying over. "Thank you, but really, I already had plans. Go enjoy your day." I was planning on taking the second part of that ridiculous CPA exam.

"Are you sure?"

"Positive. What do you have planned?"

He pinked a little and stood up straighter. "Just hitting the golf course."

Odd. Very odd. "That sounds like fun."

He turned around hastily. "Just golf."

I was curious about his strange behavior, but I was still too wrapped up in my own thoughts about Ryan, so I didn't fish for details. I lazily ate and chatted with my dad about all subjects non-Ryan related. I could tell my dad wanted to broach the subject, but I got the feeling he, too, felt like the less he knew the better. I cleaned up the kitchen while he got ready.

He was ready before I even had a chance to mop the floor.

"So how does your old man look?"

I looked him over from head to toe. He was awfully dressed up to be going golfing. He was wearing nice dress shorts and a button-up, collared shirt. "You look very distinguished. What's the occasion?"

"No occasion," he waved off my scrutiny, which only made me scrutinize him more. He was acting different.

"If you say so."

He briskly walked my way and met me at the sink where he kissed my head. "Are you sure you're okay with me leaving?"

"Yes, Daddy. I've been on my own for a long time now."

"All right. Well, have a good day, and don't let Ryan bother you.

I'm sure whatever it is, you two kids will work it out." He was too chipper.

I didn't disagree with him, at least not out loud. I knew we wouldn't be working it out, and I'll be honest, that thought sucked, because I really liked him. At least I really liked him when I wasn't an embarrassment to him. I tried my best not to think about him as I cleaned and started laundry. Unfortunately, my blouse from the previous night smelled like him and I couldn't help but drink it in. After I tortured myself, I threw it in my basket and decided I better start looking for my own place. I knew I would have to work with Ryan for a while. My dad paid me too well, and I needed that money if I wanted to go back to school and not go into major debt. As an accountant, and someone that could calculate interest, I instructed myself not to go that route. But the less I had to be around Ryan, the better I would be.

Krissy called as soon as I settled on the couch in the basement with my laptop, ready to take part two of my exam. I sighed and debated answering. I wanted to talk to her and even vent, but it was kind of humiliating that Ryan was embarrassed to be seen with me. It wasn't helping my self-esteem, I'll tell you that.

I answered.

"Chance called the bowling alley in Loveland and got us a time at seven. Will that work for you guys?" She only let me get in a hello.

"I'm sorry, but it will only be the two of you."

"What? Why?"

I threw my pride out the window and told her the whole mortifying tale.

"Oooo. Should I bring ice cream over?"

"Thanks, but no. I don't think ice cream will cure this."

"CJ, maybe it's not as bad as you say. You have to admit, it's got to be a little weird for him. I mean, you served punch at his wedding."

A little laugh escaped. "Yeah, that is weird, but do I look and act like some teenage girl?"

"No. You're all woman, honey. Ask all of Chance's friends who, by the way, would all love to show you a good time."

"Pass."

"Why don't you come out with us anyway? I think they even do karaoke at this bowling alley."

"I love you guys, but I can't bear to be the single friend of newlyweds. Maybe once you're over the whole honeymoon phase we'll talk."

She sighed deeply.

"Yeah, I know." I wasn't sure those two would ever get out of that phase. "By the way, good luck at your audition on Monday."

"I'm so nervous, but excited," she squealed.

"You'll be terrific. And maybe if you make it, you can introduce me to an attractive single football player."

"You know I will."

I'm sure she would, but knowing me, I wouldn't be interested.

On that dismal note, I started taking my exam. Was it conceited to say it was easy? Long and boring, yes, but definitely not challenging. To make myself feel better, I opened my *Psychology Today* issue online and read a fascinating article on how conflicting goals can make you a better decision maker. It was a timely article for me. Then I read the nine most common mistakes couples make in a relationship. There wasn't anything helpful, as we weren't a couple or in a relationship.

My dad came home late for just golfing—it was dinner time. He was wearing a big ol' grin and sporting a nice little sunburn, but I hadn't seen him happy like that in years. He was even whistling to himself.

"Wow, you must have shot like a seventy."

"Nope." He kissed my head. "Ninety."

"Then why are you so happy?"

"Because it's a beautiful day and my beautiful daughter and I are going to go to dinner."

"We are?"

"Yes, we are, so go get ready. I made reservations at the 4th Street Chophouse."

"You really are in a good mood."

I ran down to my room and put on my pretty red sundress, threw up my hair, and touched up my makeup. I had just put on my lip stain when my phone's text alert chimed. I reached into my bag and pulled it out. It said I had two missed calls in addition to the text, all from my neighbor.

Charlee, I wish you would answer my calls.

I threw my phone back in my bag. I had no intention of answering his calls. I was surprised he'd called. I guess talking on the phone could be done privately, without anyone knowing that he was actually talking to me.

I walked upstairs to find my dad dressed well in pressed slacks and a dress shirt. He was still wearing his smile too.

"There's my beauty."

His smile and compliments were infectious. Dads were way better than ice cream, I decided. We laughed and talked our way through filet mignon, salmon, and six-layer chocolate cake. I had made up for the six weeks of limiting my calorie intake. I needed to run, but I would have to start doing it at night or hit my dad's treadmill in the basement.

"Are you sure you don't want to talk about Ryan?" my dad asked on the way home.

I blew out a large breath. "Ryan has some reservations about dating me."

"Too beautiful, too smart?"

"No, Dad."

"Ahhh . . . too young."

"Bingo."

"He'll get over it."

"It doesn't matter."

"I told you this wouldn't be easy, kiddo."

"You were right. But you failed to mention how short-lived it would be."

"You think so, huh?"

"I know so."

He reached over and patted my knee.

I grabbed his hand. "I love you, Dad."

He squeezed my hand tight. "I love you, kiddo."

Fixing my relationship with my dad righted my world in a lot of ways. It brought me a peace that I had long missed and that sense of belonging I craved. I wondered how he was going to take it when I told him I didn't want to be an accountant and that I was planning on moving out.

Sunday was a rare day in Colorado; it rained all day. It fit my mood perfectly. As much as I didn't want to care about Ryan, I did. I spent most of the day as a slug on the couch holding onto a throw pillow and watching old westerns with my dad. I was about ready to get on the treadmill and run, when the doorbell rang. I looked over and my dad was sound asleep on his chair, snoring away. A bomb could have gone off and he wouldn't have stirred. I guess that meant I was getting the door. I dragged my lazy butt off the couch and ran up to tell the poor solicitor we weren't interested. I opened the door and found I was interested, well, at least partially interested.

My favorite redheaded three-year-old stood under the cover of our porch as the thunderstorm raged. "Cherry!" He ran straight to me and hugged my legs.

I picked him up and held him to me. "Hey, big guy."

I glanced at his daddy, who looked hopeful. He wore a tentative smile. "Charlee," he started to say.

I turned my attention back to his son.

"Will you play with me, Cherry?"

"Of course." I snuggled him close and shut the door on his daddy. I walked Josh downstairs to the family room to the sound of the knocking door. I nudged my dad awake and he startled. "Sorry, Dad, but someone's at the door."

He was still groggy when he sat up. "Josh?"

"Josh is here to play."

My dad rubbed his face. "Then who's knocking on the door?"

I grinned wickedly and walked off with my playdate.

"Bye-bye." Josh waved at my dad.

I heard the doorbell ring a few more times, but I ignored it and walked Josh down to the basement. "I've missed you this week." I rubbed his nose with mine, making him giggle. I loved this kid. His dad, not so much. I looked over the basement, not sure what we would do. It wasn't exactly a kiddie haven. I eyed the pool table and thought that could be fun. I set Josh down. "Okay, big guy, you're going to have your first lesson on how to shoot pool. Believe me, you'll thank me someday, the chicks dig a man who can shoot pool."

"Is that so?"

I looked up to find a smug looking Ryan walking down the stairs.

I turned from him and tried to find the shortest cue stick we had for Josh.

"I'm going to play pool, Daddy." Josh informed his dad.

Ryan picked up his son and tickled him. "Why don't you let Charlee and me play and you can watch."

"I don't think so." I nixed that idea.

Ryan smiled over at me. I was working on properly racking the balls, not that Josh would know the difference. "Come on, Charlee." He walked over to me with Josh in his arms and stopped inches away from me.

I really hated that he smelled and looked so good. It wasn't fair. "Why are you even here? I would hate to ruin your reputation."

His dazzling smile faded. "So I'm an idiot and I'm sorry."

"Now that we've settled that, I guess you can go home."

He caught me off guard and pulled me to him and Josh. Thankfully, Josh giggled about it because Ryan's look was my undoing. It was a mix of serious and impassioned, and whoa, did it work for him. It almost made me feel lightheaded. Why did he have such an effect on me? I tried to play it cool, but I'm pretty sure I failed miserably. I cracked a small smile. I tried to cover it up with indifference, but he noticed and grinned.

"Please forgive me and come out to dinner with us."

"Where? Denver?" That was at least a good hour away.

He pressed his lips together. "Charlee, I'm sorry."

"Fine, I forgive you, but I still don't think we should date."

He thought for a moment. He still held me and Josh to him. I thought I should probably back away, but I was conflicted and the butterflies were vetoing my mind.

"How's this? We play one game of pool and if I win, you agree to go out to dinner with us."

"What if I win?"

"That's your choice."

"Fine, you're on." I was great at pool, so I liked my odds.

Ryan set Josh on the couch. "Watch and learn, buddy."

"I want to play," Josh whined.

"You can help me," his daddy offered as an alternative. He let Josh chalk the end of his cue stick. It sort of appeased him.

Ryan met me back at the table where the balls were racked tight and perfectly.

"I'll let you break." I was more than cocky.

"Oh, no. We're going to flip for it, so when I beat you, it will be fair and square." He pulled a quarter out of his pocket. "I'll flip, you call."

I had to admit I was kind of turned on by this in-control Ryan, but I shrugged my shoulders. "Have it your way."

"Believe me, I plan to." He flipped the coin high in the air.

"Heads," I called.

He caught the coin and laid it flat against his left hand with his right hand hiding it from view. He grinned at me before he lifted his hand to reveal the coin tail side up. His eyes lit up, and he wasted no time positioning his cue on the table. He used the open bridge method and his stance was perfect. He lined the cue ball up and broke the balls with commanding force. So, maybe this wasn't going to be as easy as I thought.

Three balls went into the corner pockets, two striped and one solid. He called stripes. He stood up, proud of himself.

"I'm impressed, but don't count me out."

"Never."

I let Josh chalk my cue stick too. I had him kiss it for good luck. He thought that was funny. Ryan and I took turns entertaining him between turns. I elicited Josh's help in making lots of noise while it was his daddy's turn, but that wasn't working. Ryan was good, even better than my dad, who had some mad skills that he had passed on to me.

"Where did you learn how to play?" I asked him after his fifth ball went in flawlessly on the right-side pocket.

"Here in this basement."

"Really?"

"It was cheaper than therapy."

I looked between him and Josh, who sat on my lap. I felt very sorry for them both. I knew how it felt to have your world uprooted. "I'm sorry."

Ryan stood up from his stance over the table and locked eyes with me. "I am sorry, Charlee. I'm not embarrassed to be with you. I know I have some things to get over, but I enjoy spending time with you. There's something about you."

"And what's that?"

"For starters, you have this way of making everything and everybody come to life around you." He gave me that charming smile of his. "Please come out with Josh and me?"

"Well, since it looks like I'm going to lose anyway . . . Apparently, my dad has been holding out on me."

"I don't know about that. I just needed a good friend at the time."

"I can relate to that." I squeezed Josh.

"So, I'm starving. Do you want to go?" He set down his stick.

I raised Josh's arms up. "Daddy wins."

"Yay!" Josh shouted.

We let Josh sit on the table and push all the balls into the pockets. I'm not sure if my dad would appreciate it, but it kept Josh occupied for a moment while his dad kissed me. "I missed you this weekend," he whispered against my lips and held me close.

"You sound surprised."

"As always, with you."

Sixteen

CHARLEE AND RYAN TAKE TWO. So this was where we stood. It was interesting ground. My dad was right, dating a divorced dad was a little tricky. Ryan and Victoria had agreed that if ever they dated someone that they would be introducing Josh to, they would get approval from each other. I guess I was lucky woman number one, and from the sounds of it, Victoria wasn't thrilled with the idea, which was odd since I had spent a lot of time with Josh before I started dating Ryan. In a way, I could understand. I didn't mind that Ryan made her aware of me, she was the mom and I respected that. I didn't appreciate when she called me and lectured me about how to treat her son, that he would never call me mom, and my favorite part, "I just assumed you were his babysitter from the way Josh and Ryan talked about you. I'm surprised that Ryan would even consider dating someone so young."

I bit my tongue. I figured having words with her wasn't going to help my cause any, besides, it wasn't like we were planning on anything serious. We were only dating. She didn't need to worry about Josh calling me mom, I was quite fond of Cherry.

I didn't mention the call to Ryan. I assumed he knew it took place since he gave her my number, which I didn't love him for, but I got it. I would be protective of my kid too, but I hoped that I would be a heck of a lot nicer than she was. I would hope I would try and be friends with the other woman. Hopefully, I would never be in that situation. I hated divorce, and I prayed I would never have one of my own, especially if there were children involved.

Ryan and I weren't running around announcing that we were seeing each other, but in light of our first little blow-up, he avoided acting like he was embarrassed to be seen with me. Even at the office, if we would go out to lunch, he would come to my office and get me. He would even touch the small of my back as we walked out together. I knew we turned some heads, but it didn't bother me at all.

I found a confidant in Felicity, who happened to be taking a lot of interest in me. I had Krissy and she would be forever my go to girl, but it was nice to have a more mature woman's perspective. Felicity and I started having standing lunch dates on Tuesdays. It was perfect timing since Victoria had called the night before, and I was still trying to process the whole conversation, which was basically one sided. All I could think of to say at the end was that I loved Josh and I would never do anything to intentionally hurt him and that I would do whatever I could to protect him. She pretty much scoffed at it and hung up.

"So what do you think?" I asked Felicity after regurgitating the whole conversation with Victoria.

Her ice blue eyes peered at me in a maternal sort of way. She contemplated what to say. "I'm trying to leave my bias for both you and Ryan out of this," she began. "She didn't win a lot of points with me. Her behavior and attitude toward Ryan over the years when she would come in was anything but impressive. But I will give her this, she loves that little boy of hers."

"I know, and I respect her for that, but I don't want her to feel like she can walk all over me."

"She most certainly doesn't have the right to do that. What does Ryan think?"

"I didn't tell him about it. He's still trying to come to terms with me, and I didn't want to add any more doubts."

"What you mean, come to terms with you? He looks pretty smitten from where I stand."

"I wouldn't call him smitten, more like he has moments of Charlee appreciation."

She laughed at me. "I like that, Charlee appreciation."

"I would prefer Charlee infatuation, but maybe we'll work our way up to it."

She patted my hand on the table. "I'm pretty sure you're already there. If you could see the way he looks at you when you walk by or come to talk to your dad, he gets lost in you."

I liked the sound of that, but his actions didn't quite translate. I mean, sometimes I felt like that. Like that morning after we were done with our run and walking toward my gate, he reached for my hand and pulled me to him and kissed me ever so sweetly. Enough to get the blood flowing again, but as always, he cut it short. Just as I felt like we were getting to the good part, you know, the part where I sink into him and for a moment we only existed for each other. Every time I would get to that place, he would abruptly part from my lips and release me from his hold. It was frustrating.

"So what about you, Felicity? Do you mind me asking if you date?"

She sat up straighter and smiled nervously.

"I'm sorry. Did I overstep my bounds?"

"Not at all. It's just, there is somebody and it's complicated."

I held up my Diet Coke. "Well, here's to figuring it all out."

She held up her lemonade and clinked glasses with me. "Amen."

Ryan and I spent a rare evening alone at his house that night curled up on his couch watching the Rockies. And unfortunately, we were watching the game. I could think of better ways to employ our time alone, but I tried my best to enjoy being in his arms and yelling at the umps to get glasses or a new job.

"Wow, you're feisty," Ryan commented.

"Sorry, bad refs of any kind are a huge pet peeve of mine, but I come by it honestly. My dad has been kicked out of a couple of my games before."

He kissed the side of my head. "Just remind me not to get on your bad side."

"I don't have a bad side," I teased.

"True. All of your sides look good to me."

I turned and smiled at him. "Flattery will get you everywhere."

"Really? Is that all it takes with you?"

"No, not really."

"That's what I thought." He leaned in and barely brushed my lips. Did he know how frustrating that was for me? It was like he was teasing me, but it reminded me of my conversation with Felicity earlier.

"Hey, do you know who Felicity dates?"

His look asked if I was joking.

"Yeah, I know, odd change of subject, but she mentioned she was seeing someone today, but that it was a complicated situation."

"I don't know. I try to stay out of the employee's personal lives."

I arched my eyebrows. "Is that so?"

"With the exception of a couple of people."

"Really? Are you seeing someone else there I should know about?"

He rolled his gorgeous green eyes at me. "I meant your dad."

"He's all right, I guess."

"I'm kind of partial to his daughter."

"Well, what a coincidence, she's kind of partial to you." This time I took matters into my own hands and leaned in and kissed him. He hesitated, as if he had to think about it for a moment when I pressed my lips against his. I had never had a guy behave like him. I was about to ask him if he had an aversion to kissing me, but it was like something finally clicked. He reached up and placed his hands behind my head. His lips pressed firmly against mine. I sank into him and my lips parted. He responded by working his strong hands up and through my hair, in turn drawing me closer to him. *Finally*, I thought, but just as I thought it, his lips released my own. His hands found their way to my arms where he held me in place. He stared at me as though he was troubled.

"Is everything okay?" I was so confused. Maybe he thought I was a horrible kisser or maybe I had bad breath. I was pretty sure the latter wasn't the case, I brushed, flossed, and OD'd on breath mints, but I couldn't judge on whether I was a good kisser or not. I hadn't had any complaints, but who knew.

"Everything's great."

"Okay . . ." I turned from him. He resumed putting his arm back around me. I settled against him. Unease hung in the air.

That phrase pretty much described our relationship, uneasy. I wasn't sure why it was. We got along great. When we were together, our time was full of great conversations and lots of fun, but there was always this unseen barrier. I felt like he didn't want to let me in all the way, and I couldn't let him in because he was so unsure with me. That was how we rounded out July and the first half of August.

In the midst of my uncertain relationship with Ryan, I was contemplating my future plans. I decided to apply to both CU and CSU's Master of Psychology programs for a winter term start. I wrote the most amazing essays explaining why I would be a fabulous candidate. It was a little bit of a sob story, but I really, really wanted to get in. I also took the third part of the CPA exam and, not to be modest, I passed with flying colors. I was also looking at apartments online and during my lunch hours. I was saving up as much money as I could living at home, in hopes of being able to move closer to whichever school chose me, if either did. I still hadn't broached the subject with my dad. He was happy with the way things were. In fact, he was ridiculously happy, as of late. I kept asking him why, and he would always point to me, but I got the feeling it wasn't only me.

My relationship with Ryan, though, consumed a lot of my thoughts, and as much as I liked him and wanted to be with him, I was beginning to feel like it would be best if we took a step back. Again, we had a great time together, but I always felt like he was uneasy with me. I had just about decided that's what I was going to do, but then he threw me for a loop.

We had just finished a 10k before work because we were still training for the race in September. It had been a rough one for me. Ryan was a better runner, and he pushed me, which was good, but some mornings I wanted to give up. It had been one of those mornings.

We stopped when we came to his house. I was out of breath, but he was almost back to normal breathing patterns. How he did it, I didn't know. I was stretching out my muscles and trying to regulate my breathing when he approached me. He took my reddened face in his hands. "Have I mentioned lately how beautiful I think you are?"

"No, and I'm not sure that when I'm a hot mess is the right moment."

"I know I should say it more. You are beautiful and . . . hot." He rubbed his thumbs across my cheeks. His eyes looked inviting, but I had been fooled before, so I stuck to gazing into them.

"Thanks, Ryan."

He narrowed his eyes at my lack of enthusiasm. "Charlee," he whispered. He leaned his face toward mine and rested his sweaty forehead against my own. "I hope you haven't made any plans for this weekend because I want to monopolize all of your time."

"I guess I'll have to cancel all my other dates."

He groaned before his lips melded briefly with mine. "I would say that's funny, but I don't find it comical at all."

"I thought it was hilarious."

He kissed me once more. "So, I'll pick you up after I get Josh."

"Uh huh," I whispered.

"I can't wait." He headed toward his opened gate.

I walked off, shaking my head. I wasn't sure what to make of him. Did he know I was thinking about taking a step back to reevaluate? Or did he really want to be with me? Sometimes it was hard to tell with him.

At work I was even more surprised when a bouquet of white roses was delivered to me. The card read simply, *See you tonight, beautiful.* I sighed and held the card to my chest. I looked up the meaning of white roses. They are meant to express hope in the future. I liked that . . . a lot.

I instant messaged Ryan through our office's messaging system. I got the flowers, they're beautiful, and so are you. Thank you.

He replied right back, You're welcome. Prepare yourself for a weekend of fun.

I'm more than ready.

Perfect. I'll see you soon.

My hopes about our relationship soared in a way that they hadn't previously. Maybe there was some hope for us after all.

Ryan was true to his word, he had planned a super fun weekend. Friday night was laser tag, which Josh found to be amazing. I had more fun watching him trying to shoot his daddy than playing myself. I found that I missed Josh during the week. I couldn't even imagine how Ryan felt. I knew Krissy thought it was weird that a lot of our dates included Josh, but I liked it.

That night Josh asked if I would put him to bed. I was pleased and honored, but I looked to Ryan for approval. Ryan nodded and smiled.

Josh took me by the hand and pulled me toward his room. I grabbed onto Ryan's hand. "I think your dad should help."

Ryan smiled, got up, and followed us.

I didn't want to take away one of his nights. He only had a few every week.

Ryan took one side of his bed, and I took the other. I pulled Josh's light blanket over him and read his favorite book about fire trucks to him. When the book was over, Josh requested that I sing for him.

Ryan looked surprised. It wasn't the first time I had put Josh to bed, but it was the first time with his dad there. I had watched him a couple of times when my dad and Ryan had late night business meetings with clients or potential clients, and then there was that time I babysat when he'd had a date.

I brushed Josh's brow gently with my hand. He had the softest skin. I loved his curly red hair and those eyes that looked just like his dad's. "What do you want me to sing?"

"Close your eyes," he requested. Not quite the title, but close enough.

I sang softly, and Josh closed his eyes. I snuck a glance at his dad who was looking at me tenderly. I finished and kissed Josh's forehead.

He opened his big eyes. "I love you, Cherry." He had never said that before.

My heart melted into a big pile of goo. "I love you, too." I kissed his forehead once more. "Sleep tight."

I looked over to find Ryan looking unsure. He turned to his son and hugged and kissed him goodnight.

We walked out quietly together. As soon as we were in the living room, I pulled him to me until we were face to face. "Did it bother you that Josh said he loved me?"

His gaze was thoughtful. "No, I just worry."

"About what?"

"For starters, what his mom will think. This isn't easy for her. I think she feels threatened by you."

"Why?"

"Because you're young, beautiful, and fun. I think Josh talks about you quite a bit."

I couldn't help but smile about that fact. I was touched he talked about me. "I'm not trying to replace his mother. And from what I remember, she's young and beautiful, too."

"She's older than me."

"Really? So you like older women?"

"It's usually who I've dated in the past."

"Oh."

He let go of my hand and placed his on the small of my back, pulling me toward him. He smiled seductively. "But, I'm thinking of turning over a new leaf." He kissed me. Our lips matched so perfectly together, but I let him be the guide, and as always, the tour was sweet, but short.

I didn't want to be done with him. I embraced him and let my head fall on his shoulder. I had this desire to be close to him, and not just physically. I was happy when he reciprocated and drew me as close as he could. I felt the lightest of kisses on the top of my head. I wanted to stay like that forever. But this wash of warmth hit me like a tidal wave. I felt more than I should for him, at least at this point in our relationship. It scared me, for more reasons than one. I was the one to back away this time.

It was his turn to look confused. "Are you okay?"

I nodded and gave him a small smile. I tried to shake off the feeling and the temporary insanity of it, but it wasn't going anywhere as I looked at him. I wasn't sure where it was all coming from. This was new to me. I was grateful for the early day we planned on having the next day; it gave me a great excuse to leave. I wasn't ready for such feelings for him, especially since I knew they weren't shared. I told myself to relax—no one had to know but me.

I woke up feeling a little unsettled from the previous night's revelation. I had hoped I would wake up and those feelings wouldn't be there, but I did a gut check and they were alive and well. I reminded myself no one had to know but me, so it was okay. I showered and threw on my turquoise tankini with halter straps and a white sarong. We were headed to Water World today before it closed for the season. Josh was looking forward to it; he loved the water. I was, too. I hadn't been to Water World in forever. As a teenager, it was one of those places I was constantly begging my parents to take me and my friends to.

I didn't need to bother with makeup since we would be in the water and sun all day, so I threw up my hair, moisturized, and called it good. The traditional Saturday music was on; this time it was Heart's "What About Love." It was eerily fitting. *What about love?* Why did I have to fall in love with a man who was so clearly not in love with me? Sure, he liked me, I would even say he cared for me and he enjoyed being with me, but there was a serious roadblock around his heart. He did a great job of keeping me going through detour after detour. I wanted someone to talk to about it, but no one could know how much I felt for him. Not even Krissy.

My dad was singing along to the music as he made omelets. He was in such a good mood lately. He turned when he heard me approach. He grabbed his heart and his eyes widened. "Whoa, baby girl!"

"What?"

"I'll pay you to go put on a turtleneck."

I laughed at him. "Daddy."

"I'm serious."

I walked over and kissed his cheek. "I love you."

"If you love me, you won't leave the house looking like that."

I dished up an omelet and reveled in the love and protection of my dad.

"So, what are you doing today?" I sat down at the breakfast bar.

"Besides going into cardiac arrest, I'm going to hit the lake and get in some fishing."

I rolled my eyes. "Sounds like fun. Are you going with anyone?"

He looked me over again. "I think I'm going to need to have a talk with Ryan."

Why did he ignore my question? That wasn't like him, but I didn't address it. "Don't worry, Dad, Ryan's a complete gentleman." Does it sound bad that I wished sometimes he wasn't? I would love to have to tell him to slow down once in a while.

My dad looked like perhaps he didn't quite believe me.

"Really, he is."

"That's good to know, but what about all the other men that will see you today?"

"I wouldn't worry about that, either. There will be plenty of bikini clad beach babes there."

"You know what I love about you?"

"My wit?"

"There's that." He laughed for a moment. "I was going to say, you never let how gorgeous you are go to your head."

I rolled my eyes. "You are so biased."

"I have good reason to be."

Have I mentioned how much I loved my dad? It made me feel terrible for all the time I wasted hating him, especially since my mother and I were now barely speaking. She was so wrapped up in her own world right now, it was like she had replaced me, which really hurt after everything I went through with her. It was one more emotional issue not to dwell on today.

I helped my dad clean up the kitchen before brushing my teeth and throwing together my beach bag. It wasn't that much later when two of my favorite people came to get me.

Ryan stood at the door. Josh was in the car, all buckled in, with the window down. He waved to me as soon as I answered the door with my bag.

I met Ryan's gaze. "Hi."

He shook his head. "Wow, Charlee."

"Do you like my new swimsuit?"

He reached behind me, touched my bare back, drawing me to him. I was surprised because he was cautious about how much affection he showed me in front of Josh. I barely caught a glimpse of his hungry eyes before he kissed me hard, albeit briefly.

"I'll take that as a yes."

"I'm only sorry I didn't take you to the water park earlier."

I looked him over in his swim trunks and tight tee and thought the same thing. I was looking forward to that t-shirt coming off.

"Daddy, let's go," Josh yelled, breaking the fiery connection I had going with his father. This wasn't helping me keep my feelings for him under control.

"I guess we better go." Ryan couldn't help but stare at me.

"That's probably a good idea." I bit my lip.

Ryan kissed me one more time before taking my hand and leading me to the passenger side. He opened my door, but not before kissing me again. Oooh, I liked this Ryan, okay, I loved this Ryan.

"You're in a good mood today." I got in the car.

He winked before closing my door for me.

I turned back to Josh. "Hey, big guy. Are you ready to play in the water?"

He gave me a thumbs up. "But I have to stay by you and Daddy all day." We had gone over and over the rules with him last night. I was glad he remembered.

"That's right. We don't want anything to happen to you because we love you."

"I love you, Cherry."

Yep, that was never going to get old. I looked at Ryan to see how he felt about it this morning. He threw on his shades and smiled. I took that as a good sign. And did I mention how amazing he looked? He hadn't bothered to shave this morning, and I loved it. A little scruff on a man was so sexy to me, and he pulled it off with flying colors.

Once on the main road, Ryan took my hand and slid his fingers between mine—they fit perfectly. I also noticed the covert glances he snuck in when he could, but Josh occupied most of my time for the hour-long drive. We were working on the alphabet song.

"A, B, C, D, E, F, G, H, High J's," it sounded like. I also enjoyed the, Lelephant P's, which I translated into L, M, N, O, P. He was the most adorable kid on the planet.

"You didn't tell me you could sing something besides 'Ring Around the Rosy'," Ryan cut in.

"You know, I'm trying to keep a little mystery."

"So what other talents have you been hiding from me?"

"It would take the fun out of it if I told you."

"I look forward to discovering those."

I swore if he wasn't driving and if his son wasn't a witness in the backseat, I would have reached over and kissed him until we were both gasping for air. Instead, I taught Josh a new song about the "Five Little

Speckled Frogs." It was amusing to both father and son when I pretended to eat bugs and sang loudly. Josh had me singing it over and over again. His favorite word was "again," and I was a sucker for him.

Though I did a good job of entertaining Josh, he was more than excited when we arrived. He was trying to undo his car seat before his dad could get to him. I was excited, too. I finally felt like maybe some of the barriers were going to come down.

We finally made it through what seemed like a never-ending line to enter. We locked up our valuables before we applied serious amounts of sunscreen to Josh, who was fair-skinned like his mother. Ryan already had a call from her on our drive in warning him that Josh better not have even a patch of sunburn on him. Ryan promised we wouldn't let that happen. I could hear her say, "I suppose Charlee is with you." She said my name with such disdain. I was trying my hardest to not let it get to me. As weird as it sounded, I wanted us all to get along. I wanted to be part of Ryan and Josh's life, and I knew she was part of the package. I had read enough studies that showed that it's possible, and more importantly beneficial, for the children involved to see the adults in their lives behave in such a way.

Once we had Josh lathered up and in his swim vest, it was time for his daddy to remove his shirt. His chest was as glorious as I had imagined. He was defined, not like six pack defined, but well sculpted. I snuck in glances of him applying sunscreen while I applied my own to my legs. He kept looking my way, too. I think it was safe to say we were into each other.

Ryan came and sat behind me. "Let me get your back."

I happily handed over my sunscreen.

His hands felt good gliding across my back. I could tell he was taking his time. He leaned in low and whispered in my ear, since Josh was sitting in my lap. "You are beautiful, Charlee Jensen."

I turned toward him and kissed him. I barely caught a taste of his lip balm.

He gave a sexy grin. "Now it's my turn."

I was more than happy to oblige.

He took Josh out of my arms, and we switched spots. I knelt behind him and enjoyed the feel of his skin beneath my hands. I wanted to dig in and really rub his back, but I resisted the urge. "Speaking of beautiful." I hated to finish.

"You're good for a guy's ego. Not many women compliment men the way you do."

"Well, there's plenty more where that came from."

He chuckled when he stood up with Josh, who was beyond anxious to hit the water. Sunscreen was just a nuisance to a three-year-old. We didn't tell him this would be an hourly occurrence.

Since Josh was too little to ride most of the attractions, we were limited to family rides where we could all ride together in a raft or kiddie land. I didn't mind at all, I was just happy to spend the day with the Carter men. Besides, floating on the water enclosed in a floating device with the three of us was like heaven to me. Josh's squeals of delight were only icing on the cake. Everything to him was exciting and new. He particularly loved the Pharaohs ride. My favorite was the lazy river. Josh and Ryan rode on one tube. I had my own, but Ryan held my hand as we casually drifted along the slow-moving water. I could have stayed like that all day, basking in the sun and holding hands with my guy, but Josh found it to be a little too tame for his liking.

We traded the lazy river in for the shallow end of the wave pool. Josh loved it when either Ryan or I jumped in the waves with him. I loved watching the two of them together, and I loved them both. Maybe I shouldn't, but I did.

The rest of our day was spent in Calypso Cove where there was a myriad of activities, from small water slides to splash pads made for younger kids. Josh did everything. He didn't even want to eat lunch, but we made him take a break for food and sunscreen.

As we sat at a picnic table under the shade of one of their pavilions, we had a little blip. I should have known not to have gotten too comfortable around Ryan. A dear little lady was there with her grandchildren who looked to be about five and seven. They were at the table next to us, and she kept looking over at us and smiling. I think I was the only one that noticed, Ryan and Josh were busy eating.

I smiled back at her, and she said, "You have such a cute little boy; my son had hair just like that."

"Thank you. He's definitely cute, but . . ."

Ryan's head flew up. "She's not his mother." Panic raced through his words.

I *was* getting to that part.

The lady looked a little taken aback by his panicked state.

I tried to smile at her to smooth it over. I turned to Ryan, who was sitting on the other side of Josh, and he didn't get such a reception. "I know I'm not his mother. I was trying to tell her that." I kept my voice quiet. I put my sandwich down, suddenly not very hungry anymore.

At first, Ryan looked surprised at my reaction, but his eyes softened and realization settled in. "Charlee."

I turned to Josh and kissed his head. "I'll be right back, big guy." I wasn't sure where I was going to go, but I wanted a moment alone. My heart hurt a little. I wasn't hurt that Ryan would point out I wasn't his son's mother, it was the way he said it, like he had to say it. I stood up.

So did Ryan. "Charlee, I'm sorry."

I pressed my lips together and walked off. I decided I would go to their surf shop and browse. I didn't know where else to head. The whole way over, I scolded myself for falling in love with him and then wondered why I did.

I perused the store, not even remotely interested in anything they were selling. Unfortunately, I must have looked like I was mildly interested because one of their over-friendly sales clerks kept following me around asking me if he could answer any questions or help me find anything. I think I said, "No, thank you" ten times, but that didn't deter Paul, according to his name tag.

"So do you live around here?" Paul asked.

"Uh, no. Not really."

"That's too bad."

I picked up an azure blue towel and looked it over. "Why?" I looked up at him, and he was a tad red. I smiled. He seemed like a nice kid, and I mean kid, like high school kid. I was so glad when I heard my name being called. I needed a graceful way to exit this uncomfortable, yet kind of flattering, situation.

"Charlee," Ryan called my name as he walked over.

Josh ran to me. I picked him up and cuddled him as soon as he got to me.

"Oh, you're a mom?"

"No," I responded, almost in exasperation.

Ryan joined us, looked at Paul, and kind of snickered. That sent my little admirer scurrying away. Ryan faced me as soon as he left and shook his head at me. "Poor kid."

I rolled my eyes.

"I can't say I blame him. He has excellent taste."

"Can we go back in the water now?" Josh asked.

"If it's okay with your dad." I didn't want to overstep my non-parental bounds.

We both looked to Ryan to answer.

Ryan's face registered understanding. "I'm not in charge."

"You are of Josh."

"I'm in charge," Josh countered loudly.

I smiled at him, kissed his cute cheek, and set him down, but made sure to take a hold of his hand. I may not have been his mother, but I cared about him and worried over him.

Ryan took my other hand. "Charlee," he whispered.

I faced him. "What?"

"I'm sorry. I didn't mean for that to come out so harshly back there."

I shrugged my shoulders as Josh tugged on me anxiously. I followed Josh and let go of Ryan's hand. Ryan trailed behind us out into the bright sunny day and back to Calypso Cove. He didn't say anything more to me until we were all back in the water. Ryan and I sat in the water and watched Josh splash and play in front of us.

"Victoria is having a really hard time with this situation. She's really sensitive right now, and it's making me overly so."

"I'm sorry she's having an issue with me. I'm not trying to step on her toes or take her place."

Ryan scooted closer and kissed my bare shoulder. "I know that."

We sat quietly for another moment and watched Josh interact with some of the other children there. He was kind of shy, which surprised me.

"Can we please hit the reset button?" Ryan said close to my ear, which drove me crazy. "As sexy as you are angry at me, I want you happy with me."

I turned and stared straight at him. Did I fail to mention how attractive, wet and shirtless Ryan was? I couldn't help but grin. "I'm not angry. I'm thinking."

"Either way, you're still sexy." He looked me over from head to toe.

"So what am I when I'm happy?"

He kissed me on the lips. "Irresistible."

"I think you just like my swimsuit."

He laughed. "No, I love your swimsuit."

I nudged him with my shoulder. "You're such a guy."

"Guilty."

So we hit the reset button and spent a lovely, but exhausting, day in the sun and water. Josh was so tuckered out that he fell asleep almost as soon as we hit the highway on the way home.

"Hey." Ryan reached over and held my hand as we zoomed along I-25. "I had a great time today."

"Me, too. Thanks for inviting me."

"Are we okay?"

"Yes."

"You know this is unchartered territory for me, right?"

"I know. Me, too."

He rubbed his thumb gently across my hand. "Do you want to cross some new territory tomorrow?"

I gave him an inquisitive glance. "What does that mean?"

"Some friends of mine asked me to meet them at a sports bar in Longmont to watch the Broncos play one of their preseason games. I would love it if you would come with me."

"You want to introduce me to your friends?"

"You sound surprised."

"I am."

"What's the use in dating someone young and beautiful if I don't show her off?" He winked.

"I hope that's one of your gems."

He laughed at me. "So, will you come?"

"What about Josh?"

"I was going to see if your dad could watch him for a few hours."

"I'm sure he would love to."

"Then it's a date?"

"Absolutely."

Seventeen

WHAT I SHOULD HAVE SAID was absolutely not, but how could I have known the outcome? All I could think of was how thrilled I was that Ryan wanted to introduce me to his friends. It was a great sign that he wanted me to be part of his life. Every romantic advice column in Cosmo would tell you that's the case. I rue the day I ever clicked on "Ten Ways to Know if a Guy is Really Into You." It's all lies!

So what happened?

It all started off so terrific. I was looking super cute in my Bronco's jersey and nice fitting white shorts that showed off my long tan legs. Ryan was pleased, let me tell you. I even curled my hair a little glam. I had to say, I was rocking it. I wanted to make a good impression in front of Ryan's friends.

Ryan pulled me to him before he opened my car door. "You look amazing."

I wrapped my arms around his neck. "I'm glad you approve."

"I'm glad my friends are married." He brushed my lips.

"Darn it. And here I thought I would get to expand my horizons."

"Sorry, you're stuck with me."

I kissed him and lingered for a bit. Gosh, I loved his lips. "It's not a bad consolation prize."

He chuckled and let me go. "We better get going before the neighbors really start to talk."

Oh yes, we had been the talk of Mulberry Lane. Ann Lawton was the instigator I'm sure, but I loved her too much to be upset with her. Let's just say, the old timers found it interesting that the girl next door was dating the older and divorced Ryan Carter. Some of the new families just found it intriguing, but I know a couple of people had questioned our integrity, meaning I was the reason for his divorce, and perhaps Ryan had always had a thing for me. It was nonsense, but everyone loved a good story, even if they had to make it up. Ours would be completely boring without the embellishments.

We were meeting Alec, Rob, and Hayes, all guys that he had known as a married guy. It gave me a little pause, but I reminded myself that I loved this man and I wanted to be part of his life. All his life.

"Do your friends mind that you're bringing a woman to this thing?" I asked on our drive over.

He looked over and flashed his perfect white teeth at me. "Are you kidding me? They wish their wives liked football."

"So, what you're saying is, you're lucky this chick digs sports?"

"And, let's not forget, understands the game."

"You really are lucky." Though I didn't think I was that rare of a breed.

"I know." His tone was serious, taking all the playfulness out of it. Sometimes I couldn't figure him out.

We arrived in twenty minutes.

I took a deep breath and reminded myself I had nothing to be nervous about. I was wrong, but it was a nice try. You see, it wasn't just the guys we were meeting. Alec was an idiot and brought his wife, Trixie. Does that ring a bell? Well, it should. Trixie was the maid of honor at Ryan and Victoria's wedding. Oh yeah, and she was still Victoria's best friend. From the moment she greeted me, I knew she had been sent there on purpose.

She still had the peed-on-Cheerios look going for her. I think it was like a club. She eyed me carefully with contempt.

I looked to Ryan to help ease the awkwardness of it, but all he did was drop my hand as if he was uncomfortable. It was not what I was looking for. It was as if suddenly he wasn't feeling so lucky he was there with me. Rob and Hayes were nice to me, and Alec pretty much ignored me.

I settled myself between Ryan and Hayes at the tall table with high back chairs. Hayes was nice enough to pull out my chair for me. Ryan was lost in his thoughts, and I could tell Trixie took note. Again, who names their kid Trixie? I wish I could say she had gained a bunch of weight and looked like crap, but I couldn't. She didn't look like she belonged on a runway anymore, but she was still attractive with her tresses of long brown hair and high cheekbones. Okay, so maybe she was beginning to get a little bit of a double chin, but that was just petty on my part.

Our server came by and took Ryan's and my order since we were the last to arrive. I was wishing we never came.

"I'll take a Diet Coke. Thank you."

"It must suck to still be underage." Trixie laughed to herself.

I gave her a scathing look that said, are you for real?

Everyone uncomfortably laughed when she responded, "Just kidding."

Ryan ordered a beer, which surprised me. He had said on the way over he wasn't going to drink since he was driving. My eyes questioned his change of plans, but instead of responding to me he turned to the TV to watch the kick-off, making me feel more alone.

"Ryan said you're an accountant too." Hayes spoke to me after several minutes.

I turned my attention his way. "Yes, I am," I said it without cringing.

"Must be nice to have daddy as your boss," Trixie threw in.

Who invited her into this conversation?

I gave her an incredulous glance before ignoring her and turning back to Hayes, who was taking the same approach with her. "My dad and Ryan are both great to work for."

Hayes smiled at me.

"So, what do you do for a living?" I asked in return.

"I'm a physical therapist."

"That's a great field. Do you specialize in a particular practice?"

He raised his eyebrows at me. "Most people don't even know to ask about specialty fields. They think all physical therapists are the same. I specialize in pediatrics."

"Smart choice. I think dealing with children some days is much better than adults."

"Agreed," Hayes said.

"And what do you know about dealing with children?" Trixie asked.

Hayes grimaced at me.

I turned my attention back to the vile woman. "I've taken my fair share of child development classes, and I have several step nieces and nephews. And, I spend a lot of time with Josh." I had to say it.

She whipped out her phone so fast. Her fingers moved at lightning speed. I didn't have to guess who she was texting.

I looked at Ryan to see if he had any reaction at all. He looked at me, but I couldn't read him. He took a long drink of his beer.

The screen caught my attention. They had just flashed the cheerleaders. "I think Krissy is still pretty upset about not making the squad," I said to Ryan.

"I'm sure she'll get over it." He wasn't all that sympathetic.

"I told her I'm sure it was for a reason, that something better would come her way."

Ryan shrugged his shoulders.

This wasn't how I wanted this to go at all, and if it didn't change soon, I would be exiting the party.

I had a nice surprise in the form of an old teammate who, unbeknownst to me, was a waitress at the restaurant. She recognized me and came my way. I jumped off my seat and hugged her. "Ivy, it's so good to see you."

She hugged me tight. "Same here. I didn't know you were back in Colorado."

I released her. "Since May."

"Well, you look terrific. What have you been up to?"

I almost hated to say it with my audience, but I wasn't ashamed. "I graduated with my MBA in the spring, and I'm working for my dad right now."

"Look at you." She was impressed. "We missed you our senior year. The team was never the same after you left."

I felt a pang in my heart. "I missed you guys, too."

"We should get together sometime."

"Absolutely. Let me put your contact info in my phone."

She gave me her number and I promised to call. I sat back down, and everyone was looking at me. I guess I should have thought to introduce her, but I wasn't really feeling the love, if you get my drift. I tucked my hair behind my ear. "We went to high school together and played on the basketball team."

Rob and Hayes nodded like that was cool. Alec ignored me and turned back to the game, but his wife. Oh, his wife. I think hate was a good word.

"I don't understand why women play basketball. Their outfits are atrocious and unfeminine," Trixie said.

"I don't know why chicks want to play sports meant for guys, period," her idiot husband chimed in while watching the screen.

I looked at Ryan like this would be a good time to jump in, but he didn't. Fine. "Basketball *uniforms* are designed for comfort and to keep you cool, not for fashion shows. And as far as women playing the sport, I averaged thirty points a game, led my team to the state championship as a junior, and I would take on anyone at this table that wanted to go."

Ryan looked stunned, but stuttered out, "She's really good on the court."

It was something, but not enough.

I looked at Trixie who sneered at me.

"Thirty points a game. That's amazing," Hayes said.

I was so grateful the game got exciting and everyone turned their attention toward the screen, except Trixie, who obviously didn't like the sport. She kept looking at me and then texting. I could only imagine what she was telling Victoria. Unfortunately, I got to find out after halftime. I had a feeling I should have called Krissy to pick me up earlier, but I stayed because I wanted to give Ryan the benefit of the doubt. I wanted to see if he could and would get comfortable with me by his side, but the only thing that happened was he talked to his friends about things that didn't involve me. You know, all the stuff they used to do as couples together, like a couples' trip to New Orleans.

The other thing that kept happening was Trixie drank like a fish, and it emboldened her. Just as the third quarter was about to start, I noticed Trixie smiling evilly at her phone; you know, like the Grinch. She looked up at me, and I knew she was going in for the kill.

"Ryan, remember a few years ago when you said you hoped your kids never grew up to be like Charlee?"

I whipped my head toward Ryan, and he looked at me with eyes agape. "I don't think that's exactly what I said." Ryan reached for my hand under the table.

I didn't bother asking for clarification, besides I didn't need to speak. Trixie was on a roll. Even her husband was embarrassed and telling her to lay off it. Oh, but she wasn't going to. "I remember, Ryan. You said you hoped you never raised such a spoiled brat that couldn't stand on her own two feet." She laughed at how funny she thought she was.

I willed myself not to cry. Is this what Ryan really thought about me? I couldn't even look at Ryan. I yanked my hand away from him, stood up, grabbed my purse, and left.

I heard Ryan say to Trixie as I walked away, "That was completely uncalled for." Hayes and Rob agreed, but it was too little, too late.

I desperately wanted out of there. I pulled out my phone to call Krissy as soon as I made it outside. I was starting to dial her number when I heard Ryan call my name. I walked away. He was the last person I wanted to see.

"Charlee, where are you going?" He easily caught up to me.

"Why do you care?"

"Let's go home." He let out a heavy sigh.

I didn't answer him, I waited for Krissy to answer her phone, but she never did. I threw my phone in my bag and huffily walked toward his car, and he followed. He opened my door for me, but I refused to look at him or thank him for the gesture. I got in and faced the window and took deep breaths and reminded myself that I didn't let men make me cry.

"Don't you think we should talk?" Ryan broke the minutes of dead silence.

"Sure. We can talk about why you let your friends humiliate me or why it is that you think I'm a spoiled brat who can't stand on her own. Or if you choose, you can talk about why you ignored me. Take your pick." I glared at him.

"Well, what about you?"

"What about me?"

"It's not like you were being very friendly to Trixie either."

"Are you kidding me? She was terrible to me from the get go. I'm sorry if I didn't sit there and take what she was handing out, but you know, maybe if you showed some deference toward me, she wouldn't have felt like she had the right to talk to me that way."

"So this is my fault?"

"Yes."

He stewed for a minute. I could see his grip on the steering wheel get tighter and tighter. "You know, maybe Victoria was right. Dating you was a mistake. You don't know the first thing about life. It's been handed to you. Everything is just for fun for you, and maybe she was right about you just dating me for an out. You don't even know how worried your dad was about you during college. And now you won't batten down and take your CPA exam and . . ."

I didn't hear anything else he was rambling on about because the blood was rushing through my head. I couldn't believe he was saying these things to me. I couldn't believe my dad had talked to him about me, and I couldn't believe Victoria's accusations. The tears started to form, and as much as I wanted to stop them, I couldn't. No wonder he had been so cautious with me, I kept thinking.

He pulled into my drive and forcefully threw his car in park, before turning it off. He was opening his door, but I wasn't having it. He was going to hear the truth.

"Ryan."

He stopped, turned, and looked at my tear-stained cheeks with some emotion. He almost reached out to comfort me, but stopped himself.

"You say I don't know the first thing about life and maybe you're right. And maybe my dad had reason to worry about me, but he was worrying for all the wrong reasons. He should have been worried that I was living with a mother that sometimes didn't come home or worse yet, sometimes she did come home and she brought with her the most worthless men you would ever meet. Or how about a mother that accidentally, or on purpose, it was hard to tell, overdosed on sleeping pills and alcohol? So maybe I didn't know what I was doing, and yes, I took advantage of my dad's money and guilt, but I was just trying to get by and be the adult. You know, the one that paid all the bills and did the grocery shopping and cleaning. The one that made the dean's list every year."

His mouth fell open and he uttered, "Charlee."

"Looking back, yes, I wish I would have done things better, but I'm sorry I'm not perfect like you and Victoria. I was doing the best I could at the time. I was trying to get by and not lose myself or even stop to think, because if I thought too much, I would have lost it."

He reached out to touch my arm, but I batted it away.

"So I got a degree I hate because I didn't have to think about it. I took a job I hate because it was my only option, and by the way, I passed my CPA exam. I was waiting to get it in the mail so I could surprise you and my dad with it."

His shoulders dropped and he hung his head. "I'm sorry."

"I don't want to hear your apologies, and I don't want to see you anymore." I unclicked my seatbelt, wiped my eyes, and opened my door. "Don't come in to get Josh. I'll have my dad bring him over to you."

"Okay." He spoke into his lap.

I whipped back around. "Oh, and if I wanted an out, believe me I wouldn't have chosen you. For your information, I could have been married by now to a man who loved me more than anything and he would have never let his friends treat me the way yours did, if an out was what I was looking for. So don't flatter yourself, Ryan Carter!" I slammed the door, but I had a second thought and opened it back up. "And by the way, you and your friends and your ex-wife can all go to hell!"

He looked up, stunned. I slammed his car door again and ran in.

I marched down to the family room, and there were Josh and my dad.

"You're home early, honey. What's wrong?"

I stared at him hard. "Don't talk to me." I was so not happy with him.

"CJ?"

"I mean it, don't talk to me. You need to take Josh over to Ryan."

I picked Josh up off the floor where he was playing with his blocks and snuggled him to me. He gently touched my face. "Why are you crying, Cherry?"

It only made me cry harder. I kissed his cheeks. "I'll see you later, big guy."

"I love you." He was the sweetest kid.

"I love you, too," I choked out.

I set him down and glared at my dad, who stood nearby looking as confused as ever. I ran down to my room and grabbed my basketball.

Eighteen

As soon as I heard my dad leave with Josh, I headed back upstairs with my basketball. I thought about leaving, but I was too emotional to drive. I couldn't even talk to Krissy I was so upset. So this is what everyone thought of me? Maybe they had good reason to, but they had no idea what I had to put up with and struggled through. No wonder Ryan treated me so indifferently at times, and especially today. Believe me, I wasn't excusing him, oh, no. I hated him with a burning passion.

I shot basket after basket after basket while thinking about my next move. For sure, I was moving out as soon as possible. New job, definitely. Dying a little inside because the man I fell in love with was the wrong man, check. Every time I hit the backboard I pictured Ryan's perfect face. I would have loved to chuck the ball at his actual head, and my dad's for that matter. How dare he talk to Ryan about me like that! This was all his fault in the first place, the philanderer.

I don't know how long I was out there, but it was getting dark, and my dad still hadn't come back. I assumed he was still at Ryan's and they were probably talking about me. No matter, I was washing my hands of the idiots.

I was working on my layups when my dad came walking home. I ignored him. I was in no mood to talk to him or anyone with a Y chromosome, unless they were three years old.

"Hey, baby girl," my dad called out tentatively as he neared.

I ignored him, went up for my shot, and missed. Ugh! I hadn't missed one until he showed up.

"You didn't follow through." Only kindness filled his voice.

"Don't talk to me." I dribbled back, turned, and shot from the three-point line. The ball hobbled in and through the net.

My dad grabbed the ball before I could rebound it.

Whatever. I turned and walked toward the house.

"CJ, please talk to me," my dad called out.

I ignored him and kept on walking.

"Why didn't you tell me?" I heard him say.

I turned from where I stood near the porch. "Because I wasn't going to give you the satisfaction of knowing what you did to mom."

He dropped the ball, looking dumbfounded. "Honey." He walked closer to me, kicking the ball onto the grass. "How could you think that? I loved your mom. I still do. And, more importantly, I love you. Had I known what was going on, I would have brought you home and gotten your mom the help she needed. I would have never allowed you to go through that."

I held onto the rail of the porch, and the tears started up again. My dad took that at his cue and took me up in his arms. I didn't even bother fighting him. I let him hold me. I soaked his shirt with my tears. I'm sure we were giving the neighbors more to talk about.

He stroked my hair. "Baby girl, I love you so much. I'm so sorry."

"I'm sorry too, Daddy. I'm sorry I took your money."

He hugged me tighter to him. "You don't have anything to be sorry about. I knew something wasn't right. I should have done more to find out. I'm sick thinking about what you went through."

"I survived."

He kissed the top of my head. "Yes, you did, but it wasn't right."

He walked me in. We sat on the living room couch, and he held me as I got out eight years' worth of tears. I also talked about how much I disliked accounting and how what I really wanted to be was a psychologist. He was disappointed, but he understood. He even offered to help pay for grad school again. I declined. He did talk me into staying with him until I could qualify for in-state tuition.

"You know, I wish you would have told me you hated being an accountant."

"I probably should have, but everyone around me was telling me what a terrible idea majoring in psychology was, and I just couldn't deal with it," I said through the never-ending tears.

He rubbed my arms.

When I finally stopped crying, I sat up.

My dad softly touched my tear-stained cheeks.

"I'm thirsty."

My dad chuckled. "I can fix that at least. Are you hungry, too?"

It was well past nine, and neither of us had eaten dinner.

I nodded my head.

He stood up and helped pull me up. We made our way to the kitchen.

"Have a seat and I'll make us some grilled cheese sandwiches," my dad offered.

I kind of melted into the stool. I was exhausted, emotionally and physically, but I mustered up a little enthusiasm for dinner. My dad made grill cheese sandwiches with bacon. He was a genius.

"You know you need to talk to Ryan." Dad was pulling the ingredients out of our fridge.

"I don't think that's a good idea."

"He feels terrible, you know."

"He should. He didn't treat me very well today."

"I know. I'm not happy about it."

"So why do you want me to talk to him?"

"Because everyone makes mistakes, kiddo, and he's feeling pretty rotten right now."

"Will you think I'm terrible if I say, 'good'?"

"No, I'd think you're human and more than justified."

"We're done, Dad." That came out brave, but inside I hurt. A lot.

He set the griddle in front of me. "I think he got that message loud and clear. Are you okay?"

I shrugged and tried not to cry.

"That's what I thought."

"Do you think I could call in sick tomorrow?" I somewhat teased.

"If you want to, but I don't think that's going to make you feel any better. And usually, running away from our problems only makes them worse." His eyes were so full of concern when he spoke.

"Yeah. Unfortunately, I know that from experience."

"CJ, I'm proud of you, and I'm sorry that I let anyone think any different."

"Daddy, you had cause for being concerned, and I *was* being selfish. I felt like you owed it to me, and I'm sorry for that."

"Don't apologize to me, baby girl."

I lay in bed that night with dueling emotions. I was completely heartbroken, I'm not going to lie. For whatever dumb reason, I loved Ryan Carter and I loved Josh. I wondered if I could get in on the whole shared custody deal. I knew I couldn't, because his mom hated me. Any respect I had for her went out the window today. How immature was it for her to sit there and text her friend? If she wanted Ryan, she should have just stayed married to him.

As heartbroken as I was, I also felt lightened. My dad finally knew the truth, and I think I could finally move on from the past. I felt free. The best part was, my dad was going to help me realize my dream of becoming a psychologist. Now I just had to get into a program.

He also gave me some more insight into my mom. It didn't help me feel better about what she put me through, but it helped me to understand a little better. I guess she battled depression more frequently and severely than I knew growing up. She and my dad had done a great job hiding it from me. I think that, more than anything, made my dad feel worse about letting me leave with her. I guess he had been counting on me to say something. Too bad he forgot how stubborn I could be.

I woke up later than normal. I sure as heck wasn't running with my moronic neighbor who I was in love with. I really needed to get over that, like as soon as possible. I knew it wasn't happening, though. I supposed if it was quick and easy, it wouldn't have been real love. I dreaded going into work and seeing him, but I had goals and I needed that job. My dad was going to help me come up with a plan. He was willing to work around my school schedule once I started. It looked like I would be putting my CPA license to use, at least for a little while.

I rode in with my dad. I figured if I ran into Ryan, at least my dad would be with me. On our way in, my phone went off. I nervously picked it up. I thought perhaps it was Ryan, but I was pleasantly surprised to see that it was Jay.

"Hello."

"How's the most beautiful woman in the world?"

Why wasn't I in love with this man? "I don't know, I'm not sure who that is."

"Well, you're the only one that would know." That was his usual response.

I laughed as I always did. It was nowhere near true, but he honestly felt that way.

"Tomorrow I'm passing through there on my way to Wyoming. Do you think we could have lunch together?"

"Yes, please."

"Great. Give me the address to your office and I'll swing by and pick you up around noon."

"I'll text it to you."

"I can't wait to see you."

"Me, too. Bye."

"Who was that?" my dad inquired.

"Jay."

"Jay, as in the guy that wants to marry, you, Jay?"

"Yes. He's coming through town tomorrow and wants to take me to lunch. Do you mind if I take a long lunch tomorrow? I'll stay later and work."

He reached over and patted my knee. "You're a good kid. Just be careful tomorrow."

"What does that mean?"

"Your emotions are running high, and I don't want you to do anything you'll regret."

I sighed. I knew what he was getting at. "Thanks, Daddy. I wouldn't do anything to lead Jay on. I've already hurt him enough, but I do wonder if there's something wrong with me. Why can't I be in love with Jay? He would have never treated me the way Ryan did."

"I don't know, baby girl. Love is a fickle creature. I'm not going to pretend I like how Ryan treated you, and I'm not going to tell you that you need to give him another chance, but Ryan's a good man. He has some issues he needs to work out, but I don't think he's irredeemable. He, too, fought a long, hard battle. Maybe on a different front than you, but the last eight years were anything but a cake walk for him."

I didn't say anything back. I leaned my head against the cool glass of the window and pondered my life.

As we walked in, my dad said, "I'll tell Ryan to give you some space today."

"Thanks, Dad."

He kissed the side of my head and opened the office entrance for me. We parted ways, and I started my very long day. Mondays were the worst, but this Monday beat out all the other Mondays. Not only was I worried I would run into Ryan, which thankfully I didn't, but there seemed to be never ending issues from my computer freezing up to the internet being down at the precise moment I needed to transmit a report to the IRS. It was normally stuff I let slide off my back, but I was tired.

I was looking forward to a relaxing evening at home, but I had two calls that prevented that. First up, my mother. She called while I was changing out of my work clothes into some more casual attire. She was not happy at all. I guess my dad called her and gave her the what for. I wished he hadn't, but there was nothing I could do about it now.

"I can't believe you told your father that I was a terrible mother."

"I never said that to him."

"Well, that's what he thinks. He is such a hypocrite. And you. After everything I went through, this is how you repay me. Mark is very upset with you, young lady."

"For what? Telling Dad the truth? And what does Mark have to do with it anyway? I don't remember him being the one in the hospital with you praying that you would wake up. He also wasn't there to clean up your puke after you came home falling down drunk all the time, either. And don't even get me going on the parade of men."

"Enough. I don't deserve this." Here came the tears.

"No. You know who didn't deserve any of this? Me."

She hung up.

I walked upstairs for dinner. Her calls didn't even rattle me anymore.

I started the meat for taco salad, and my dad soon joined me. We both liked to change when we got home.

"When did you call mom?"

"This morning."

"She's not very happy with me now."

"I'm sorry for that, but what she did was wrong. I'm sorry my horrible mistake ended our marriage and broke up our family, but her taking you and not caring for you the way she should have is inexcusable. Had I known, I would have fought tooth and nail for you."

"I just want to forget about it and move on." I chopped some lettuce.

"Your old man is going to need some time. I'm still livid about the situation."

"I get that, but quit calling Mom. She and I already have enough issues."

"We don't have anything left to say to each other." My dad was angry, but there was some sadness mixed in.

I had never seen my dad really angry before. He was a pretty even keel sort of guy. I had no idea this would shake him so much.

During dinner, my second phone call came. It was Krissy, and I could barely understand her. "Please come over," I made out during her hysterical crying.

"Are you okay?"

"Just come quick," she begged.

I jumped up. "I'm headed to Krissy's. She's crying, and I don't know why."

My dad's brow scrunched together. "You don't think it's anything domestic, do you?"

"No," I laughed. "She probably burned dinner and Chance said he didn't like it."

My dad laughed in return. "Well, have fun then."

I stopped at the store and got her favorite ice cream, cookies and cream. I thought about getting some Midol, but she should have already had her period for the month, so I decided against it. Instead, I bought my favorite ice cream, fudge revel, because I was nursing a broken heart.

With a grocery bag full of goodness, I knocked on the door of her new digs. She answered the door almost instantaneously and pulled me in. "What took you so long?" She was already dragging me back to her bedroom.

"What are you doing?" I laughed. "I have ice cream in my hand."

"Just follow me."

I let her pull me into her master bath.

"Okay, this is weird. I didn't need to see your love den."

She stood there, looking pathetic. Her eyes were puffy, and she was wearing sweat pants and an ill-fitting t-shirt.

"Are you okay, honey?"

"No," she cried and grabbed onto me for dear life.

I dropped the ice cream bag and held onto her. "Did Chance do something to you? Because if he did, I'll kill him." After him, I'd kill Ryan for good measure. If you're going to kill once, you might as well do it again, I figured.

"Yes," she howled. "He got me pregnant."

Whoa! I was not expecting that. "Krissy, that's terrific."

She let go of me and handed me her peed-on pregnancy test stick.

"Um . . . thank you. I always wanted to touch your pee."

She cracked a small smile.

I looked at the two very distinct lines. "Well, you sure didn't waste any time."

"We weren't planning on having kids for at least two years." She sat on her toilet and cried some more.

I set down her pee stick and washed my hands. "So you're having a surprise blessing. What does Chance think?"

"He's so happy about it."

"Well, that's great."

"No, it's not. I'm not ready to be a mom. I've barely been a wife. How can I be a mom? And what are people going to say when I have a baby before we've even been married a year?"

I knelt in front of her and took her hands. "Krissy, you're going to be a great mom, and who cares what people say. Most people today don't even wait to get married to have kids."

"I'm not ready."

"Well, ready or not. And I'll be here every step of the way."

"You're such a good friend."

"I am, aren't I?"

She laughed a little.

"Wash your face and let's have some ice cream."

"Okay," she said obediently.

We sat on her couch, each with our own carton of ice cream.

"So, if it's a girl, you're going to name her Charlee, right?"

She grinned at me and shook her head no.

"Fine. I don't know why you don't want your daughter to have a strong, masculine name."

"How about a middle name?"

"I'll take it."

"So how are you and Ryan? You never told me how your weekend of fun was."

I looked down at my half-eaten carton. I was going to regret that. "Oh . . . We're not seeing each other anymore."

"Why?"

I told her the whole ugly story. Like a true friend, she interrupted when she should, and was outraged on my behalf.

"I guess it's for the best," I sighed when I finished.

"Are you sure?"

"No. Honestly, this hurts like hell."

"Why didn't you call me?"

"I was going to, but it hurts to even think about it. Plus, my dad's been hovering over me. He's totally freaking out about everything that happened in Kansas. He even had it out with my mom this morning."

"Wow."

"Well, at least it's all out there now. But enough about me. Let's talk about your baby. I can't believe you're going to be a mom."

"I know."

"Have you told your mom?" I could see Ann now. She was going to be beyond excited.

"No. I want to wait for a few weeks."

"My lips are sealed."

She set down her ice cream and reached for my hands. "CJ, you're the best person I know. You just make sure Ryan treats you that way."

"Ryan and I are over."

"We'll see," she countered.

We spent the rest of the night watching one of those reality shows where they show live births. Maybe it wasn't the best thing to do. My insides hurt just watching the process, and Krissy looked a little squeamish. I think she was hoping they could just knock her out and then wake her up when it was over and hand her a perfectly cleaned up baby. I left as soon as Chance got home from work. I'd never seen him look so happy and proud of himself. It was like he wanted to high-five over the fact he knocked up his wife. What the heck, I high-fived him.

I knew there was a reason she didn't make that squad, I just never guessed this would be it. Note to self, when it comes to birth control, don't believe your husband when he says trust me.

Nineteen

I KEPT LOOKING AT THE time on my computer, waiting for noon. I needed a drama-free friend at the moment. At a quarter 'til noon, a man happened upon my doorway. I looked up, expecting to see Jay, but I was surprised.

"Charlee."

"Ryan."

He bravely stepped into my office. He didn't look well. I mean, he looked gorgeous as usual, but his demeanor was solemn, and he looked tired. He rubbed the back of his neck. "I know I told your dad I would give you some space, but I'm finding that difficult. Will you please go to lunch with me?"

"I can't."

"Can't or won't?"

Looking at him, my heart ached. Part of me wanted to jump up and hug him, the other part wanted to punch him in the gut. "Both," I answered, but I kind of regretted it. He looked miserable.

"Charlee, please."

It was then that the man I expected earlier graced my doorway. I smiled at him, but I think Ryan mistook that for him and looked relieved. That was, he did for a split second.

Jay wasted no time coming to me. I stood up, and he picked me up and swung me around. "You're a sight for sore eyes, beautiful."

He set me down, and I straightened my dress. He was always a little too exuberant. I looked between the two men who were now in a full-on staring contest. "Jay, this is . . . my dad's business partner and neighbor Ryan. Ryan, this is my . . . Jay. We went to grad school together."

Ryan looked at me. He seemed hurt and unsettled by my introduction. I didn't know what else to call him. I was never his girlfriend, and we weren't seeing each other anymore, but friend or coworker seemed weird to say. Jay, too, seemed disappointed. Why did Ryan have to come in here?

Jay reached out his hand to Ryan, and Ryan reluctantly held out his own and shook Jay's. "Nice to meet you." He didn't mean a word of it.

"Same," Jay said.

"You ready to go?" I asked Jay.

Jay put his arm around me. "Anywhere with you."

I looked at Ryan, who looked worse than ever. "See you later."

"Count on it." He glared at Jay.

I walked out with Jay, but my eyes and heart were on Ryan. Ryan didn't move, he just watched us leave. Awkward didn't even begin to cover that little scene.

Jay led us to his loaded-down truck.

"What's all this?"

"I'm meeting up with some buddies in Yellowstone for some hiking and camping."

"That sounds like fun."

"Do you want to come?" he half-teased.

I rolled my eyes at him.

He laughed and helped me into his truck.

He ran around and jumped in the driver's side. "So, where to, my lady?"

I gave him directions to my favorite burger joint. I knew he would love it.

"You going to tell me what's up with Ryan?" he asked on our drive over.

"What do you mean?"

"Don't play coy with me, Charlee Jensen. That guy was about ready to punch me."

"He was not."

"You don't know men very well."

"Believe me, I know."

"Are you dating him?" He sounded like he didn't really want to know.

"Jay, I don't think you and I should talk about him."

"Charlee, I know you don't love me. I saw the way you looked at him, and it's the way I always wished you would have looked at me."

"Jay."

"I'm okay." He reached over and took up my hand.

I squeezed it tight. "You're one of the best guys I know. I never meant to hurt you."

"I know. This isn't your fault. I always knew. I just hoped."

"I hoped, too."

"So, are you going to tell me what's going on with your 'neighbor'?"

I laughed. "No."

"Actually, I think I'm good with that."

I needed a lunch with Jay. He always made me laugh. He was a big goofy kid at heart. The two hours passed quickly, and I found myself back in my office questioning my sanity again. I felt like I should get on an episode of Dr. Phil called, "Women Who Can't Find Love with Perfect, Available Men."

I tried not to dwell on it as I crunched numbers the rest of the day. I also helped my widow friend again.

At five, my dad came by. "Don't stay too late."

"Oh, I won't."

He chuckled. "All right. See you later, kiddo."

I only planned on staying until six. I was trying my best not to look like the boss' kid. I knew my dad didn't care if I took a two hour lunch and came home on time, but I didn't want the other employees having any contempt for me or my dad about it. And heaven forbid anyone think I'm a spoiled brat. Yeah, I still wasn't over that one yet. I still wasn't over Ryan, either.

I don't know how much extra work I got done as I sat there and thought about him and what happened on Sunday. My heart ached.

A half hour later, the man who occupied way too much of my thoughts called, but I didn't answer. Part of me really wanted to. I wanted to hear his voice and tell him about my day. I wanted to hear about his day and Josh, but he'd really hurt me.

Within a couple of minutes, my phone let me know I had a voice message. I tried to resist listening to it, at least for a few moments, but I gave in.

"Charlee, I'm sorry. I know that doesn't make this right. I guess I just want you to know I'm thinking about you and I miss you. I'll try back later."

I'll admit, part of me wanted to call him right back, but I couldn't. I wasn't ready to talk to him.

I had a lot of messages over the next week, not to mention the flowers and his frequent visits to my office to test the waters. No matter the cold reception or the number of times I declined to have lunch or dinner with him, he still came back for more.

After a good ten days, my dad intervened on his behalf, although he wasn't happy with his partner and friend. My dad reached over and held my hand on the way into the office. "I've noticed a decline in productivity the last week and a half."

I turned to him, somewhat taken aback. "What do you mean? I'm actually ahead of schedule with most of my clients."

My dad chuckled and squeezed my hand. "I'm not talking about you. I meant my partner."

"Oh."

"I'm not telling you that he deserves another chance, but could you at least talk to the guy?"

My dad had no idea how much I wanted to talk to him. I missed him and Josh, although he did let Josh come over on Saturday for a bit to jump on the trampoline with me. My eyes started watering. They had been doing that a lot lately.

"Honey, people make mistakes. I know that better than anyone, but not all mistakes are fatal and sometimes there's greater happiness to be found on the other side of our stupidities. Mistakes are the best teachers."

"So what are you saying?"

"I just want you to listen to your heart. That's all."

I thought a lot about what my dad said during the day, but it wasn't until the next day I acted upon it. We drove in separately because I had to stay late. I promised my widow friend I would help again, but she couldn't meet until after hours. After our call ended, I had a visitor. I thought he would have left when my dad did, but I guess not. He was looking pretty miserable, standing there at my door. "Your dad said you were working late."

"He was right."

Ryan gave a hint of a grin. "Do you want to grab dinner?"

"No, thanks."

Ryan boldly walked in and perched himself on the edge of my desk.

I looked up at him from where I sat. "What are you doing here?"

"Isn't it obvious? I want to talk to you."

"I don't know why."

He took my hand that had been writing down a calculation on my scratch pad. I looked up at him, annoyed, and he smiled. "Charlee, I've missed you. I want to see what I can do to make things right between us."

I took my hand out of his, and rubbed my face. "It's never going to work between us."

"Why? Because of Jay?"

I wasn't expecting that comment. "You almost sound jealous."

"I haven't wanted to punch anyone since junior high until I saw the way that guy looked at you, so I guess you could say I'm jealous."

I guess Jay was right. "I don't understand why you would be."

He edged closer to me and took my hands in his. "I'm sorry. I know that comes nowhere close to making this right, but I am. My behavior toward you at the sports bar was inexcusable and it in no way reflects how I really feel about you." He pulled my hands up to his heart. "How much I care about you. I've been kicking myself for the last week and a half. And Hayes and Rob were less than impressed with me. Hayes read me the riot act over the phone afterward."

"Well, I'm sure Trixie and Alec will sing your praises if you're looking for some comfort."

His head dropped and he sighed. "I deserve that. I should have never let them talk to you that way. I don't know what got into me. Alec did call, though, after he sobered up, and he asked me to apologize to you."

"How kind of him."

"Charlee, I'm sorry for what I said and didn't say that day and I'm sorry for believing things about you that were false, but most importantly, I'm sorry for what you had to go through. I had no idea."

I removed one of my hands from his grasp and wiped at my eyes. "How would you have known?"

He stood up, took my hand back, pulled me up, and held me against him. "Regardless," he whispered in my ear. "I hate thinking of what you had to go through and I hate that I misjudged you. And you know what else I hate?"

"What?"

He released me enough to peer into my eyes. "I hate that you introduced me as your dad's partner and neighbor."

"Well, that's what you are."

"I was hoping since we made out, I would get a better title." He grinned like an idiot.

I backed up, but he held firm. "You and I have shared some very nice kisses. We've never made out."

His brow furrowed. He pulled me closer, and like a moron, I let the butterflies in my stomach override my head. Our foreheads met.

"Charlee, I'm sorry if I've given you the impression that you're anything but desirable to me. I want to more than make out with you, and if I were younger, I would have already acted on that. But I'm a father now, and I look at things differently. I don't want to remake past mistakes, especially with you."

"Maybe you should have asked how I felt on the subject."

"You're right. I should have, but it wouldn't have changed my mind."

"You're assuming things about me you shouldn't."

"I'm confused."

"I wouldn't have slept with you even if you'd wanted to."

He straightened up and zeroed in on my eyes. "Why?" He sounded offended.

I laughed at his reaction. "Don't take it personally. It's not just you."

He arched his perfectly shaped eyebrow at me. "Are you saying what I think you're saying?"

"I don't know, am I?"

"You really are an unusual girl, I mean woman."

"No. I just decided a long time ago after watching my parents make huge mistakes when it came to sex, that I didn't want that for myself. When that time comes, I want that person to be fully committed to me in every sense of the word."

He took my face gently in his hands. "I wish, at your age, I was as wise as you."

"So, you weren't perfect?"

"Anything but. Victoria and I got married because she was pregnant," he admitted reluctantly.

I felt my own eyes dilate. I wasn't expecting that piece of information. I was speechless. It did explain a lot, though; especially her behavior before and during the wedding.

"We didn't tell anybody because Victoria was . . . less than happy about it. She didn't want people to think that I had to marry her. It's not that I didn't want to, but I would have waited to ask."

"She didn't look pregnant at the wedding, and what happened to the baby?"

"We rushed to get married before she started showing. She miscarried two weeks after our wedding."

"I'm sorry."

"We both took it hard, but she questioned our decision. I think she stayed because of how it would have looked if she left, so we muddled through, and eventually we had Josh. I thought that would fix things, and for a while it made things better between us, but her indifference for me returned, and she finally called it quits."

"I'm sorry, Ryan."

He gently slid his hands back and through my hair before he leaned in and barely grazed my lips with his own. "Charlee Jensen, you are intelligent, beautiful, and irresistible. I'm sorry if I made you feel anything less." His lips met mine again, but this time harder.

I pushed him away, just barely.

"I'm sorry. Do you not want me to kiss you?"

"I should probably say no, but that would be a lie."

He grinned.

"I told my dad I wouldn't make out with you in the office."

"I have no intention of ever mentioning it to him." His lips met mine.

My arms found their way around his neck, and my hands found themselves happily tangled up in his hair. They had wanted to for so long. He wasted no time in parting my lips and removing any available space between us. My body easily sank into his, heightening the intensity of his kiss. When his lips finally left mine after several minutes of bliss-worthy kissing, they found their way to my ear and then down my neck.

I sighed deeply as he reached the base of my neck and then worked his way back up to my ear. "I hope this makes me worthy of being called more than your neighbor," he whispered in my ear.

I needed to take a breath before I could speak. "What do you want to be called?"

He didn't hesitate. "Charlee's."

Twenty

SO WHAT ARE WE ON? Charlee and Ryan take three? I warned him this was the last take. If we didn't get it right this time, it wasn't happening. I also warned him I didn't date men that made me cry. He thought that was unrealistic, but agreed to do his best not to let that happen again, unless of course they were the happy kind of tears. I was a complete sucker for him, so I agreed after lots of groveling, and making out. He was better at it than I imagined, and much more willing to do it now that he knew I didn't want it to go further. Who knew that would take pressure off a guy? It was also helpful for him to know that I wanted to be close to him. Not surprisingly, Victoria was a cold fish and not very affectionate. He was afraid to be overly so with me. I guess rejection gets to guys after a while. I told him to pile on the affection.

For a while, things were a little tenuous between my dad and Ryan. There was an uneasiness that hadn't been there before. My dad was being extremely protective of me in light of past revelations. I knew he loved Ryan, but I think he wanted him to know not to mess with me. Ryan took it in stride and did his best to prove to my dad he was "worthy" to date his daughter.

Ryan was also doing his best for me. The uneasiness between us diminished almost completely. I don't know what exactly changed for him, but it was like a switch flipped and the door to his heart opened. I loved having access to it.

We had just finished running the course where the 10k was taking place the next weekend. It was the first trial run, and I didn't die, so that was a plus. It was hillier than I would have liked, but I thought doable. Ryan ran it like a pro and was breathing like a normal person.

I knew I was red in the face and breathing like I had been smoking for forty years. I laid out in the cool grass of the evening and tried to recuperate. Ryan sat down next to me and smiled down at me.

"Why is this so easy for you?" I lamented.

"You just need to work on your breathing patterns."

"Or not do it."

"You've come this far, and your time is great. You can't quit now."

"Well, I could, but I'm too prideful to."

He laughed. "Knowing you, you'll probably show up and beat us all."

"Your faith in my running ability is highly misplaced."

He scooted closer and leaned his arm over me.

I smiled up at him. "We probably look like two old people showing way too much PDA now."

"Anyone that sees you wouldn't blame me."

"So maybe flattery will get you everywhere."

He leaned down and kissed me. "Perfect, because I have something to ask you."

"Shoot."

"My friends have invited us to watch the game with them on Monday night."

I narrowed my eyes at him. "What friends?"

"Same as before, minus Trixie."

I sat up. "Didn't you inherit any other friends in your divorce?"

He scooted closer and ran his strong hand across my cheek and up through my sweat drenched hair. If that didn't say a guy liked you, I don't know what did. "Have I mentioned how beautiful you are lately?"

"Yes, so if you're trying to flatter me into saying yes, you better come up with something better."

His forehead scrunched together, and he thought for a moment.

"Is it really that hard to think of something?"

He groaned and kissed me hard. "No, there's too many good things, it's hard to pick only one."

"Uh-huh."

"Come on, Charlee. Please. I need to prove to my friends that I'm not some jerk of a boyfriend to you."

"Since when did you become my boyfriend?"

He smiled sexily, leaned in close, and kissed his way to my ear. He so knew he was getting his way. "Ever since we started making out."

Goosebumps erupted, and I sighed. "Okay . . . but I think you have to give me your class ring or something to make it official."

He laughed softly in my ear. "Deal."

We had a great weekend with Josh, who was super excited to start preschool the following week. He was only going two afternoons a week on Tuesdays and Thursdays, but for a three-year-old, that was big news.

"Cherry, will you take me to school with mommy and daddy?" he asked while we had dinner at Ryan's house on Sunday.

I looked over, smiled at him, and began to tell him, "I would love to." I was thrilled he asked me to, but Ryan cleared his throat loudly and gave me a meaningful look. "Can I talk to you for a minute?"

I set my fork down on my plate. "Um, sure."

We both got up and walked to the kitchen where we could still see Josh in the breakfast nook. We stood by his immaculately cleaned granite counter top.

Ryan's eyes were full of worry.

"What's wrong?" I kept my voice down.

He moved a tad closer. "Nothing's wrong. It's just, it's probably not a good idea for you to come on Tuesday."

"Why not?"

He looked unsure of how to proceed. He rubbed his neck and stretched it from side to side.

I waited.

"Charlee, I want you there, but . . ."

"I get it. Victoria doesn't."

"I'm sorry. This is a big deal for her, and she wants it to be just us."

"Us?"

"You know what I mean, Charlee."

"I do know what you mean. But if you ever want 'us' . . ." I pointed between him and me, "to ever really move forward, you're going to have to let me be involved in your whole life, including Josh." I walked off and joined Josh back at the table. "Hey, big guy, I'm sorry I can't make it, but I'll send a surprise with your daddy to give to you for your big day. Okay?"

He looked up at me with those big green eyes. "Okay." He was disappointed for a second before his eyes lit up. "Don't forget my surprise."

I ruffled his hair. "I won't."

Ryan joined us again, took up his seat across from me, and gave me a sheepish smile.

I smiled back close lipped and wondered.

Victoria arrived a couple hours later to pick up Josh. He ran to the door yelling, "Mommy."

I watched from the great room when she picked him up at the door and held him to her. She eyed me and wasn't pleased I was there. I smiled at her. What else could I do?

Ryan looked between the two of us, and I smiled at him as well. He turned back to his ex-wife, who was looking to make a quick exit.

"I'll walk out with you." Ryan grabbed Josh's bag.

"Bye, Cherry." Josh waved from his mother's arms.

"Bye, big guy." I waved back to their retreating figures.

I sat on the couch and sighed. I knew it didn't have to be this way. There were lots of people that got along with their ex's girlfriend, boyfriend or significant other.

Ryan returned a few minutes later and dropped next to me on the couch. He pulled me onto his lap and kissed me with fervor, without saying a word. I was more than okay with it. I liked non-verbal communication. By the time I pulled away, my heart rate was up and I was breathing harder than normal. I settled my head against his chest. "What was that for?"

"I didn't know I needed a reason to kiss you."

"You don't, but there seemed to be some underlying emotion in it."

He rubbed his hand gently against my arm. "Charlee, I'm trying."

"I know you are. Do you still . . . love her?" I had wanted to ask him that for so long.

He paused, and my heart skipped a few beats waiting for him to answer.

"No . . ."

"What does that mean?"

"Charlee, she's the mother of my son and we were married for seven years. While I'm not in love with her, my feelings for her are complicated." There was that word again. I was beginning to dislike it very much.

"Okay."

"Hey, my feelings for you are not complicated. I'm happy we're together. Which reminds me, I have something for you." He extracted himself from me and walked toward his bedroom. He came back carrying a jacket. He stood in front of me with a playful grin and held up his letterman's jacket. "I didn't have a class ring, but I thought maybe this would work."

I laughed and took the maroon and gold jacket out of his hand and admired it. I ran my fingers across the S with all his track and field patches and pins. "Looks like you were quite the star."

He sat next to me and relived some of his high school glory days with me. I liked to hear him talk about his track meets and accomplishments and even failures that he learned from. I liked it even better when he took the jacket from my hands and placed it around my shoulders. It smelled yummy, like him.

"Now you're mine." He kissed me.

Twenty-One

MONDAY EVENING ARRIVED, AND I was nervous. I dressed more conservatively, in jeans and a Bronco t-shirt this go around. The evenings were getting chilly now that we were into September. Even running in the mornings was getting a little too nippy for my taste. Ryan was sad I had to retire my pink running shorts for the season.

My dad insisted on getting the door when Ryan arrived to pick me up. I insisted he not, but I lost. My dad was still on the overprotective kick, and since Ryan was taking me back to the same place where he blew it, he felt the need to flex his dad muscles.

I let my dad talk to him alone. I figured it would be less embarrassing for Ryan that way, and honestly, I didn't want any part of it.

After five minutes, my dad called to me and let me know Ryan was there, like I didn't know already. I stopped myself from running upstairs. I found I just wanted to be near Ryan, but I acted mature and sauntered up at a casual pace.

Both the men in my life turned my way. One greeted me with a look of fatherly affection, the other was anything but fatherly. It was more like a "maybe we should be alone tonight" kind of a look. I recognized it because I felt the same way when I looked at him. He looked great in his well-fitting jeans and his own Bronco t-shirt that stretched nicely across his toned chest.

Ryan reached out his hand to me and I gladly took it. My dad kissed my cheek as if he were letting Ryan know who the boss was.

"Goodnight, Dad."

"You kids have a good time."

"We will." At least I hoped we would.

"See you later, Jeff," Ryan said to his friend and partner.

Ryan led me out the door into the crisp evening. It was starting to smell like fall, and I loved it.

Once we were both settled in the car, he kissed me.

"Sorry about my dad."

"It's all right, I suppose I deserved it. Hopefully he'll forgive me soon."

"I'm sorry our relationship has caused discord between you."

"It's not your fault. It was my own doing. Your dad is being a good dad, and I respect that."

"I know, but you guys are partners and friends."

"And we still will be."

He turned to start the car, but stopped suddenly. "I forgot, I have something for you." He reached back, grabbed a silver colored gift bag, and handed it to me. "I picked it up during lunch today."

I took the bag. I knew what was inside of it. He insisted on having my CPA license professionally matted and framed when it had come in the mail last week. I told him a frame from Target would do, but he adamantly disagreed. I pulled out the black framed license that made me a legit certified public accountant and looked it over. I looked back up to a proud Ryan. I grabbed his shirt and pulled him to me. "I would kiss your face off right here if the neighbors weren't so gossipy."

"Let them talk." His mouth landed on mine.

I didn't exactly kiss his face off, but close enough. I wiped my lipstick off his lips, and he grinned.

"When you get your Master's in Psychology, I'll get it framed to match."

We were never leaving the driveway if he kept talking like that. That was the biggest turn-on ever. Not only did it say he supported me in my goals, but he thought we would be together when it happened. "I lo . . .like you . . . a lot." Oh, I got careless. I wasn't sure if he caught that.

He smiled. "I'm glad, because I like you, too . . . a lot." He kissed my cheek before he started his car.

I took a deep breath and reminded myself to watch it, but it was getting more difficult. I was truly, madly, deeply in love with him.

When we pulled up to the sports bar, he turned off his car and turned toward me. He rested his hand against my cheek. "I really am sorry about last time, but tonight I plan on making up for it."

I arched my eyebrow. "Oh, really?"

He leaned over and his lips teased mine before he pressed his mouth against mine. He took a moment to soak me in before my lips parted. He gave me a small taste of what I hoped I had to look forward to the rest of the night. He had a hard time pulling away. "We better go." He didn't sound convinced.

We walked in hand-in-hand, but this time when we met his friends, he kept a hold of me. In a somewhat comical gesture, Hayes and Rob took me from him and placed me in between them. I thought it was cute, Ryan not so much. He took me right back, led me to the other side of the table, scooted his chair as close as he could to mine, and draped his arm around me. It kind of broke the ice and awkwardness, and we all settled in for a night of football. Alec was even somewhat polite. He was a lot better without his wife around. I was so relieved she didn't show up again. That had been my biggest worry.

My other pleasant surprise of the evening was that Ivy was our server. This time I made introductions. I loved saying, "This is my boyfriend, Ryan."

Her eyes said she approved. Who wouldn't? He was a credit to the male species.

I got crazy and ordered a virgin daiquiri, and Ryan ordered a Coke. Yeah, we were really wild. Alec gave him a hard time for not drinking, but he brushed it off. I knew it wasn't the best thing for either of us to be drinking sugar laced beverages since we were training for a race that weekend, but oh well. I was going to die either way, and Ryan was going to be amazing.

"Congratulations," Hayes yelled across the table to me. The game had started and everyone was shouting at the TV. "Ryan told us you passed your CPA exam."

I smiled over at my proud boyfriend before answering. "Thank you. Now I'm trying to get back into school."

"MBA not enough for you?" Hayes asked.

"No." I smiled.

"She's going to be a psychologist," Ryan added before kissing my head.

I loved this Ryan.

"Did we come here to watch the game or not?" Alec barked.

We all turned our attention to the game, but not before we thanked Ivy for bringing our drinks and the most ginormous platter of nachos I had ever seen. Rob had ordered them and told us all to help ourselves. No one needed a second invitation. The spicy meat and cheese concoction was oh, so good, but I'm sure super bad for you. I washed it down with some of my other unhealthy choice for the night. I took a large drink of my daiquiri and something was different. At first I thought maybe the jalapenos had burned off my taste buds, so I took another sip. It was still different, but yummy, so like an idiot I kept drinking it. I didn't realize that perhaps the burning sensation wasn't the spicy nachos. Besides, I was having such a great time with Ryan that everything else was secondary. And like a bigger idiot, I had more than one daiquiri.

I had a great time yelling at the refs and cheering on my favorite football team. Ryan kept smiling over at me.

"Am I embarrassing you?"

"Are you kidding me? I'm not sure if you've ever been sexier to me."

Suddenly I was feeling warm and fuzzy; it was kind of an odd, freeing sensation. Ryan had that effect on me and I loved it. I didn't care that we were with his friends, or in a room full of people, I leaned into him and let my lips fall on his. I saw him grin right before our lips met.

He kissed me once, but pulled away. "You taste different, and my lips kind of tingled."

I laughed like it was the funniest thing he had ever said.

"You did say virgin daiquiri, right?"

"Of course."

He looked over at my almost completely empty glass and picked it up. He took the final sip, set it down, and laughed. "Charlee, there was nothing virgin about that drink."

I leaned into him again, I couldn't help myself. "What do you mean?"

He pulled me closer, and kissed the top of my head.

Ivy walked by to ask if we wanted our drinks refilled.

"What did you bring Charlee to drink?" Ryan asked her.

"A virgin daiquiri like she asked."

Ryan shook his head. "I don't think so." He handed Ivy the glass.

"I guess the bartender misunderstood me," she said, or at least I think that's what she said.

My brain was swirling, and I wasn't sure I heard her right. All I could focus on was Ryan, and even that was becoming difficult. "Ryan, I don't feel so hot." I continued to lean against him.

He took a hold of me. I think his friends were asking what was going on and the verdict was I was trashed. Ivy was profusely apologizing and Ryan was chuckling and stroking my hair. "She doesn't ever drink. Now I see why."

His friends were laughing at me. I knew I should probably care, but my head was pounding.

"Ryan," I managed to say. "I don't feel right."

"Can you stand up?"

I stood up, and the whole room seemed to move. Ryan wrapped his arm around me and I clung to him. "Let's get you home."

"I'm so sorry," I heard Ivy say.

"Don't worry about it," Ryan replied for me.

Ryan began to move, but I didn't want to. I felt like the world was spinning and if I moved, I would fall.

"I have you. Come on, Charlee."

I trusted his voice and made my legs move. It felt like it took forever to make it outside. The place was crowded, and with each step I felt unsure.

As soon as we made it outside, Ryan picked me up as if I weighed nothing.

I leaned my head against his shoulder. "I'm sorry."

"Don't be. I kind of like this arrangement. Your dad may kill me, though."

"I would laugh, but my head hurts and I feel like I'm going to toss my cookies."

"Let's see if we can't get you home first."

When we reached his car, he carefully set me in and buckled me like I was Josh.

I leaned my head against the cool glass of the passenger side window and willed myself not to throw up in Ryan's car. I was so embarrassed. Why did I keep drinking those stupid drinks?

Ryan reached over and held my hand. "Are you okay?"

"Not really."

It felt like the longest car ride ever, but at least I didn't throw up. I was never ever drinking again. I didn't know how people did it. I wanted to curl up in a ball and die.

Ryan came around and, with as much care as he used to place me in the car, he picked me up.

I groaned and sank into him.

"Now the neighbors really are going to talk," he teased.

"I'll laugh about that later."

Ryan kissed my head and walked us up the porch. He deftly rang the doorbell with me still in his arms. We waited, but no answer. That was weird. My dad hadn't mentioned he was going anywhere. Ryan gently set me down, but kept a hold of me, so he could reach into his pocket. I guess he had a house key, which was good since I left my purse in his car.

We barely made it in and to the guest bathroom in the hall before I lost it. As soon as I felt better, I was going to be mortified. What was worse, or the sweetest thing ever, was he stayed in there with me and held my hair. I felt like I was going to die. The vomiting wasn't helping me feel any better, either. After I lost everything I had eaten in the last ten years, I collapsed on the cool tile floor of the bathroom.

"Charlee," Ryan whispered and stroked my head. "Where do you keep your toothbrush?"

"Downstairs in my bathroom," I barely muttered.

"I'll be right back."

I lay still in a ball and wished for the nausea and head spinning to go away. I was so stupid. Why did I keep drinking those delicious drinks? I had never felt so miserable in my life, and the man I loved just witnessed my stupidity and probably the grossest thing that had ever happened to me. I won't even talk about the smell of it all. I wanted to die, literally and figuratively.

Ryan returned in no time at all with my toothbrush and tooth-paste. He set them down near the sink. He bent down and basically picked me up. I didn't want to move. I felt like in doing so I really would die. "Come on, honey. Rinse out your mouth and brush your teeth, and then I'll take you to the couch."

"Please, just let me die," I moaned.

He chuckled softly. "Sorry, no can do." He hoisted me up gently. He even put the toothpaste on the toothbrush for me.

I felt like Josh.

I slowly lifted the toothbrush and brushed my teeth at a snail's pace and then rinsed out my mouth. I wasn't sure that horrible taste was ever going anywhere, or the burn in my throat.

"Do you want me to carry you to the couch?" he asked.

"No, I've got it."

He wrapped his arm around me, and we slowly made our way to the living room couch. I fell on the soft cushions of the light blue fabric couch. Ryan joined me and placed my head on his lap. He had also thought to bring up a blanket from my bed. He was the greatest boyfriend ever, though he was probably thinking of breaking up with me after my little exorcist event in the bathroom. Why couldn't I be like a normal twenty-something who could drink alcohol without any issues?

"By the way, I love your bathroom decorations. I think the lacy pink one is my favorite."

Could this night get any better? First vomiting, and now all the bras I had hand washed earlier that morning hanging all over my bathroom. I moaned as I lay there shivering. "I'm so embarrassed."

"Why? I've seen plenty of bras in my day."

"The bras are the least of my concerns."

He gently brushed my hair with his hand. "You know, I kind of like this part of you."

"The pukey, incapacitated side?"

"No, the vulnerable side."

I turned carefully to my other side, so I could see him. He was looking down at me so sweetly. He rested his hand on my clammy cheek.

His look was my undoing. "I . . . I" I so badly wanted to tell him that I loved him. I almost did. I had never felt it stronger.

"You what?" He ran his thumb across my cheek.

"Thank you, Ryan." I chickened out. Thank you seemed entirely inadequate for the situation, but I didn't know what else to say.

"You're welcome."

I closed my eyes to his gentle touch. "You know, I had the biggest crush on you when I was growing up." I felt like I needed to offer him something. Something to the depth of how I felt about him.

He stopped stroking my hair and face for brief moment.

I didn't bother opening my eyes to see his reaction.

"Really?" He took up touching me ever so softly again.

"It's true."

"Can I tell you something?"

"You can tell me anything."

"That summer I got married, I used to look at you and think someday you were going to make some guy a very lucky man. Who knew it would be me?"

I curled up tighter against him and almost told him that I loved him again, but I stopped myself. "If I could sit up, I would so kiss your face off right now."

"I'll take a rain check on that. You rest." He pulled the blanket around me. I settled into him and drifted off to sleep, wishing that I had him to fall asleep to every night.

I'm not sure what time it was when I was awakened to the sound of Ryan and my dad talking. I heard the tail end of Ryan telling my dad what had happened. At least my dad was laughing. I was afraid he may be upset with Ryan, although it wasn't even close to his fault. He was the best caretaker ever. I didn't open my eyes or move away from Ryan. I liked where I was at. I didn't say anything until my dad left. I did wonder, though, where my dad had been.

"What time is it?" I asked Ryan as I stirred.

"Just after midnight."

It was late for my dad to be getting home.

I tried to sit up, but my head pounded. Instead, I groaned.

"Can I get you anything?"

"No. You've already done more than enough."

"It's late, I should probably go home."

"Please don't." I opened my eyes to see his reaction. I wasn't even sure why I said that, but I wasn't ready to say goodbye.

He looked at me with eyes that looked like burning evergreen bushes. He didn't say anything. Instead he kicked off his shoes and maneuvered me gently until we were both comfortable on the couch. I snuggled into him. I wanted to stay there forever.

"You know, I'm risking my life for you."

"My dad is all talk."

He kissed my head. "Maybe, but I can't think of a better way to go."

"That may be the sweetest thing anybody has ever said to me."

He pulled me closer to him, and I easily fell asleep with him holding me.

I stayed asleep until a little past five when Ryan woke me up by kissing my forehead. "I hate to go, but I better."

My head still pounded, but I felt a little better. "Okay." I peered into those eyes of his. I wanted to wake up to that every morning. I wondered how he felt about eloping. "Thank you for everything."

"It was my pleasure." He sat up. In the process, I sat up, too.

He put his shoes on while I leaned against him. "I don't think I'm going to make it in to work today."

He laughed. "I don't think so, either. I'm only working half the day. Josh starts school today."

"Don't forget to give him my gift and tell him I can't wait to hear all about it this weekend." I found him the cutest little fireman outfit and fire truck to go with it. I thought it was perfect. He loved his fire truck book and always got excited if he saw one while we were driving.

Ryan didn't say anything, he just turned and kissed me once on the lips. I hope I didn't have morning breath. I'd never kissed anyone first thing in the morning. It must have been okay because he smiled sexily when our lips parted. "I'll call and check on you later, and then I'll come by tonight."

I nodded, but even that hurt.

As soon as he left, I laid back down and thought, *I'm the luckiest woman in the world.*

Twenty-Two

THAT NIGHT NOT ONLY SOLIDIFIED my feelings for Ryan, but it also carried me through the lingering doubts the next few months would bring as we tried to make it work as a couple. But we weren't just a couple, there was a third and fourth party. The third party I loved more than anything, the fourth party not so much. That night also helped me with another member that had joined the party.

My dad woke me up before he left for work. He was all smiles when he touched my head like he was checking for a fever.

"Dad, I don't have the flu. I think this is what they call a hangover."

He laughed. "Your mom could never hold her liquor, either."

I knew that from experience, but didn't mention it.

"So where were you last night? Do you have a girlfriend you're not telling me about?"

His smile dropped, and he fidgeted next to me.

"Dad?"

"Baby girl." He stared at the wall. He took a deep breath and let it out. "I wasn't sure how to tell you, but Felicity and I . . ."

"Felicity? As in your secretary Felicity?"

He reluctantly turned his attention back to me. "Yeah, that Felicity."

"Why didn't you tell me? How long have you been seeing her?"

"For a while, on and off."

I sat up slowly. My dad leaned back, and I rested on him.

"You could have told me. I'm not a child."

"No, but you're my child, and I wasn't sure how you would feel about it. I can tell you don't like Mark, and I didn't want to rock the boat with you. You're the most important person to me, honey."

"Daddy, I'm happy for you. And I really like Felicity. I guess I know why Felicity has been so friendly to me."

"That's not the only reason. She thinks you're the best."

"I guess I was the complication she told me about when I asked if she was dating anyone."

My dad wrapped his arm around me and laughed.

"So, do you love her?"

There was a long pause before he answered. "Yes, I think so. She's quite a bit younger than me, but I've known her for a long time. I think we're a good match."

"Does Ryan know?"

"No, but I suppose he will soon."

I kind of laughed. I still felt horrible, I wasn't up for real laughter yet. "Yeah, I don't know if I could keep this juicy secret to myself."

"I don't want to advertise it in the office, I think we have enough inter-office dating going on as it is. So how's it going with you and Ryan?"

I sighed dreamily.

"That good, huh?"

"Yeah."

"Well, don't go losing your head."

"I won't."

"Do you need me to stay home with you?"

"Remember? Adult."

"I know, but sometimes I wish you were still my little girl."

I felt the same way sometimes. In the coming months, I would feel like that more often than I liked.

Don't get me wrong, there were so many things that were terrific about Ryan's and my relationship. Like I loved how he supported me. He finished the 10k in a beautiful time of just under thirty-five minutes and came in second place over-all. I ran it in forty-eight minutes, which was a respectable time, but nowhere near his level. But that didn't matter to him. He was the first one there to greet me when I crossed the finish line. He even had enough strength to pick me up. I loved our sweaty kisses. The look of pride on his face was priceless.

The day of the race was also the first time Felicity entered our world outside of work. She came to the race, and she and my dad watched Josh while we ran. I liked having Ryan with me as I got used to my dad being with another woman. I liked Felicity, a lot more than I ever liked Mark, but it was still weird. I mean, she was only seventeen years older than me and eleven years younger than my dad. Ryan was quick to remind me that I was also dating an older man. In a way, it was weird that my life and my dad's life were paralleling each other that way. I never thought we would be dating at the same time and to top it off, both co-workers.

When I saw Felicity with Josh, it got me thinking. What if my dad and her married and she wanted kids of her own? Would my dad want to? I mean, he was fifty-three.

Ryan laughed at me. "You could have kids at the same time," he teased.

I almost asked him if he wanted to be the dad, but I felt it was too forward and I was a little put out with him. The day before the race I found out from Josh that his dad hadn't given him my gift on his first day of school, but waited until he picked him up that day for the weekend. After Josh went to bed that night, I questioned him about it because he was really uncomfortable when Josh mentioned it at dinner that night. I was proud of myself for not lambasting him right there.

"Why didn't you give Josh my gift on Tuesday?" I asked as we were curled up on the couch together watching *Pretty in Pink*.

"Honestly?"

"No. Please lie to me."

He paused the movie and paused himself for a moment. "I was planning on it, but Victoria was in a mood when I went to pick them up. She had been talking to Trixie that morning about the night before and it was over-exaggerated."

"You're kidding me, right?"

"I set her straight. I told her you weren't drunk, well at least not on purpose."

"Not that I would ever, but even if I was, that isn't any of her business. I wasn't driving and I'm an adult."

"An adult that spends a lot of time with her son."

I sat up and stared straight at him. I saw a touch of 'maybe I said the wrong thing,' in his eyes. "And when have I ever been anything but responsible and loving with Josh?"

"You've been great with Josh, but she's his mom and she worries."

"Well, you're his dad. Do you worry about me being with your son?"

"No, never. You're amazing with him."

"She's never going to believe that unless you help her to see that." I turned back around and faced the TV, which hung above the fireplace.

"You're right." Ryan pulled me to him. "I'm doing the best I know how to keep everyone happy."

"I'm sorry for the pressure this causes you. And just so you know, it's not your job to make me happy. That's my job."

"Really?" He kissed my neck. I felt his warm breath against my skin. "Because you make me happy." He worked his way up to my ear. "Very happy."

I was in my happy place. I sighed deeply. "Ryan . . ."

"Yes?"

"I'm happy we're together."

"Me, too."

Twenty-Three

AS THE NEXT COUPLE OF months progressed, I tried not to let the fourth party get in the way, but it was hard at times. It wasn't anything big, more like minor annoyances, like the way she sneered at me anytime I saw her, or when she threw a fit with Ryan because he placed me as one of Josh's emergency contacts at school.

Felicity became my sounding board. She knew a thing or two about waiting for a man and dealing with an ex-wife. Not that my mom and Victoria interfered in quite the same way, but I guess my dad's love for my mom lingered over their relationship for a long time. They had been seeing each other for a lot longer than I knew at first, like two years on and off. I was surprised Felicity had stayed working for my dad. It sounded like an emotional roller coaster. It made me like her more. She was patient and understanding, but she was no doormat. I loved how she didn't push my dad, but she held her own ground. I tried to follow her example with Ryan.

We were well in the throes of autumn, and some days it felt like winter as we headed into November. The holidays were fast approaching, and so was Josh's fourth birthday. He was beyond excited. Not only was his birthday going to be at one of those places where they had a variety of bounce houses, but his Grandma Kaye was coming in honor of him. I was looking forward to it too. I hadn't seen Mrs. Carter in forever, and it felt kind of big that Ryan was introducing me as his girlfriend now to his mom, even though she already knew me.

Ryan and I weren't professing our love to each other, although I really wanted to. I was straight up in love with him, but I wasn't sure how he felt. At times I thought he was in love with me, too, but it was

245

as if there was this nagging question in the back of his mind about me. Like how he was nervous that he was taking me to Josh's birthday party with his ex-wife there and her friends and family. He never came outright and said it, but I could tell he was uncomfortable with it. He kept giving me warnings about them. I even asked him if he was trying to scare me off, but he denied it.

I wasn't going to miss it. I promised Josh I would be there, and I bought the best birthday present ever for him. A Nugget's jersey and three center-court tickets to see them. The Nuggets were my all-time favorite professional team, and I had been priming Josh to follow in my footsteps. I had even bought one of those standing toy basketball hoops so we could play inside when it was cold and dark out. He was getting pretty good at making baskets. His dad and I used it after he went to bed. I loved kicking Ryan's butt at hoops, and I loved the way he tried to distract me from making my shots. We ended up kissing way more than shooting.

I was also excited about Josh's birthday because that was the day I was going to tell Ryan I made it into grad school again. It took some finagling on my part and some evaluations, but CSU finally agreed to let me enter their Master's in Psychology program. I had been such a stress case about it, but Ryan kept encouraging me to keep pressing forward and not to take no for an answer. He even helped me craft some of my correspondence with the school. More reasons to love him. I had wrapped up my acceptance letter when I wrapped Josh's gifts. I also included two ski-lift tickets for Thanksgiving, as a gift for Ryan. This was the first year he wouldn't have Josh for that holiday, and I knew it was hard for him. I figured a day on the slopes and some fireplace and hot chocolate action were in order.

Kaye arrived on Friday, the day before Josh's party. Ryan asked me to come to the airport with him and Josh to pick her up and take her to dinner.

There Kaye stood at Denver International Airport, with her designer luggage, waiting for us at arrivals. She still looked fabulous. It was like she hadn't aged at all. She exuded elegance and grace as she stood there in her long woolen black coat, with perfect shining, bobbed, black hair.

Josh recognized her immediately and yelled out, "Grammy," before Ryan even stopped the car.

Ryan and I both got out; Ryan to retrieve the luggage and hug his mom, me to move to the backseat, but before I could, Kaye happened upon me and hugged me. "You are a vision and more beautiful than ever." She held me to her.

I loved this woman and was about ready to name her my mother-in-law. "I was thinking the same thing about you."

She stepped back and touched my cheek. "I think we will be the best of friends."

I nodded. I thought so, too. Or at least I really, really hoped so.

I held the front car door open for her and motioned for her to take my place.

"No, no. I want to sit in the back with my grandson."

I liked her even more.

Ryan smiled over at me and held my hand before he drove off. All felt right in the world.

I was even hopeful the next day when we headed to the party. Josh chatted nonstop on the way there. He was excited about all aspects of the party from the bounce houses, to the cake and ice cream, to the presents, and his friends. He had made a few friends in preschool, and he had a cousin close to his age coming.

I will admit I was a little nervous, but having Kaye there made me feel better. She was pretty anti-Victoria. She made sure not to say anything in front of Josh, but after he went to bed last night, she opened right up. Kaye wasn't thrilled with Victoria at all. She thought she took too much of Ryan's money and that the custody arrangement favored her. But for me, she had nothing but praise. I was apparently smart, beautiful, and charming, and not even the annoying kind that Ryan claimed me to be. She told me privately while Ryan was in the kitchen last night that she always wished I was older, so one of her sons could date me. I guess if you wait around long enough, we all get older. She was tickled Ryan and I were together. "There's this light about him now that you're in his life," she said.

I hoped so.

Ryan was fidgety on the way there. I reached over and rubbed his neck. "Are you okay?"

"Yeah." He nodded.

"Good, because I have some exciting news." I was going to wait until after to tell him, but I was already bursting.

He glanced my way and smiled.

"CSU admitted me into their Master's in Psychology program. I start in January."

I could see him smile as he kept his eyes on the road, but he reached over and placed his hand on my leg. "I'm proud of you."

I placed my hand on top of his. "Thank you."

"That's wonderful," his mom said from the backseat.

Ryan and I retrieved the gifts from the back of his car while his mom tried to reign in Josh, or at least tried to keep him from getting ran over in the parking lot. With our brief moment alone, I tugged on his shirt until my lips pressed against his. He joined in by wrapping his arms around me and kissing me deeper.

He grinned after our brief, yet passionate, kiss. "I've been missing your lips."

"Yes, I was thinking our lips should get together more often."

"It's a date," he said playfully.

"By the way, I have a surprise for you later."

"Like after my mom and Josh go to bed kind of surprise?"

I raised my eyebrow at his seductive comment, even though I knew it was innocent, at least mostly. "If you want it to be."

He winked at me.

I took that as a yes.

We walked in loaded down with gifts. I had fun shopping with Ryan for them. I hoped someday we would be buying the kind of gifts that were from both of us. Regardless, I had a lot of input, so I guess in a way they kind of were. But I was taking all the credit for what I bought for him. I wouldn't even let my dad go in on it. I made him purchase his own gift for Josh. Or more like I shopped for it and my dad paid for it. I was surprised he didn't have Felicity do it for him. Those two were like teenagers in love. I was kind of jealous. My dad seemed so sure about Felicity now that he knew he had my blessing. I wished Ryan would tell me he loved me like my dad told Felicity all the time, except at work. They were trying to be covert there, but believe me, people were talking.

Once we entered the fun zone, it was anything but fun for me. Right off the bat, there was this horrible tension when we walked into the party room. Victoria greeted her son with hugs and kisses and then was glued to her friend Trixie (yes, that dear showed up) and her sister-in-law, #wickedwitchOsanna. Osanna was married to Jonathon, Victoria's brother. Jonathon and Alec were semi-decent to me, but you could tell it made them uncomfortable, just like Ryan. I couldn't figure out what this hold was that Victoria had on everyone.

Ryan was good to me, but he wasn't as affectionate as he normally would have been. And I guarantee, those women were talking about me. They were all dressed to the nine's and I was dressed nice, but casual. This was a kid's birthday party after all, not the Academy Awards. I looked down at my vest, scarf, jeans, and boots and thought I looked cute and stylish.

My saving grace was Kaye. She never left my side. I had a feeling she had a diatribe on the tip of her tongue for her once-upon-a-time daughter-in-law. She kept looking at her and tsking. I could tell Ryan was torn on how he should behave, or should I say who he should be with. I figured it was his son's birthday, so I didn't make a fuss when it seemed like Victoria needed his help with everything. Apparently, lighting candles is a tricky business, as is moving chairs.

My heart had a little twinge of pain when we sang to Josh. He was flanked by his mom on one side and his dad on the other. They looked like the perfect little family. As soon as my favorite four-year-old blew out the candles on his Spiderman cake, both his parents kissed him on the cheek. They both looked at each other afterward, and there was this weird tension. Victoria gave Ryan this look. You know that look that sometimes wives give husbands. The one that says how you really feel about that person. Ryan didn't reciprocate, but it was awkward for me.

Kaye squeezed my hand as several eyes focused on me. I nervously tucked my hair behind my ear and smiled. What else could I do? I wished that was the worst of it. Presents were next. Victoria wanted to get that out of the way before the kids went to play. I don't know if that was a good call. They were all chomping at the bit to head out to the bounce houses. Not even cake or ice cream seemed very enticing to them. Josh's friends were generous, and it was all well and good until Josh liked my present more than his mom's. She had bought him some educational tablet that I'm sure was very expensive. Josh kind of tossed it aside and then opened my gift. He immediately wanted to put on the jersey, and he was really excited about going to the game. Victoria wasn't happy at all. She wished me dead with her eyes when Josh ran to me and hugged me.

"Thank you, Cherry."

"Her name is Charlee," his mom corrected him.

"I don't mind him calling me Cherry," I said quietly.

"I want him to talk properly."

I looked up at Ryan, who was standing near Victoria trying to get some guidance on how to proceed.

"It's just a nickname he has for her." I knew he didn't want to say anything. I was surprised he did.

"Well, I think it's darling." Kaye squeezed her grandson before he ran back to open the rest of his gifts.

The other adults in the room were looking between the two camps like this was some sort of ping pong match. Thankfully, Victoria left it alone. I didn't want to have to tell Josh he couldn't call me that. I was quite fond of it.

I was happy when they released the kids to the play area. The party room had become suffocating to me. Kaye and I stood nearby and watched Josh play with his friends. Ryan joined us after he oversaw the cleaning up of the party room.

He surprised me by standing by me and holding my hand and kissing the side of my head. "I'm looking forward to taking Josh to that game with you."

"You think the third ticket was for you?"

He smiled and squeezed my hand.

"Me, too." I squeezed back.

All was well and good for about two seconds.

Josh came running up to me. "Cherry, will you bounce with us?"

I felt Ryan squeeze my hand tighter, so I looked at him before answering his son. He didn't say anything, but it was like his eyes pleaded with me not to.

I shook my head at Ryan. "I've never been one to stand on the sidelines. I'm not changing that for anyone." Especially not Victoria.

Ryan's eyes registered understanding, but I knew what he was thinking. Victoria wasn't going to like it.

I let go of his hand and turned back to Josh. "I would love to."

"Me, too," said Kaye.

I turned to her and smiled. "Rock on, Grandma."

We both took off our shoes to the turned-up noses of Victoria and her cronies. I didn't care. I was tired of this game. I took Josh's hand, and we made our way to the bounce house that looked like a fire truck—it was his favorite. I didn't even bother looking at Ryan. If he wanted me to be someone I wasn't around Victoria, then we had a problem, a big problem.

I had a great time bouncing with Josh, his friends, and his wonderful grandma. Josh had me teach his friends "Ring Around the Rosy". They all giggled as we all fell down. I didn't bother looking at the adults. I knew they were staring at me. I could feel it, but this was who I was.

When Josh and his friends moved on to the ball pit, Kaye and I took up seats on one of the benches while Ryan talked to Alec and Jonathon.

Kaye looked between her son and me. "You know, a long time ago he would have been the first one to jump."

I met her concerned eyes. "I think I embarrass him."

"Nonsense. He would be a fool to be embarrassed by you."

"I don't know. Sometimes I feel like he wants me to be someone else."

"I hope you don't mean Victoria."

"That's exactly who I mean."

"No. He was miserable with her."

"Are you sure?"

She took my hand. "I'm sure. I see the way he looks at you. Sometimes people get into patterns with how they deal with people. They're unhealthy habits, and they're hard to break."

"Maybe you should be the psychologist." I smiled.

"No. I've just been around for a long time. Getting older has some benefits."

"I don't think Ryan sees their relationship as anything but healthy."

"Well, then he's a fool."

Maybe, I thought to myself.

The car ride home was pretty quiet. Josh was worn out and sleeping, and Ryan's mom was texting her husband.

Ryan reached over and held my hand. "Hey, thanks for coming today and for the great gift you gave Josh."

I didn't say anything other than to nod my head in acknowledgment. I was watching the clouds roll in. There was a storm coming. You could feel the snow that was brewing.

"Jonathon and Osanna invited me over for Thanksgiving so I can be with Josh."

My heart sank. I was happy for him, but I guess my plans for skiing and getting cozy in front of the fireplace went out the window. I was also hoping we would spend one holiday together. I knew he and Josh were going to D.C. for Christmas to spend it with his family.

"That's nice." I stared out the window. My insides churned, like the gathering clouds.

"Do you think that's wise?" his mom asked.

"I don't see any harm in it," Ryan answered. "I'm thankful for the invite. I hate spending the holidays away from Josh."

"Hmmm," his mom replied.

I stayed silent. I hated that he had to be away from Josh, but something seemed off about all of it. I felt like Victoria had ulterior motives, but what could I say about it?

Ryan came around and opened my door for me when we got to his house.

"Thank you." I kissed him on the cheek. "I think I'm going to head home. I'm tired."

"What about my surprise?"

"Oh . . . it was nothing. I'll see you later."

He reached out for my hand when I walked away and pulled me back. "You can come back later if you want."

"Thanks."

"Charlee?"

"I'm fine," I lied, and he knew it. His eyes were full of concern.

I walked home slowly and wondered what I was doing and if there was any hope for Ryan and me.

Twenty-Four

THE FOLLOWING WEEK WAS THANKSGIVING, and I had kept my distance from Ryan. I was confused. Josh's party had made me realize that I had perhaps been more optimistic about our relationship than I should have been.

Felicity and my dad had tried to get me to talk to them, but I didn't know how to put it into words. Heck, even Ryan tried to get me to talk about it, but I didn't know what to say to him exactly.

I took to spending my time with Krissy, who was now past the puking stage. She had a nice little baby bump going. She was due on April 6 and had just found out she was having a girl. Ann was in pink heaven, and the baby already had two wardrobes. I admit, I had bought my fair share, too. Baby girl stuff was too cute. The Lawtons and now the Wallaces, took pity on me and invited me for Thanksgiving. I was benevolent and gave my tickets for a romantic day on the slopes to my dad and Felicity.

I think they felt a little guilty taking them. My dad was torn about whether he should spend the holiday with me, but I insisted. Being around the two lovebirds was making me green with envy. It's a sad life when your dad has a hotter romance than you do. I was kind of used to it. I watched my mom date more than me through college. I had a feeling I would soon have a stepmother. I might even consider Felicity a stepmom if she and my dad got married, although I didn't like that title; I would think of her as mother the second. Or maybe mother the first if my own mom didn't straighten up. She was still ignoring me since the summer when my dad let her have it.

Can you see why I needed to become a psychologist? I lived a functional dysfunctional life.

Ryan asked me to go for a run with him Thanksgiving morning before we each went our separate ways. I felt like I couldn't say no. I had been putting him off since Josh's party. I had made sure I stayed busy with Krissy, which meant I had a lot of ice cream the past week, so a run was in order. And it's not that I didn't want to see him. I did. My problem was I was in love with a man, but I wasn't quite sure how he felt about me, and to top it off, he came with an ex-wife that got in the way in more ways than one.

We met behind the fence. It wasn't a bad morning for November. It was clear and crisp, but not cold.

Ryan greeted me with a kiss on my cheek. "There's my long-lost girlfriend. I was beginning to think I would only see you in the office."

I smiled, but I didn't really feel it. "I've been busy."

"I've noticed."

I took off running, and he followed.

"Charlee, are you upset with me?"

"No."

"Are you upset that I'm spending Thanksgiving with Victoria's family?"

"No. I mean I don't know. I'm happy you get to be with Josh, but how would you feel if, say, I was spending the day with Jay?"

He thought for a moment. "It would be off-putting for me, but this is different."

"How?"

"Because these people are family to me."

I didn't answer him. I guess he had a point. Not as valid as he thought, but I didn't push it further.

"Do you want to come with me?" He was more than hesitant to ask.

"We both know that's not a good idea."

He gave me a knowing look.

I sighed.

Our run was mostly a silent affair.

At the end, he pulled me to him and wrapped me up. "Charlee," he whispered in my ear. "Please tell me what you want. I don't like it when we're apart."

I sank into him. I missed him, too. "Ryan, I want to know that we're on the same page."

"What page is that?"

"The one where I mean as much to you as you mean to me."

"My mom told me that you thought I was embarrassed by you. Is that what this is all about? Because that's not the case. Any man in his right mind would be proud to call you his girlfriend, and I am."

"It's more than that, Ryan, and you don't need to answer right away, but I need to know how you feel about me."

"Charlee, where is all this coming from? I'm happy with where we're at. You know how much I care about you."

I reached up and kissed him once, softly on the lips. "Have a Happy Thanksgiving."

He cradled my face in his hands and peered into my eyes. "You, too. I'll call you later, or better yet, I'll come by. Please say yes."

I nodded my head. He smiled and kissed me goodbye.

The whole next week I just went along with him and pretended like everything was grand and I had nothing to worry about. Ryan was doing his best to be overly attentive. Normally I would have been into it, but it didn't come from the place I wanted it to come from. He was doing it because he was worried. I had no doubt he cared for me, but I knew he didn't love me and I loved him, and that was a problem for me. If he loved me, he would have said it Thanksgiving morning. Right?

I almost did, just to get it out in the open and because it was hurting me to keep it inside. There was the part of me that said, *Quit sweating this, you've only been dating for just over four months, you have plenty of time.*

It didn't matter because the following Friday it all came to a head. It's funny how life has a way of working it all out, even if it sucks. Ryan was in major boyfriend mode. Lunch dates every day that week, flowers, major make-out sessions in front of his fireplace. Then I got a very interesting phone call Friday afternoon as I sat wanting to poke my eyes out and reminding myself that in a month I would only be doing this part-time and I would be studying my favorite subject (other than Ryan).

"Hello."

"Charlee, sweetie, it's Kaye."

"Hi. It's so nice to hear from you. How are you?"

"Perfect, dear. I was calling to get some ideas from you about what kinds of foods you like and if there is anything special you want us to have here while you visit."

"I'm sorry, I'm a little confused. I mean, I would love to come and visit you, but I didn't know I was."

She paused. "Oh . . . Well I guess I thought Ryan would have asked you by now. I told him before I left there that I wanted you to come with him and Josh for Christmas."

My heart hurt, literally. It was beating wildly out of control. "I guess this is awkward. Ryan hasn't mentioned anything."

"I'm sure he will," she said without any confidence.

"It's okay."

"No, it's not. I need to have a talk with my son."

"Oh . . . please don't."

Before his mother could respond, the pig showed up at my door, all smiles. "Hey, Charlee."

"Can I call you back? Your son is here."

Ryan's smile faded when I glared at him and he realized who I was talking to.

"Don't go easy on him," she said before I hung up.

"That was your mom."

He shut my door and approached me cautiously.

"She was asking me what kinds of things I liked, you know, for our trip there during Christmas."

He stepped closer and sat at the edge of my desk. He looked like a kid who got caught with his hand in the cookie jar. "It's not what you think. I was going to ask you, but Victoria has never been away from Josh on Christmas and it's difficult for her and she asked if maybe she could come and—"

"And you told her no, right?"

"I told her I would think about it. It's not like we would stay together. She would get a hotel room."

I shook my head. "Do you hear how ridiculous this sounds? I can't do this anymore."

He reached out to touch me. I scooted my chair back and away from him.

"Don't do this, Charlee. I want to talk to you about this, but I have an important meeting in ten minutes. I was coming to ask you if you could get Josh for me," he said sheepishly. "His school is closing early because of the winter weather they're predicting, and Victoria's driving back from Denver and won't make it back in time."

I rolled my eyes. "Fine." I stood up.

"As soon as my meeting's over, I'll come home and we'll talk."

I ignored him and grabbed my purse and coat.

He embraced me, but I stayed stiff. "Be careful. I'll see you soon. And we'll work all this out. I promise." I felt him kiss the top of my head.

I almost sucker punched him before I walked off, ignoring him.

I stomped to my car. The snow was beginning to fall. I wrapped my coat tightly around myself and willed myself not to cry. I did not cry over men, especially stupid ones.

On my drive over to Josh's preschool, I kept running through my head all the things I wanted to say to Ryan later. First on my list was how blind he was to Victoria's manipulation. She said jump, and he asked how high.

The roads were decent on my twenty-minute drive over to the school, but the snow wasn't letting up and it was cold enough to stick. I hoped they wouldn't get too bad before we got home.

Josh was excited to see me. It was the highlight of my day seeing him running toward me and wrapping his arms around my legs. It made my heart ache, though. Ending things with Ryan meant not having Josh in my life, and I'll admit I had been picturing myself being in his life forever. I thought maybe we could trade Cherry in for mom one day, even though I knew his mom would hate it. *Don't cry,* I told myself.

"Are you ready to go home, big guy?" I bent down and helped him with his coat and gloves.

"Yes." He nodded that cute head of his.

I realized how much he had grown since the summer. His cheeks weren't as chubby anymore and he had gotten taller. I kissed his smooth cheek before I stood up and took his hand. We braved the cold and snow. The wind had picked up. It was almost white-out conditions. I carefully buckled Josh into the high-back booster seat I had been keeping in my car. Krissy had made fun of me, telling me I was such a mom. I wouldn't mind being one. I couldn't imagine loving a kid more than Josh.

"Will you make psghetti tonight?" Josh asked from the back seat as I carefully exited the school parking lot.

I smiled. I loved how he still said words wrong. He did that less and less now. I was going to miss it when he started speaking correctly all the time. "Yep. Will you help me?"

"Yes," he said like it was obvious. He loved helping us cook, even if it was something simple like stirring. *Us*, I sighed. I didn't know if after tonight there would be an us.

The roads were getting slick, and fast; it was also getting harder to see. The school was only ten minutes from both our homes, but everyone was driving at a snail's pace, which was good. I was a ball of nerves as we drove. I hated driving in this kind of weather. Josh, on the other hand, was enjoying himself. He was singing "Frosty the Snowman" in the backseat. He was missing half the words, but I liked it that way.

Halfway home, I slid a tad stopping for a red light. The car jerked a little, but it was okay. I took a deep breath. Only a couple more miles I told myself.

"Fire truck." Josh pointed out.

I looked over to see the newly built fire station. I bet they were going to be busy today with accidents. No sooner had I thought it then I looked in my rearview mirror to see a car behind me that was going a too fast for the conditions. It was like slow motion, although it happened so fast. They tried to brake, and then lost control. I braced myself, which probably wasn't the best thing, but it all happened so fast, and all I could think of was Josh. I called his name when the car hit the back of my car, sending my car into the back of the truck in front of me.

"Cherry!" Josh cried out.

My airbag didn't deploy, though it should have. I hit my head on the steering wheel. "It's okay, it's okay," I said after the shock wore off, like I was willing it to be that way. As soon as everything came to a halt, I whipped around to look at Josh who was crying, but he didn't look hurt. I reached back and took his hand. "It's okay, honey. Everything's okay."

The driver of the truck came out and checked on us. I didn't think it was safe for him to be out of his vehicle. "We're all right," I told him through a crack in my window. I wasn't rolling it all the way down for him. I didn't know who he was, and I kept thinking, *Keep Josh safe*. I didn't even unbuckle him. "Stay put, honey."

Thankfully, we were conveniently in front of the fire station. I saw lights flashing, and they made the short trip across the street. That at least got Josh to calm down.

"Are you hurt, honey?" I asked him.

He shook his sweet head no.

I felt sore, especially my neck, but I was okay, too.

Within a minute, I had a fireman at my door, opening it up. When they realized Josh was in the back, another one came our way. They both checked us over and cleared us to be moved. My car was not so lucky. It was in bad shape, but it kept us safe, so I wasn't going to complain.

What was a scary experience for Josh quickly turned into his dream. We were going to get to wait at the Fire Station.

Once there, I got Josh wrapped up in a blanket on my lap before I had a chance to call Ryan. We were waiting in the commons area of the fire station.

I didn't even get to say hello. "I've been worried, are you guys okay?"

"We're fine, a car plowed into me, but Josh is perfectly fine," I tried to ease his mind.

"Where are you?"

"We're at the new fire station on Balch. Josh is in heaven."

"I'll be there as soon as I can."

"Please be careful."

I called my dad next. He was ready to call out the cavalry to rescue us. I told him there was no need, Ryan was on his way. Besides, Josh was ready to move into the fire house. The firemen were making him balloon animals, and they gave him a toy fire hat. He was set for life.

I watched from the window as they towed my Jetta away. I loved that car. I hoped it could be repaired, but she didn't look too good. I also watched my least favorite person arrive before her ex-husband. I wasn't counting on that. I figured Ryan would call her, but I didn't expect her to show up, and first at that.

She tore across the parking lot like she was on a mission. She threw open the station doors and homed in on Josh. She was to him in two seconds flat. She wrapped him up and began to bawl. Trey, the fireman and Josh's entertainment, tried to tell her he was perfectly fine, but she was inconsolable. That was, until she turned her sights on me. Through her hysterical crying she went off on me. "You will never see Josh again. I knew something like this would happen with you."

I stood there, dumbfounded.

"Ma'am," Trey said politely. "The accident wasn't her fault."

"I don't care whose fault it was." She pulled Josh tighter to her.

I heard Josh say, "Mommy, Cherry took care of me."

She didn't care.

I was at a loss for words, but the next scene was worse in comparison. Within a minute Ryan was there. We all looked his way as he strode across the entrance to the common area.

Victoria was still crying when she set Josh down. Ryan looked between me and her, and he looked torn, even pained as to what he should do. In the end, he didn't choose me. He took Victoria up in his arms where she cried and cried, and in between, she cursed me.

I watched him tenderly try to quiet her for just a moment before I walked away to the front. I stood by the window. The tears that had been desperate to fall were finally shed. The words the old man spoke to me at the street fair over the summer rang in my head. "You know how to tell if a man is in love. He will look at you like you hold the moon and the stars in your eyes." That was how Ryan looked at Victoria. I couldn't see the forest for the trees because I was blinded by love, a misplaced love.

I grabbed my phone and called my dad. I wasn't going anywhere with Ryan. "Dad, can you come and get me?"

"Yes. Did something happen to Ryan?" He was worried.

"No, he's fine. He's here, but I don't want to go home with him."

"Honey, what happened?"

"I don't want to talk about it right now."

"Okay, baby girl. Hang tight."

Ryan, Victoria, and Josh all came walking up toward the entrance. I looked at the little family and tried to hide my tears.

"Josh is going to go home with Victoria tonight. I'm going to walk them out and I'll be right back," Ryan informed me.

I shook my head. "Don't worry about it. My dad's coming to get me."

Ryan stopped in his tracks with confused eyes. He walked my way, leaving Victoria and Josh at the door. "Charlee, what's wrong?" He reached up to touch my tear stained cheek.

I turned so he couldn't touch me. "The fact that you have to ask says it all. Just go, your family's waiting for you."

His eyes went from confused to worried. "I'll be right back."

I turned from him and sat down in one of the chairs near the window. I heard Josh say bye to me. I couldn't say it back. I felt like every part of my body hurt. I had this horrible hollow feeling in my chest.

"Are you ok, ma'am?" Trey approached me, handing me a tissue.

I reached up and took the tissue. "Thank you. I'll be fine." I always was.

Ryan returned quickly, and Trey took his leave, but not before giving me a sympathetic look.

"I told you my dad was coming."

He sat next to me and tried to take my hand, but I wasn't having it. "Charlee, please let me take you home."

I shook my head no. "I don't want to see you anymore."

"What do you mean?"

"Exactly what I said."

Ryan looked around at the few firemen and others that had been stranded by the accident. "Can we please have this conversation elsewhere?" He kept his voice down.

"There's nothing left to say."

"I don't understand. Please come to D.C. with me and Josh."

"That's the problem. You don't understand. You don't really want me to come. You don't really want me."

"Charlee, that's not true. Please, I'm trying here. I don't want to lose you."

I couldn't believe it. "You made your choice today. I saw it in your eyes and in your actions. So take Victoria to D.C. and put your family back together," I choked out.

"Charlee . . ."

I looked into his beautiful green eyes once more before kissing his cheek. "I love you, Ryan Carter. I hope you'll be happy."

He looked at me with wide eyes and touched his cheek where my lips had left a slight lipstick stain.

I stood up stoically and walked over to the window and watched the snow fall gently to the ground. In the midst of the snowflakes, I watched Ryan walk out of my life.

Twenty-Five

I CRIED THAT NIGHT LIKE I hadn't in recent memory. My dad held me on the couch and was smart enough not to say anything. Nothing he could have said would have made it better. The only thing he offered me was the ability to work from home, and I gladly accepted. The thought of having to see Ryan every day was more than I could handle at the moment.

I felt stupid, like the teenage girl that dyed her hair red so that a certain someone would notice, but he never did. Even when we were together, I'm not sure if he had.

Breaking up with the person you love really puts a damper on the whole holiday season. Not like they had been real cheerful for me in recent years, but I had hoped that perhaps this year would be different. Nope . . . it sucked worse than ever.

That first weekend I basically lived on the couch. My dad and Felicity took turns comforting me and trying to get me to eat something. I was also feeling the effects of being in a car accident. I was sore and stiff all over. It was a great combination. Not really.

The following week must have been the Lawtons' turn to take pity on me. Every day I had a visit from at least one of them. Krissy, Ann, and Maviny were all trying their best to help me feel better. I felt very loved and quite pathetic.

By the following weekend I declared my pity party and self-loathing over. I gave myself a good lecture that went something like this: *You knew you were in love with a man who didn't love you back. You only have yourself to blame for sticking around. So, now it's time to move on. You've been through worse, you'll survive this. Think about all that you have to look forward to. You even get a new car out of the deal.* It was a totally lame pep talk.

After Saturday chores to the music of 38 Special, I decided to wear real clothes and do my hair. My dad looked relieved when I came up the stairs looking like a human being and not a slug on the couch.

"What do you say we go car shopping today?" My dad was trying to be enthusiastic.

"I guess we better. I also need to finish Christmas shopping."

"Great. We'll make a day of it."

It was a perfect winter day in Colorado, bright, sunny, and cool. That was the great thing about Colorado. It could snow one day and be sixty degrees the next.

When we pulled out on the street, Ryan and Josh were walking out. Of course. I hadn't seen them in a week, and the first time I left the house, there they were. Josh waved and waved, making my heart ache. I loved that kid. I missed him as much as I missed Ryan.

I waved back at Josh. Ryan and I locked eyes. He put his hand up as if to say hi and I see you. He looked good as always, but there was a seriousness to his mannerisms.

I had to turn from both of them before I lost it. I reminded myself the pity party was over.

My dad reached over and held my hand as we drove away. "You okay, kiddo?"

"Yeah."

"You're lying."

"How could you tell?"

"I'm not sure who's more miserable, you or Ryan."

"Why would he be miserable? He's with Victoria again."

"That would be miserable for him, but he's not back with his ex-wife."

"Well, what he does now is his own business."

"He asks about you every day."

"I hope you didn't tell him I was living on the couch."

He squeezed my hand. "Your secret's safe, but I wouldn't be surprised if he was doing the same thing."

"Oh, Dad. He didn't feel for me the way I felt for him."

"You think so, huh?"

"I know so. I don't want to talk about him."

My dad squeezed my hand again and let the subject drop.

Our first stop was the car dealership. My dad was excited about it. It was like he was longing to be there.

"Dad, why haven't you bought a new car?" I asked him on our way into the VW dealership.

He wrapped his arm around me and gave me a little squeeze instead of answering.

"What's the mystery?"

"No mystery." He smiled down at me.

"Then why?"

"It seemed unnecessary while you were in school," he admitted.

I paused and looked up at the best dad in the world. "Dad, now I feel terrible."

"Don't you dare. It was money well spent."

"Why don't you give me your car and you get something new today."

He kissed my head. "Not a chance, baby girl. I want you to have something new and with four-wheel drive since you'll be driving back and forth to school soon."

"I don't think that's in my budget. I was planning on getting another Jetta."

"Think of this as an early Christmas gift."

"You're too good to me."

"You're the only kid I have to spoil."

"Speaking of which . . . Not that it's any of my business, but you don't plan on having any more kids, do you?"

He stopped before he opened the door to the dealership entrance. He had an interesting gleam in his eye. "No."

I let out a huge breath. I don't know why that thought bothered me, but it kind of did.

"But, I was going to talk to you. I've been thinking about asking Felicity to marry me. How would you feel about that?"

I looked up into his hazel eyes that matched my own. "I think that's terrific. I'm happy for you and Felicity."

His eyes lit up at the sound of her name.

"It's weird, both of my parents beating me to the altar."

He lifted my chin. "Your time will come."

"Yeah, maybe." My eyes began to water. *No pity party,* I reminded myself.

After our day of shopping, I ended up driving home a beautiful cherry red Tiguan, four-wheel drive with more bells and whistles than I needed. My dad ended up with an engagement ring. It was an odd thing, helping my dad shop for rings, but I knew Felicity would love her Christmas present. I tried not to be jealous. I think I would have rather had the ring than the car. Not a ring from my dad, but you know what I mean.

My dad had plans with Felicity that night, which left me home alone, sitting by our Christmas tree and wrapping gifts. It was kind of depressing. You shouldn't wrap gifts alone. At seven my phone went off. I picked it up, it was a text from Ryan.

Can Josh please come by and see you? He has something for you.

My heart ached. I wanted nothing more than to see Josh, but I knew it wasn't a good idea. *Victoria said she didn't want Josh around me.*

That's not her call. Please, just five minutes. He misses you. I promise I'll wait by your mailbox.

I held the phone to my heart, my broken heart. *Okay.*

Within two minutes, there stood my big guy, wrapped in a coat at my door. He was holding a gift bag. I knelt down and tried my hardest not to cry. He immediately flew into my arms. I held him to me and let the tears fall. I loved him with all my heart.

"I made you something, Cherry."

I set Josh down. I looked up and caught Ryan's eye. He was standing by our mailbox. He held his hand up and waved. I turned my attention back to Josh.

Josh handed me the little green bag.

I eagerly looked inside and pulled out the most beautiful noodle necklace I had ever seen. I put it right on. "I love it. It is my most favorite gift ever."

Josh's eyes danced with delight.

I pulled him to me again and kissed him all over his cheeks until he giggled loudly. "I love you so much."

"I love you, Cherry."

More tears flowed. "I have something for you, too." I handed him a large gift bag.

His eyes were wide with anticipation before he peered in and pulled out a largish remote-control dinosaur. "Yay!" he exclaimed.

"Merry Christmas, Josh."

"What do you say?" Ryan called out.

Josh threw his arms around my neck. "Thank you."

I stroked his head and held him to me. I didn't want to let him go even though I was freezing. I didn't think to wear a coat. "You're welcome."

"Josh, we better go," his dad called to him.

"I don't want to go," he yelled back.

I looked up at Ryan, who, from where I stood, looked torn about what to do.

I wanted to ask if he could stay with me for just a little while, but it wasn't my place. I hoped Ryan would offer, but instead he hung his head. "We need to go, son."

"No, Daddy!"

I had never seen Josh behave in such a way. He was usually an obedient little guy.

I knelt down again. Josh looked determined as he clung to the dinosaur that was almost as big as him. "Please, can I stay?" he pleaded.

It was almost my undoing, but I couldn't undermine Ryan. "I'm sorry, honey, you better go with your daddy."

"But I miss you. I want you to come over and play with me, and you didn't make me psghetti."

"No, I didn't, and I'm sorry."

By this time Ryan was walking up the porch.

I wiped at my tears, but I'm sure he had already seen them.

Ryan gazed down at me. He acted as if he wanted to say something to me, but he didn't.

"I don't want to go, Daddy." Josh dropped the dinosaur and clung to me.

I held onto him like a vice. "I love you."

"I love you the mostest."

I looked up at Ryan, and if I wasn't mistaken, I saw tears in his eyes too. I wasn't sure why he would be emotional.

I kissed Josh one more time, and Ryan took him from my arms. Josh howled. It shattered what was left of my broken heart.

"I don't want to leave." He was kicking and thrashing about.

Ryan was trying to calm him down, but it wasn't working.

I placed his dinosaur back in the bag and tried to hand it to Ryan, but Josh was really out of sorts.

"Hey, buddy. Calm down," Ryan tried to soothe him.

"I want CHERRY!" he wailed.

I approached him and stroked his head. "It's okay, Josh." I was too close to Ryan. My whole body was drawn to him.

Ryan's eyes were warm as they met mine. "He's got good taste."

I tucked my hair behind my ear. "That's a matter of opinion."

"Charlee?"

Why did he always say my name like a question?

I handed him the bag. "I better get in." It was freezing outside, though I was feeling some heat as Ryan and I stared at one another. It was as if, for a moment, there wasn't a little boy between us throwing a tantrum. And for a moment, I foolishly thought it looked like he wanted me. "Goodnight," I choked out before I ran in.

I could hear Josh cry from the other side of the door. It trailed off the farther away they got. I stood against the door and said to heck with not feeling sorry for myself. I stood there and sobbed until my insides hurt, holding on to my noodle necklace that I was never taking off.

Twenty-Six

SO, ALL IN ALL, IT was not the jolliest of Christmas seasons, but I survived. At least my dad was blissfully happy; Felicity said yes. I tried my best to be happy for them, and I was. But it's hard to see the people around you so dang happy and in love. It seemed like everyone was. Krissy and Chance were still in the honeymoon phase, even though she was getting big. The baby had nowhere to go but out. She was a cute pregnant lady, and Chance waited on her hand and foot. Even Maviny and Mason had significant others.

I didn't see Ryan and Josh, though I did have some contact. On Christmas morning I received a text with a picture of Josh opening his gifts and a message that read, *Merry Christmas. We miss you . . . I miss you.* I didn't even know how to respond to that. It was weird he would say such a thing with Victoria with him. I hoped she was treating him well—she never seemed to, yet that's what he wanted. Idiot.

My dad also wouldn't let me off the hook when it came to corresponding with Ryan at work. My dad got me set up with a secure connection at home, so I could work from there, but I still had to report to Ryan. It was all business, but I found myself staring at his dumb name on my screen more often than I cared to admit.

My mom finally got around to calling me. I guess she missed me for Christmas. She didn't apologize, she kind of pretended like nothing ever happened. I was too emotionally exhausted to do anything but play along. She wasn't happy I was going back to school. Psychology was a useless degree in her mind.

Going back to school was the only thing that kept me from going crazy. It was a reminder that someday I wouldn't have to be an accountant or work with Ryan. It gave me something to look forward to. I mean, sure I was looking forward to yet another wedding, but I already warned Felicity if she even thought about tossing me her bouquet, she would rue the day. She touched my cheek in that "my poor, poor girl" sort of way. And then there was the baby who was going to have the best middle name ever, to look forward to, but I needed something of my own, and school was it. I was a nerd and bought my textbooks early and took to reading them. It's not like I had anything better to do. Watching my dad and Felicity canoodle on the couch was getting nauseating.

The basement and Krissy's townhome became my go-to places. It was nice that Chance had to work a lot of evenings. I needed Krissy now more than ever. We did things like yoga for pregnant mommies. My pelvic floor muscles were stronger than ever from all the Kegel exercises we were doing. I wouldn't be wetting my pants anytime soon.

"You know, Aidan is still available," Krissy said as we lay on the floor strengthening our lady areas.

"I'm surprised. He seems like a great catch."

"Just not for you."

"I know, I have issues." I rubbed the noodle necklace around my neck to prove my point. People thought I was ridiculous for wearing it everywhere, but I didn't care.

"I don't know about that. Ryan is pretty yummy. Jerky, but yummy."

"I wouldn't call him jerky, maybe blind and stupid."

"Obviously."

"It isn't only Ryan, though. I miss Josh, too. I more than miss him. I ache to hold him in my arms."

She looked over at me with pity. "Are you sure it's not for the best? I mean, do you really want to be a mom right off the bat?"

"Yes." I didn't even have to think about it. "I never imagined I would, but just having a taste of it was so amazing. Krissy, you're so lucky you get to be a mom. I know it was sooner than you wanted, and I know I wasn't Josh's mom, but I saw myself someday being a mother figure and being married to his stupid dad, who I love and can't get out of my head."

Krissy reached over and held my hand. I turned to her and cried like a baby. I did that more often than I wanted to admit. For someone that didn't cry often, I had more than made up for it the last month.

"Oh, sweetie. It will be okay."

"Will it? Because sometimes I wonder, which is stupid because it makes me sound pathetic." I was snottily crying now, and Krissy's shirt kind of became my Kleenex.

She patted my back. "You're the least pathetic person I know. I promise, it will get better. I know it may not seem like that now, but it will. Do you want some ice cream?"

"No," I laughed. "I haven't run in a month. I need to purge ice cream from my diet."

"Are you sure? Because the baby really wants some."

"I love you, Krissy."

"I know, CJ. Now let's have ice cream."

I know most people didn't look forward to starting school, but for me it was a lifeline. I was even a dork and set out my clothes the night before I began and I had my bag packed to perfection.

Ryan sent me a little note with my last email of the day before I started classes. I was working Monday, Wednesday, Friday and going to school on Tuesdays and Thursdays. He said, *CSU is lucky. Good luck.*

It was nice, but I wanted it to say, *I love you and I can't live without you.* It was a pipe dream, I know.

So school . . . it was amazing and just what the doctor ordered. I needed something else to focus on, and my teachers were more than happy to give out plenty of homework. It did the job well, kind of.

I was waiting for my behavioral psychology professor to cover the material that would give me the magic bullet that would fix my Ryan disorder, but no such luck. It had only been a few classes, though, so maybe we would get to it. It was my favorite class. Professor Yost was a retired therapist who I guess wasn't quite ready to hang up his hat. He had the best stories to tell. I pegged him for the kind of professor you could get to go off on a tangent, which would keep you from the real work at hand. That could be good and bad.

I was getting into a routine. Tuesdays and Thursdays, I could be found on campus all day; if I wasn't in class, I was set up on one of the empty tables in the social science building studying. I was a freak about getting A's in every class, so I put a lot of effort and energy into school. I kind of got lost in it, which is why I was more than startled when I had a visitor one Thursday afternoon. I was engrossed in my chapter on substance abuse before my behavioral psychology class, and it was like he fell out of the sky. I looked up, and to my ever-living surprise, there sat Ryan.

I was too stunned to speak. He sat there across the small table from me, with his dazzling smile, like this was normal. Gosh, did he look good. He was wearing his long gray wool overcoat. I always found it sexy.

"Hi." He simply greeted me.

I closed my book and inadvertently touched the noodle necklace around my neck.

Ryan looked at my hand and smiled.

"What are you doing here?" The butterflies in my stomach said, *Who cares? Yay, our Ryan's here.*

"Well, I walked past your empty office today and, like always, I missed seeing your beautiful face, so I asked myself what I was going to do about it. Then your dad walked by and told me he was tired of seeing the two of us mope around and that if I was half the man he thought I was, I would fix the mess I created between the two of us. So, here I am."

My heart was beating erratically, but my brain was not going to be overridden by it this time. It had been fooled more than once before. I began gathering up all my things for my next class.

Ryan reached out and grabbed my hand when I went to pick up my notebook. "Charlee, I know I don't deserve any more chances, but I think what we had is worth not giving up on."

I pulled my hand away. "I don't know, you seemed to do a good job of it." I hastily shoved all my books and belongings into my bag. I left him at the table and headed toward my class.

Ryan caught up and followed right alongside me. "I deserved that, but I also feel like we deserve another chance."

"I don't know what makes you think that. I told you the last time, one more chance was it, and I meant it. You blew it. End of story."

"Yes, I admit I blew it, but giving up on what we had seems like more of a mistake. Don't you think?"

"And what was it that we had?"

He pulled on my arm gently and stopped me. We came face to face. He looked as serious as I had ever seen him. "The best relationship either one of us has ever had."

I rolled my eyes and pulled away. "How can you say that? You're still in love with your ex-wife." I didn't give him time to answer. Instead, I walked away again.

Like an idiot, he followed. Now people were starting to watch us with interest.

"I don't love Victoria." He followed me down the corridor to the lecture hall.

"Please. Yes, you do."

"I don't think that's your call."

"Well I'm not blind or dumb."

"In this case, you are."

I stopped dead in my tracks and gave him my deepest look of loathing. "Did you just call me dumb?"

He grinned. "I wouldn't dream of it."

"Will you please go away? You're going to make me late for class."

He shrugged his shoulders. "I'm not leaving. That was my mistake before, and I'm not going to do that again."

"Ugh! Suit yourself." I threw my hands up in the air and marched away.

He followed silently all the way to the hall where my class was held. I turned to him before I opened the double doors leading in. "You can't come in here."

"Watch me."

I wasn't sure what to do with this bold Ryan. I called his bluff and walked in. He followed me and took the seat next to mine in the second row of the amphitheater-type seating. I looked over to him, sitting there smugly. I narrowed my eyes at him. He leaned in closer and smiled. I leaned in too. "You need to leave," I whispered.

"Not happening."

"You're not a student here."

"People sit in on classes all the time."

"Please just go," I begged.

He pulled delicately on my noodle necklace. "Josh and I want you in our lives. It hasn't been the same since we've been apart. We haven't been the same."

The mention of Josh's name pierced my heart, but I knew it wouldn't work with Ryan and me. We had tried, and it was nothing but trouble. Lots and lots of trouble. "Josh is welcome at my house anytime."

"That's a nice offer, but we want more."

He was killing me, but thankfully my brain was still my voice of reason. I sat up stiffly, looked forward, and tried to ignore him. He didn't budge when Professor Yost walked in.

I quietly spoke from the side of my mouth. "Now you really need to go."

He leaned closer to me and whispered in my ear, "I'll go if you promise to meet me afterward to talk and work this out."

I had to stop myself from shivering. He knew how much I loved it when he talked low in my ear. "There's nothing to work out."

"Guess I'm staying."

In a huff, I got out my laptop and notebook. I couldn't believe him, and unfortunately, my professor was observant. I guess that had kind of been his job, to be observant of human behavior, but it wasn't real handy today.

"Ah . . . it looks like we have a new student. I thought it past time for schedule changes," he directed his remarks toward Ryan.

"I'm not a new student, I'm here with Charlee."

I turned and gave him my vilest of looks, but he kept flashing those pearly whites at me.

"Ms. Jensen, is that correct?"

I nodded my head.

"Is there a particular reason you've brought a guest today?"

"No, sir. I didn't invite him."

Professor Yost looked between the two of us with interest.

I was going to kill Ryan. The whole class was looking at us.

Ryan smiled at me before turning to my white-haired professor. "Charlee didn't invite me. I'm here of my own accord."

"Mr.?"

"Carter, but please call me Ryan."

"Well, Mr. Ryan Carter, to what do we owe the pleasure?"

Ryan looked my way again. "I'm here to convince Ms. Jensen to give me another chance."

I put my hand over my face. He was so, so dead.

"Ah. So you're interrupting my class in the pursuit of love, or perhaps lust?"

Who uses words like lust anymore? It didn't matter, I was so beyond embarrassed.

"Definitely both, sir," Ryan answered. The whole class laughed.

My eyes bore into Ryan.

He flashed me an innocent smile.

"By the look of it, I take it, Ms. Jensen, that you're torn by his request."

I whipped around to face my professor. "No. I'm not."

"Well, the way you lean toward him, tilt your head, and blush, says something entirely different. So where is your conflict coming from, Ms. Jensen?"

"Please, sir, I'd rather not discuss that."

"Intriguing. Well, class, how would you like a real-life demonstration in couple's therapy today?"

There was a murmur of approval. My professor looked delighted.

Ryan also looked happy. I was so the opposite. "We're not doing this," I informed him.

"Please, join me up front, Mr. Carter and Ms. Jensen."

I felt like I had been caught passing notes in class. "Professor Yost, please, this isn't necessary. Ryan was just leaving."

Ryan stood up, to my relief, but he held out his hand to me. "Shall we, my dear?"

The class laughed at his attempt at wit. His little gem was anything but funny.

"Come now, Ms. Jensen, we are wasting valuable time," my professor called out.

I stood up, but not before throwing Ryan the dirtiest look ever. He laughed and followed me down, touching the small of my back. Professor Yost set out two chairs for us that faced each other. Ryan and I each sat down at the same time. I didn't want to look at him, which was saying a lot. He was beautiful, but I was furious with him. I liked this class, and now I was going to have to drop out of it.

"As we are not in a private setting, I will not ask you to go into any intimate details," my professor said quietly to us.

That didn't make me feel any better, considering that wasn't even an issue. Ryan winked at me. I'm sure he was thinking the same thing.

"Class, please take notes on posturing, mannerisms, and tone. As you can see, Ms. Jensen is a bit tense, and her posture suggests she's on the defensive. Mr. Carter, on the other hand, is eager and even relaxed. So our first job here is to make Ms. Jensen feel comfortable, make her feel like she can open up to her partner."

Ryan smiled at the title. I grimaced at him.

"Did you notice that class?"

Great, I was in a fish bowl, and I felt like I was on trial and losing.

"So, Ms. Jensen, tell me about your first date."

I turned to him, surprised. "What? Why?"

"Very good question, and I'll answer after you do."

He was no longer my favorite professor. In fact, I was going to login to ratemyprofessor.com after this and give him the worst review ever. I took a deep breath and thought back to that perfect night back in July. I felt so stupid doing this, but I looked at my professor and felt like I didn't have a choice. I closed my eyes for a moment. "He took me to see a One Republic concert."

"We need more detail."

Okay. "It was at Red Rocks in July. Before the concert, we had dinner."

"And do you remember what you ate?"

"Grilled salmon salad and apple pie with ice cream." I felt myself smile at the sweet memory, but then I looked at a grinning Ryan and frowned.

I noticed my classmates were furiously taking notes . . . on me.

"Good choices, Ms. Jensen. What do you remember most about that night?"

I let out a deep breath and thought about lying, but I couldn't, not about that. "It began to rain just as the concert ended, and we ran back to his car. When we reached the car soaking wet, he pulled me to him and kissed me and then apologized for being too forward."

"Aww," I heard someone say.

It really was sweet.

"Someone, please tell me what you noticed when Ms. Jensen spoke."

Several hands went up, and he called on a random person in the first row. I still couldn't believe this was happening. Ryan sure looked like he was enjoying the show.

"Her eyes were bright when she spoke and she smiled often. She also inadvertently looked at him when she remembered being kissed."

I did?

"Very observant. And what does this say to you?"

"If I had to guess," my classmate said, "I would say that she still has favorable feelings toward him."

"I would agree with you, Ms. Hart." Professor Yost turned to me. "When couples would come to me for counseling, Ms. Jensen, a great way for me to gauge if there was any hope for the couple was for me to ask them to tell me about their first date or the day they got married. If they responded negatively, that was usually a good indication that counseling might not be very helpful, but when someone responded like you just did, it was usually a good tell-tale sign the couple would be able to work things out."

Ryan smiled and nodded. I wasn't sold on the idea.

"Mr. Carter, please tell Ms. Jensen what you believe your biggest obstacles as a couple are."

I wanted to say we're not a couple, but I wanted to get this over with more, so I didn't object. And I knew how therapy worked: when it was the other person's turn to speak, you were not supposed to interrupt.

Ryan leaned forward and toward me in his seat. His eyes were warm and inviting, just like I loved them. "Charlee, honestly I don't see any obstacles other than you being willing to give us another chance."

I refrained from rolling my eyes, because that wasn't true. I had a laundry list on the tip of my tongue, just waiting for my turn.

"Hmmm, interesting," my professor said. "Now, Ms. Jensen, it's your turn."

I sat up straighter. "For starters, he's in love with his ex-wife."

"I'm not—" Ryan interrupted.

"Sorry, Mr. Carter, it's not your turn. And Ms. Jensen, you need to address your partner, not the class."

I smirked at him. "You are in love with your ex-wife. You took her to your parents' home for Christmas instead of me."

Ryan tried to interrupt again, but was stopped again by Professor Yost. There was also a gasp heard among my classmates after I revealed that little tidbit. That's right, I wanted to say. He's not as wonderful as you think.

"And at the fire station, you went to her first, even though I was the one in the accident *and* the one you were supposed to be with." I tried to keep my voice calm and steady, but it was difficult. I also felt completely embarrassed, which reminded me. "I know you're embarrassed of me and our age difference, among other things." That was enough. I still couldn't believe I was bearing my soul in class. I was never coming back.

"Is it my turn now?" Ryan was eager to talk again.

"Not quite." Professor Yost smiled. He turned his attention back toward me. "What is your age difference?"

"I'm eight years younger."

"Are you a mother, Ms. Jensen?"

"No." I could hear the regret in my own voice. "But why do you ask?"

He pointed to my necklace. "The only women that wear home-made necklaces like that are moms."

I looked at a smiling Ryan. "This was given to me by Ryan's son, Josh."

There was a low murmur among my classmates, and my professor, by his look, also found it interesting.

"So, there is an added dimension to your relationship."

Ryan and I both nodded.

"Mr. Carter, am I correct in assuming your ex-wife is the mother of your son?"

Ryan nodded again.

"Obviously, your ex-wife is an obstacle for Ms. Jensen. Why do you think she feels that way, and why do you feel it's not an issue?"

Ryan faced me again. "Charlee, first of all, Victoria didn't come with us for Christmas. You don't know how sorry I am that I didn't ask you in the first place. Believe me, you were more than missed. And the day of the accident, you're right, I should have gone to you first, but I had conflicting emotions. When I saw you standing there, you were so strong, as always, and Victoria had already been threatening to take me back to court over Josh because of you. I panicked when I saw her crying and yelling at you. I was trying to keep both of the people that mean the most to me in my life, but I failed." He reached out and took my hands in his. I didn't pull away. "And I've never been embarrassed of you. I've just acted very poorly out of fear, but I'm done with that because what I fear most already happened when I lost you."

"Aww . . ." seemed to be the consensus of the classroom.

I pulled my hands away and thought for a moment. I wasn't sure if I could believe it. I had seen the way he looked at her, and I told him I loved him and he didn't say anything back.

My contemplation was interrupted by my professor. "What are you thinking, Ms. Jensen? You seem hesitant."

I looked directly into those eyes I'd loved for almost half my life. I noticed both hope and fear in his expression. "I don't want Josh to be taken away from you because of me, and I've seen the way you look at Victoria. You look at her like she holds the moon and the stars in her eyes. You don't look at me the same way."

Ryan didn't even wait for the professor this time. He scooted his chair closer, reached up and rested his palm on my warm, embarrassed cheek. His sole focus was on me as if we were alone. "You're right, I don't look at you the same way. I never felt for Victoria the way I feel for you. You are my sun. You make everything brighter and warmer in my life. Since we've been apart, the light has gone out of my life."

A single tear drop fell down my cheek and onto Ryan's hand. He smiled and rubbed his thumb gently across my skin. "And Josh isn't going anywhere. If Victoria even tries . . . I promise you, it won't end favorably for her."

I sat back and tried to let everything he said sink in. I was a mixed bag of emotions, everything from peaceful to confused. I was grateful Professor Yost decided to end his little experiment there. I didn't know what to say in return.

Ryan and I both stood up. Ryan kissed my cheek. "I need to get back to the office, but I'll see you later," he whispered in my ear.

I nodded numbly and took my seat back on the second row. I didn't pay attention to anything else that was said. I'm not sure if my classmates did either. I think they all took turns staring at me. After class, a couple of women remarked that if they were me, they wouldn't let such a catch go and that I was a lucky woman. I sat there and thought about that for a moment.

"Ms. Jensen," Professor Yost called, bringing me out of my swirling thoughts. "May I speak to you?"

I put away my things and joined him at the front of the room.

"I hope I didn't embarrass you too much today."

"I'm sure I'll eventually get over it."

He laughed. "You will have to forgive this hopeless romantic for trying to help."

"Don't be surprised if I transfer out of your class."

He smiled again. "Just in case you don't come back, let me give you a few statistics you may find interesting. A majority of men choose younger women to marry the second time around. It can be beneficial, you know. Younger women like to talk more freely, and older men are more settled and better listeners. And you would be surprised how many men learn from their first divorce and try to do better the second time around."

"Thank you, but Ryan and I have never talked marriage. He's never even said he loves me."

"Maybe not in words." Professor Yost strode out of the classroom, leaving me standing there daring to hope.

♡Twenty-Seven

I DON'T THINK I LEARNED a thing the rest of the day. Going to my next class was pointless. All I could think about was Ryan, which wasn't unusual, but he was all I could focus on. His words kept ringing in my head.

When I arrived home that evening, it looked like he was home. I didn't know what I should do. Should I go talk to him? Should I smack him? It was a toss-up. I decided to do what I always did when I was stressed and unsure. I changed into some athletic pants, a hoodie, and my basketball shoes and hit the court. It was dark and cold outside, but basketball was like medicine for my soul. It helped me not go crazy with my thoughts. I started playing a stupid game in my mind . . . he loves me . . . he loves me not . . . but instead of petals on a flower, it was he loves me if I made a basket and he loves me not when I missed. If we went by that, he really did love me, but I was a good basketball player. I tried not to put too much in it, but I really wanted to.

After thirty minutes of shooting hoops, I noticed Victoria pull into Ryan's drive. She had Josh with her, and as soon as he saw me, he ran to me. I took him up into my arms. He looked like he had grown in the month since I had seen him, and he had gotten his hair cut. I missed the curls, but he was still the most handsome little boy.

"Cherry." He wrapped his arms around my neck.

"Josh, I've missed you."

"I missed you."

His mother joined us, and I thought she would be furious, but instead she looked stoically beautiful. She looked like she was trying to be brave.

"Charlee, may I speak to you?"

I thought for a second. I felt like I was entering the danger zone, but I knew I could take her if I needed to. "Sure."

She walked closer and eyed her son in my arms. I could tell she wasn't overly fond of it, but she didn't say anything.

"Can we play basketball?" Josh asked.

I looked to his mom to reply. I wasn't sure why they were there. Typically Ryan only had Josh Friday through Sunday.

"Sure, honey. Why don't you play with the ball while I talk to Charlee."

I set Josh down and handed him my ball. He was getting better at dribbling.

Victoria stood tall and proud near me. "Ryan called me today. It was the first time I think he's ever been truly angry with me, and after everything we've been through, that's saying a lot. It speaks volumes about how he must feel about you." She paused and looked off into the distance for a moment. Before she directed her attention back toward me, she let out a very long, drawn out breath. "This is really hard for me to say." She ran her fingers through her flawless red hair while grimacing at the noodle necklace around my neck. "But I owe you an apology for my behavior toward you."

I felt my own eyes dilate. "Thank you?"

"I'm going to be honest, I probably won't ever like you, and I'll always be jealous of your relationship with Josh and maybe even Ryan, but my mother and Ryan reminded me that I had made choices and there are consequences to them, and I'm fortunate that Ryan has found someone that loves Josh and treats him well."

I looked over to my big guy dribbling so well. "I do love him."

"I know." Her words were cold. "I know you love Ryan, too, and he deserves someone that loves him the right way and for the right reasons."

Her forthrightness was throwing me for a loop. I wasn't quite sure how to respond, but I don't think she was looking for a response. I think, in a way, she was warning me.

"Come on Josh, your daddy is waiting for you." She stared at me with that peed-on-Cheerios look of hers. "Don't forget, I will always be Josh's mother."

"I'm not looking to take your place."

She held her head up, took Josh's hand, and began walking him over to Ryan's, but not before Josh waved and said goodbye to me.

"Bye, big guy." Saying those words didn't hurt now because I felt like they weren't permanent. It was a see you later.

I ran my ball back into the house and waited for Victoria to leave. I stood there, for a moment, looking at Ryan's house, asking myself if I really wanted to give us another chance. I rushed next door. I barely knocked before I found myself being pulled in and wrapped up in Ryan's arms, where I belonged.

"I was just coming to get you." He kissed my cheek.

He felt warm against my cold body, and I sank into him. Josh wormed his way in between us, and we just stood there in the perfect silence, not saying anything for several moments. I think Josh went as long as he could. "Can you please make me some psghetti?"

Ryan and I both laughed and reluctantly pulled away from one another. Ryan wiped at my cheeks. "I hope those are happy tears."

I nodded before looking down on the little man in my life. "Are you ready to make some spaghetti?"

"Yeah!" he shouted.

I took his little hand in mine.

His daddy pulled me to him for a hard, but brief, kiss. "I've missed your lips."

"I look forward to making up for lost time."

Ryan flashed me his sexy smile. I hoped Josh was tired tonight.

We spent the perfect evening together doing nothing but enjoying each other's company and eating. It took longer than normal to get Josh to go to bed. He had a lot to tell me, from his trip to D.C., to all his Christmas gifts, to school. Then he had to be read three different books. It was funny watching Ryan be almost exasperated at his son prolonging bedtime.

"Are you anxious for something?" I teased as Ryan raced through the third book.

He looked up at me with those passionate eyes, and the butterflies said, *Ahhh.*

As soon as Josh was tucked in, kissed, and sang to, we made a quick escape. The moment Josh's door was shut, I found myself being picked up and kissed thoroughly as Ryan walked us toward the couch. I never knew he was so talented to kiss, carry, and walk all at the same time, but dang, he was good. I think my toes even curled as he explored every inch of my mouth, face, and neck. We settled nicely on his couch, and there we stayed for several more hours as our lips got reacquainted. Not a word was spoken, even after our lips finally parted. I sank against him and enjoyed being near him.

He was so quiet and still, I thought perhaps he had fallen asleep. I knew I felt like doing the same. Sleeping in his arms was like heaven to me. But then, in the still of the night, I heard the most beautiful words ever spoken against my ear, "I love you, Charlee Jensen."

"Did you say that because you thought I was sleeping?"

"I said it because I mean it. I should have told you a long time ago, but I was afraid of moving too fast like I did with Victoria. I'm sorry I hurt you."

"And let's not forget embarrassing me today."

He pulled me closer to him. "I'm not going to apologize for that. It was the smartest thing I've ever done."

I looked up into those smiling eyes of his. "I'll give you that one, but only because I love you."

"Say it again."

"I love you, Ryan Carter."

Epilogue

I RUSHED HOME FROM KRISSY'S baby shower at the Lawtons', a shower that I threw in conjunction with her sister, to get ready for my Valentine's Day date. I'd had the two most handsome men ask for the pleasure of my company tonight, and I couldn't wait. I wanted to look fabulous, so Krissy and I had spent the previous weekend picking out the perfect outfit. She was now waddling and was to the point where she was tired of being pregnant. I think she had a twinge of jealousy while I tried on non-maternity clothes.

"You'll be back in regular clothes before you know it. Just enjoy it, and your large chest."

She threw a red dress at me. "I never thought I would say it, but I think your boobs can be too big."

"Well, I'm sure Chance is enjoying it."

She blushed, and we left it at that. Thankfully, she didn't feel the need to discuss that facet of her relationship.

We decided we better go more flirty than sexy since Josh was part of the date. Valentine's Day fell on Saturday this year, and it was one of Ryan's nights. Thankfully, Ryan was getting more nights now with Josh. Ryan was now insisting that the original terms of the custody agreement be in force, and that meant they switched off every other week getting Josh for four nights. I liked that arrangement much better. Victoria, not so much. But like she said, she'd made choices.

I chose a flirty belted pleat dress in berry that hit me right above the knee. It was fun, child appropriate, and I felt pretty in it, so we went with it.

I don't know why I was so excited. I knew we were just staying in, but it was our first Valentine's Day together and everything had been going so well. We had practically been inseparable. I had even gone back to working at the office on my work days. I'll admit, I kind of threw out the whole "I won't make-out in the office" rule, but I had a feeling my dad and Felicity had thrown that one out too, so I didn't feel too guilty.

When I went to put on my lip gloss, I glanced at the two dozen white roses Ryan had already had delivered to me earlier that morning on my dresser. I couldn't help but pick up the card that came with them. I opened the pink card with the same anticipation I had from the first time I read it.

Charlee Jensen,

I've been trying all day to come up with something witty or clever to say to you, but as you know, my gems are usually inadequate. So I hope you will settle with me trying to express the depth of what you mean to me, what you've meant to me all along. I knew I was in trouble from the first moment I laid eyes on you in your dad's truck that first day you came back. I couldn't believe how incredibly beautiful you had grown up to be. I know you hate it when I say grown up, and I know I was an idiot to keep saying it to you, but I was trying my hardest at the time not to be attracted to you. It was the one thing I'm glad I failed at.

One thing I wish I hadn't failed at was letting you know how much I cared for you right from the beginning. If I could go back, I wouldn't let a day go by that I didn't tell you what you meant to me, how beyond lucky I felt that you found me worthy to be by your side. I wish I would have told you the moment I knew I loved you, that night as we danced in the crowd at the mall.

Charlee, I just want to say thank you for sticking it out with me, for loving me like no one ever has, and for showing me what real love is. You've made me a better man and father. I hope someday I'll truly be deserving of you. Until then, I hope you'll choose to stay by my side.

Know that I ardently love and admire you. Please be my Valentine.

With all my Love,

Ryan

I set the card down and dried my eyes again. I had read it so many times I almost had it memorized word for word.

I looked at the time and threw on a sheer layer of lip gloss. The doorbell rang and I had just enough time to grab Ryan's card with a gift certificate to his favorite running store. I ran upstairs to the door and opened it. There stood my men, decked out in suits and ties, looking oh, so fine. Josh looked so stinking cute in a suit and Ryan . . . let's just say the butterflies were back to swearing and making me feel like I was going to puke. I loved it.

"Well, hello." I smiled at my men.

Ryan started to hand me a large bouquet of white roses, but his son beat him to the punch.

"I made you this card." He handed it up with a large heart-shaped box of chocolates.

I took them and admired them both. I bent down and hugged and kissed him. "I love them. Thank you."

"Happy Valentime's Day." He was the cutest kid ever.

"Happy Valentine's Day to you."

Ryan had been patient long enough. He handed me the flowers and then crushed them between us as he kissed me. "That," he whispered against my mouth, "is for starters, the rest will have to wait until after we put someone to bed."

I smiled and kissed him once more. "Something to look forward to."

He groaned and released me.

Don't get me wrong, I loved dating Ryan and Josh, if you know what I mean, but sometimes it was tricky. There really was something about anticipation, though.

My men walked me back to their place; each had taken one of my hands. We walked in, and the mood had been set. Low lighting and a table set in front of the fireplace filled with a cheese fondue pot, breads, meats, vegetables, and chocolate fondue with assorted fruits. It was perfect. Ryan lit the candles and started the gas fireplace.

Ryan helped me in my seat and whispered in my ear, "You look like perfection tonight." He kissed my neck, and the goose bumps appeared. When was Josh's bedtime again?

"Thank you, handsome."

I sat between them and ate the best meal ever. Nothing is better than melted cheese and gorgeous men. They are perfect paired together, and who could forget the chocolate? Not Josh. We would be getting his suit dry cleaned as soon as possible.

Finally, bed time rolled around and Josh was gratefully sleepy. I guess Ryan had purposely played hard with him all day in hopes of him being tuckered out. It worked like a charm. That left his daddy and me to slow dancing and kissing in front of the fireplace. The first song of the evening was the first song we had ever danced to, "Thinking Out Loud" by Ed Sheeran.

"You remembered."

He pulled me close and we began to sway. "A man never forgets the first time he dances with the woman he loves."

"That is the sexiest thing I've ever heard."

From then on, it was a lot of nonverbal communication. That was until Josh cried out, "Cherry!"

Our lips parted and we stopped swaying.

"He'll go back to sleep." Ryan didn't sound convinced.

"I better check on him."

"You know he only does this when you're here."

"I'm here every night he is."

"I know." Ryan smiled.

I kissed him. "I'll be right back."

He groaned, but smiled and reluctantly let me go.

I watched him watch me walk off. Have I mentioned how sexy he was?

I quietly crept into Josh's room to find him sitting up, crying in bed. He looked so cutely pathetic. I went to him and wrapped him up. "What's wrong, honey?"

"I had a bad dream."

I held him against my chest and stroked his head. "What about?"

"Scary dinosaurs."

I was going to strangle that teenage babysitter Victoria hired last week. Who shows a four-year-old *Jurassic Park*? I was at least grateful that wasn't on our watch. Where Victoria was better, she still wasn't easy to deal with. She would have raked me over the coals for this if it had been our fault.

"It was just a dream, honey. Remember those dinosaurs aren't real. Dinosaurs don't exist anymore. Do you want me to sing to you?"

He nodded his head.

I laid him back down in his now full-size bed; he had way outgrown the toddler bed. I laid next to him and wiped his tears as I began to sing. He snuggled against me, and I felt this amazing rush of emotion for him. It almost made me forget his daddy's arms were waiting for me. It took longer than normal to calm him down. Just as I was ready to leave, Ryan joined us. He laid on the other side of his son and faced me. The bed really wasn't made for three, but somehow, we all managed to fit.

Ryan kissed Josh's head rested against me. He looked up at me with the most intense gaze. My insides melted as he smoothed my forehead.

"I was just thinking," Ryan whispered.

"About what?"

"I was thinking about how I would like you to be the mother of my children."

"Like right now?" I smiled.

"I was thinking as soon as possible."

"Aren't you forgetting something first?"

"Will you share my bed with me, minus Josh?"

I smiled wider. "Um . . . aren't you forgetting something else?"

He rested his warm hand against my cheek. "Charlee, please be my wife, best friend, lover, stepmother to my son and mother to our children. Did I forget anything that time?"

I shook my head no and cried some of those happy tears.

"So what do you say?"

"I say yes, but . . ."

"But?" He looked worried for half a second.

"We need to think up another name besides stepmother."

He laughed and thought for a moment. "How about goddess?"

"I can work with that."

"Perfect." His lips met mine.

And it was.

More Trouble in Loveland

"DON'T EVEN GET ME GOING on his breath," the woman told Dr. Mallard. Then she turned to her husband. "Why can't you brush your teeth at night? Is that too much to ask?"

Her husband looked up from his dress shoes. His eyes said *why am I here*? He sat as far away from her as possible, hugging the arm of the couch. It wasn't a good sign.

Dr. Ginny Mallard, whom I was shadowing, was at a loss for words. The wife had spent the last forty minutes of this session unloading on her husband. Did she ever have a laundry list— everything from his lack of help around the house to their lackluster sex life. And who could forget her diatribe about how he wasn't ambitious enough? She couldn't understand why, at thirty, he wasn't making at least six figures. Unrealistic expectations, anyone?

The husband hardly offered a word the whole session, not even in his defense.

I wanted to whisper to Dr. Mallard that the situation was putting the husband in an unfair position. She should have never given the wife so much time. But what did I know? I was only a student in my practicum. And Dr. Mallard hated students.

I had to do something. Technically, I was allowed to speak. Or at least, I was supposed to be able to. Dr. Mallard had basically told me to keep my mouth shut before the session started. But if there was any hope for this couple, the husband needed a reason to try, and the wife, who'd dragged him there, must want to save the marriage. Right? She was the one who asked— or probably more like demanded— they attend couple's counseling.

I took a deep breath and went for it. "Danica, tell us about your first date."

Dr. Mallard's head whipped my way. Her icy stare tried to intimidate me, but she had nothing on my husband's ex-wife. I didn't even flinch.

I faced the couple in crisis and waited for Danica's reply. She was taken aback by the request. I remember feeling the same way once upon a time when I was asked the same question, by my favorite teacher and mentor, Professor Yost. One of the best days of my life.

Jake, the husband, became mildly interested, looked at his wife, and waited for her to say something. Curiosity, and maybe fear, played in his worn eyes.

Danica ran her fingers through her luxurious blonde hair and thought for a moment. But as soon as her gray eyes narrowed and face tightened, my hopes for ending this session on a good note went out the small window in the office.

Danica let out a disgusted breath before she let it all out. "It was every girl's dream date." Sarcasm clung to every word.

Jake's brooding brown eyes hit his shoes.

"First, he was an hour late picking me up. We missed our dinner reservation, so we grabbed a pizza, and he drove me up to the mountains for a picnic instead."

Sounded like my kind of date.

"Of course, it started to rain." Danica was a downer.

That would have been excellent news for me. Dancing in the rain, or making out in the rain, or both at the same time— because we were talented like that— were some of my favorite things to do with Ryan.

"And to top it all off, he called me Leah when he dropped me off." Ouch.

That perked Jake up. His head turned toward her, a sinister smile playing on his lips. Oh, that couldn't be good.

Yep, he snapped. Jake sat up, and it was like an imaginary hose had filled him with spite. Not that I could blame the guy, but after his forthcoming confession I could confidently say there were bigger reasons this marriage wasn't working. I was sure this would be their last marriage counseling session. They were headed for divorce court.

"Leah," he said her name like I would say Ryan's. "I should have married her instead of you."

The fire in Danica's eyes was unquenchable, and it shot out at everyone in the room. "That's my sister you're talking about, you—"

"Tell me something I don't know," Jake interrupted. His stare was scathing. "No, let me tell you something." Then he pulled the pin out of his grenade. "Leah and I are sleeping together."

In that moment, all the air was sucked out of the room in a silent but deadly blow.

Not even Danica uttered a word, but tears filled her eyes. Maybe a hint of remorse glimmered in Jake's, but I mostly saw relief.

When Danica came to, she grabbed her bag and left, slamming the door on her way out.

Dr. Mallard and I focused on Jake, who shrugged. "It was a mistake to marry the hot sister."

As a professional in training I had to keep from wrinkling my nose at his distasteful comment.

Jake proceeded to unload three years of misery and told how he had fallen in love with Leah, the cute but sweet sister who idolized him.

The upcoming holidays were not going to be fun in that family.

Dr. Mallard gave Jake a homework assignment to read a book about how to save a marriage in crisis. His smirk said he wasn't going to read it. I was surprised she recommended it. Professor Yost said that was a sign of an unskilled counselor. She needed to be recommending divorce counseling. It was apparent Jake had no interest in saving his marriage, which was probably dead on arrival. But I sat like a good student again and took notes.

Once Jake left and it was time to fill out the paperwork, I got an earful from Dr. Mallard. I knew I would. I was in favor of a client-centered approach, and obviously she didn't like adapting during a session.

"Why would you ask such a ridiculous question? Did you see what happened?" Her beady, dark eyes bore into me.

I stood my ground, or at least sat up tall in the uncomfortable, high-back chair I was sitting in. "My professor—"

Dr. Mallard rolled her eyes. "This is why I dislike dealing with students. Your professors aren't living in the real world. They preach from glass towers."

"Professor Yost was a practicing therapist for several years."

That shut her down, at least for the moment.

"He believed a good way to tell if a couple had a chance in therapy was to ask them about a time like a first date or the wedding day so he could gauge how they remembered it and what stuck with them. Danica was obviously resentful, and I would say she never felt confident or comfortable in their marriage. And her behavior reflected her discontent and unease."

Dr. Mallard stood up in clothes that screamed she hadn't been shopping since 1985. Who still wore shoulder pads? "You have a lot to learn, and, thanks to you, the divorce rate will be holding steady. Don't forget to fill out the paperwork."

I let out a huge breath when she left. Why was I paired with her today? My last day of my practicum for the semester, and it had to be with her. All the other counselors and psychologists at the clinic loved me.

Before I finished up the case and psychotherapy notes, I pulled out my phone and called my favorite number. "I love you." I didn't even let him say hello.

"Rough sessions today?"

"How did you know?"

"Because I know you."

The butterflies in my stomach still erupted when he talked to me like that. Some of them had been on a 24/7 bender ever since we were married six months ago.

"I could move some meetings around and come have lunch with you," Ryan offered.

"Sounds perfect, but I have my last study group in an hour. I can't wait until finals are over at the end of this week. And then we get Josh all to ourselves for two weeks. It's going to be perfect."

"Even with all the wedding chaos?"

"Thanks for reminding me." My dad and Felicity were finally getting married on Christmas Eve. Their love affair had been a series of ups and downs. They had planned on getting married in May, but they broke up in April, only to rekindle in June at my surprise wedding. Summer was mostly good for them. The beginning of fall was iffy, but supposedly this was a done deal. I wasn't so sure, but I was trying to keep my personal and semi-professional feelings out of it. I loved Felicity. I loved my dad. But they had more trouble in Loveland than most couples, as my dad liked to say. Not unlike Danica and Jake, my dad and Felicity had insecurities too. Unfortunately, a lot of them were fueled by Felicity's mom. That dear needed to get a new hobby and stop bashing my dad. But I couldn't think about it right now. I had finals, a husband who adored me, and a stepson I loved to pieces.

"I'm sorry. Take a breath, Charlee. I love you. And if you aren't too tired tonight after Josh's Christmas concert, I'll show you exactly how much."

The butterflies were now swearing. "I'll do my best. Sorry I've been so exhausted lately, you know it's not you, right?"

"I've been wondering," he teased. "I know you've had a lot on your plate lately."

My schedule had been insane. Between school, practicum, wedding, Ryan, Josh, Victoria (Ryan's ex-wife), my best friend Krissy and her baby Taylar Ann (Krissy reneged on naming the baby after me. She went with her mom instead. What could I say to that?), I was wiped out. I fell asleep every night as soon as my head hit the pillow. I was being a pitiful newlywed, which was a shame because I loved every part of Ryan, and he was a rock star in the bedroom. "You're always my main course."

"I love it when you talk dirty to me like that."

I laughed. "I love you. I'll see you tonight."

"You have no idea how much I look forward to it."

Believe me, I did.

If you enjoyed *Trouble in Loveland*, here are some other books by Jennifer Peel that you may enjoy:

Merry Little Hate Notes
The Spy Who Ghosted Me
The Proximity Factor
Forgettable in Every Way
The Valentine Inn
All's Fair in Love and Business
My eX-MAS Emergency
The Holiday Ex-Files
My Not So Wicked Stepbrother
Facial Recognition
The Sidelined Wife
How to Get Over Your Ex in Ninety Days
Narcissistic Tendencies
Paige's Turn

*For a complete list of all her books,
visit her Amazon page.*

Jennifer Peel is a *USA Today* best-selling author who didn't grow up wanting to be a writer—she was aiming for something more realistic, like being the first female president. When that didn't work out, she started writing just before her fortieth birthday. Now, after publishing several award-winning and best-selling novels, she's addicted to typing and chocolate. When she's not glued to her laptop and a bag of Dove dark chocolates, she loves spending time with her family, making daily Target runs, reading, and pretending she can do Zumba.

***

If you enjoyed this book, please rate and review it.
You can also connect with Jennifer on social media or join her
Facebook readers group, Jen's Book Besties:
Facebook
Instagram
Jen's Book Besties

To learn more about Jennifer and her books, visit her website at
www.jenniferpeel.com.

Made in United States
Orlando, FL
07 January 2025

56989408R00165